Rachel West *and the* Fallen Starlet

Rachel West *and the* Fallen Starlet

EMMA MILLS

BERKLEY MYSTERY
NEW YORK

BERKLEY MYSTERY
Published by Berkley
An imprint of Penguin Random House LLC
1745 Broadway, New York, NY 10019
penguinrandomhouse.com

Book design by George Towne

Library of Congress Cataloging-in-Publication Data

Names: Mills, Emma, 1989-, author
Title: Rachel West and the fallen starlet / Emma Mills.
Description: First edition. | New York : Berkley Mystery, 2026.
Identifiers: LCCN 2025035387 (print) | LCCN 2025035388 (ebook) |
ISBN 9780593954379 (trade paperback) | ISBN 9780593954386 (ebook)
Subjects: LCGFT: Detective and mystery fiction | Novels
Classification: LCC PS3613.I56816 R33 2026 (print) |
LCC PS3613.I56816 (ebook) | DDC 813/.6--dc23/eng/20250917
LC record available at https://lccn.loc.gov/2025035387
LC ebook record available at https://lccn.loc.gov/2025035388

First Edition: May 2026

Printed in the United States of America
1st Printing

The authorized representative in the EU for product safety and compliance is Penguin Random House Ireland, Morrison Chambers, 32 Nassau Street, Dublin D02 YH68, Ireland, https://eu-contact.penguin.ie.

For all those who are iceberg types—
one-eighth above the surface,
seven-eighths below the surface

Rachel West
and the
Fallen Starlet

prologue

★ MARCH 2008 ★

I FIRST MET MOLLY BYRNE AT A HOT NEW CLUB CALLED LITHIUM, WHICH WAS the successor to a formerly hot new club called LA$ER, which was the rebrand of a presumably tepid club called Entity.

I wasn't into the club scene, but I was there with Anton on a mission to see a deejay who was supposed to be the next big thing in house music, or the love of Anton's life, or both. Anton, an early and enthusiastic adopter of Twitter, followed this deejay, who tweeted under the handle @BEATDRAGON and shared photos of his washboard abs along with hashtags like #beatgasm and #letmyrhythminsideyou.

I didn't particularly want BEATDRAGON's rhythm inside me. But it was a Saturday night and I had no other plans to speak of. Although I'd been in LA for more than a year, Anton was still my only friend—a fact he was well aware of when it came time to find a wingwoman for missions to see internet-famous rhythm artists with exhibitionist streaks.

Unfortunately, there seemed to be very little to differentiate Lithium from either LA$ER or Entity. Having been to all three at Anton's behest, I could report that Lithium was every bit as loud, dark, crowded, expensive, and obnoxious as its predecessors. Anton fought the crowd at the bar and got us drinks that were fluorescent green and served in test tubes. They looked like something you'd take before a radiological scan.

"To your past life," he shouted over the pounding music.

We each threw back a test tube. Barium might have tasted better.

"Yum!" Anton yelled.

"I can't feel my tongue!" I yelled back.

BEATDRAGON didn't take the stage until after midnight, and when he did, it was with a series of smoke bombs and dizzying laser light cues. I was not drunk per se, but I was buzzed enough to be somewhat dazzled by it. Anton and I pulsed along with the crowd as BEATDRAGON mixed and spun and confronted us with his rhythm.

As one track melted into another, Anton gestured toward the deejay booth. "Let's get closer!"

I waved him on with a reply of "Restroom!" Brevity was best in this type of situation.

The women's restroom at Lithium was all black—the walls, the ceilings, the floor, the stalls, and the toilets inside them—and lit by bare halogen bulbs hanging from electrical cords. The faucets were inexplicably shaped like lions' heads.

I was reapplying my lip gloss when I heard someone throwing up. A quick retch, the flush of a toilet, and then one of the stall doors swung open.

And there she was, in all her glory. Molly Byrne teetered out on sky-high stilettos, a silver lamé minidress hanging limply from her frame.

She had the look of someone who hadn't consumed a carbohydrate in the past five years. She was beautiful—disarmingly so—but in a fragile sort of way. I was reminded suddenly of my grandmother's apple strudel recipe. Grandma insisted that the dough had to be rolled out until you could "read a newspaper through it." You might've been able to read a newspaper through Molly Byrne.

I couldn't help but gape. My first boyfriend in college had an *A Is for Arnold* poster hanging over his dorm room bed. It featured Molly in a tight cropped tank top and extremely low-rise jeans, her back arched as she threw a seductive look over her shoulder at the film's pale, underfed male lead. The tagline read: *He's got the grades . . . but can he get the girl?*

(Spoiler alert: Arnold gets the girl. They have sex on a waterbed, and as Arnold climaxes, the mattress loses structural integrity and the resultant spray of water propels them wholesale through a second-story window and into the aboveground pool below. There's a one-liner about squirting. An All-American Rejects song plays. Credits roll.)

"I know exactly what you're thinking," Molly said to me as she stuck her hands under one of the lion's-head faucets. For a split second, I wondered what the chances were that she and I had forged some sort of psychic connection through that *A Is for Arnold* poster.

"I'm not bulimic," she continued. "And I'm not drunk either. I think I had a bad wheatgrass shake earlier—too much wheat, not enough grass." She pumped the soap dispenser twice and shot me a wry look. "That was a joke."

I couldn't reply. Fourteen months as a copy editor at *Icon* magazine, and my only real brush with celebrity was the time Jessica Biel asked me where the bathroom was.

Molly dried her hands, and then examined her reflection in the mirror. She touched her lips, assessing some invisible flaw, and then glanced over at me again. "Could I use that?"

I stared down at my lip gloss. It was YSL Glossy Stain in Corail Aquatique, and it had cost me twenty-eight dollars. I was not in a financial position to justify buying twenty-eight-dollar lip gloss, but sometimes a crappy day at work felt like justification enough. "Uh, sure."

I offered her the tube and she took it, smearing some gloss on her lips with the wand. Then she extended it back toward me.

I honestly don't know what possessed me—if it was the fact that she was Molly Byrne, the fact that I was a little tipsy, or the fact that she had just thrown up. Maybe it was some mix of the three.

But I said, "Keep it."

She looked at the lip gloss, and then up at me. "Really?"

"Sure."

"Thanks." Disconcertingly, her eyes suddenly took on a liquid shine, as if this were some incredible act of kindness. "Thank you." She regarded me with more recognition now. "What's your name?"

"Rachel."

She leaned back against the sink. "What brings you here, Rachel?"

I glanced toward the stalls. "Well, traditionally . . . waste disposal?"

For a moment, she just looked at me—my life hung in the balance—and then a smile broke her face. It changed her entire look. It was the kind of smile you could imagine a fairy-tale princess bestowing on a villager. That villager's family would tell the story of it for generations to come.

"I meant, here in LA."

"Oh. I, uh . . ." How do you share the fact that you work for a tabloid with someone who frequently appears on the cover of that tabloid? "I work for a magazine."

"Which one?"

"*Icon*."

Molly's smile dimmed. "Shitty gossip rag."

That was undoubtedly true, but it was *my* shitty gossip rag. The one that was going to be my jumping-off point. My foundation. My *experience*, the kind I so desperately needed in order to get anywhere in this industry.

"They pay shit for pictures," she continued when I didn't speak. "That's what Dax says, anyway."

It was a strange time. Paparazzi were becoming celebrities in their own right, and Dax Van Sant was right at the forefront. How you go from lurking in the bushes outside someone's house to dating them, I would never understand, but Dax had somehow made it happen with Molly.

"Your boyfriend?"

"For now." Her eyes twinkled. "You know what my mom calls the guys I date? 'The Mayfly Men.' They live for a day."

I smiled.

"You're not from here, are you?" she asked. "I have this sense about people, you know. I can tell you're not from here."

"I'm from St. Louis."

"Are you trying to do movies? Is being a—" She gestured, to prompt me.

"Copy editor," I supplied.

"Is that the new 'waiting tables'?"

"No. Or, at least, not for me. I would be terrible in movies. I want to be an entertainment journalist."

"*Icon* doesn't do journalism. It's all *Jennifer Aniston: Pregnant, or Just an Unflattering Blouse?*"

A breath of laughter escaped me.

"You don't want to write that sort of garbage, do you?" Molly continued.

"I mean, it would be great to skip ahead to writing profiles for *Vanity Fair*, but I've got to start somewhere. I didn't come in with much experience. I, um. I kind of took the long way round."

"What does that mean?"

"I used to . . . I actually thought I wanted to be a doctor. I was premed in college. I even—" Why was I telling this to five-time Teen Choice Award–winner Molly Byrne? Was I drunker than I thought? She looked at me, her expression unwavering, and for whatever reason, it just continued to pour out of me: "I even got into medical school, and I went. For two and a half years. I don't know if you're up on the price of med school these days, but suffice it to say, it's not a great idea to start and not finish. 'Fiscally irresponsible' is what my dad said."

"Do you have loans?"

"My loans have loans," I replied. "If I miss one of the payments, Sallie Mae comes to my apartment and cuts one of my fingers off."

One side of her mouth curved upward. "How do you go from med school to staffing for *Icon*?"

"You have a sick brother when you're a kid." The words tumbled out of my mouth before I could stop them. I was definitely drunker than I thought. "So you spend a lot of time in hospitals, reading *People* and *Entertainment Weekly* while he gets treatments. And when you grow up and your first plan fails—the one where you were going to become the smart, capable doctor who helps other sick kids—you think of the thing that brought you comfort back then. The thing that made you happy at a time when . . . nothing seemed happy."

She considered me for a long moment. Even in the insufficient light of the halogen bulbs, her eyes were a piercing blue.

"That's a cute bag," she said finally, her gaze sliding to where my knockoff Chanel purse rested on the counter next to me.

Instantly, I felt embarrassed. Sort of like in school, when everyone has the name-brand sneakers and you've got the Payless version—the Adidas Superstars with an extra stripe, the Chuck Taylors without the star. I was certain she knew the purse was a replica, and sure enough, she grabbed it and tilted it up to the bare bulbs above the sink, peering at the front of it.

"The stitching tells the tale with Chanel. But it's a pretty convincing fake." Molly's eyes shone with a mix of amusement and something else, something I couldn't quite place. "Just like me."

I didn't know what to say, so I said nothing.

She set the purse down, and then looked up at me. She put on a smile, but this one was different than before—much more rote. "Well. It was nice meeting you."

I was a little thrown. "You too," I replied, and watched as Molly stole one last glance at herself in the mirror and then exited the bathroom.

It felt almost like a dream. There was no one around to witness it. I had no proof of meeting Molly Byrne. But it had happened.

That was only the beginning, of course.

WWW.CELEBRITEASE.COM

June 17, 2008
07:03 AM PST

A warning for you, dear reader: this is not a hearts-stars-and-horseshoes kind of obituary. Molly Byrne was known for telling it like it is, and by God, we'll do right by our sweet silicone goddess in death.

First, the details—Former Disney darling Molly Byrne, 24, was found unresponsive in her Beverly Hills home early Tuesday morning and pronounced dead at the scene. While authorities have yet to confirm a cause, the star's death is rumored to be the result of a drug overdose.

While we here at the Tease would never make light of a tragedy such as this, we just have to put it out there: things have been rough for Molly, and this sort of tragic finale is not nearly as much of a "shock" to the Hollywood community as all those mags and tabs will have you think.

Recall if you will the three-in-a-row box office bombs. The straight-to-cable flick dubbed "unwatchable" by *The Hollywood Reporter*. Not to mention all that business befuddling Miss Molly's personal life . . . the rumored drug and alcohol abuse, the paparazzi love affair, and who could forget all that Byrne family drama-rama-rama?

Remember Molly's long-standing feud with little sister Amy Byrne? Unfortunately, if Molly Byrne was lightning in a bottle, then Amy Byrne is static electricity in a Capri-Sun pouch. The (ahem) competitive spirit between the sisters led to a legendary backstage spat at the Kids' Choice Awards in '03, a brutal red-carpet snub at the VMAs in '05, and an all-out screaming match on a particularly messy night at 1OAK earlier this year.

But not even Amy at her greenest-with-envy can deny that Molly was, at one point, a genuine sensation. The dawn of the new millennium saw our nation gripped by a Molly Byrne zeitgeist. After nearly a decade spent cutting her baby teeth on Juicy Juice commercials, guest-starring roles on family-friendly sitcoms, and a stint on the (extremely ill-advised) *Mickey Mouse Club* rip-off *The California Kids Crew*, we watched a teen Molly blossom as Betsey Blue in the Disney Channel original series *All Bets Are Off*. After three seasons of record-high viewership, she kicked Mickey Mouse to the curb and had breakout success of a different sort in the raunchy teen comedy *A Is for Arnold*. Molly went on to star opposite mega-hunk Nick Hart in the mega-huge summer blockbusters *Robot Wars* and *Robot Wars 2: Rise of Omnitron*. Her boobs were fake but the explosions were real, and so was our love for Miss Molly.

But fame is fickle, as is the media (cough cough), and it's awfully hard to maintain top billing when you show up to set still marinating in last night's Cristal and popping Xannies like they're Mentos. While she continued to top tabloids with her increasingly desperate shenanigans, producers stopped coming a-knocking, and Molly's rep switched from hard-working to hard-partying, from box office draw to production poison.

There seemed to be a glimmer of hope for Molly in recent months—amid her very public breakup with (notoriously vile) photog Dax Van Sant and her puzzling friendship with (bottom-feeding) *Icon* reporter Rachel West, Molly's latest film, *Sun City*, set to release next month, is already drawing awards-show buzz. In a gritty story of revenge and redemption from Oscar-winning director Adrien Ford, Molly's turn as a young single mother desperate for justice is a best-actress nom waiting to happen. Alas, it seems that promo will fall on the shoulders of her *Sun City* costars, including former on-screen flame Nick Hart (and as we all know, those are some very broad shoulders).

It's been a rough road for Molly, and an even rougher fall from grace. But look at it this way: things could've been worse. Somewhere in it all, she could've married K-Fed.

Rest in peace, Molly dearest, and way to dodge that bullet.

1

I learned of Molly Byrne's death the same way I learned the top ten exercises for toned abs, or what movies were playing at the nearest Cinemark, or whether my ex-boyfriend from college was currently seeing someone. In short, it was the internet that told me Molly was dead. Not a friend, not someone from her staff, not even the anchor of my usual morning news show. It was the internet, cold and unfeeling, in badly kerned Helvetica font. The home page of my web browser announced that she had been found early that morning, and a quick search turned up any number of articles from sources ranging from the Associated Press to the soul-sucking realm of Celebritease.

I lived alone, so there was no one to share the news with. Molly was dead. She had died. She was just . . . gone.

There was a feeling of absolute unreality about it. Like if I closed my laptop, it would no longer be true. Or if I picked up my phone and called Molly right now, she would answer.

More than three months ago, the idea of having Molly Byrne's phone number would've sounded absolutely absurd to me. But somehow, remarkably, we had become friends.

In fact, I had seen her just last night. Just over twelve hours ago.

And now . . .

It didn't make any sense. I couldn't believe it. I didn't want to.

I grabbed my cell phone and brought up her contact info, even though I knew it was nonsensical. As the phone rang, I looked at the headline currently front and center on the *People* home page—large, bold letters above a photo of Molly exiting an SUV, one hand held up to shield her eyes from flashbulbs:

MOLLY BYRNE DEAD AT 24, FAMILY 'DEVASTATED'

The phone clicked midring. For a second, my breath caught.

"Your call has been forwarded to an automatic voice message system," a robotic preset message said. Her number was *"not available. At the tone, please record your message, and when you are finished recording you may hang up or press one for more options—"*

I hung up.

I had brewed a cup of tea before I sat down and opened my laptop. It was stone-cold now. I picked it up and took a sip anyway. I thought of Molly's kitchen, and her mismatched tins full of bags of Earl Grey and English breakfast.

Tears pricked my eyes, but I forced myself to blink them away. I was not a crier. I prided myself on that, though part of me wondered if I never allowed myself to cry because I knew that once I started, it would be extremely difficult to stop.

There was a knock at my door.

I squeezed my eyes shut. Anton, maybe? He would enter in a haze of lavender, and he would make me new tea, and tell me that everything was going to be okay. I wouldn't believe him, but it would help to hear it anyway.

Regrettably, it wasn't Anton. When I opened the door, two people were standing on the concrete walkway outside my apartment—a man and a woman, both wearing generic, crime-scene-procedural-type clothes.

"Rachel West?"

The guy was tall and good-looking, shades of David Boreanaz circa *Angel.* The woman had an athletic build and an attractive face, an Eva Mendes type.

Celebrity bullshit gets into your bones. It replaces the marrow. I thought briefly of the med school dreams of a Rachel West past. Then I cleared my throat.

"Yes?"

"I'm Detective Lee," the man said. "This is Detective Ruiz. We're with the LAPD." They each gave the perfunctory flash of a badge. "We'd like to speak with you about Molly Byrne."

Detective Ruiz's tone was clipped. "May we come in?"

I opened the door wider to let the detectives in. As I went to close it behind them, I caught sight of one of my neighbors taking a bag of trash out to the dumpster. She was peering my way with interest. This was surely not the first time the cops had ever visited the Palm Vista apartment complex, but it was definitely the first time they had come to see me.

I shut the door quickly and turned to face the two detectives.

They were surveying my apartment: the trays from half-eaten frozen meals in the sink of the little kitchenette, the ladybug Pillow Pet on my thrift-store couch, the well-worn sneakers and slides in a haphazard pile by the door. I'm sure they easily noted the things that didn't fit—the Fendi sunglasses on my coffee table, the stack of Louboutin boxes next to the TV.

Then they looked at me, and maybe they knew I was Rachel West, recently minted entertainment reporter for *Icon* magazine. Probably they were judging me, trying to understand a situation in which one plus one somehow added up to negative five.

Ruiz had beautiful uptilted eyes that were perfectly lined. She looked like someone who drank kale juice and did the Bar Method. She was definitely judging me.

Lee's expression was deliberately neutral. He was certainly good-looking, though how conscious he was of that fact, I couldn't tell. In my experience, there was kind of an inverse relationship to it here in LA—the less aware of being handsome a guy was, the more attractive he became.

I realized that no amount of useless analysis of this pair was going to change the situation. So I cleared my throat. "Do you want to sit down?"

Ruiz gingerly moved my Pillow Pet to one side. Both detectives sat down on the couch. I took a seat in the adjacent chair.

"We've got witnesses placing you at Molly Byrne's house yesterday evening," Ruiz said without preamble. "Her security team says you were there between eight and eight thirty. Is that correct?"

The feeling of unreality intensified. I was being interviewed by the *police*. About Molly. Because she was . . . because she had . . .

"Yeah. Is she—" It was pointless to ask. I knew it was. But that didn't stop me. "Is she really dead?"

"Yes," Ruiz said bluntly, at the same time that Lee said, "I'm afraid so," in a somewhat gentler tone, and then they both glanced at each other for a fraction of a second, as if each was disappointed by the other's approach.

"How did Molly seem last night?" Lee asked.

"What do you mean?"

"Was she upset? Acting differently than usual?"

A lump had formed in my throat. "Is it true? What everyone's saying." I gestured toward my computer, like that somehow encompassed it. *Everyone*. "That it was—that she overdosed."

"The investigation is ongoing," Ruiz said.

"Was it on purpose? Or was it an accident?" Their answer seemed imperative. *Just how oblivious were you last night, Rachel? Just how stupid were you not to realize that she was struggling?* "Do you think she did it on purpose?"

Ruiz's expression was unyielding. "I'm afraid we can't share that kind of detail at the moment."

"How did she seem?" Lee pressed, but not unkindly. I met his eyes, which were a warm brown.

"I mean, kind of on edge, but . . . also kind of far away, I guess?" I swallowed hard. "But she would get like that sometimes. I just thought she was . . ." The words stuck in my throat. "She's been doing a lot of promo lately. I just thought she was tired."

"What was the nature of your relationship with Ms. Byrne?"

I had known Molly Byrne for three months. It felt like much longer, but at the same time, now, impossibly short.

"Friends," I said. "We were friends. I . . ." How could I describe the bathroom at Lithium? The Corail Aquatique and everything that came after? "We met at a club, and then later, I ended up interviewing her for the magazine where I work. She gave me an exclusive."

"About what?"

"Her breakup with Dax Van Sant." A pause. "Her sobriety." I blinked against the fresh sting in my eyes. "We kind of just . . . hit it off. She doesn't—didn't—have a ton of friends. Neither do I." My heart squeezed painfully at the realization: *Now I have one less.*

The two detectives proceeded to ask me a slew of questions. Was anyone else at Molly's house when I arrived? Did I know of any medications or recreational drugs that Molly was taking? Did I see her take any last night? Where did I go after I left her house? Could anyone vouch for my whereabouts?

When the questioning finally wound down, both detectives

stood and thanked me and then headed toward the door. Ruiz had her hand on the knob, but Lee lingered for a moment.

"I'm sorry," he said. "About your friend."

I nodded. He was the first person to say this to me.

"If you think of anything else, this is my number." He handed me a card. I accepted it, and then watched as the pair headed away.

2

IN COMPLETE SHOCK, Anton texted me.

He always texted in all caps, as he considered case-sensitive to be "too much hassle." Once, I pointed out that he could type entirely in lowercase letters instead. He replied that lowercase was INCOMPATIBLE WITH HIS LIFESTYLE.

My phone buzzed again, three times in short succession.

IM DEVASTATED FOR YOU
AND FOR MOLLY
SHE WAS SO VIBRANT

It was the same kind of thing people were saying on TV and online—*She was a beautiful soul. So full of life. She will be so missed.*

And the think pieces were pouring in already: *Hounded by paparazzi, crucified by the media—is the entertainment industry to blame for the death of Molly Byrne?*

But this was personalized: *I'm devastated for you.*

I'm sorry about your friend.

My phone screen swam before my eyes. I looked away, blinked hard, and then typed back:

I know. It's terrible.

And that was completely insufficient. But what do you say in a text? How could I possibly sum it up? *This horrible, weird, bad thing has happened, and I don't know what to do with myself*?

I had no clue. So I did what I'd do on any other morning: I went to work.

Icon's offices were on the fourteenth floor of a high-rise on Wilshire. "Is it just like *Ugly Betty*?" my little sister, Natalie, had asked me over the phone when I first got the job, more than a year ago. She was a college freshman at the time, still living at home in St. Louis, with our parents.

"Yes," I had replied, "down to the very floor tiles. All magazine offices are like that. In fact, people can barely remember what magazine offices looked like *before Ugly Betty*, and did you know that they're contractually obligated to hire an America Ferrera look-alike—"

"Okay!" she squawked. "I get it! Silly question. Also, I hate you."

"I hate that we don't talk about *Ugly Betty* as much as we should."

In reality, *Icon* was not particularly glamorous. Besides the view, I suppose, but that was only for the privileged few in the private offices along the perimeter of the floor. All the lower editorial staff were stuck in a bullpen in the center of the floor, with the characteristic fluorescent lights and gray industrial carpeting of myriad office suites across the country. My old desk and Anton's backed right up to each other. I had to crane my neck to catch a sliver of window through one of the open office doors when I got up to make a copy.

Since my recent promotion to entertainment reporter, I now shared one of the windowed offices with a lifestyle editor named Tyla. She was very into health and fitness, and was obsessed with what she referred to as *wellness*. This involved things like drinking lukewarm water with lemon in it, sitting on an exercise ball in lieu of a desk chair, and refusing to eat anything that contained Red 40.

Tyla's desk was empty this morning, and I was secretly relieved. I had encountered many well-intentioned condolence givers on my way into work. So many tilted heads, so many *I just can't believe it*s and *How are you holding up*s.

It made me irrationally angry and I couldn't even articulate why. Maybe because I didn't deserve condolences—I had known Molly for only a few months, while there were so many people who had known her and loved her for longer—or maybe because I hated having to hear them in the first place. I hated the fact that Molly was gone.

I had just settled in at my desk when Irina stopped by.

She was my boss, and the chief entertainment editor at *Icon*. Irina's office was indeed glamorous, and Irina herself was intimidatingly glamorous. "She's got the kind of beauty that's completely timeless," one of the art directors remarked once. "Like she'd be considered just as beautiful in ancient Rome or Regency England or imperial Russia."

"True, I can totally see her plotting the downfall of the Romanovs," Anton had muttered to me, and I stifled a laugh.

Right now, Irina gazed at me with icy blue eyes that revealed nothing. She wore her hair in a blunt-cut bob, perfectly straight, and it moved as a unit, a pale blond curtain, as she gestured in the direction of her office. "Shall we chat?"

I followed her.

"Please sit." She indicated one of the uncomfortable chairs in front of her desk. It was made of padded leather and had a very low back, so you had to either sit perched forward or lean awkwardly back. I opted for perching forward.

Irina offered me a Fiji water, which I waved off, and then she took a seat behind her desk. She twisted the cap off her own Fiji, and then immediately screwed it back on without taking a drink.

"I'm so sorry about Molly," she said. "I know you two were close."

"Thank you," I replied, which felt both completely wrong and completely inadequate.

"This is an incredibly difficult situation, but obviously we need to move forward with a memorial issue. I'm wondering if you would be interested—" Irina paused, pursing her lips. "That's not the right way to put it. I'm wondering if you would be *willing* to contribute a short editorial about Molly. Something about your friendship with her, how close you became in such a short time—"

"I . . ." The thought hadn't even crossed my mind yet. Of course they would scrap the current issue.

"And before you get started, it would be immensely helpful to me if you could reach out to the Byrnes." Irina clicked one manicured nail against the cap of the Fiji bottle. "Tish, Doug, Amy—it doesn't matter who, as long as we get something from one of them. *People*'s already got a 'source' who's 'close to the family'"—Irina lived and died by air quotes—"but I know we can get something directly from the Byrnes if you work your magic."

"My magic?"

She waved a hand. "That aw-shucks Midwestern schtick. It works so well for you. Bring them a casserole and get as many pull quotes as you can. By early afternoon, if possible."

"Their daughter just died."

"Yes, and I imagine they'll have something to say about that."

I didn't speak.

"I know this is a delicate situation, Rachel. But the truth of the matter is that nothing sells a magazine quite like a beautiful dead starlet. Look at the Piper Standish murder—those issues smashed our sales records for the past five years. Right now we stand poised to beat even those records if we do this right. And Molly was undeniably a valuable source for you—"

"She wasn't a *source*. She was my friend."

Irina just smiled, a small, patronizing thing. "Yes, of course. And I know this is difficult—"

"Stop saying that."

"—but this is the industry you're in. You wanted to be an *Icon* reporter. What exactly did you think your job would entail? Drinks at Chateau? VIP passes? I can assure you, it's not always glamorous or fun or pleasant. If you're going to have any kind of a career here, you need to understand that."

Is the entertainment industry to blame for the death of Molly Byrne?

My heart pounded. I could hear blood rushing in my ears.

"I do. I do understand that." I stood up. "I quit."

3

This was not the first career I had walked out on. As I took the elevator downstairs, I wondered how I was going to explain it to my family this time around. Last time, it had been haltingly, on the phone, as I sat hunched on the floor of the visitors' parking garage at Memorial Hospital: *I can't do this. I can't. I can't. I can't.*

A buzzing sound pulled me from the memory. I opened my bag and reached for my phone—a beat-up blue Nokia that I had been carrying since college.

It was Irina. "You're not thinking clearly. Come back and let's talk."

She was right—I wasn't thinking clearly. But not about quitting. With the adrenaline from my extremely abrupt resignation still coursing through me, I wasn't paying attention to where I was going. Instead of heading for the door to the garage, I'd pushed through a set of glass double doors, out onto the sidewalk out front.

"I have nothing else to say," I told Irina. "I'm not—"

I did not immediately spot the half dozen people clustered nearby, but they definitely saw me.

"Rachel!" someone yelled, and then shutters clicked, flashes bursting in my eyes as the group descended upon me.

It was an influx, all at once: "Talk to us about Molly!"

"What were her last words to you?"

"Do you know how she died?"

I ended the call with Irina and threw my phone back in my bag as I attempted to head down the street. The crowd moved with me, the questions and flashes and whirring of cameras unrelenting. I quickened my footsteps, but the group quickened theirs to match.

"Do you know why she did it?" One photographer's voice, flat and strident, carried over the others. "Did she leave a note?"

My lungs tightened. It was too much. The flashes were too disorienting. I rounded a corner, and suddenly someone grabbed my arm with a hurried "This way." Before I could react, I was pulled abruptly through an open doorway.

I wrenched out of the person's grasp and stumbled away from them as a door swung shut behind us, the crowd of paparazzi on the other side of it.

Except for one.

A young man, outfitted in a T-shirt, black skinny jeans, a beat-up leather jacket, and even rougher-looking black Converse, stood across from me. He wasn't much taller than my five foot five—he probably told people he was five eight, but it was an aspirational, Tom Cruise kind of five eight. He had shaggy brown hair that curled around his ears, and although he was slim, there was a softness to his features; his cheeks still had a roundness to them. I wouldn't have put him at much more than twenty.

He held up his hands in placation. "Sorry. Just trying to help." A black bag was slung across his chest. I knew what was in there.

And I realized, startlingly, that I knew who he was. I flashed on a lunch at a café in Malibu, sitting at a patio table with Molly. I had leaned toward her, trying to be discreet: "There's a guy over there taking your picture."

Molly cast a surreptitious glance over her shoulder and then waved a hand, her expression clearing. "Oh, that's just Casper. He's totally harmless. He's been trailing me for ages."

"Casper," I had repeated.

"I know, right? It suits him. He's like a friendly little ghost."

"Does it bother you? That he follows you around?"

"The rest of them, sure—the ones waiting for me to slip up or lash out or accidentally flash my vag or whatever. They fucking bother me. But Casper's different."

"How?"

She paused before answering. "Why wouldn't I want to control my own narrative?" Her eyes shone. "Plus, there's that thing people say: Better the devil you know than the devil you don't."

Now Casper and I stood opposite each other in an ATM vestibule next to a Chinese restaurant. He moved past me toward an exit at the other side of the vestibule and opened the door, revealing an alleyway. "Go this way. You'll avoid them."

I pushed by him and started down the alley.

"Hey, wait—"

Annoyance flared in me. "What? You want something for helping me?"

"No, listen—"

I turned back. "Go ahead—take my picture, send it to *Us*

Weekly, get it the fuck over with. Better yet, send it to *Icon*. Ready?"

I held up both middle fingers.

He was unfazed. "I need to talk to you about Molly."

"Of course you do."

"She was murdered."

I blinked.

4

I'm sorry, what did you just say?"

"She was murdered," Casper repeated, with utmost gravity.

"Yeah, okay, see, I thought maybe I heard you wrong, because I was expecting to hear something based in reality."

Casper cast a brief glance down the alleyway. "We shouldn't talk about it here. There are paparazzi everywhere."

"Yeah, I'm looking at one right now."

"It's not like that."

"Are you recording this? Trying to get a quote?"

"Fuck the camera, okay, I'll leave it." He threw his bag on the ground. "I need to talk to you. No one else will believe me, but Molly didn't overdose."

I couldn't help but give a bitter snort. "Let me guess. She faked her own death. It's all an elaborate publicity stunt for *Robot Wars Three: The Bride of Omnitron*. You'll never guess what they do to Tokyo in that one!"

"She was murdered," he said again, his expression unwaveringly serious. "Everyone's biased against her. She was seen as a train wreck, so everybody's assuming she did it to herself. You know that saying, when you hear hoofbeats, think horses, not zebras? Nobody's thinking zebras. But they should be."

"Why?"

"Yesterday, Molly had lunch with her manager and her agent. Cal Price and Damon Maxwell. You know them?"

I gave a terse nod. I had met Calvin Price on several occasions. He was a brusque, heavyset man in his early fifties. He wore polo shirts almost exclusively and kept his cell phone in a holster attached to his belt. He had been Molly's manager since the very beginning of her career, arranging her schedule and supervising her day-to-day. She once slipped up and referred to him as "Uncle Cal" in one of our conversations—apparently she used to call him that as a kid. She seemed to view him generally with fondness, partially tempered by exasperation.

"He's never been married, you know," she told me over drinks one night. "Amy says he's holding out for me. Like I'm some long-term investment he's waiting to cash in on. Can you imagine?"

"Uncle Cal and Aunt Molly," I mused, and she gave an exaggerated shiver.

"Please, God, don't even."

"You know, they say compound interest is a remarkable thing."

"Rachel, I will banish you from this table."

I had never met Molly's agent, Damon Maxwell, but I had witnessed Molly's side of their phone conversations a handful of times. Damon's job, according to Molly, was to help her land jobs and to do "the boring stuff—negotiations, contracts, the legal mumbo jumbo—to make sure I'm getting my fair share. And, of course, he stays motivated so that he can get his fair share too." Like many agents, Damon seemed to exist entirely on the phone—Molly was either annoyed because he was calling too often, or vexed that he wasn't calling enough.

"I saw the three of them," Casper said. "I was having lunch there too."

"How convenient."

"Something was wrong. They were having a conversation that looked pretty intense, and suddenly Molly got up. She was really upset. She said she wasn't going to promote *Sun City*, and if they didn't like it, she'd fire them both. She said something about how . . . the movie didn't matter anymore. The truth was the only thing that mattered. Then she stormed out, but Price and Maxwell stayed behind. I couldn't hear everything they said, but I definitely heard this—Maxwell said that they would have to deal with Molly sooner or later. He said, 'If we don't stop her here, it'll be the end of all of us.' And then she just happens to turn up dead less than a day later?"

It *was* suspicious—if it was even remotely true. "And I'm just supposed to take your word for it?"

Casper picked up his bag and pulled out a small, very pedestrian-looking digital camera. "I have pictures."

I couldn't help it: "Aren't you supposed to carry something a little more high-tech?" It was the same kind of camera I had given to Natalie for Christmas last year, and while it was definitely a foolish splurge on a budget like mine, it wasn't exactly something you'd expect a professional photographer to use.

He moved closer, tapping one of the camera's buttons to shuffle through images. "I have other cameras. It's not like I can roll into a restaurant with a telescopic lens."

"Oh yeah, no, you need to be discreet when you're infringing on someone's privacy."

"Molly and I had an agreement."

"I know. You were her 'friendly little ghost.'"

He met my eyes for a moment. "She said that?"

He looked just as young up close. His cheeks had a healthy bloom to them, like someone who had just taken a brisk walk in refreshingly cold weather.

"Show me the pictures," I said.

He extended the camera toward me. On the small view screen was a photo of Molly seated at a round table with Cal Price and Damon Maxwell. Cal was wearing his requisite polo shirt, a pair of folded-up wraparound sunglasses hanging from the collar. Damon was in a crisp, slim-fit dress shirt with the sleeves rolled up, a shiny Rolex on one wrist. Molly sat between them, casually dressed in a long tank top and jeans. As I clicked through the photos, a scene unfolded: Molly standing up, her expression fierce; turning to Damon, her eyes blazing, mouth parted in speech; then looking at Cal with scorn; and finally she was walking away, head held high, expression defiant.

I handed the camera back to Casper. "So they had lunch together." Seeing Molly—knowing that these pictures were from yesterday, her last day alive—stoked a leaden feeling in my stomach. "That doesn't prove what was said. They could've been talking about anything."

"But they weren't."

"And why should I believe you?"

"Because you wrote this." He reached into his jacket, pulled out a folded sheet of paper, and held it out to me.

I took it. It was a page from April's issue of *Icon*. My exclusive with Molly. One of the pull quotes, offset in a large, stylized font, read, "I'm on a new path, and I feel better than I ever have. I'm only looking forward now."

When Casper spoke again, his voice was soft. "They're saying there were half a dozen pill bottles on her bedside table. But she was clean. She'd been clean for months."

I knew that. I did. I thought of an alternate passage I had suggested for the pull quote: "It's so easy to slip back into old habits. But I don't want that. I don't want to live that way anymore."

"Someone set her up," Casper said quietly. His expression—the look in his eyes—was earnest. "Someone did this to her. You have to believe me."

I wanted to. I really did.

When I spoke, my voice came out rougher than I meant it to. "What do you want from me? What am I supposed to do?"

"You knew the people around her. You have connections. We could investigate."

I let out an unhappy breath of laughter. "Investigate. Right. Why don't you just go to the police?"

"Because they're not going to take me seriously," he said. "Horses, not zebras, remember?"

I didn't speak.

"This is my info." Casper pressed a small black rectangle into my hand. CASPER JONES was printed on it in sleek white letters. "Just think it over. You can call me anytime."

Then he was gone.

★ MARCH 2008 ★

IT WAS A SATURDAY NIGHT WHEN I MET MOLLY BYRNE FOR THE FIRST TIME, at Lithium. The following Monday, I arrived at work to find a package on my desk.

Anton was already seated at the desk across from mine, with his hands gathered under his chin, his expression expectant.

"Open it."

"Sorry?"

"I have to know what's in there."

I set my purse down and surveyed the box. It didn't have a shipping label.

"It was delivered by *courier*," Anton added with relish.

I was just as curious. So I opened it, and inside I found another box—black, with two white interlocking *C*s on the top.

"No way," Anton breathed.

I lifted the lid and there it was—my bag. The purse I had carried to Lithium that weekend.

But not really. It was the *real* bag. The real Chanel. The classic quilted double flap with rose gold hardware. I was almost too awed to touch it.

I took it out of the box nonetheless. A few other people from the bullpen had gathered around, and they collectively let out a soft gasp when I held it up, as if I had just uncovered the Ark of the Covenant.

"Holy shit, Rachel," said Stacia, another copy editor. "Did you get a sugar daddy?"

"Is there a card? Check if there's a card," Anton urged.

There was no card in the box. I opened the bag—the leather was smooth and flawless—and inside was a handful of YSL lip stains. All Corail Aquatique.

A note was tucked inside the inner pocket:

An authentic bag for an authentic person.
—MB

"No fucking way." Anton peered over my shoulder at the note. "Is that—"

I hurriedly stuffed the note back into the bag. "It's—um, it's a birthday present," I told the assembled crowd. "From . . . my aunt."

They dispersed, disappointed. I could hear Stacia saying, "Definitely a sugar daddy," in an extremely unsubtle whisper to another coworker.

Anton grabbed me by the wrist and pulled me through the bullpen and into the nearest stairwell. I was still holding the bag. Truth be told, it made far more sense with Anton's current outfit than with my own. He was resplendent in typical Anton fashion: an elaborately patterned black-and-white shirt with one too many buttons undone to be strictly work appropriate, black True Religion jeans with contrast stitching, a ring on nearly every finger.

He had worn his hair in twists when we first met, but he kept it close shaven these days. He often described himself as "too thick to model, too handsome to be a character actor." He also jokingly liked to refer to us both as "Midwest tens."

"Seriously?" His eyes were comically wide. "You *actually* met Molly Byrne at the club?"

"You didn't believe me?"

"You were drunk! I thought there was at least a sixty percent chance you met some girl who *looked* like Molly Byrne!"

I shook my head. "It was her."

"It was! And she sent you a Chanel!" In an impressively short turnaround, Anton's expression shifted from awed to suspicious. "*Why* did she send you a Chanel?"

That was the question at the forefront of my mind as well. "I . . . I don't know." I thought of Molly at Lithium, reaching for my bag on the bathroom counter, turning it toward the light. *It's a pretty convincing fake. Just like me.*

"She knew mine was fake," I said.

Anton raised his eyebrows skeptically. "Yeah, so? I know Stacia's 'Cartier' watch is actually a 'Schmartier,' but you don't see me upgrading her to the real thing. Why would Molly Byrne, *the* Betsey Blue, forever known as the only legitimate reason to watch *Robot Wars*, and esteemed singer of 2002's best gay club anthem, 'Polaroid Girl (Shake It, Drop It, Pop It),' do that?"

"Wow, did you memorize her Wikipedia page?"

"Molly Byrne is Hollywood's most perfect intersection of glamour and mess, and I'll have you know I shook it, dropped it, and popped it with the best of them in 2002. Why on earth would she send you that bag?"

The club bathroom . . . the Corail Aquatique . . . "I . . . I gave her my lip gloss. At the club."

"So? I gave Stacia a pen once, and you know what she gave me in return? Norovirus."

"I feel like you have a lot of pent-up feelings about Stacia that we need to work through."

"To know Stacia is to be annoyed by her, Rachel." Anton tapped the bag. "Why? Tell me. I need answers. I might actually die of anticipation."

"I . . . don't know. Seriously. I don't." I looked down at the purse. *The stitching tells the tale with Chanel.* The stitching was perfect.

For a moment, I imagined myself pushing through the doors of *Icon* dressed in some unbelievably chic outfit, this bag on my arm as I swanned through the bullpen on the way to my own private office. This was a bag that Rachel West, entertainment reporter, would own.

This was reality, though. It was not a bag meant to belong to Rachel West, copy editor. "I have to give it back."

"What? Why?"

"I can't accept this! She doesn't even know me. Why would she—" I shook my head. "It's too much. I have to give it back to her."

"How? It's not like there was a return address."

I paused. "Who's her agent?"

It took only a quick search to find that Molly was represented by Damon Maxwell, head of Maxwell Artistic Management. When I dialed the number for the agency, the phone rang only once before a woman with a nasal voice answered.

"Maxwell Artistic Management. This is Veronica. How may I direct your call?"

"Hi, my name is Rachel West. I'm calling about a gift from Molly Byrne—"

"I'm sorry, but the agency no longer accepts gifts on Molly's behalf. Thank you so much for—"

"It's not a gift *for* Molly, it's a gift *from* Molly. I need to return it."

"Pardon?"

"It's a Chanel bag. It was delivered to the *Icon* offices this morning. It's really kind of Molly, but I—"

"What did you say your name was?"

"Rachel West."

"Rachel . . ." There was a pause, and a muffled conversation. Then, "Hold, please."

The ringback music was one of Molly's Disney singles. Her singing voice was not particularly strong, but like all Disney Channel original tunes, the song was an infectious bop. It was not "Polaroid Girl"—her breakout shedding-the-child-star-image release that came post-Disney—but it was upbeat and fun.

"Go your own way, strike your own chord, write your own song," a teen Molly chanted enthusiastically to a peppy backing track. *"Beat your own drum, pave your own road, find your own—"*

"Are you still there?"

Veronica was back.

"Yes."

"You can bring the bag to LaSalle's on Melrose at two."

"I don't—"

"Ask the hostess for Anna Scott."

"But—"

Veronica hung up.

LaSalle's was a small restaurant in West Hollywood, tucked between an olive oil boutique and a bakery for dogs. The interior was dark paneled but warm, with a European kind of vibe.

After I asked the hostess for Anna Scott, as instructed, I was led to a table in the back of the restaurant, where Molly Byrne was already seated.

She was dressed in a cropped white peasant blouse and a tiered skirt. Suitably trendy boho chic. As I approached the table, she looked up from her phone—an iPhone, the likes of which I had only cradled lovingly at the Apple Store in the Glendale Galleria. "You're late."

"I . . ." It had taken me fifteen minutes to find a parking space, and another ten to walk to the restaurant from the space I finally found. Anton had totally mastered the mental calculus involved in the timing of travel around LA, but I hadn't quite gotten it yet.

I shook my head. "I'm sorry, I—What are you doing here?"

"Having lunch." She gestured to the empty seat across from her. "With you."

"I—"

"Are you vegetarian? Vegan?"

"No."

"Sit," Molly said. "You're making me nervous."

I sat.

"Why . . ." I wasn't quite sure how to finish the question. *Why are you here? Why am* I *here?* There was no reason on God's green earth why film and TV star Molly Byrne would have any interest in a med-school dropout with sixty-seven dollars in her bank account, a mountain of student loan debt, and persistent mildew on her bathroom ceiling that the landlord was somehow always "just about to get around to."

Maybe *Why are you wasting your time on me?* was the appropriate question.

Molly waved a waiter over. He had a ponytail, and large tattoos on his forearms, and he gazed at Molly in a way that made me think that if she asked him to bring her Snow White's heart, he would definitely do it. Though I couldn't imagine a scenario in which the mirror would declare anyone but Molly to be *fairest in the land.*

"We'll have a Perrier and . . ." She looked at me expectantly.

"Just water."

"Still? Sparkling?"

"Still."

The waiter went away, and for a moment, Molly simply assessed me with that cool blue gaze, her expression unreadable.

"So you don't like the purse?" she said finally.

I had brought the Chanel box in a brown paper H&M bag that Anton found under his desk. It was currently resting at my feet. "I do! Of course I do. I just . . . I can't accept a gift like this. We don't even know each other."

"So if we knew each other, you'd accept it."

"No. I mean—that's not it. It's really kind. Honestly. But I'm . . . not worth it."

Molly's tone didn't change—it was still conversational, nonchalant—but curiosity flashed in her eyes. "Why would you say that?"

I tried to match her. Light and conversational. Not nerve-racked in the least. "Why would you spend that much money on a stranger?"

"Because I have a lot of it. It's kind of like that thing where you say a word enough times and it loses all meaning."

"Semantic satiation," I said. Molly blinked at me. "That's what it's called," I clarified, and then instantly wished I hadn't. I felt like that annoyingly smug pedant at parties who's always one *well, actually* away from alienating everyone in the room.

Luckily, the waiter returned with our drinks at that moment.

Molly ordered food, and then gestured to me. I hastily scanned the menu and picked something at random.

"Have you heard of Vivian Grayson?" Molly asked when the waiter had once again retreated.

I shook my head.

"She leads these wellness retreats that have totally changed my life. She told me I need to focus on manifesting authentic experiences. I need to draw genuine and authentic people into my life." She looked at me. "I know it sounds weird, but I can just tell—you're authentic. You're your own person."

"Who else's person would I be?" I asked. I was not trying to be funny, but Molly smiled anyway.

We ate lunch together (her: a kale salad with no dressing; me: a five-cheese and bacon macaroni casserole served in a cast-iron skillet). Molly asked me polite questions about what it was like to work at *Icon*, how long I had lived in LA, what I liked to do in my free time. It felt a bit like a job interview, or maybe even a first date—that initial, semi-awkward, getting-to-know-you encounter. I asked questions too—about Molly's latest movie, about her future projects—and her answers were polite but uninformative.

When the waiter brought the check, I fumbled with my wallet, but Molly placed a card down and the waiter whisked it away before I could get my own card out.

"Thank you," I said. Suddenly, I remembered the purse at my feet. I picked up the bag and held it out to Molly. "And for this too, but it's still too much."

Molly took the bag and stood. "What are you doing right now?"

I blinked. "Sorry?"

"Do you want to run an errand with me?"

"Um . . ." It seemed like a no-brainer. What was I doing right now? Just finishing lunch with a celebrity. And what was next on my agenda? Going back to the office to proofread a listicle on the top ten favorite luxury items of celebrity dogs. And then going to my apartment to sort through my belongings for the umpteenth time and figure out what I might reasonably be able to pawn in order to pay my electricity bill this month. Glamorous.

But still I hesitated, and I didn't know why. "Sure," I said finally, and Molly smiled. It was a real one, a broad one, that fairy-tale princess smile.

"Great."

5

Someone set her up. Someone did this to her. You have to believe me.

I made my way back to the Palm Vista apartment complex in somewhat of a daze. The day felt surreal. In a matter of hours, I had learned of Molly's death, been questioned by the police, quit my job, had a paparazzi run-in, and heard an insane theory that I couldn't believe, but at the same time . . . couldn't stop thinking about.

I half expected another crowd of photographers to be waiting for me at Palm Vista, but luckily, the only person out front when I returned from *Icon* was a bored-looking teenage boy wearing a backpack and headphones and holding a skateboard. He didn't spare me a second glance as he threw the board down on the sidewalk, hopped on, and effortlessly glided away.

If only I could glide away from my problems like that.

Once inside my apartment, I kicked off my shoes, tossed my bag on the chair, and then collapsed onto the couch.

Someone set her up echoed again in my mind.

And: *You wanted to be an* Icon *reporter.*

And: *An authentic bag for an authentic person.*

And: *I'm sorry. About your friend.*

I lay there for a moment, one arm flung over my eyes, before suddenly sitting back up.

I retrieved the card from Casper and crossed over to my kitchenette. I placed it side by side with the card from Detective Lee. Two phone numbers in a single day. It was unusual for me under normal circumstances.

However, these were far from normal circumstances.

I picked up the rectangle from the detective. BENJAMIN LEE, it said in a straightforward font, with a phone number stamped underneath. A second number was handwritten in pen on the back.

He must've prepared it before he came to my apartment—or else he had taken the time to write his phone number on the back of every business card he had. Was it a "personal touch" that was supposed to make people want to open up to him? I flashed suddenly on the mental image of Detective Lee sitting at his kitchen island (probably a decently nice granite), carefully writing his phone number on the backs of a whole stack of business cards.

I dialed. It rang twice. And then:

"Lee."

I used to think people answered the phone like that only on TV, but I had talked to enough publicists by now to know otherwise. It was certainly more succinct and less absurd than how a celebrity rep I had spoken to recently answered the phone, with a harried "Go for Marcus. Catch me up." Anton swore he was going to adopt *Go for Anton. Catch me up*, but then he just as quickly abandoned it: "Should we bring back *ahoy-hoy* instead? More importantly, did we ever have it?"

"Hi, this is Rachel West. We spoke earlier today? About Molly?"

"Yes. What is it?"

No small talk, then. Okay. That was fine.

"Were there pill bottles on her bedside table? Half a dozen of them?"

A pause followed.

"Is this something you remembered from last night?" Lee asked carefully.

"Just something I heard around. Is it true?"

"Ms. West—"

"Rachel's fine."

"Rachel. I'm sorry, but I know you're a member of the press—"

"I'm not asking as a reporter. I'm not even—I just quit my job. And even if I was still with *Icon*, I don't think they even count as the press. Unless the press as a whole is preternaturally obsessed with pictures of Faith Hill at IHOP."

There was an exhalation that may have been a laugh.

Encouraged by that maybe-laugh, I continued. "I just . . . need some clarity. About what happened to my friend."

"There's going to be an official report released later today," Lee said. "But . . ." He let out another breath, one that was definitely not a laugh this time. "Since you're a friend of hers, I'll just say—strictly off the record—this appears to be a pretty cut-and-dried case. Molly had a history of prescription drug abuse—"

"She was clean, though."

"Relapse is not uncommon—"

"You didn't know her." It came out more sharply than I'd intended. I couldn't help it.

Lee continued, unfazed. "The ME will look for any underlying medical conditions. It's always possible that she—"

"I heard she had an argument. With her agent and her manager. Yesterday, at lunch." It flew out of my mouth before I could second-guess it. "Have you talked to them yet?"

"Why didn't you mention this earlier?"

"I didn't know about it. I didn't hear it from Molly. Just . . . around."

There was a tinge of amusement in his voice. "Wow, it really sounds like *around* is the place to go for info these days. Should I be getting around more?"

I might've laughed under other circumstances. But I just pressed ahead: "Did you interview them? Did they mention the argument? Because if they didn't, that could mean—"

Lee cut me off. "We're following up with everyone who interacted with Molly yesterday. If something was amiss, we'll find it."

"Something was *obviously* amiss. She's dead."

"Rachel—"

"I take it back. *Ms. West* is fine."

"I know this must be hard—"

"Never mind."

I hung up. But that didn't feel definitive enough, so I threw my phone across the room for good measure. It hit the couch, bounced once, and landed on the floor with a thud.

I flashed on Molly, holding up her iPhone. *I know it's the latest thing and the wave of the future or whatever, but how am I supposed to hang up on people with any kind of actual satisfaction? Just poking at a screen isn't going to do it. But apparently, if I slam this thing down on the table the screen'll crack and I'll be out six hundred dollars.*

I remembered the wry smile that followed. *You know what, though? That might be gratifying in its own way. I might want to get six hundred dollars' worth of mad someday.*

ICON ONLINE

JUNE 17, 2008

Following the heartbreaking news of actress Molly Byrne's sudden passing, an outpouring of love has come from the Hollywood community, with many celebs posting messages in tribute to the star online.

On Twitter, *Sun City* costar Alessandra Delgado tweeted: "This is unfathomable. RIP sweet girl."

A Is for Arnold costar Noah McFarlane shared: "Such a great girl, gone way too soon. Life just isn't fair sometimes."

Robot Wars costar Nick Hart added: "Heaven has a new angel today. We will never forget you, Mol."

A representative for *Sun City* director Adrien Ford told *Icon*, "Our thoughts and prayers are with the Byrne family, and with everyone affected by the loss of such a bright young talent."

A statement issued by Maxwell Artistic Management, the agency representing the actress, requested a reprieve from media speculation: "We ask for care, compassion, and respect for the Byrne family's need for privacy at this very difficult time."

6

That night I got an email from Molly's assistant, Alyssa. The subject line read, "FW: Funeral information—STRICTLY PRIVATE."

The message at the top read simply: "FYI."

That feeling of unreality swept over me again as I scanned the details.

I ate part of a microwave dinner. It tasted terrible. I turned on the TV, mindlessly watched a few minutes of a *Friends* rerun, switched it off. The laugh track was grating.

I felt numb. Which seemed better than feeling . . . anything.

I needed to get out of my apartment. Down the street there was a gas station that I visited for snacks from time to time. I didn't keep a lot in the way of groceries; I didn't cook often even in the best of times.

"Just remember, the ride won't last forever," Anton said to me once at work, casting a sidelong glance my way as I scarfed down a Hostess Sno Ball at my desk. He was only five years older than me, but he never missed an opportunity to share the wealth of wisdom those additional five years had brought him. "I remember being twenty-five and thinking I was invincible. But no one's immune to scurvy, Rachel. Try to eat something with a little vitamin C in it every now and then."

"Do lime-flavored Chewy Sprees count?"

"I know you're playing with me right now, but I would genuinely urge you to start a multivitamin."

I was walking up to my apartment door, Star Crunches and Doritos successfully obtained, when I heard a loud *pssst* from nearby.

I ignored it, fumbling with my key in the lock.

"Psssssssssst." Several units down, a head of curly dark hair stuck through the front door. "Honestly, who ignores a *psssst*?"

I couldn't ignore the *psssst*—or its progenitor—now. A woman stepped out of the apartment. She was short and round, with dark chin-length curls, and deep brown eyes that shone behind rimless rectangular glasses. Her age was hard to pinpoint; I would guess she was somewhere in the latter half of her thirties, but she had what my mom would call a baby face. She wore a brightly colored crocheted patchwork sweater and a pair of black gauchos. She was holding last week's issue of *Life & Style*, flipped open to a spread on star sightings.

"That's you, right?" She looked at me, her eyes bright with curiosity. Then she glanced at the page on the left, the bottom half of which showed Molly and me leaving a club. "Don't get me wrong, I didn't pay for this. I'm not the kind of person who subscribes to *Life and Style.* It got delivered to my box accidentally, but holy shit, this is you. Who knew? You're a little bit famous, and you live right here at Palm Vista. That's LA for you, isn't it?"

"Yeah, well" seemed like the only thing to say. I fumbled with my keys again.

"I'm Fadia." She pointed to her door. "From 102. You're 105. I see you taking your trash out sometimes. Man, you eat a lot of frozen food."

"Not much of a cook," I said. And then as an afterthought, because it felt rude not to, I added, "I'm Rachel."

"I know." She referred to the magazine. "'Molly Byrne leaves Hyde with gal pal Rachel West.'" She raised an eyebrow. "Gal pal, huh?" Before I could respond, she went on: "Hey, that must mean . . . I saw that she died. Did you—is that why the cops were here this morning? Because you knew her?" Her gaze softened. "Are you okay?"

It somehow hit harder than any of the *how are you holding up*s I received at *Icon* this morning. Maybe it was how Fadia's eyes, already large to begin with, were magnified by her rimless lenses, amplifying the surprisingly genuine concern there.

"I'm fine." I guess it was par for the course for me to outright lie to people now.

"I'm really sorry she passed."

I nodded. I was too. More than I could possibly express.

"How'd you meet her, anyway?"

I thought of Lithium. The bathroom. The Corail Aquatique. Then I thought of what followed.

"Just around. You know."

She looked amused at that. "Can't really say I do. Did you—"

It was suddenly too much. This interaction. This day. All of it. "Have a good night," I said, and went into my apartment, shutting the door swiftly behind me.

★ MARCH 2008 ★

MOLLY'S "ERRAND" AFTER OUR FIRST EVER LUNCH TOGETHER TOOK US TO the Chanel store on Rodeo.

"We can return your bag and pick up mine," Molly told me as she expertly angled her Mercedes into a space that looked far too small for it. "I'm not usually a Chanel girl, to be honest, but I guess you kind of inspired me. I went ahead and ordered my own when I got yours, but they had to overnight it from New York. It's from the limited collection. And before you say it, yeah, I could have my assistant pick it up, but, like, where's the fun in that? Half the point is the hunt, after all." A marimba melody suddenly filled the car. Molly pulled her iPhone out of her purse and glanced at the screen. "Speak of the devil." She swiped a finger across the screen and accepted the call. "Everything's fine," she told the person on the other end of the line. A brief pause followed. "Don't worry about it." Another, slightly longer pause. "Yes, I'll be there. No, listen—it's fine. Take five calming breaths and drink a kombucha, okay? I'll be there, I swear."

She ended the call without hesitation, and then threw the phone back into her purse.

"My assistant," she said, her tone a mix of beleaguered and fond. "Alyssa. She's great—don't get me wrong—but sometimes it feels a bit too much like babysitting."

I couldn't help but smile slightly. "Is she babysitting you, or are you babysitting her?"

Molly's eyes shone. "A little of both."

She reached into the back seat and grabbed the Chanel bag she'd given me. "Look, no offense whatsoever, but you can't go in there carrying that." She lowered her gaze to indicate my own purse, which sat on my lap. It was not the knockoff Chanel clutch I had carried at Lithium. It was a tattered canvas Coach bag that had been a high school graduation present from my grandmother. It had logged an impressive number of miles since then. "To be clear, it's not because it's wretchedly out of season. It's because it looks like it was run over by a semitruck." She poked at a hole that was starting to wear through the fabric, and then glanced up at me, her eyes sparkling. "Seriously, Rachel, do you use this to wash your car?"

It was a little mean, in a way that intimidatingly beautiful girls could be sometimes. But it was also funny, and humor was a direct line to my heart.

Molly handed me the Chanel purse. "Just carry it into the store so I won't be embarrassed if we get papped."

So I moved my wallet (from Target) and phone (the battered Nokia) into the new bag. I half expected it to vomit them back out, demanding higher-quality contents.

"Great." Molly looked satisfied, and then added, "Don't worry about your shoes. There's no time to do anything about them anyway."

I peered down at my well-worn ballet flats, and then back up at her. Whatever my expression was, it made Molly burst into laughter.

"Kidding." And, as she opened her car door, "Mostly."

Just as Molly had predicted, a photographer descended on us as soon as we got out of the car. He was probably mid-thirties, tall and rangy, with long blond hair and a patchy beard.

"Molly! How are we doing today?" he called brightly, revealing a British accent that I was about seventy percent sure was authentic.

"You're quick on the scene," she replied conversationally. "Did you follow us here?"

"At a safe distance, darling. You know we always treat Dax's girl right."

It hadn't crossed my mind before, but Molly's dating a paparazzo meant that she was probably frequently running into . . . his coworkers.

"Out shopping today? What are we in the market for?" the pap continued.

Molly's lip curled. "'Dax's girl,'" she repeated, ignoring the questions. "Why isn't he 'Molly's boy'?"

The pap grinned. "Feisty. I like it. Can you smile for me, love? Who's your friend?"

For a moment, I wondered if Molly was going to tell him to get lost—or something more colorful. But instead, she flashed a perfunctory smile and looped her arm through mine. "This is Rachel. Just one more."

The pap's shutter whirred a dozen or so times, rapid-fire, and then Molly pulled me in the direction of the store.

The sales associates gathered around us as soon as Molly and I stepped inside. A willowy woman who seemed to have a little more of an authoritative air than the rest—maybe she was the manager—stepped forward and greeted Molly with air-kisses.

"Molly, honey," she gushed. "Look at you! You're radiant as always."

Molly just smiled—a reserved one. "What a relief."

"We've got your new baby in," the manager said as she led us farther into the store. "It's to die for."

Molly's "baby" was a small black leather shoulder bag with a scattering of metal detailing across the front: a number five, cursive script spelling out *Chanel* and *Monaco*, a shiny turtle. It had a chain strap that Molly slung over her shoulder immediately.

The manager clasped her hands under her chin. "What do we think?"

Molly assessed her reflection in a nearby mirror. For a moment, the air in the Chanel store turned tense in anticipation of her judgment.

"It's perfect," she declared.

Relief flooded the manager's face. "Isn't it just?"

Molly set the purse on the counter and began transferring the contents of her current bag to the new one. "While we're here," she said offhandedly, "we want to return that one." She gestured in my direction.

The manager's eyes widened. "Oh. Was there—"

"You know what, though?" Molly's expression transformed into a concerned pout. "I bet we can't, because it's already been used. Isn't that right?"

"Well, I—" the manager began.

"That's a shame, but I totally understand." Molly shot me a look, completely unapologetic. "See, their hands are tied, Ray. I guess you have to keep it."

I realized in that moment that I was now in full possession of two unexpected things from Molly Byrne: the Chanel bag and a nickname.

I pushed back on the former. "Or you could keep it." I held the bag out to her.

"Why would I do that?" Wide-eyed, Molly clutched her own, newly filled bag to her chest. "I already have my new baby." She slid her old purse in the direction of the manager. "Could you box this one up? Thank you so much."

We left the store with the new purse on Molly's arm. She tossed the old one in the back of her car.

"You tricked me," I said. I was equal parts chagrined and impressed.

"It's not like I could actually return it anyway. Cynthia would lose her commission. Do you really want to take bread out of the mouths of Cynthia's seven children?"

"She has seven kids?"

"She *could*," Molly said innocently. "Face it—the bag's all yours now. I certainly can't take it back. I don't wear anything pre-owned unless it's vintage."

"Oh, so I just need to hold on to it for . . . twenty-five years?"

Molly grinned. "It's a deal. Up for another stop?"

We visited most of Rodeo that day. I followed Molly from store to store, witnessing the adulation of fawning salesperson after fawning salesperson, and watched as Molly tried on a seemingly endless parade of dresses, jackets, shoes, hats, scarves, necklaces . . . She dismissed options without hesitation, and purchased with equal authority. I had never witnessed a shopping spree carried out with such impunity.

And at every store we went to, she'd turn to me and say, "You should try on the green halter; green is really your color," or "I want the suede sandals in blue; I'll get you the same in burgundy."

I turned down everything she offered, but that didn't stop her from requesting the second pair, in burgundy, and then gesturing to the sales associate to hand them to me.

"What is this?" I asked, finally relenting and taking the box, as I seemed to have no other choice. Molly was already putting on another pair of shoes—peep-toed platform heels in bright vermilion. "A *Prince and the Pauper* situation? Are you trying to butter me up so I'll switch places with you?"

"Don't be silly. No one in their right mind would believe that you were me." She stood up and took a few steps, considering the shoes. "More like *Cinderella*. Or . . . *A Cinderella Story*, if we want to stay current."

"Are you the Chad Michael Murray in this scenario?"

Her eyes gleamed. "Would you like that?" She moved toward the full-length mirror that stood between two shelves of shoes. I watched as she turned slowly in front of it, examining the peep-toed heels from all angles. "You know, I was up for that part."

"Really? I mean, Chad is the more traditional casting choice, but I'd applaud the studio for their forward thinking—"

Molly grinned at me. "Hilary Duff's part. But they said I was too sexy to play PG." The grin faded. "I heard that a lot after *A Is for Arnold*. *We want puppy love, not Playmate of the Year.* I guess that's what happens when you get screwed on a waterbed and jet-packed through a window. Changes your whole career trajectory. I haven't even done *Playboy*, for the record. Not to say I haven't been asked." She bit her lip, her eyes falling back to the shoes. "They pinch my toes. I'm trying to figure out if they're cute enough to overlook it."

"If they're not comfortable, you won't wear them," I said

automatically. It was something my mom always said when I was a kid.

Molly met my gaze in the mirror, amused. "Well, that's just categorically untrue. It's all relative to how good they look. Or, more importantly, how good I look in them." She took a few more steps, and then declared, "Worth it." To the sales associate: "Add these too, please? Thank you so much."

It was after our last stop—the Fendi store—that Molly let out a sigh and said, "I don't know about you, but I'm starving."

It had been a few hours since lunch. And Molly had eaten a flavorless kale salad, whereas I was still going pretty strong on that cast-iron skillet full of mac and cheese.

"I know a place," she said. "It's kind of a drive, but it's worth it. Are you in?"

Of course I was.

Molly's "place" was a taco truck near Santa Monica Beach. We got massive tacos—carne asada for me and al pastor for Molly (the kale salad now a distant memory, seemingly)—and ate at a picnic table nearby. A few heads turned in Molly's direction—it was the same everywhere we went—but no one approached her.

"It'll last a little while, if we're lucky," Molly said. She had pulled her hair back into a loose ponytail and donned a baseball cap and sunglasses before we left the car. "It's that thing where you don't expect to see someone, so you're not exactly sure if it's really them or not. But as soon as the first person steps up and breaks the spell, it could turn into a total mob scene."

"What do you do then?"

Her tone was wry. "Hope for the best."

The sun was just beginning to set as we sat and ate, the light slanting across the sand. It was my favorite time of day—golden hour.

"So what's your plan?" Molly asked between bites.

"What do you mean?"

"How are you going to break out of tabloid copy editor hell?"

"I wouldn't call it *hell.*" Last week, at a staff meeting, Irina had ranted for a full, uninterrupted seventeen minutes about our unwillingness to *engage beyond the bare minimum*, and the subsequent *shit pile of mediocrity* that had resulted from it. "I mean, not exactly."

"But you want to be a reporter, don't you? You can't be stuck fact-checking and proofreading for *Icon* forever."

I couldn't keep the surprise out of my voice. "You know what a copy editor does?"

She gave me a withering look. "I'm not dumb just because I'm pretty, Rachel."

I couldn't respond.

"What if you got a really big story?" she continued. "You'd probably get promoted, wouldn't you?"

"I don't know . . . Maybe?"

"How about an exclusive?" She held a hand up, indicating the words in the air above her. "'Molly Byrne Tells All: Rehab, Her Recent Breakup, and Everything in Between.'"

"You broke up with Dax?"

"Not yet." Her eyes shone. "Let's be real, though—it's just a matter of time."

I considered Molly for a moment as she sat across the table from me. I was reminded again of the *A Is for Arnold* poster that had hung above my college boyfriend's bed. The girl from the poster—from the movie screen, the magazine covers—was sitting here with me, casually polishing off a taco. We might be overrun by fans or paparazzi or both at any moment. She might vanish in front of my very eyes, some kind of vitamin-C-deficiency-induced hallucination. But we had spent the day together. And here she was, offering to help me. But why?

I spoke, and it wasn't with suspicion but with genuine curiosity. "Why would you give me an exclusive?"

She wiped her mouth delicately with a paper napkin, and then said, "Why not? I told you, Ray. I'm *manifesting authentic experiences.* And what's so bad about using the influence of my extremely *in*authentic experiences up to this point to help my new friend level up at her shitty job?" She gave me an assessing look. "And can I tell you something else? If you really want to work in this industry, you have to be a shark. You have to be fucking relentless. You don't ask, *Why would you give me an exclusive?* You ask, *When can you give me the exclusive?*"

I swallowed. "When can you give me the exclusive?"

Molly smiled. "Much better."

7

I slept poorly the night after Molly died. I managed to drop off eventually, but the sleep that followed was restless, and although I couldn't remember my dreams when I awoke, the unsettling feeling of them lingered.

The sun was up and I had been awake for some time when a knock sounded at my front door. I was still in my pajamas. I had been scanning news sites since I got out of bed. Detective Lee had told the truth on the phone yesterday—a report had been released by the LA County coroner's office.

The articles all said the same things: *Pronounced dead at the scene. No evidence of trauma or foul play. Release of a cause of death will be deferred until toxicology results are available.*

A second knock sounded, this one more insistent. I looked toward the door. Yesterday it had been Lee and Ruiz. Who would appear today?

I crossed over and looked through the peephole. One brown eye peered back at me, equidistant from the peephole on the other side.

"I know you're home."

It was Anton. I opened the door.

"Why the hell weren't you answering your phone?" he demanded.

My phone. After calling Lee yesterday—after throwing my phone at the couch—I had completely forgotten about it. I went over to it and picked it up off the floor. The battery was dead.

"Ran out of battery." I moved to the kitchenette, fished the charger out of a drawer, and plugged it into the wall as Anton toed off his shoes and came inside the apartment.

"Natalie called me," he said. "Your negligence forced your nineteen-year-old sister to make an actual phone call."

"When did she call?" My phone sprang to life, and a series of notifications flooded in: missed calls, texts, voicemails. I felt guilty seeing that a number of them were from my sister.

"This morning. I said I'd come over and check on you." His expression softened a little. "How are you?"

I shrugged. I genuinely didn't know. But the look on my face must have spoken for me, because Anton crossed over to the kitchen and folded me into a hug.

"This whole thing is shit, isn't it?" he mumbled into the top of my head. I just nodded, closing my arms around his waist and gripping the back of his shirt.

Anton was a copywriter and three years my senior at *Icon*. He had shown me the ropes when I first started working there. At our first lunch together, he asked me why I wanted to work at *Icon*. I didn't tell him the whole story—just that I had found comfort in magazines when I was a kid.

"Oh, honey, that's sweet," he had replied, before taking a long pull from a Jamba juice. "I mean, the internet is definitely going to kill print media, but still. Sweet."

I knew then that we would be friends.

Anton was a Midwestern transplant himself. He grew up in Michigan, went to college in Chicago, and eventually followed his then-boyfriend out to LA.

"We had big California dreams," he told me once with a wry smile over drinks. "He was going to be a fashion designer, and I was going to be a fashion designer's boyfriend, and maybe I'd do TV or write a memoir or start my own line of sneakers that effortlessly transition from day to night. Obviously, I hadn't put a lot of time and effort into developing this plan. And then the thing that always happens happened."

"What thing is that?"

He waved a hand. "Arguments. Broken trust. Inevitable heartbreak on my side, relative indifference on his side. And he somehow ended up with the apartment *and* custody of the friend group. Didn't seem fair in the least, but that's life sometimes. As my grandmama liked to say, *fair* is a place with cotton candy and carousels."

According to Anton, it was all for the best in the end. "Turns out I have the soul of an Angeleno. Thank God the ex didn't move us to New York instead. Can you imagine me there? What would I have even done? Finance? I'd have to wear a vest and watch *Mad Money* and complain about rush hour at Grand Central. It's too upsetting to even contemplate."

Right now, I leaned into him. He smelled like lavender and mint. I tried not to think about the fact that the last person I had hugged was Molly.

He pulled back after a moment and held me at arm's length, assessing. "What are we gonna do with you, huh?"

I broke away and crossed over to close my laptop—currently displaying an article titled "Initial Report from Coroner Deems Molly Byrne's Cause of Death 'Uncertain'"—and then I sank down onto the couch.

Anton, who usually sat beside me on the couch during our TV nights watching *America's Next Top Model* or *Project Runway*, took a seat in the armchair (a dumpster find, slipcovered at Anton's urging). Which signaled to me that the hug did not mean he had forgiven me for going AWOL.

I knew I was probably meant to say something like *I'm sorry for going AWOL*. But I was terrible at apologizing, and the past twenty-four hours certainly hadn't made it any easier to articulate my feelings. So we just sat until Anton spoke.

"You quit your job."

"Yes."

I hadn't exactly considered all of the ramifications of that spur-of-the-moment decision. I didn't regret it, but I did regret leaving Anton. He was more than my work friend—he was my *friend* friend, and I had grown accustomed to seeing him every day, having lunch together, sharing work gossip, bouncing ideas off each other. I had grown to depend on all of that, actually. In giving up *Icon*, I had given that up too.

I wondered if Anton was thinking the same thing. If he was annoyed with me or . . . hurt.

His face revealed nothing. He was remarkably expressive, but he knew just how to control his expression when he needed to. He never gambled, but he once told me, "If I had chosen to become a professional poker player, I'd have been amazing at it."

"Okay, Lady Catherine de Bourgh," I had replied with a grin. I had seen the latest film adaptation of *Pride and Prejudice* more times than I cared to admit.

"You're just . . . done," he continued when I didn't elaborate. "At *Icon*."

"Correct."

"And . . . how do you feel about that?"

It felt a little too much like a therapy session. I shook my head. "I don't know how I'm supposed to feel about anything right now."

Anton nodded. "Fair." He was quiet for a beat. "What happened with Irina? When I got in yesterday, she was in the middle of a Grade A bitch fit—targeted at the design department and ostensibly about font choice, but honestly, everyone could tell it wasn't *really* about the fonts."

I rubbed my temples. "I couldn't handle it. Her. Any of it."

"So you just quit?"

So you're just quitting? My mother's voice popped into my head, an echo of the past. *Just like that? Everything you've worked toward, down the drain?*

Another job—or the pursuit of it—down the drain indeed. I was the kid who quit softball after three practices. I stopped showing up to my high school summer job at an ice-cream shop after a particularly heated argument with my manager about proper scoop sizes. I ended my last relationship via text message.

"Yes," I replied. "Classic Rachel West avoidance tactic. Now I just have to figure out how I'm going to pay rent next month, and what I'm going to do for work, and—oh yeah—whether or not Molly was murdered."

Anton's eyebrows ratcheted up. "Come again?"

It seemed crazy when I said it out loud. But at the same time . . .

I told Anton about Casper, the "friendly little ghost" paparazzo, and the fight Casper overheard at the restaurant the day of Molly's death, and the call with Detective Lee.

"Seriously, though," Anton said, his expression reflecting that sentiment exactly. "What would anybody gain by killing Molly?"

"I don't know. But . . ." I ran a hand over my eyes. "Is it so fucked-up that part of me thinks it's better to believe she was murdered than to believe she overdosed?"

Anton didn't reply. Maybe he knew the question was rhetorical. Maybe there was no good answer.

My phone rang, cutting through the silence. I went over to the kitchen counter and picked it up. *NAT* flashed across the screen.

There was probably enough charge now to take the call, so I unplugged the phone and headed into the bedroom, even though the particleboard door was unlikely to provide much privacy.

"What the fuck, Rachel," Natalie said by way of a greeting.

"I'm sorry."

"Are you okay? What happened? I saw some stuff online, but, like, what actually happened?"

Natalie was nearly seven years younger than me, and ten years younger than our brother, Sam. She had been a "surprise" according to our mom and dad, a happy accident for parents who were already a little older to begin with.

"She's the consolation prize," Sam liked to say, in a way that might've sounded mean if you didn't see the mischief alight in his eyes when he said it. "God knew I had a factory defect, so he threw in another kid to make up for it."

Natalie was more easygoing than either Sam or I had ever been, more optimistic, more inclined to express her feelings rather than keep things bottled up. Sam was funny and bright but deeply private; there was this feeling you got with him sometimes like you were barely scratching the surface of what he truly thought or felt. "The iceberg type," Molly once told me when I'd described him to her. "I've dated guys like that before. It never works out. *I want more, Tony. All eight eighths.*"

"Sorry?"

She had stared at me as if I had three heads. "You've never seen *The Band Wagon*?"

She would later make me watch *The Band Wagon*—her favorite film, a 1953 classic about the making of a movie. At one point during shooting, the "genius" director demands more commitment from the film within a film's star, Tony, leading to Molly's favorite quote from the movie: *"Now, look, Tony. You know about icebergs, don't you? One-eighth above the surface, seven-eighths below the surface. That's you, Tony. Now, I'm greedy. I want more. I want all eight eighths."*

I didn't know if it was possible to get all eight eighths out of someone, but Molly was right about Sam. And if he was the iceberg type, then Natalie was the opposite: she certainly gave more *eighths* than he did.

I was more inclined toward that middle-kid brand of independence—holding my tongue to smooth things over or mediate, taking care of myself so as not to pull focus or be a bother because I knew that Sam and Natalie needed more attention.

"I'm fine," I told Natalie now. "And I don't know what really happened with Molly."

"I thought you said she was doing well."

I thought she was echoed in my mind. And then I immediately amended: *No. She* was.

But all I said was: "Mm."

"Are things really crazy at work?"

I knew before I answered the phone that I wasn't going to tell Natalie about quitting *Icon*. She would worry, and tell our parents, and they would worry, and then I'd be fielding calls and reassuring everyone, and I just didn't have it in me to do that at the moment.

"I'm taking a little time off," I said evenly.

"That's good. You could come home if you wanted."

I hadn't been back since Christmas. I didn't have the money for a flight, and even if I did, I wasn't sure how comforting I would find going home.

"I'll think about it."

"You always say that. And it always means no."

"Not always."

"Rachel." She didn't sound exasperated. But she sounded more serious than she should have at nineteen years old.

"Hm?"

There was a pause before Natalie spoke. "Just . . . make sure you're taking care of yourself. You're important, okay?"

It was embarrassing that my baby sister felt the need to give me affirmations. It was supposed to be the other way around. I was supposed to affirm her. I was supposed to be the role model. But what kind of role model had I ever been? I hadn't lived at home since she was twelve years old. She'd spent her entire adolescence apart from me. Maybe that was why she was so much more well-adjusted.

When I ended the call and returned to the kitchen, Anton was standing at the counter, eating from a blue ceramic casserole dish that was not mine.

Last night, an hour or so after I had arrived back from the gas station, a knock sounded at my door. When I peered through the peephole, Fadia from 102 was standing there, holding a dish covered in aluminum foil. "It's me, from before," she called brightly.

I opened the door.

"I brought you some food. I had some leftovers from dinner, and that gas station stuff you had earlier kind of bummed me out. Plus, you look kind of . . . drawn. Figured a home-cooked meal couldn't hurt."

"That's—"

"It's not poisoned, don't worry." She peeled back the foil, pulled off an edge of something noodle-like, and ate it. "See? Mmm. I'm a good cook—great, some might even say."

I didn't feel like I could refuse it, so I took the dish. "Thank you."

"No worries. Enjoy!" And with that, Fadia headed off.

I had stuck the casserole dish in the fridge, where Anton had now clearly discovered it.

"I can't believe you actually cooked something," he said, mouth full. "And not only is it edible, but it's actually pretty damn delicious. Seriously. What else have you been hiding from me?"

"I didn't cook it. The woman from 102 brought it over."

He dropped his fork. "Do we trust the woman from 102?"

I shrugged. "She ate some of it in front of me."

"Kinky."

I sat down on the couch again. Anton brought the casserole dish over and sat next to me (I knew then that I was forgiven). He held out a forkful of food, which I ate without hesitation. It was lasagna, and it was indeed delicious.

We polished off the rest of it, and then I took the casserole dish to the sink and washed it. "I'll take it back to the neighbor."

"She's probably at work, don't you think?"

"Exactly. I'll leave it outside her door."

"Classic Rachel West avoidance tactic," Anton called as I left the apartment.

I headed down three doors to 102 and placed the dish on Fadia's doormat, which was made of jute and printed with a bold diamond pattern. As I turned to leave, the door swung open.

Fadia stood there, wearing a phone headset and holding a cordless phone. She waved at me.

"Yes . . . the premium plan is at a *slight* price differential compared to the— No, no . . ." She pointed to the headphones and held up one finger. I glanced around, not sure whether I should stay. "Absolutely . . . Yes . . . Now, is there anything else I can help you with? . . . Thank you so much. Have a great— Yeah, okay, then."

She lowered her headphones. "Can't even get out *have a great day* anymore before they hang up on you. People these days, the state of society, blah, blah, blah . . ." Then she cast a sunny smile at me as I picked the dish back up. "So, how was it?"

"It was really good. Thank you."

"No worries."

I was going to hand her the dish and leave—that was the natural thing to do—but then I caught a glimpse inside Fadia's apartment.

My own apartment, a Palm Vista utility unit, had one bedroom, a minuscule kitchen, and a bathroom that was probably too small to qualify even as minuscule. "I didn't know they made sinks that small," Anton had commented the first time he came over. "Was it manufactured by Playskool?"

Fadia's unit had the same components, laid out in the mirror image of mine. But that was where the similarities ended. While my general interior-decoration aesthetic was defined by its total lack of cohesive interior decoration, Fadia's apartment was . . . atmospheric.

The living room walls were a deep forest green, with an intricate pattern stenciled in gold paint. There were vintage movie posters hung in gilt frames, a midcentury-style couch, a marble-topped coffee table . . .

She noticed me looking. "Oh, you want the tour?"

"No, I—"

"Come on in. If a call pops up, I'll just grab it real quick."

She held the door open wider and, against my better judgment, I entered.

"No shoes in the house," Fadia commanded, so I left my slip-ons by the door before stepping onto the lush, multicolor area rug.

"How long have you lived here?" I asked, eyes raking over the tall chestnut shelves filled with DVDs and old VHS tapes. Next to the TV was a display of vintage video cameras.

"Four, five years? Five. I used to live in Venice, but the rent here is way better." She took the casserole dish from me and carried it to the kitchen. I couldn't believe we lived in the same building. This place made me feel like I had stepped into some chic hotel.

Suddenly, a phone rang, and Fadia winced. "Sorry. Give me a minute." She pulled her headset back on and tapped the left earphone. I could hear her as she disappeared into the bedroom: "Elite Enterprises. This is Stephanie. How may I be of service to you today?" She cast a wink at me as she closed the door.

I walked over to examine one of the shelves. There was a running theme among its contents. DVD sets of the *Halloween* films, the *Nightmare on Elm Street* films, and the *Scream* trilogy stood side by side. Perfectly pristine VHS tapes of classics like *The Exorcist*, *The Shining*, *Carrie*, and *The Birds* stood alongside a whole slew of movies I had never heard of before, with titles like *Santa Slasher VIII*, *House on the Hill of Death*, and *A Clown's Revenge*.

I was contemplating the illustrated cover of a film called *Endoscope of Terror*—a doctor in blood-spattered scrubs extending a tube toward the viewer with a sinister gleam in his eyes—when there was a knock at the front door. I jumped.

Anton stuck his head in tentatively. "Ahoy-hoy!"

"What are you doing?"

"You didn't come back right away. I thought maybe you got kidnapped."

"And you thought *ahoy-hoy* would be a good icebreaker?"

Anton's eyes roamed the room. "Holy hell, look at this place."

"Right?"

The bedroom door swung open and Fadia appeared. "Sorry on behalf of Pete from Albuquerque," she said. "I mean, I did just save him two hundred dollars, but frankly, he didn't seem all that appreciative." Her gaze landed on Anton. "Hi. Who are you?"

"Anton. Originally of Ann Arbor, currently of Los Feliz. I'm Rachel's dearest friend."

"Fadia. Charmed."

"Likewise. Are you the horror movie buff?"

Amusement flashed across Fadia's face. "What makes you ask that?"

Anton, who had by this point fully entered the apartment and shut the door behind him as if he had been invited in, pointed to a large gilt frame centered on the wall behind the couch. "Is that an original poster for *Psycho*?"

"Yup. Mint condition."

"And the walls?"

"Hand stenciled. It's the same pattern as in the *Silence of the Lambs* house. I changed the colors, though, and added the gold detailing. I like a little more pizzazz."

Anton looked impressed. "I know we just said who we are, but, like, who *are* you?"

Fadia shrugged. "Film enthusiast? Food enthusiast? Corporate drone? Pick a card."

"How are you at murder investigations?" Anton said, and I shot him a sharp look. He blinked back at me innocently. "What? It's just speculation, right? Should we be keeping it a secret?"

Fadia looked between the two of us with interest. "Is this about Molly Byrne?"

"How did you know that?" I asked, at the same time that Anton said, "She's a witch! Or a psychic! Tell the truth—are you a psychic witch? You have to tell us now or it's entrapment."

Fadia grinned. "Sadly, I'm no psychic witch. Just the recipient of a misdelivered *Life and Style*."

Anton cocked his head.

"It *is* about Molly." Fadia pinned me with an assessing look. "You think she was murdered?"

"I don't know." I swallowed. "Maybe."

It was quiet for a moment.

Then Fadia's gaze brightened. "I know exactly who can help. Richard from 203. He's the one who drives the old yellow Beetle? He's always ordering Vietnamese food at random hours?"

I couldn't say that I was particularly aware of the goings-on of the other residents of the Palm Vista apartment complex. But then, I didn't work from home like Fadia clearly did.

Anton turned from where he was now browsing Fadia's movie collection. "Is he a cop or something? A retired PI?"

"Better. He used to be a writer for *Crime Scene LA*. You know, the show with the guy from that thing? Richard plotted the murders—it was basically his entire job. He'll definitely have ideas. And he knows a lot about how the whole investigative process works, since he literally had to script a murder or two and how to solve it every week."

"Some episodes even have *three* murders," Anton told me.

I blinked. "You watch *Crime Scene LA*?"

"Of course. I love the guy from that thing."

I turned back to Fadia. "We don't need any help. I mean, thank you. For the suggestion. But we're not—this is all just speculative. Thanks for the food," I added. "Really." And then I ushered Anton out of the apartment.

WWW.CELEBRITEASE.COM

June 18, 2008
4:25 PM PST

Rally up, dearest readers! It's time for (drumroll, please) . . . Celebrity Hypocrisy: "Thoughts and Prayers" edition!

Every letter on the list from A to D to triple Z (we see you, booted *Rock of Love* contestants) is clamoring to make their requisite public display of sympathy in light of Molly Byrne's tragic passing, including folks that MB herself thought extremely little of in life. You can practically hear her "girl, please" from the beyond.

Recently dumped ex Dax Van Sant, who was papped (friendly fire?) outside Guy's the night after Molly's passing, told TMZ: "She was amazing. Just the best. I'll never find a girl like her again." [At least there's a hint of self-awareness?]

Former *All Bets Are Off* costar Madison Vaughan told *Entertainment Tonight*: "I'm in a state of shock. Molly was like a sister to me." [A sister you notably snubbed outside an after-party for last year's MTV Movie Awards? Although, let's be real—that *is* pretty typical Byrne sister behavior.]

Sun City costar Alessandra Delgado told *Us Weekly*: "She was such a kind and unique soul. There will never be another Molly Byrne." [Okay, as far as we know, Miss Mol had no beef with bombshell Alessandra, and if we're being fair, her quote's probably true. But don't tell Amy Byrne, whose entire life and career have been dedicated to the single-minded pursuit of becoming Another Molly Byrne.]

8

The morning of Molly's funeral was bright and sunny. Clouds and rain would've been a little too on the nose, I guess, and after all, it was LA. *How's the sunshine?* My dad asked whenever we spoke on the phone. *Honestly, could anyone ever get tired of it?*

It rains here too, Dad, I'd reply, even if those showers were few and far between.

I wanted to bring Anton with me, but the email from Alyssa had said that Molly's service was "strictly private." So I went alone, in the same black pantsuit I had worn to interview at the UCLA School of Medicine—the first and only time I had ever been to LA before I moved out here. The suit was a little tight now, and a little uncomfortable, but everything about this experience was uncomfortable, so I figured it didn't make much of a difference.

As I entered the venue, I could hear Molly's voice in my head, her tone light but disapproving: *Really, Ray, a polyester blend? To my* funeral*? Don't we both deserve better than that?*

I tried to silence that voice. To empty my mind completely. It hurt too much otherwise.

The service was held at a place called Eternal Promises—a stately limestone building that opened onto sprawling grounds dotted with elaborate marble headstones and mausoleums. The central feature of the grounds was a long, narrow reflecting pool with a tall white stone monument at one end that was oddly reminiscent of the Washington Monument. White chairs were arranged in rows along either side of the reflecting pool, all facing a pulpit that had been erected in front of the monument.

I braced myself for the sight of Molly's casket, but it wasn't there. Instead, a large portrait of Molly stood next to the pulpit, surrounded by dozens of flower arrangements.

As "strictly private" as the service was, the gathered crowd was massive. And for as many people I didn't recognize, there was at least an equal number that I did—famous faces from movies and TV and music, actors from shows I watched as a kid engaging in polite small talk with reality TV stars and musicians and celebrity chefs.

I was not there to mingle, and I certainly wasn't of any interest to anyone else. So I took a seat toward the back.

It all felt surreal. It wasn't just the staggering assortment of celebrities, or the lavish venue, or the brilliant blue sky doubled in the reflecting pool. It was the notion that this was for Molly. As the title of the program an usher handed me proclaimed, it was Molly's "Celebration of Life." It was weirdly absurd. I had seen her just days ago. And now she was gone, and we were celebrating her life, and there was not one iota of me that felt like celebrating in any way whatsoever. I felt so acutely devastated that I knew I couldn't let myself feel anything at all.

Eventually the service began. A number of people got up to speak about Molly. An *American Idol* runner-up sang an ad-lib-heavy version of "Candle in the Wind." Adrien Ford, the director of Molly's latest movie, told the story of Molly's first audition for him. Molly's manager, Cal Price, got up holding several crumpled index cards, started to read from them, and broke down in tears partway through. He left the pulpit without finishing his speech.

Nick Hart, Molly's costar in *Robot Wars* and *Sun City*, was up next. It was an odd breath of fresh air to see someone so put together after seeing Cal, who was so clearly fraying at the edges. "That's what actors do," Molly told me once. "That's our job. We deliver when it matters most, because we have to."

"Hello," he said. "My name is Nick. When I was asked to speak here today—when Tish, Molly's amazing mom, asked me to speak, she asked me to share a good memory of Molly. So I want to talk about the first time I worked with our girl."

"Nick is like . . . the high school quarterback who everyone loves," Molly told me once. She had never attended regular school, so all of her references to the school experience were much closer to what you'd see on TV or in movies than to anything actually resembling real life. "He's pleasant, he's nice to look at, he made the amazing throw at the homecoming game or whatever. But he doesn't really stir up any major feelings, at least for me. He's like . . . Malibu Ken. Honestly, we probably should've slept together at some point, but, like, I don't know. Maybe there's something wrong with me, but I'd rather have someone fucked-up but interesting than someone perfect but boring."

"People say you two have good chemistry, though."

"Ray, I could have chemistry with a lamp. It's no credit to Nick."

"As I'm sure many of you here know, films shoot largely out of order," Nick said now. "You might even shoot a major climactic moment before you shoot the opening scene of the film. It's a lot to keep track of—a character's journey, their motivation from scene to scene, even from shot to shot—but Molly was a wizard at it. In our first film together, we shot this huge scene really early on. It was an emotional scene and it demanded a lot of Molly. And she was just willing to do it over and over again, as many times as it took to get it right. As funny and as smart and as beautiful as she was, I think that's what was most special about Molly. Her work ethic. Her refusal to give up. She was like that at work, and she was like that with people too. Despite how she was painted by the media, no one was as considerate on set as Molly. No one cared as much about the crew, about the people around her. She's touched so many people's lives"—his voice grew hoarse—"including mine. It's heartbreaking that her life was lived out of order, with this ending scene coming so much sooner than it should have. But I think the best way to honor her memory is to stay determined. And to be kind."

When Nick stepped away from the pulpit, Molly's mother stood and approached him, her arms outstretched. She hugged him, ragged Kleenex clutched in each of her hands.

And then Amy Byrne stepped up to address the crowd.

She was wearing a black strapless dress with a large slit up one side, and an elaborate black hat. She was just as thin as Molly was but taller, and although she was the younger sister, she looked undeniably older. *World-weary*, my dad would say.

She unfolded a sheet of paper and began to speak.

"Molly was a lot of things to a lot of people," she said in a quavery voice. "To some people, she was a first crush. A goddess. Someone to look up to. Someone to be like. But to me, she was just . . ." Her voice caught. "She was just my sister. That's all that I wanted from her, to have her as my sister. To have her here. I wish . . . I wish she had known that."

"Maybe she would've known that if you had actually told her," a woman behind me muttered. "Maybe then she wouldn't have killed herself."

"Oh, stop," a male voice murmured back.

"Seriously, though. It's always *Who could've predicted that this very predictable thing would happen? How could we have ever prevented it?* And it's like, well, maybe you should've been more upfront with your loved ones when they were alive instead of sobbing about it in hindsight."

"They don't know if it was really suicide, though."

"Even if it wasn't, how many people here looked the other fucking way while that poor girl snorted herself into oblivion? And you know it was suicide. Of course it was. Even if she didn't do it with the intent to die, she took the drugs that killed her. She did that on purpose. That's killing yourself."

I could hear it—a buzzing. Like a swarm of bees growing closer. Suddenly, I felt too hot. My pantsuit was too tight, it was absorbing too much sun—it was so bright out—why did it have to be so bright, relentlessly so, all the fucking time—

"I just don't get why she'd kill herself when it seemed like things were finally turning around for her," the man whispered.

"Yeah, that's how it seemed on the outside. But who knows what was going on behind closed doors? Who knows how she really felt?"

I stood up, too abruptly. My chair tipped backward. The man behind me caught it and gave me an odd look.

I burst into the aisle and hurried away.

9

I didn't make it all the way to the parking lot—my legs gave out partway there and I fell against the side of a marble mausoleum that was lined with Grecian columns.

"Hey," said a voice from nearby. "You okay over there?"

I needed to put my head between my knees. I needed air. I needed to be somewhere else, anywhere else. I needed to jump into an alternate timeline, one in which none of this had happened.

"Hey," the voice repeated, closer now.

I opened my eyes. Malibu Ken was staring down at me.

"You good?" he asked.

Nick Hart was even more handsome up close than he had been from afar, addressing the crowd from the pulpit not ten minutes ago. Part of me understood Molly's assessment. Nick was chiseled and muscled, square in the jaw, broad in the shoulders. He had dark blond hair and blue, blue eyes. It was almost as if he had been engineered—*print me one Hollywood Hunk to go, please.* I couldn't fully agree with Molly on all counts, though. I don't know what it said about me, but someone who was perfect but boring didn't sound so bad.

Right now, there was concern in his eyes. I could hear a strange sort of wheezing from somewhere very far off. It sounded like a goose in distress.

Then I realized it was me. That sound was coming from me.

He crouched down. "Do you need help? Should I call someone?"

I shook my head violently. I did not want to go to the hospital, because I didn't want to have to pay for having gone to the hospital. But the lack of oxygen was concerning. My vision was narrowing.

"Hey, look right here." Nick put one hand on my shoulder and pointed to his left ear. "Focus right here. This earlobe. Take a breath, a big one."

I tried. The wheezing persisted.

"For five seconds. Focus on my ear. Breathe. One . . . two . . . three . . . four . . . five."

In that way, shockingly, *People*'s Sexiest Man Alive 2006 helped me come down from the panic attack.

"I'm okay," I choked out eventually, when the wheezing had mostly subsided and my field of vision had widened. "I'm fine."

"You sure you don't want me to call someone?"

I shook my head again, and because I was me, asked, "Why did you have me look at your ear?"

He smiled. "Because if you'd looked into my eyes, you might've fallen in love with me."

It was cheesy but effective. Or maybe it was the smile that was effective.

"What's your name?" he asked.

"Rachel."

"I'm Nick. You should get your blood sugar up. Here." He reached into his suit jacket pocket. "Don't tell anyone I gave you this."

I stared down at the object he extended toward me. It was an unopened king-sized Payday bar. When I took it, it was disconcertingly warm from his body heat.

I gave him a curious look, and his expression turned sheepish. "I'm shooting a *Men's Health* cover next month. I'm not supposed to go within five square miles of a carb. It's skinless, unseasoned chicken breasts all the way down."

"Then why do you have this?"

"Because I lack willpower. I sneak out and buy one once a day and eat it in secret like some kind of cursed snack gremlin." He dropped his voice to a whisper, leaning in conspiratorially. "If I'm being honest, sometimes it's the highlight of my day."

I opened the Payday bar and broke it in half, offering one half back to him. "I'd feel bad if I took all of your highlight."

He took it and sat down next to me, leaning back against the wall of the mausoleum.

"Molly would've done the same thing," he said, and then took a big bite and talked around it. "Did you know her?"

"I wouldn't be here if I didn't, would I?"

"You'd be surprised. Lot of people treating it like a fucking social event. It's disgusting. Molly doesn't deserve that." He shook his head. "We lost a really good one."

"Yeah, but how?" I murmured, mostly to myself, voicing the thought that had been on my mind since I saw the first gut-wrenching headline: MOLLY BYRNE DEAD AT 24. "How did we lose her?"

Nick finished his half of the candy bar in another large bite, chewed in silence for a moment, and then crumpled up the wrapper.

"Everybody's got their secret candy bar," he said. "I guess you just hope to God it's not something that could end you."

I took a small bite and chewed for a moment. "You're in *Sun*

City, aren't you?" Molly's final movie, the Adrien Ford picture that was already getting awards-show buzz.

He nodded. "It's a supporting role. My agent pushed for it. I mean, it's Adrien Ford, you kind of can't say no. He's one of the greats—even if he is totally batshit."

"Why do you say that?"

"Oh, you know. He's one of those *do seventy-two takes to get it right* guys. You can't just act, even though that's your job. You have to have some kind of *lived experience*. I can't knock the process, because he's got the Oscars to back it up, but it's a little much, if you ask me."

"Did Molly have a tough time on set?"

"I don't know. We only had a couple scenes together. Our storylines are kind of parallel. She's the single mom, I'm the brother who's just gotten back from Iraq . . . The whole thing's sort of an ensemble piece. It was nice getting to work with her again, though. And nice to be in a situation where neither of us had to, like, try to have a heart-to-heart with a tennis ball attached to a fifteen-foot pole." I shot him a questioning look. "It's how they did the CGI for Omnitron in *Robot Wars*."

"Ah." A pause. I thought back to the conversation Casper overheard between Molly, her agent, and her manager the day of Molly's death. *She said she wasn't going to promote* Sun City, *and if they didn't like it, she'd fire them both. She said something about how . . . the movie didn't matter anymore.* "Do you know . . . is there any reason why Molly wouldn't want to promote the film?"

Nick glanced over at me, his perfectly shaped eyebrows drawn together. "No. Why?"

I shook my head. "I don't know. I just . . . I don't understand why she would relapse. Why now? After everything?"

"I don't know," he said regretfully. "But it's a real fucking shame."

He got to his feet and extended a hand to me. I grasped it and climbed to my feet.

"You feeling better?"

I nodded. "Thank you."

He gave me a smile in return, touching two fingers to his forehead in a salute. "Anytime."

It was such an awkward gesture—one that so completely contradicted the rest of Nick Hart's whole deal—that I couldn't help but smile back.

FROM THE *ICON* ARCHIVE:

OCTOBER 4, 2005

In this week's Quick Takes, Nick Hart, star of the upcoming *Robot Wars 2: Rise of Omnitron,* catches up with *Icon* to discuss costars, dating, and of course, giant-robot slaying.

ICON: Three favorite roles as an actor?

NH: Oh, that's tough. I definitely have to go with Trek Lahure, what with *Robot Wars 2* coming out this Thanksgiving—see it at a theater near you [winks]. Jet Mannings in *Never Twice* was definitely my breakout role. And Des Johnson in *Bootstrap City.* It was a small part, but it was my first, so that will always be a special role to me. You know what they say—you never forget your first!

ICON: Three spoilers for *Robot Wars 2*: *Rise of Omnitron*?

NH: Boom. Boom. Boom.

ICON: . . .

NH: That was three explosions. You know how Mike McColm movies are—he takes those practical effects mega seriously. Mike always says, if you want to see something blow up, then why not blow something the #$%& up?!

ICON: Three words to describe your *Robot Wars 2* costar Molly Byrne?

NH: Sexy. Firecracker. Takes no shit.

ICON: That's five words.

NH: That's Molly, though! She plays by her own rules. Three words just won't cut it.

ICON: You have a bit of a reputation as a ladies' man. Any sparks on set (or off) between you and Molly?

NH: [laughs] Believe me, I could never land a girl like Molly Byrne. She's in a class of her own.

10

Following the service, a reception was held in the large stone building on the grounds of Eternal Promises. In its wide lobby, tables covered in white tablecloths stood loaded down with platters of charcuterie. Waiters circled with trays of champagne flutes. People gathered in small groups, talking and laughing. If not for the general style of dress—black on black on black—this might have been some pre–award show cocktail party.

I wasn't quite sure why I was still there. I stood alone, clutching my champagne flute, the drink growing warm from the heat of my hand. I scanned the room, looking for . . . I don't even know what. Something suspicious. Someone acting strangely. Something—anything—that could help explain what had happened to Molly. Some possibility that her death wasn't exactly what everyone was saying it was.

Eventually I caught sight of Cal Price, standing by himself at a high, round table. Like the other cocktail tables, this one had a small glass votive holder on it, a flame flickering inside. Cal had cupped one hand around the votive holder and was staring down at the flame. It must've been hot.

I don't know what possessed me, but I moved toward him.

"Mr. Price?"

He looked up at me. He released the votive holder. The palm of his hand was an angry red.

"Sorry?" he said hoarsely.

"I'm Rachel, a friend of Molly's. We've met before, at the Ivy?"

Recognition flickered across his face. "The reporter."

I nodded.

"I have nothing to say. I have nothing for you."

"I'm not collecting quotes." In an echo of every well-wisher who had unintentionally angered me the day after Molly's death, I continued: "I just wanted to express my condolences. I'm so sorry for your loss."

It didn't seem to anger Cal. He looked at me with slightly more acknowledgment now. "It is my loss too, isn't it?" he said dully. "She was every bit as much family to me as—" He broke off, shook his head. "Maybe even more so." His face crumpled.

Compound interest is a remarkable thing.

"I'm so sorry," I repeated. And then . . . "Do you think . . . Was there anything unusual about the day Molly died? Anything out of the ordinary you noticed, or . . . any conversations you had that seemed . . . off?"

Suspicion sparked in his eyes. "Why?"

"I just . . . want to understand what happened."

"I told you I had nothing for you. I'm not doing this."

"I'm not with *Icon* anymore. I'm just asking as Molly's friend, as someone who—" Suddenly, I felt flames of panic flickering again at the edges of my mind. *Someone who should've been there for her.*

And suddenly it was just like before—too warm in there, too bright.

Cal's expression shifted. "Hon? You okay there?"

"Yes." I took a step back, stumbled a bit. He caught my arm.

"Here." He led me over to a nearby chair positioned against one of the walls. "Sit." He headed away, and then returned a moment later with a bottle of water, untwisting the cap and handing it to me.

I gratefully accepted the bottle and took a few small sips.

"Does Cal drive me nuts sometimes? Sure," Molly told me once. "But if I'm being honest, he's just what you want out of a manager. It's better they care too much than not enough."

"I just feel terrible," I admitted now as I looked up at Cal. I have no idea what drove the truth out of me, to him of all people: "I feel like I failed her."

Maybe it was that he, of all people, might understand.

"You and me both, kid." He took a shaky breath and let it out. "Don't think it hasn't crossed my mind about a thousand times since Tuesday. Why wasn't I there? Why did I have to go in then, at the worst possible damn time—"

"Go in where?"

"To the hospital," Cal said. "I had to have an angiogram, so I couldn't go to the *Sun City* promo event with Mol that afternoon." He ran a hand over his eyes. "Why did it have to be then? Why couldn't I have scheduled it for any other day? What kind of sick joke from the universe is that? The *one time* I try to look after myself is the day that she—" He cut himself off.

"Did you have lunch with Molly beforehand?"

"Yeah . . ."

"And . . . was she upset about something?"

He considered me for a moment before responding, "You said it was Rachel?"

"Yes. Rachel West."

"Rachel West, I've gone toe-to-toe with enough publicists, reporters, paparazzi, and just plain busybodies in my day not to know when I'm being questioned."

"That's not—"

"Yes, it is. So tell me exactly what it is you want to know and why."

I hesitated. "Could something bad have happened to Molly?"

"Something bad did happen. This fucking industry. And I fucking helped." All of a sudden, his eyes glazed with tears. "She was the sweetest kid." Then he blinked rapidly, shaking his head as if to clear a memory. "I'll run through it for you quickly. Yeah, I had lunch with Molly that day. Yeah, I went to Cedars for an appointment afterward. My cardiologist is Dr. Rajesh Pandey, and you can go ahead and call him to confirm. Yes, Molly was upset at lunch, and no, I don't really understand why, just that she thought the film would get buried when 'the truth came out.' The truth about what? I have no idea. That's it. She wasn't making sense. If I had known—if I had realized that she had fallen back into . . . old habits . . ." A tear slipped from one of his eyes. He quickly dashed it away. "If I could build a time machine, I'd go back in time to Monday and do anything I possibly could to keep her alive. Except that's a lie, because actually I'd go back to 1992 and tell her parents to get her the fuck out of this business. Give her a life she was willing to live." His voice went hoarse. "Spare us all the heartache."

"But why—"

Before I could continue, a voice rang out, high and harsh, above the general thrum: "*You.*"

And suddenly, Amy Byrne was cutting swiftly through the crowd, heading straight in our direction, one manicured finger pointed right at me.

We had never met in person. I'd seen her in framed photos at Molly's house, and on TV occasionally. In the tabloids often. But this was the first time I'd come face-to-face with Molly's little sister.

Up close, I could see rings of mascara under her eyes, as well as dark smudges that indicated a lack of sleep.

"How *dare* you show your face here?" she snarled.

I got to my feet, still clutching the water bottle. "I—"

Her finger, still aimed at me, was shaking. "You knew her for *three months.* Three months! You're a filthy fucking gold digger, and if you think I'm going to let you touch a *single* thing she owned—"

"Amy, come on, now, kid—" Cal started.

"Don't fucking call me that," Amy snapped.

For a moment, Cal looked as if he were about to snap back, but instead he just let out a breath and then walked away.

"Honey, please." A woman appeared at Amy's side and put an arm around her in an attempt to guide her away. It was Tish, Molly and Amy's mother.

"She's a leech, just like the rest of them! She wasn't Molly's friend. She wasn't anything but the next new, shiny thing, and Molly would've gotten bored of her if she hadn't—"

"How do you know what Molly would've done?" A man cut in between Amy and me. "Honestly, you didn't give a solid gold shit about Mol or who she spent her time with when she was alive, so why do you care now? Except that there's money on the line?"

It was Dax Van Sant.

"Dax . . . I mean, what can I even say about him?" Molly said once. "It's one of those things where it's like, yeah, we have nothing in common, but he's damn sexy, so does it really matter? Like, at least we have *that* in common."

If I was Molly's "next new, shiny thing," then Dax Van Sant was Molly's last Mayfly Man.

We had met just once before, after my exclusive with Molly came out. Molly and I were leaving a club as Dax was heading inside. She had greeted him, all smiles as she pressed a kiss to his cheek and did a quick round of introductions, and then she grabbed my hand and pulled me in the direction of her waiting car. "Well, that was awkward," she said with a grin after we piled inside. The interaction made it onto the home page of TMZ the next day: MOLLY BYRNE STEPS OUT WITH NEW PAL AND EX VAN SANT GETS THE BRUSH-OFF.

Right now, Amy regarded Dax for one long moment, her eyes red rimmed and blazing, her lip curled. "Fuck off, Dax," she said finally, and then stormed away.

Dax turned to me. He had a close-cut beard and long, thick golden-brown hair, half of which was piled into a haphazard bun at the back of his head. I wouldn't have deemed anything about his outfit particularly funeral appropriate, except for the color scheme: a black knit shirt that fell open at the chest, black skinny jeans with large rips at the knees, and a skull-printed Alexander McQueen scarf draped around his neck. The dazzling watch on his wrist belied the casual nature of the ensemble.

"Finally," he said. "Someone who's just as unwanted here as I am."

That shitty Celebritease obituary flooded back to me: *Her very public breakup with (notoriously vile) photog Dax Van Sant and her puzzling friendship with (bottom-feeding)* Icon *reporter Rachel West . . .*

A waiter passed by with a tray. Dax grabbed a champagne flute, and then clinked it against my bottle of water. "To a fellow persona non grata."

I took a shaky sip of water. "What was that even about? 'Money on the line'?"

"Rumor has it that Amy got cut out of Molly's will."

"What? Why?"

He shook his head. "No idea. But if it's true, it's not gonna endear her to someone who benefited a fair bit from a relationship with her sister."

Anger flared in my chest, but part of me knew he wasn't wrong. Molly had done so much for my career. Not to mention all the gifts she had given me, even when I tried to refuse them. *Especially* when I tried to refuse them.

I met Dax with a hard stare. "Are you talking about me or you?" I asked.

His mouth curved into a smile. "Touché."

Suddenly, above the buzz of the room came the sound of voices growing louder. I cast a look around. Nearby, Cal was advancing toward a man in an expertly tailored suit. The man took several steps back, holding up his hands in placation.

"Let's be reasonable here."

"Go to hell, Damon," Cal snarled. "Molly's dead, and you want me to be reasonable?"

Without thinking, I moved toward them. The man in the suit was Damon Maxwell, Molly's agent. He looked to be in his mid-forties, with thick dark hair that was artfully slicked back. The watch on his wrist rivaled Dax Van Sant's. His shoes were so polished that they were practically mirrored.

"You're not in a good state right now," Damon said calmly.

Cal pushed a finger into Damon's chest. "Molly's gone, and you're saying I should be fucking reasonable. What if you're the reason this happened? If we had just *listened* to her—"

I had gotten close enough that I could see the perspiration beading on Cal's forehead. Damon was right—he really didn't seem to be in a good state. I wondered about the results of that angiogram.

Damon was unwavering. "Let's not do this here."

"No, let's." Cal gave him a shove, and Damon stumbled backward into a waitress, who then stumbled back too, her tray falling to the side and sending a number of champagne flutes flying in the direction of the closest person, who was, unfortunately, me.

If there was anyone around who was not already paying attention, the crash of the tray hitting the ground and the shattering of glass was enough to draw the attention of the rest of the crowd.

Cal stood there, his chest heaving.

"You get one of those," Damon said, righting himself and brushing off his jacket. "Because you're grieving. But next time, don't expect me to hold back."

He cut through the crowd and disappeared.

I went to the restroom to try to tackle the large blotches of champagne now adorning the front of my jacket and pants. A mission that was doomed from the start. I had given up and was about to leave when I heard voices outside the door. Two men, speaking in hushed tones.

"—was I supposed to do?" one was saying. The voice was familiar. "They *asked* me."

"Is this some kind of joke to you?" the other replied in a harsh whisper. "Do you not understand what's on the line here?"

"That's not what I—"

"Look, I don't know what kind of game you're playing, but if you don't get your shit together, I swear to God, we'll be right back here with you as the guest of honor. Nothing—and I mean not a goddamned thing—is going to jeopardize this film. Got it?"

The reply was bit out: "Yes."

"Good. Then stop trying to be clever, and keep your fucking mouth shut."

Footsteps retreated. I cracked open the door. Someone was still standing there.

The familiar voice—it was Nick Hart.

He looked shaken. He smoothed down the front of his suit jacket, and just as I was about to step out and ask him what had happened—why he was being threatened—there was a muffled ring. Nick pulled a phone from his pocket and, after a brief glance at the screen, accepted the call.

"Baby, hi." His tone was totally normal—upbeat, untroubled. It was a jarring contrast to his expression just a moment before. Could actors really reverse course that quickly? *We deliver when it matters most, because we have to.* "Good, yeah. Better now that I'm talking to you."

He headed away.

Once I reached my car, I pulled the black rectangular card out of my wallet. The one with CASPER JONES printed across it in a small sans serif font.

I dialed the number, my hands shaking.

He picked up on the second ring, slightly breathless, as if he had dived for the phone. "Hello?"

"What do we do?" I asked. "Where do we start?"

11

I met Casper that afternoon at a coffee shop near Eternal Promises. He was dressed almost identically as the day I met him in the alley, and I wondered briefly if his approach to fashion was like that of a cartoon character—sets of identical black T-shirts and jeans lining his closet like some kind of emo Doug Funnie.

I was still wearing the ill-fitting pantsuit, and it still reeked of champagne. I looked like I was interviewing him to join me as an associate at a boozy Ann Taylor store.

"So, someone's threatening Nick Hart," Casper said. "The same person could've threatened Molly too."

"I have no idea who it was, though. I didn't recognize his voice. And Nick disappeared before I could talk to him."

Casper considered this for a moment, tapping one finger against the table. "We need to work backward," he said. "Retrace Molly's steps on her last day. Talk to everyone she interacted with."

"First things first," I replied. "I need to know who you are."

Why exactly are you interested in working at Ann Taylor After Dark?

"I told you, my name is Casper—"

"And you're a pap—"

"I'm a photographer."

I couldn't quite keep the disdain from my voice. "Yeah, okay."

He took a quick sip of his drink, an iced Americano. "I'm twenty-four." Four years older than I had initially thought. "I was born in New York. Moved here when I was a kid. Went back east for school, dropped out, came back out here. I've been working in photos for about three years now."

"And you followed Molly around."

"Sometimes."

"Why? Why her?"

Casper leaned back in his chair, ran his fingers through the condensation on the side of his cup for a moment. "She was my first paycheck. Picture-wise. I had just started, and I . . . got lucky."

"How?"

"I was waiting outside a club, and she happened to show up. It was right around *Robot Wars Two*, and she was in the news a lot then for . . . partying and stuff."

That was putting it kindly. I remembered the coverage from that time, back before I knew her. It seemed like every week there was a new tabloid cover photo of Molly accompanied by some sensational headline about her "out of control" partying.

"Her pictures were selling really high at that point," Casper said. "A big crowd rushed forward trying to snap her. I got pushed down and someone stepped on my hand. Broke two fingers."

"That doesn't sound particularly lucky," I said wryly.

"Molly saw it happen. Instead of going into the club, she doubled back and had her security guy grab me. Said they'd drive me to the hospital. On the way there . . ." He paused.

"What?"

"She felt bad. Like, responsible for what had happened, even though it wasn't her fault in the least. So she had the driver stop at a McDonald's. She let me take pictures of her ordering food at the counter. I sold them for an obscene amount of money." He shook his head, his lips curving into a small smile. "I could barely hold the camera up, but it was totally worth it."

That sounded just like Molly. The Molly I knew.

"So, what then?" I asked. "You just followed her around after that?"

"Yeah," he said. "I did. And you did too, right?"

It wasn't two broken fingers. But there was the bathroom at Lithium. The Chanel bag. The exclusive article. Molly liked helping people. And there was that thing she liked to say: *I have this sense about people.*

So maybe she had a sense about Casper. Maybe I could trust him.

That was a tall order, though, and not because of Casper specifically. I didn't trust very many people.

"What do we do first?" I asked.

"We need her schedule," he replied. "Can you get ahold of her assistant?"

WWW.CELEBRITEASE.COM

June 19, 2008
02:59 PM PST

Heads up to anyone who thinks they're remotely anyone here in Tinseltown:

Hollywood's most star-studded event of the year is not the Emmys, the Globes, or even the Oscars. We here at the Tease can report that if you missed Molly Byrne's funeral, your List status has automatically been downgraded. All A-listers are now Bs, all Bs are now Cs, and all Cs are now Ds (particularly fitting for Mol's sister, Amy, who already went from As to double Ds last summer, as if we all weren't going to question the sudden late-onset puberty).

At Eternal Promises (*not* a rehab facility, we eternally promise), MB was laid to rest amid a crowd of reportedly three hundred of her nearest and dearest. Among the attendees were numerous stars of the silver and small screens, from booked and busy A-listers who made time in their packed schedules to attend, to former reality show contestants willing to trade their firstborn for the privilege. Molly's *Sun City* costars Alessandra Delgado, Nick Hart, and Sam Hong were spotted clutching Kleenex and champagne flutes alike, in conversation with *Sun*

City's big-time serious director, Adrien Ford, and *Robot Wars*' big-time explosion director, Mike McColm [SEE BELOW].

What do you wear to a celebrity funeral? If you're little sister Amy Byrne, you wear a Balenciaga peplum dress with a slit from here to kingdom come. If you're Molly's former BFF of the Week, *Icon* reporter Rachel West, you wear a tragic pantsuit that would be much more befitting of a mannequin at JCPenney than MB's erstwhile bestie. You'd have thought that along with her cast-off Louboutins, Molly would've gifted Rachel dearest something more suitable for a formal affair.

(You'd be wrong.)

12

When I arrived back at my apartment, there was an envelope waiting for me on the ground by my front door.

The first thing I did when I got inside was change out of that godforsaken pantsuit. And then I sat down on the couch and opened the envelope.

The letter was brief:

Dear Rachel West,

You have been named as a beneficiary in the will of MOLLY MARIA BYRNE. Please contact the offices of Walther & Peck for further information.

Sincerely,
Bobbi Peck

I read it, and then read it again. *You have been named as a beneficiary in the will of MOLLY MARIA BYRNE . . .*

It made approximately zero sense. Why would Molly put me in her will? What's more, *when* did Molly put me in her will?

I called the number listed at the bottom of the letter. A smooth male voice answered and told me to "Hold for Ms. Peck."

Ms. Peck answered after several minutes.

"Rachel West?"

"Yes. Hi. That's me."

"You're calling about the Byrne estate."

"Yes."

"Can you come by my office today?"

"I—sure, yes."

"Great. Four o'clock. Brooks will get you the details." There was a click, and then the receptionist returned with more information.

~~~

The office of Walther & Peck was full of glass and chrome and had a wealth of uncomfortable chairs that Irina would've coveted.

Bobbi Peck was a whippet-thin woman in her fifties. She wore a black Diane von Furstenberg shirtdress and a large statement necklace in silver and turquoise.

"Brooks can grab you something to drink," she said when I took a seat in front of her desk. "Water? Tea?"

"No, thank you."

"Great." She waved Brooks away, and then flipped open a folder on her desk. "So. I don't know how much you know about the situation, or if you had any conversations with Molly prior to the amendment of her will—"

"I don't know anything. She never—we never talked about it."

"Well, bare bones: Molly had her will amended last month." She leafed through the file. "Disposition of property . . . To Rachel Elizabeth West—that's you, yes?"
~~~

I nodded.

"—at South Halm Avenue—relationship to testator, friend—I bequeath the following: the property at 357 Riverside and all belongings therein, and five million dollars to be paid in a single sum."

"I . . ." My stomach dropped. I didn't know it was possible to feel lightheaded and leaden at the same time—simultaneously floating away and sinking into the earth. It didn't make sense. Nothing Bobbi Peck just said made any sense whatsoever. "I'm sorry," I said, voice thick. "What did you say?"

"Disposition of property to Rachel Elizabeth West," Bobbi repeated crisply. "The property at 357 Riverside and all belongings therein, and five million dollars to be paid in a single sum."

"I don't understand. I don't . . . I don't know why she would do that. There must be a mistake. Her family—"

"The remainder of her assets have gone to her parents," Bobbi said. "It's a considerable amount. But so is this." She tapped the folder. "I won't lie to you, the Byrnes are absolutely going to contest the amendment in probate. It won't be easy and it won't be pretty."

I thought of Amy at the funeral: *You're a filthy fucking gold digger, and if you think I'm going to let you touch a single thing she owned—*

So this was what she meant. She already knew about the will—which meant that the rumor Dax had shared was likely true. If the rest of Molly's estate went to her parents, then Amy really might have been cut out.

My throat suddenly felt extremely dry. "I don't want it. I don't—"

Bobbi Peck made a sudden loud, grating sound, the kind you would make to warn a dog away from a plate of food, or to rush a cat off your counter.

"I—"

She made the sound again.

"I really don't—"

"Ms. West, don't say it out loud. Don't even *think* it loudly. You don't mean it, and you'll regret it."

"What do you mean?"

"You're grieving, yes? We're all grieving. Molly was a firecracker. I know I'll miss her, and she didn't leave me a house on Riverside and five million dollars. You're not in the right state of mind to make a decision regarding whether or not you want this inheritance. Don't throw away any claim you might have to it just because you're sad. What Molly wanted"—she tapped the folder again—"is printed here in black-and-white. And as her friend, you owe it to her to see that through."

I swallowed. "So, what am I supposed to do?"

"Do you have a lawyer?"

I shook my head. I didn't even have a primary-care doctor.

"Well, I'd suggest you get one."

"Holy shit, Rachel." My cousin Jonathon was a lawyer who lived in the Bay Area. I called him as soon as I left Bobbi Peck's office. "Are you kidding me?"

"No."

"Wow. Just . . . wow."

"I know. She's saying I should get a lawyer. Will you . . . can you represent me?"

"Rachel, this is so far outside my area of expertise, it's basically on another continent." Jonathon was a public defender.

"But aren't lawyer skills . . . somewhat transferrable?"

"Do you want your podiatrist diagnosing your melanoma?"

"I hope to have neither, but I get your point."

He let out a breath. "I have a buddy from school who went into estate law. I'll see if I can get in touch with him."

"I can't pay him much." A statement that required immediate revision. "By which I mean I can't pay him anything."

"Well, if you get this inheritance, you sure can." I didn't respond, so he went on. "I'll see what I can do, okay?"

"Thank you. Also, please don't tell anyone about this—your mom, or my parents."

"This is a pretty big thing to keep secret."

"I just want to . . . process it on my own first. Okay?"

He sighed. "Okay. Yeah. Fair enough."

★ MARCH 2008 ★

"I'M JUST TELLING YOU RIGHT OFF THE BAT, I'M NOT TALKING ABOUT AMY," Molly said. We were at Molly's house—a modern two-story mansion north of Sunset—in the back, by the pool, meeting for what would be the first of several interviews I would conduct for her exclusive with *Icon*.

I hadn't brought the idea to Irina yet—I wanted to have the article written in its entirety first. I was too worried that as soon as Irina found out I had Molly Byrne "on the hook" (her words for landing a major story), she would try to scoop the interview for someone else on staff. Someone with more experience. Or any experience, actually. Molly was right—if I wanted to get by in this industry, I had to be a shark.

So here I was, swimming.

"I'm sure you saw she's been running her mouth to the tabloids," Molly continued. She was stretched out on one of the pink and white chaise lounges that flanked the pool. I was in the chaise next to hers, ready with my notebook and tape recorder.

I had indeed seen the video that TMZ posted of Amy leaving

Les Deux just the night before. *"How's Molly?"* the pap behind the camera asked. *"Are she and Dax getting engaged? Is she pregnant?"*

"How the hell would I know?" Amy had replied. *"I don't even have that bitch's phone number."*

This of course sparked dozens of online articles to the tune of BITTER FEUD REIGNITES BETWEEN BYRNE SISTERS.

"If your article lands at the same time she happens to say something stupid to the media, they'll just pull out whatever I say about her and your interview will get buried. It'll devolve into another rehash of our *rivalry* or whatever. As if it's a rivalry."

"It's not?"

"You have to be on even footing to be rivals, Ray. I'd have to sword fight with my left hand."

The Princess Bride was another favorite movie of Molly's, and the sword fight between Inigo Montoya and the Dread Pirate Roberts was a particular highlight for her. She'd later tell me that she would chop off her pinkie toe to be as beautiful as Robin Wright was as Buttercup.

"Why don't you and Amy get along?" I asked, and Molly cast a glance at me, one eyebrow arched in question. "This isn't for the article, I promise. Just curious."

"Do you have siblings?" A pause. "You do. You have a brother."

How on earth does she know that? was my first thought, and then I remembered: I had mentioned Sam the night we met at Lithium.

"You remember that?"

"I have a fantastic memory," Molly said airily. "And perfect nail beds. God really gave with both hands."

I smiled. "I have a younger sister too. Natalie."

"Do you get along with her?"

"Yeah. But we haven't lived in the same place since she was in junior high. We're six years apart."

"That probably helps." Molly's expression was wry. "It's not that Amy and I hate each other. I mean, we do, but she's still my sister. I still love her. Of course I do. But . . ." She was quiet for a moment. Molly wielded silence extremely effectively. She knew how to build tension, how to capture attention. "She's always wanted everything I have, but without having to work for it." She shook her head. "Don't get me wrong, I understand her struggle. It was kind of a done deal from the start."

"What do you mean?"

She pursed her perfect lips for a moment, and I realized she was wearing Corail Aquatique. "Imagine Valentino puts out a pair of limited edition pumps in . . . royal blue satin, with gold accents. Gorgeous. Everyone loves them; everyone wants a pair. It's the shoe of the moment. Then, three seasons later, they release the same shoes in a different color. Yeah, maybe there's a chance that those shoes could be even better and more popular than the first pair, but, like, there's also the chance that everyone who wanted them already got them, or they've moved on to a new style, or they're just not going to care as much about something that's only a little bit different than something they've already seen. They've already filled that spot in their closet." A pause. "If Amy and I were less similar, it might've turned out better for her. I mean, it's certainly possible. Famous siblings have made it work over the years." Something in her eyes danced. "Maybe if Amy were a better actor." She adjusted the pillow behind her on the chaise, and then looked over at me. "What does your sister do? Is she into magazines too?"

"She's in college, back in St. Louis. She's studying graphic design."

"How did you even end up in LA? I always wonder what brings people out from all those, you know, down-home, country-style states."

I would not describe St. Louis as "down-home" or "country,"

but I imagine in Molly's mind, the whole swath of the Midwest probably looked something like a Cracker Barrel, with a rolling backdrop of cornfields.

"I came out here when I was interviewing for med schools a few years ago," I explained. "I ended up going to school back home, but I liked it here. And when everything kind of . . . went sideways . . . I ended up moving back out."

"Like, *Fuck it, I'm starting over, this is my new life now*?"

"Basically, yeah."

"Bold. I like it. I don't know if I could do something like that. I've always lived here. Though I did move out of my parents' house the minute I turned eighteen. I was dying for my own place, away from them. And from Amy." She paused. "For the record, she does have my phone number." Another beat. "I think."

As if on cue, her phone rang. Molly looked at the screen and then made a face. "Sorry," she said. "Duty calls."

I jotted down a few more interview questions on my already healthy list while Molly had a phone conversation that was much like the one I had witnessed in her car outside the Chanel store: "Yes, I will be there" and "Don't worry, it's covered" and "Take five deep breaths and drink a kombucha." I was certain it was Molly's assistant, Alyssa, on the other end of the line.

"Sorry about that," Molly said after she hung up. "Just logistics. Alyssa worries, and I don't, so we kind of balance each other out. It can be hard to gel with an assistant, so when you find a really good one, you have to hold on to them."

"Why's that?"

"Well, I'm sure it's easier if you're a businessperson or whatever. But as an actor, you have to find someone who's organized and competent and all that jazz, but also willing to be that close to fame and not want any of it for themself. Someone who's totally comfortable being behind the scenes."

"Kind of like being on a stage crew?" A part of the production that's rarely seen by the audience but is absolutely indispensable for a successful show.

"Exactly. You don't want to be the virtuoso—you want to be the person who helps the virtuoso be the virtuoso."

"And Alyssa's good at that?"

"She's amazing. Especially back when . . . well, you know." Molly looked uncharacteristically embarrassed. "Back in my party days or whatever. She stuck it out, even though she just as easily could have jumped ship." She clapped her hands together as if to redirect the conversation. "But enough about Alyssa, I'm sure she's not making it into your article." Molly's eyes shone. "Ask me about me."

13

After a day that included Molly's funeral, an unexpected inheritance, the start of a (potential, unofficial) murder investigation, and a meeting with a lawyer who probably charged more per hour than I earned per week, food from the Circle K just wasn't going to cut it for dinner. So I went to a Thai restaurant near Palm Vista, even though I didn't remotely have the budget for dining out.

Except . . . maybe now I did?

I didn't know. I tried desperately not to think about it as I pushed through the door of Sawasdee. It was a long, narrow place, with small two-tops crowded along one side, next to windows that looked out onto the street. A long counter extended along the opposite side. Whenever I came here as an exceedingly rare treat, I always sat at the counter, I always brought a book, and I always ordered tofu pad thai with extra lime wedges, and sometimes—if the day had truly warranted it—a beer. Tonight was definitely a beer night.

Tonight's book was a contemporary romance about a woman

who owned a bakery and a man who was the CEO of a major corporation but was hiding that fact due to his fatigue with women who were only interested in him for "the wrong reasons." The secret-millionaire trope was supposed to be sexy, but thus far I mainly found the love interest's mistrust of women to be off-putting. And the protagonist's inability to question how this "regular Joe" drove a Bugatti was, frankly, baffling.

As much as I tried to focus on the story, to savor my food, to not down my beer too quickly, I was too steeped in the meeting with Bobbi Peck and my conversation with Jonathon afterward. Bobbi Peck's words kept echoing through my mind: *What Molly wanted is printed here in black-and-white.*

Was *I* a secret millionaire now? Was I going to be one? Certainly, Bobbi was right that Molly's family wouldn't let that happen without a fight—Amy's reaction to me at the funeral backed that up wholly—but would a court of law support Molly's amendment to her will?

Why had she amended it? Why did she include me? What on earth would possess her to do that?

I was so deep in thought, my paperback eventually cast aside, that I didn't notice when someone took the seat two spots down from me at the counter.

In fact, he had already placed his order by the time I finally clocked him.

He was in business-casual slacks and a button-down. He might've been a character in some basic-cable drama about lawyers or sports agents or lawyers who are also sports agents. He could've even been the secret millionaire from my romance novel (if the millionaire wore off-the-rack as part of his ruse).

"Detective Lee," I said, unable to keep the note of surprise out of my voice.

"Ms. West," he replied, and then added, "just Lee is fine."

I wasn't going to take mine back and say that Just Rachel was fine after I had already revoked it during our frustrating phone call about Molly. Plus, Rachel was undoubtedly Not Fine.

Lee was just as good-looking as I had remembered—perhaps even more so. Or maybe I was able to appreciate it more this time because he wasn't here to question me about a friend's death.

Unless . . . he actually *was* here for that.

"What are you doing here?" I asked, trying but failing not to sound suspicious.

"Applying for a deep-sea fishing license," he replied. It surprised a brief smile out of me. "I live nearby," he added, as our server set a bowl of *panang* curry down in front of him. "And I was hungry."

So this wasn't about Molly. "Then you've come to the right place," I said. "I've heard the food at the deep-sea-fishing licensing office sucks."

One side of his mouth ticked up. He nodded toward the seat between us.

"May I?"

I hesitated. I don't know why. The restaurant was pretty busy. Soon someone could be seated in between us and we could each enjoy our meal alone, as we had seemingly both intended.

But maybe it wasn't the worst thing in the world, to eat with someone. Or next to someone, at the very least.

I nodded.

Lee moved his bowl and his own bottle of beer down the counter and shifted to the seat next to mine.

We ate in silence for several minutes. I couldn't decide if it was awkward or companionable. If I wasn't sure, then that must have meant it wasn't quite companionable. But at the same time, it didn't feel particularly awkward. I thought about Lee and his partner, Ruiz, seated side by side on my couch, and the look they had shared after their mismatched responses to my asking about Molly's death.

"So," I said finally. "How long have you been working with your partner?"

His brow furrowed. "Ruiz? About three years now."

"But you've known her for much longer."

"Yes." He looked at me curiously. "How'd you know that?"

I shrugged. "Educated guess."

"Based on . . . ?"

"When you two were interviewing me, you exchanged . . . a look."

"What kind of look?"

It was hard to explain, and I said so.

"We went to school together," he said. "So yes, we go way back. I've known her for years." A pause. "I thought you were an entertainment reporter, not an investigative one."

"You think being an entertainment reporter doesn't involve investigation?"

"I don't know. Isn't it just a lot of . . . pictures of celebrities at the grocery store? People who accidentally wore the same outfits to different events? A movie star punching a photographer outside a club?"

"To be fair, you have to do some investigation to read the room on the club fight, to clock those duplicate outfits, and to be at the exact right grocery store at the exact right moment when Orlando Bloom decides to buy a spinach salad."

"You think Orlando Bloom hits up the grocery store salad bar?"

"I know it for a fact," I said. "Because I'm good at my job."

Amusement shone in his eyes when I met his gaze. There was a freckle under his left eye that was more disarming than it had any right to be. "What got you into magazines?"

I looked at my bowl so I wouldn't contemplate the freckle any further. "I really liked them as a kid." I stabbed a piece of tofu. "Why did you become a detective? Wait, let me guess. Your high school sweetheart-turned-fiancée was murdered by some mafia kingpin."

He looked at me aghast.

"That's the kind of thing that always motivates men in procedurals," I explained. "That, or your father was a detective, and you had a complicated relationship with him, and then he was killed in the line of duty. Probably by some mafia kingpin."

"No. To both of those scenarios. Good Lord."

"Then why? Deep sense of justice? Knack for crime solving?"

"I really liked *Law and Order* when I was a kid."

I blinked. I thought maybe he was making fun of me, but it was said without artifice. "You became a detective because of television?"

"You became an entertainment writer because of magazines."

"Well, yeah. Mine seems like a pretty natural progression—you consume the media; you like the media; you want to create the media."

"Mine's not a natural progression?"

"I mean . . . you consume the media; you *become* the media? That's a little different." I shook my head. "It's just . . . surprising. I always thought people in criminal justice had these complex backstories."

"Some people do. Like Ruiz."

"Her dad was a cop?"

"Her mother was murdered. When she was a kid."

"Ah." That was not at all funny. I wondered why I was joking about murder in the first place. It was too much at the forefront of my mind at the moment.

I decided to take the opportunity: "So. I've been thinking. About Molly."

He picked up a slice of bell pepper. "What about Molly?"

I chose my words carefully. "I remembered something. About the night I was at her house." It had flashed suddenly into my mind as I was driving back from Bobbi Peck's office earlier: the winding road from Molly's house, a pair of headlights streaking by. "I passed a car on the road near her place when I left. Did someone come by after me?"

"We've interviewed everyone who was at Molly's house that night."

"Including the person who showed up after I left?"

"Yes."

"Who was . . . ?"

"Not a person of interest."

"Are there people of interest, then?"

"Rachel, no. I just meant, it was a family member—not a hired hit man."

I didn't point out that he had called me Rachel instead of Ms. West. Instead I followed a hunch: "It was Amy, wasn't it?"

The surprise that flickered across Lee's face told me exactly what I needed to know. I wondered how he had gotten this far as a detective, being so readable.

"No one showed up after her?" I asked.

He considered me briefly before saying, "No. The security guard confirmed it."

"Will there be a tox screen?"

"What do you know about tox screens?"

"I know they're performed when someone's cause of death is unclear."

"God, *Crime Scene LA* has a lot to answer for. Everyone thinks they're an ME now."

"What about an autopsy?"

Lee took a pull from his beer before responding. "Molly's family is against it."

"Why?"

"To put it in nice terms, they want to preserve her body as it was. To use their own words, they don't want 'some pervert carving her up and trying to sell her organs on eBay.'"

I raised an eyebrow. "Is that something that happens often?"

"Oh yeah, the LA County coroner has a real flourishing eBay presence, more than a thousand five-star reviews. You don't want to get your spare kidneys there, though—Ventura County's office has way better deals."

"Funny."

"You smiled, though."

"Did I?"

"Mm." He took a bite of food, glancing sidelong at me. "You did."

I looked down at my bowl again, the memory of the last date I'd been on springing suddenly into my mind. It had been a setup—some guy that Stacia from work knew and swore would be just my type. How Stacia thought she had any sense of what my type was when I didn't even really understand that myself, I have no idea. But apparently she thought my type was stunningly unfunny marketing guys who think having an in at an industry party is impressive.

I don't know why I was even thinking about dates in this moment. This was not a date. It was an accidental encounter. I needed to focus.

"How does the ME determine the cause of death without an autopsy?" I asked.

"Well, like you said. A tox screen should be pretty enlightening."

"When will the results come out?"

"These things take time," Lee replied. "*Crime Scene LA* doesn't exactly show that part, does it? Where Detective Clarkson has to wait four to six weeks to find out exactly what was in the victim's system? It's so much more expedient for him to put on his sunglasses, make a pun, and get comprehensive blood tests back in three and a half minutes."

"Oh, so you watch *Crime Scene LA* too. Do you have a Detective Clarkson poster on the wall by your desk at the precinct?"

"Yes," he replied, without skipping a beat. "Right next to a framed photo of Jerry Orbach."

I couldn't help but smile now.

As we continued to eat, the conversation wound back to more neutral topics. Eventually the man behind the counter brought our checks by. I set my credit card down for my own.

The man returned shortly thereafter. "Sorry," he said, pushing the card back toward me. "Declined."

"What?" That wasn't possible. I had paid last month's bill, I was certain of it. And I hadn't gone over my limit this month, had I?

I reached into my wallet. Empty. No cash.

Lee pulled out his wallet.

"Don't. It's—I'll—" I turned to the man. "Can you try running it again?"

"Here." Lee handed him cash. "No change." The man headed off to the register.

"That wasn't necessary," I told Lee.

He blinked at me. "He deserves the change."

"No, I mean you didn't need to pay for me."

"Don't worry about it."

"I have cash at home."

"It's really fine."

It didn't quite feel fine. "I don't like owing people things."

"Then you can get the next one."

"Give me your address and I'll send you the money."

He looked at me for a moment, and then nodded. "That works too."

He borrowed a pen from behind the counter and wrote his address on the back of another of his business cards. Now I had a matching set.

I stared down at his neat handwriting. Then I actually took in the address.

"This is right near Palm Vista."

"I said I lived nearby." His lips quirked. "I didn't think to bring it up during our first meeting. Not exactly the appropriate context for a *Howdy, neighbor.*"

"Are you renting?"

He shook his head. "I have a house."

"Really?"

"Yeah, they'll give a mortgage to anyone these days. Thank God the coroner cuts me in on a percentage of those organ sales." He blanched. "I'm sorry, we probably don't know each other well enough for me to keep joking like that. For the record, I'm not actually involved in any black-market organ harvesting."

"That's probably for the best. I might've asked you to cut me in too." It was funny, but saying it was probably a mistake, because it raised the specter of my declined credit card. I could see on Lee's face that he was likely thinking of the same thing. "It's just . . . lately, money is a little . . ."

"You don't have to explain."

We walked out of the restaurant together and stood out front. The sky was dark overhead.

I wasn't sure how to end the interaction. "Thanks for"—*Having dinner with me? Paying?*—"covering me," I decided, and then felt like that was probably the wrong choice of words.

Lee just shook his head. "Don't mention it. You know that

thing people say—'Everyone you meet is fighting a battle you know nothing about.'"

"*Be kind always*. Yeah, I kind of hate that saying."

"Why?"

"I'm a proponent of kindness, obviously. But I guess I want to think that there are people out there who *aren't* fighting battles. Maybe there are people who just get to be happy. Wouldn't that be nice?"

It was quiet. I had turned it awkward. So in another classic Rachel West move, I doubled down. Sometimes, instead of making a tactical retreat, I couldn't help but keep digging. "I mean, you must be happy, right? Steady job, nice house where you live with . . . let me guess. Your attractive girlfriend, soon-to-be fiancée, and your charming golden retriever named . . . Cooper."

He let out a breath of laughter.

"Am I onto something? You've got an engagement ring—a respectable number of carats but not ostentatious; you went for clarity over size—in your sock drawer, inside a novelty pair you know she'll never touch. You have an anniversary coming up, and you'll surprise her during dessert at her favorite restaurant. She'll cry. June wedding next year, Cooper is the ring bearer, honeymoon in Barbados, pregnant within the following year, congratulations—it's a boy." I didn't glance over at Lee until the end of my monologue, and it was only then that I saw the stricken look on his face. "Are you—"

"Yeah," he said, his expression quickly clearing. "Am I that easy to read?"

"Yes." I felt ambivalent, and I wasn't quite sure why. "Did I nail it?"

He shook his head. "It wasn't during dessert. It was during the appetizers. I was too nervous. I couldn't wait."

"During the apps, that's bold. What if she had said no?"

He gave a half smile, one dimple appearing on the corresponding cheek. Like the freckle under his left eye, it was not to be contemplated. "Then it would have been a very lonely shrimp cocktail." He hesitated for a moment. "Do you . . . need a ride anywhere?"

"I'm good, but thank you."

He nodded. "Then I guess this is good night."

I nodded too. "Good night."

I did not interrogate the slight feeling of disappointment I felt watching him walk away.

14

The following morning, Casper and I met with Molly's assistant, Alyssa, at a café on Sunset.

Alyssa was in her late twenties, and was not quite conventionally pretty but had the makeup skills and grooming to carry her well into *attractive.* Through our limited interactions, I knew that she was incredibly efficient, had very little sense of humor, and was extremely competent at her job, except in the moments when she got overwhelmed, in which Molly would prescribe her some number of calming breaths and a kombucha.

Alyssa approached our table at the café carrying a large designer tote bag. She had only just taken a seat when I realized that the bag was whimpering softly.

"Is that—"

"Rainbow Pup, yeah." Molly's toy poodle. Rainbow Pup had the personality of a block of uncooked tofu. He was only slightly more sentient than a rock. I watched as Alyssa pulled him out of the bag and sat him on her lap. He showed no interest in Casper or me, choosing instead to stare blankly at the overhead lighting.

"How are you holding up?" I asked, because it was the kind of thing that people asked.

Alyssa shrugged. From up close, I could see that her eyeliner had been shakily applied. "It's all really surreal. There are a ton of things to deal with, and on top of that, I'm out of a job, so . . ." She glanced at me. "I heard you quit *Icon*."

I nodded.

"What are you going to do now?"

"I have no idea."

"Yeah, same. I don't even know how to get my last paycheck." She gave a hollow laugh. "It's all so messed up, honestly."

"Did you—" I clasped my hands in my lap to steady them. "Were you the one who found Molly?"

"Yeah. Paulie and I did, that morning." Paulie was the head of Molly's security team. "She was supposed to have an early shoot and she wasn't answering her phone. So we both went in and she was there in her bedroom, it was—" Her voice cracked. "I thought she was asleep at first. But there was just . . . I don't know, it sounds crazy, but there was just this . . . *emptiness* in the room." She shook her head. "I'm sure I'll talk about it in therapy for years to come."

"Did anything seem out of place?" Casper asked.

"Like what?"

"I don't know . . . anything unusual in the room? Signs of a struggle?"

Alyssa frowned. "What are you getting at?"

"We're just . . . trying to understand what happened," I said.

She eyed Casper. "I'm sorry, who did you say you were?"

"He's my . . ." I paused. "Cousin," I finished, at the same time that Casper said, "Boyfriend."

We looked at each other.

Alyssa looked between us. "Yeah, no. This is weird."

Honesty seemed to be the best way forward. "We think maybe something bad happened to Molly."

"Well, obviously."

"No, I mean, we think that somebody might have . . . wanted to hurt her. Do you think that's possible?"

"Of course it's possible. There are people out there mailing her their fingernail clippings." Alyssa's eyes narrowed. "Are you trying to get some kind of story out of this? You just said you quit *Icon*."

"I did. It's not for a story. I just want to help Molly."

"I think you missed the boat on that one."

"I want to find out the truth," I amended. "I just don't believe that . . . I don't believe Molly would do that. Do you? You spent so much time with her. Do you really think she overdosed?"

Alyssa pursed her lips in contemplation. "I did think she was in a good place. But . . ."

"What?"

"She was really private. She didn't talk about her feelings much. She always kept it professional, at least with me. But. I could tell . . . I don't know, I did have this feeling the past few weeks that something was bothering her. So I wonder if maybe . . . you know, maybe that was it. Maybe she was struggling."

I wouldn't have said that Molly "kept it professional" with me. We were friends. But, thinking back, I hadn't gotten that same feeling as Alyssa. Then again, in the weeks before Molly's death I had received my big promotion. Things had ramped up at work. I was going to more events, conducting more interviews. Had I been too busy to notice that Molly was struggling?

I pushed the thought away for now. It hurt too much to consider.

"I just want to rule out every possibility," I said. "And you can help."

Suspicion reignited in Alyssa's eyes. "How?"

"Do you have Molly's schedule from the day she died?"

She considered me for a long moment. "You swear this isn't for some bullshit article?"

It had been my second or third visit to Molly's house when Alyssa caught me in the formal living room, trying to hide a pair of Dolce & Gabbana sneakers behind a large potted fiddle-leaf fig. She had looked askance at me.

"What are you doing?"

"I, um. I was just heading out."

"I mean"—she had waved a hand in the direction of the plant—"why are you doing that?"

I knew I was well and truly caught. I picked up the shoebox and showed it to her. "Molly gave me these. But I thought . . . she might change her mind. She might want them back later." I shook my head. "She gives stuff away so freely, but I'm not really comfortable just . . . accepting it."

Alyssa had examined me for a moment, her gaze cool under twin wings of expertly applied eyeliner. "Huh," she said finally.

"What?"

"Most people come to Molly with their hands out. I didn't think you'd be any different."

I had just shrugged, unsure of what to say.

Now I looked at Alyssa from across the café table. There was no guarantee that she would believe me, that this wasn't for *Icon* or any other tabloid story. That we really just wanted to help Molly. But I tried to put the truth of it, my sincerity, into my reply: "It's not for an article. I swear."

Another moment of evaluation. Then Alyssa nodded. "Yeah. Okay." She fished around in her purse and pulled out a BlackBerry in an aquamarine case.

She tapped at it for a moment. "Okay, Monday." Casper pulled a small notepad out of his pocket, and he poised a pen above it to take notes as Alyssa spoke. "Molly went to a spin class at nine a.m., at Revolution. The one in Brentwood, not the one in Bel Air. The Brentwood one is the original."

"Got it."

"I picked her up from there—I had gone to grab some wardrobe options from her stylist for the press event that afternoon—and then I dropped her off at her place. She was going to have lunch with Cal and Damon, but she wanted to drive herself. She called me afterward."

"Did she mention anything that happened at the lunch? An argument, maybe?"

"No. But something definitely seemed off. She was supposed to go from lunch to an interview with a writer from *EW*, but she had me cancel it. She said she was going to run an errand."

"Do you know where?"

Alyssa paused. "I . . . have an idea." After another moment's hesitation, she continued. "When we linked back up later, I parked her car for her. She had stopped for gas, and there was a receipt—it was from a station in west Malibu. I can't say for absolute certain what she was doing, but I know that lifestyle woman Vivian Grayson has her commune or whatever out there."

Lifestyle woman was said with the utmost contempt.

"Molly saw her a lot," I said. I had never met Vivian Grayson, but Molly had certainly sung her praises enough times.

"Yeah, Molly threw money at that woman like it was nothing, and honestly, for what? She's not even licensed in anything! Not health care, not psychology, not even yoga! She's just some hack who decided to *do wellness*, and Molly followed her word like it was absolute gospel. Seriously, if Molly had funneled even half that money into paying her *actual* employees—"

Alyssa cut off abruptly, shook her head. Rainbow Pup looked up at her, his gaze black and empty.

"I'm sorry. I know I shouldn't speak ill of the dead. And I don't . . . begrudge Molly anything. Obviously, she could spend her money however she wanted. I just . . . didn't understand Vivian's hold on her."

"Where did Molly go after she visited Vivian that day? When did you link back up?" Casper asked.

"There was a promo event for *Sun City* at the Four Seasons. It wasn't a full junket, just a handful of outlets, but it was still pretty hectic, and she showed up more than an hour late. I thought Damon was going to have an aneurysm."

"Damon was there?"

"Uh-huh. He was . . . not exactly *keeping an eye* on her, per se, but he's been really engaged with the promo for *Sun City*. He kept saying that if Molly played her cards right, it would turn her whole career around."

"Did they argue? At the junket?"

"No. Molly wouldn't even talk to him. She was definitely in a mood. She even snapped at me, and she never—I mean, she was always really reasonable, even if I made a mistake—"

"What happened?"

Alyssa looked embarrassed. "I had a lot to juggle, first trying to put out fires because she was so late, then getting her changed and into glam, and at some point I lost track of her purse. We found it pretty quickly, but she was upset—she said she'd been waiting for a call, and how could she get it if I didn't keep her phone nearby? Ignoring the fact that, like, I'm not going to stop an interview in progress just so she can answer a freaking phone call."

"But she did the event?"

Alyssa nodded.

"And did she get a call?"

"I don't know. She didn't mention it again. I took her home afterward. I wasn't feeling well, so I didn't stay long. She said she was just going to turn in early." Suddenly, her eyes filled with tears. "I should've stayed, right? Obviously I should have."

It was the same thing I felt, voiced aloud. It made my eyes burn perilously too. "No one could've known . . ." I started to say, but it echoed too much of what the woman sitting behind me at the funeral had said: *Who could've predicted that this very predictable thing would happen?*

It wasn't, though. It wasn't predictable. Nothing about that day sounded predictable. Something had obviously happened. Something was obviously *wrong*.

"Thank you," I said, as Alyssa carefully dabbed at her tears with the corner of a napkin. "For sharing this with us."

She set the napkin down, and her gaze turned steely. "If I see a word of it printed in *Icon* or anywhere else, I'll make your life a living hell."

I nodded. "Understood."

"Boyfriend?" I said to Casper after Alyssa had left the café, with Rainbow Pup stowed safely back in her tote bag.

Casper blinked innocently at me. "What, like *cousin* is so much more believable?"

"We could be cousins."

"We could be dating," he replied, and then grimaced. "Hypothetically. As a cover story. It's a plausible cover story. That's all I'm saying."

It wasn't that Casper wasn't cute. In fact, maybe that was part of the problem—there was a boyish quality to him, one that kind of made you want to ruffle his hair more than anything else.

The glare that he directed at me now made me wonder if he knew exactly what I was thinking.

"Don't," he said. "Don't say why it wouldn't work."

"The last thing I need right now is a boyfriend." It seemed to be the most diplomatic approach, and anyway, it was extremely true. "Even a hypothetical one."

"Noted," he replied. "Let's get going on the plan for tomorrow. Retracing Molly's last day. We'll start with the spin class."

15

I was on board with Casper's plan, but there was something I wanted to check out on my own first. Someone I needed to talk to, and I wasn't sure if bringing Casper along would be the best course of action.

So I went to Maxwell Artistic Management alone that afternoon.

I had never seen the receptionist, Veronica, in person, but we'd spoken on the phone several times. I couldn't have told you what I thought she'd look like, but at the same time, she somehow looked exactly like I thought she would—extremely thin and pale, with coppery red hair pulled back into a very tight chignon, and almost unnervingly big eyes.

"Rachel West," I said. "I have a three o'clock with Mr. Maxwell."

"Yes, Rachel, hi. Damon will be ready for you shortly. He's just finishing up a call."

I'd finessed the truth to secure this meeting, which Veronica had told me on the phone could last fifteen minutes "at the *absolute* most." I gave the impression that I was still with *Icon*, and asked if Damon would be willing to give me a quote about Molly.

I was hoping he wouldn't have any reason to know or care about my actual employment status.

I took a seat in the small reception area. The office, to my surprise, looked a little down-at-heels. The furniture and fixtures spoke more of the previous decade than the current one.

On the wall across from me was a pair of framed posters. One was the *A Is for Arnold* film poster, with Molly posing next to the titular nerd. The other was for the first *Robot Wars* film—Nick Hart front and center, holding a sci-fi-coded pistol, with Molly behind him, her hair windblown, her minuscule tank top artfully stained and ripped.

"It would be nice to be the star of a movie," Molly told me once, and I didn't understand it at the time. She had starred in multiple movies, after all. But her meaning was suddenly clear, seeing the movie posters side by side.

"Rachel?"

I blinked. The door to Damon's office had swung open, and there he was. He was in a dress shirt and slacks. I thought briefly of Lee—the lawyer slash sports agent look.

"Come on in," Damon said with a smile.

"Thank you for taking the time to meet with me." I took a seat in front of his desk. The chair was more comfortable than the ones in Irina's office, but not by much.

"It's my pleasure. Molly spoke very highly of you."

I pulled out a notebook. "Is it okay if I record too?"

"Of course."

I went about setting up my tape recorder. It was best to both write and record during interviews. Writing helped you remember the salient points better, which made the recording more useful later when you wanted to go back to listen for quotes. Not that any of this was for an actual article, but it couldn't hurt to be thorough in my keeping up of appearances.

"Like I told Veronica on the phone, I was hoping you could share some words about Molly."

Damon sat back in his chair. "It's hard to know where to start. It's a tremendous loss." He paused for a moment. "She lit up any room she walked into."

If this really were for an article, I would need something significantly less cliché than that. But he wasn't wrong. Molly did do that. She had that kind of presence.

"I'm still processing it all, to be honest," he continued. "Molly and I worked together for . . . oh, over fifteen years. I feel like I've lost a member of my family."

"I spoke with Cal Price at the funeral," I said carefully. "I know he felt the same way."

Something flickered across Damon's face, like he had smelled something unpleasant, but it just as quickly disappeared. "We were both with Molly from almost the start."

I kept my tone deliberately neutral—a reporter asking a benign question, nothing more. "I'm sorry to bring it up, but I saw that you and Cal had a bit of an argument at the reception."

For a second, I thought Damon might not respond. Or that he would change the subject, or ask me to leave. But then he let out a breath. "We did," he said, a little chagrined. "Cal and I both wanted what was best for Molly. Sometimes we butted heads when it came to what that meant. I can't help but be business minded; that's my job. I did my best to look out for her career."

"I saw some pap photos from the day she . . ." I swallowed, then continued: "You had lunch with Molly. It looked like things got a little heated then too."

Damon, to his credit, looked at me clear-eyed. "Molly had her ups and downs. She was an incredible actor when she was all in. Getting her to *stay* all in was another matter entirely. And there were so many points in the past couple of years when it felt like she could right the ship if she just reached out and grasped the wheel, you know? But she could self-sabotage like no other. She came to us at lunch that day saying that she wouldn't promote the film. Despite it being in her contract, despite it being a major project, one that up until that point she had been incredibly proud to be a part of. Despite knowing that other people's careers—mine, Cal's—were dependent on her doing her job. It made no sense. But it was . . ." He stopped, shook his head, gave me a rueful smile. "Not unlike her, I'm afraid to say."

I paused for a moment, considering how to push forward. "But she went to the press event for *Sun City* afterward. I guess you both convinced her to promote?"

"She did go to the event, but I don't know how much either of us had to do with that." I recalled what Alyssa had told us earlier—the receipt for the gas station on the way to Vivian Grayson's ranch. Did Vivian convince Molly to promote the film?

Damon fiddled with a pen on his desk. "If I had known when I watched her leave that day that it would be the last time I'd ever see her . . ." He cleared his throat. "Well. Life is . . . unpredictable."

"Where did you go after the press event?"

He met my eyes. "I'm sorry, I'm not sure how that's relevant?"

"I'm just trying to get a timeline of what Molly's last day was like. Did you see her again afterward?"

He shook his head. "I went to dinner with my wife. It was our tenth anniversary. I won't tell you what we got up to afterward, but I wasn't exactly monitoring my phone."

It seemed better to steer toward the lighthearted. "Did you get that watch as your anniversary gift? It's pretty snazzy."

Damon smiled down at the shiny silver Rolex on his wrist. "No, this was a gift from Molly when we got the *Sun City* contract. It really felt like . . ." He let out a breath. "Like the start of something special. Who knew it was actually the beginning of the end?"

16

That evening, I went by Lee's house to drop off some cash for dinner. Since he lived so close by, it seemed silly to mail it. So in a Classic Rachel West avoidance move, I planned to leave it in his mailbox. I could practically hear Anton telling me it was a federal crime to put anything in a mailbox without postage. I chose to ignore that.

Lee's house was a small, tidy-looking bungalow with a porch running across the front. The windows were dark when I approached, which was ideal, as it meant neither Lee nor his fiancée was home. I wouldn't have to skulk around to ensure a clandestine mailbox drop-off.

The house wasn't much like my childhood home—a brick-clad one-and-a-half-story in south St. Louis—but it reminded me of it somehow. During the winters when I was growing up, the sun would set so early that it would already be dark by the time I got back from after-school activities. The bus would drop me off at the corner and I'd hurry down the street, eager to see the windows of our house all lit up. Even from afar, the little rectangles of light made me feel warm.

Later on, more often than not I'd peer down the street from the bus stop and the house would be dark, like Lee's was now. The feeling cut both ways back then: as warm as those lit-up windows made me feel, the dark windows made me feel just as cold—empty, like the house itself.

I lifted the lid of Lee's mailbox and slid the money, folded into a sheet of paper, inside. Then I turned and walked straight into someone.

I yelped and stumbled back. A pair of strong hands reached out and steadied me. I pushed them away immediately. Then I realized the hands were attached to Lee.

He was in a T-shirt and running shorts. His face was flushed, his hair damp with sweat, his eyebrows raised in surprise.

Extremely good-looking was the involuntary thought that reverberated through my mind. Pure lizard brain.

"What are you—" he began.

"Mailbox," I burst.

"Sorry?"

"Money. In the mailbox. For the pad thai. Why the hell did you sneak up on me like that?"

"I didn't. I even said your name."

"Well, I didn't hear you. You should . . . think about . . ."

His eyes shone. "Tap shoes? Wearing a bell? I'll take it into consideration." A pause. "I told you not to worry about dinner."

"Yeah, and I told you I don't like owing people."

"Fair enough." It was quiet for a moment. I knew I should say something, or leave, or say something and then leave—that would probably be the ideal order of events—but for some reason I just stood there.

Lee broke the silence. "Would you . . . like a bottle of water? Or would you owe me for that too?"

"I—" No. Was what I should've said. But instead, I nodded. "Sure. Water would be great."

"Do you want to sit outside? It's a nice night."

"Sure."

As he headed into the house, I thought of the small act of kindness that the suggestion was. Maybe I'd feel uncomfortable going inside when we didn't really know each other. Maybe his fiancée would be uncomfortable having a strange woman in their shared space. Especially a strange woman who thought her fiancé was extremely good-looking.

An outdoor lamp flicked on as I took a seat in one of a pair of plastic Adirondack chairs on the porch. There was an array of potted plants of varying sizes surrounding the chairs and lining the perimeter of the porch. Most of them, unfortunately, looked dead, or well on their way to being dead.

"Plant enthusiast?" I asked when Lee returned and extended a bottle of water toward me. When I took it, our fingers brushed. Just barely, but my stomach still made an irrational swoop in response.

Lee settled into the other chair and glanced at the potted plants as he twisted off the cap of his own bottle. He took a drink before responding. "No, actually. I thought they might be happier out here, but I guess I just . . . can't figure out what they need."

"How often do you water?"

"Every few days."

"Most of these are succulents. That's probably your problem. They can't tolerate overwatering. Less is more."

"Are you a plant person?"

"No, but I read a lot." I tapped the side of my head. "There's a whole boatload of knowledge up here that I'll probably never use. Ask me about napkin folding or birds of the Pacific Northwest next."

Lee's lips twitched. "You should go on *Jeopardy!*"

"I'm more of a *Price Is Right* girl."

"You know, I won a furniture set on *The Price Is Right* when I was in college."

"Seriously?"

He nodded. "I had no idea you had to pay taxes on those prizes. But I did, even though I was broke and had nowhere to put it."

"Be honest, is that why you bought the house? It matches the furniture set?"

A shadow of a smile crossed his face. "It's still at my parents' place. Fits in better there. It worked out for everyone. They got a new living room set and I got a go-to truth for any game of two truths and a lie."

"What's the other truth and the lie?"

"You'll have to guess which is which."

"Fifty-fifty odds. I'll take it."

He took another sip of water. "I won a child modeling contest when I was nine." Another sip. "I cheated on my SATs."

"Child model," I said. "That's obviously the truth."

"Why?"

"Because an upstanding citizen like you would never cheat." I went on before I could stop myself: "And because you were clearly an adorable kid."

"Why's that?"

"Those dimples? Come on."

It was too close to flirting. I had to pull back. But it felt shockingly easy, sitting here in the golden glow of the porch light. Maybe it wasn't flirting. Maybe it was just . . . existing with another person. Allowing that to happen, at least for a moment. In the way that had been so easy to do with Molly.

I considered the potted plants again. The one closest to me was a withered-looking jade. The pot containing it looked handmade; pieces of colorful glass and mosaic tile were laid into its blue-glazed ceramic.

"So, is your fiancée the plant person, then?"

Lee responded after a pause: "My fiancée was the plant person."

My grip on my water bottle tightened. I looked over at him. He was contemplating another of the mostly dead plants. "Lee, if your fiancée was *actually* killed by some mafia kingpin, I will launch myself into the sun."

"She wasn't. She's just not my fiancée anymore."

I frowned. "So now you have . . . a new fiancée?"

"You know, if we say *fiancée* any more times, it'll lose all meaning. It's called—"

"Semantic satiation," we both said at the same time, and then looked at each other.

His expression was sheepish. "I read it in a crossword puzzle once."

"I have no justification," I said, and I knew that I should look away, but I didn't. "I'm just a deeply annoying person."

Lee smiled a little. "I find that hard to believe."

Silence.

"Why didn't you say?" I asked hesitantly. "When I went on about the whole thing last night." The ring, the honeymoon, Cooper the golden retriever . . . I had made an ass of myself, hadn't I?

"I didn't want to burst your bubble," he replied, and then added, a little more quietly, "and I guess I liked your version better than the truth."

"Which was?"

He shrugged. "She left."

"Why?"

He gave me another look, curiosity in his eyes.

"Occupational disease," I explained. "I ask a lot of questions. And anyway, sometimes it's easier to talk to a stranger, isn't it? Just get it all out there when the stakes are so low?"

Lee considered this for a moment. When he spoke again, he was measured. Striving for casual in a way that strayed too far into the formality that ironically often accompanied striving for casual. "She left because she met someone else. I don't know exactly when it started, but she was already . . . Well, there was obviously some degree of . . ."

"Overlap?"

"Yeah." He took a long drink of water. "I think it was someone she met through work. I never actually got the whole story of how it started."

"How did you find out?"

"She told me. Which is good. At least I didn't have to—I mean, I prefer it that way. Being up-front."

"You mean being up-front about the very not-up-front act of cheating?"

"You know what I mean, though. I didn't have to find out through mutual friends, or by overhearing some phone conversation, or . . . whatever the female equivalent of lipstick on the collar is."

"It could still be lipstick on the collar. The guy might like a lip tint."

"True."

"So, she took you out to dinner, and over the shrimp cocktail, she told you . . ."

Amusement flashed across his face at the callback, but it quickly faded, replaced with sadness. "That she didn't love me anymore. That she wasn't sure if she ever had. She said . . ." He swallowed, glanced away with a wavery smile. "Sorry, I don't know why—"

"What did she say?"

He looked for a brief moment like he was weighing whether or not to continue. And then he met my eyes.

"That it wouldn't have been so easy to cheat if she actually loved me," he said. "I guess it made her question not just us but . . . everything. What if what she *thought* she wanted wasn't what she actually wanted at all? What if it was like the plants, you know? You buy one, and then another, and then suddenly people are giving them to you as gifts and asking for advice, and now you're this *plant person*, and what if you never wanted to be that in the first place? What if you just liked what you liked in the moment, and then it becomes this identity that you don't even have a grip on?"

I felt a strange urgency to banish the sorrow in his eyes. To make him smile. "Are you the withered jade or the doomed monstera in this analogy?"

It didn't quite work, but he did point to a drooping dracaena. "I'm that one. Whatever that is." He paused. "I actually saw them together once. My ex and the other guy. After things had ended between us. It wasn't on purpose—we just happened to be at the same place at the same time, and I'm sure she didn't even know I saw them . . . Anyway, I don't know what I expected. I guess you kind of end up building the other guy up in your mind. But he was . . . just a guy. Literally just some guy."

There was that feeling again, even more powerful than before: *If I try hard enough, I can get him to stop looking so sad.* "How could he compete with a *Price Is Right* winner who was *also* the winner of a child modeling contest?"

I was rewarded with one dimple briefly surfacing. "You're right," he said. "I'm definitely better looking."

I held up my water bottle in salute. "Fuck that guy." A beat. "I mean, I guess she already did."

He shot me an incredulous look.

Shit. Not the intended effect. "Too soon?"

He shook his head. "No. I just . . . haven't been able to see much humor in it. But maybe I should."

"In your defense, it's not a particularly funny situation on paper."

"Oh, I don't know. Getting cheated on . . . broken engagement . . . living alone in the house I thought we'd raise our kids in . . . No, actually, it's a laugh riot. Get *Mad TV* on the phone."

"I knew you'd be a *Mad TV* person."

"What does being a *Mad TV* person imply?" he asked.

"That you're patently not an *SNL* person."

"I grew up on the West Coast. It airs on a delay. You don't get the thrill of live TV."

"Oh yeah, the thrill of live TV is definitely one of my favorite vices. That and forgetting to take the tea bag out of my tea."

"Okay, I don't—"

I couldn't help myself. "I also love waiting until the very last second to take popcorn out of the microwave—like, *just* before it's about to become a charred mess."

He smiled now. Both dimples appeared. It felt gratifying in a way I didn't want to think too much about. "I get it, I'm extremely boring."

I met his eyes. "I find that hard to believe."

It was quiet for a moment.

"I didn't kill the plants on purpose, though," he said. "For the record. Just because she left them behind doesn't mean I would do that to them."

"I would never assume that."

"They're innocent bystanders. I just really don't know what I'm doing."

"Succulents are hardy, though. They propagate really easily. Even if most of the plant is dead, you can pop off a branch or even a leaf and let it root. And then the plant lives on." I pointed to the drooping dracaena. "Even that one."

"That's good to know." He downed the rest of his water and then screwed the cap back on the bottle. "So, what about you?"

"What about me?"

"Boyfriend? Long-distance relationship? Failed engagement?"

"None of the above." When I moved to LA, I wasn't in the right headspace for dating, though that didn't stop the people around me—Stacia, primarily, and sometimes Anton—from trying to matchmake or wingman for me every now and then. It never got much further than awkward drinks dates with guys I had absolutely nothing in common with.

Looking back at past relationships—my college boyfriend, a brief stint with a guy in my class at the start of med school—it sometimes felt more like I was playing at something . . . romance, partnership, whatever . . . because I thought I was supposed to rather than because I actually wanted to.

"I like being alone." I took another drink. "I probably like it a little too much."

"There's nothing wrong with that."

"Mm." I thought of Molly's favorite quote from *The Band Wagon*: *"I want more. All eight eighths."* Sometimes I wondered if it was possible for me to give any more *eighths* than what was on the surface. To allow myself to be known, more than just a little bit.

When Lee spoke again, it was tentative. "Are you—"

"Any updates on Molly?"

Anton spoke in my head: *Classic Rachel West.*

"No," Lee said. If he was thrown by the sudden change in subject, he didn't show it. "Nothing new."

"Would you tell me, though? If there was anything you could share?"

He nodded.

"I appreciate that," I said. "And the water. I'll come back and leave a bottle in your mailbox sometime."

"I can't tell if you're joking."

"That's part of my charm."

He met my gaze. "The first part is okay, though. The part where you come back."

All of a sudden, it felt too . . . charged. Too significant. Lee's effortlessly beautiful fiancée, who I had envisioned blond and sun-kissed in that distinctly Californian way—shades of Cameron Diaz—didn't exist. Or, she did, but now she was with some other guy, some pathetic non-Lee. She was someone who abandoned her plant collection. And her fiancé. Lee was someone who seemingly hadn't quite moved on from that. But he was also someone who . . . thought the first part was okay. The part where I came back.

I stood. "I should get out of your hair. I've got to get up for a spin class in the morning."

"Spin class," he repeated.

"Yeah, I know. Not really my thing."

"Why are you going, then?"

Now I was the one striving for casual. "Oh, just trying something new."

★ APRIL 2008 ★

"RACHEL, WE HAVE TO GET YOU LAID, THOUGH."

Molly was aghast when she found out I hadn't been with anyone since leaving med school. We were in her kitchen, eating Pinkberry that Alyssa had dropped off. It was a facet of the celebrity lifestyle that continued to baffle me—all Molly had to do was say the words *I want frozen yogurt* and someone would bring it to her. It made you wonder where the line would be drawn. *I want a fifteen-course meal flown in from Italy. I want fresh placenta for an antiaging treatment. I want the souls of everyone who ever wronged me captured in jars and buried in my backyard.*

"I don't . . . particularly feel that way," I said.

Molly was sitting atop the kitchen island, holding her plastic spoon like a scepter. "When I was twelve, I guest starred on an episode of *Are You Afraid of the Dark?* Do you remember that show?"

I did. As a kid, I had recurring nightmares about the episode with the pool monster.

"I played a girl whose family moves into this creepy old house, and in the attic she finds this cobwebby wooden trunk just absolutely covered in dust and spiders, and when she opens it up, it leads to this narrow, decrepit old secret passageway. Then there's ghosts, et cetera, et cetera. That part doesn't really matter."

"Okay . . . ?"

"I'm saying that cobwebby old trunk is what your vagina's going to be like."

"Molly."

She laughed, and then laughed some more.

I fought a smile. "Technically, the trunk would be my vulva and the decrepit passageway would be my vagina. If we're drawing metaphors."

"Yeah, I'm super concerned about the anatomical accuracy of my idiotic metaphor. The point is, you need to hook up with someone. Want me to call Dax? He might have a friend who doesn't suck." Her eyes shone. "Or who does, if you like that."

"You just broke up with Dax."

She shrugged. "I usually stay cool with my exes. There doesn't always have to be bad blood. I might even . . ."

"What?"

She looked nonchalant, scooping up a spoonful of frozen yogurt. "Nothing. He might still be useful—that's all."

"For what?"

"For keeping my secret passageway free from cobwebs."

"Got it."

Her eyes gleamed. "And spiders. So many spiders."

"Why would there be—"

"You know, the ghost was this Victorian kid who was forced to live in the secret passageway when he was alive. So I don't know how we're going to parse that, vis-à-vis the metaphor."

"Can we talk about something else? Like, literally anything else? I just read an article about this guy who went to the dentist for a tooth infection and they found an entire second set of teeth in his jaw, under his regular teeth. Apparently he had never had an X-ray done—"

"Oh, that reminds me . . ." Molly set her frozen yogurt aside, hopped down from the counter, and headed off in the direction of the living room.

"You don't want to hear what happened when they extracted the infected tooth?" I called after her.

"No, I categorically do not." She returned with a shopping bag, which she threw at me. Miraculously, I managed to catch it without dropping my own yogurt. "Take these."

I peered inside the bag. It contained several sets of Lululemon workout clothes.

"They aren't me," Molly continued. "I'm clearly a summer, not a winter. I don't know why people keep trying to make me do jewel tones. You, on the other hand . . ."

"How did the tooth story remind you of this?"

"Because sometimes I feel like I'd rather get a tooth pulled than go to another fucking spin class."

"You should keep these, though," I said. "You might change your mind and want them later."

Molly shook her head. "Nope. You know me. I never look back."

17

The spin studio, Revolution, was tucked between a med spa and a hair salon. I met Casper there for the nine a.m. class. I had donned one of the Lululemon sets from Molly—teal yoga pants and a matching tank.

Casper arrived wearing workout shorts and a sleeveless tank top that had *Sun's Out, Guns Out* printed in neon letters across the front. He was more muscled than I expected him to be.

"I borrowed this," he said, noticing me noticing his shirt. Or, at least, he thought it was just the shirt that I was noticing.

"Sure."

"I did."

"I'm not judging." And I wasn't. I was just . . . surprised. On account of the muscles. Cameras weren't *that* heavy, were they? And considering that the only camera I had seen Casper lift thus far was the likes of a Canon PowerShot, it couldn't have been occupational muscle building. Clearly, this friendly ghost hit the gym on a regular basis.

"Have you done one of these classes before?" He gestured

toward the building, which had a large segmented front window, like a garage door.

"Yes," I replied. "Under duress." Tyla, my office mate, had dragged me to one such class last month, citing the wellness benefits of exercising during your lunch hour. I did approximately two-thirds of the class, went outside and threw up, and then got a red velvet cupcake at the Sprinkles down the street. Tyla was not thrilled at my failure to appreciate the *wellness benefits* of the class. Or my consumption of refined sugar. And carbs. And Red 40.

Casper and I entered Revolution. Inside was a metal-clad reception counter (industrial features abounded), and beyond it there were several closed doors. Behind the counter stood a tan, toned woman with a high ponytail and effortless no-show makeup. When we asked to join the nine a.m. class, she smiled, revealing teeth that were aggressively white.

"I'm so sorry, but we're not accepting new clients at this time. If you'd like to join our waiting list, we're booking about sixteen weeks out."

"So we could spin in . . . October," I said.

The smile didn't waver. "Potentially."

I glanced at Casper.

"This is the studio that Molly Byrne went to, isn't it?" Casper asked.

Something in the receptionist's expression sharpened for just a second. "Our client list is confidential, of course."

I wondered if Casper was going to try to push it, but he just gave an affable nod. "Of course. Thank you so much."

We headed out.

"So that was a bust," I said, feeling stupider by the second as we started down the street. I should've known that the kind of studio Molly would go to wouldn't be the kind to just accept random drop-ins.

Two women, one short and one tall, both in matching sets similar to mine, were heading toward us, holding water bottles and carrying designer tote bags, their heads bent with the hushed tones of good gossip. Their conversation became clear as we neared each other.

"—said that Molly was acting weird that day, but she didn't really know whether—"

As we passed them, Casper and the shorter woman knocked shoulders. Her metal water bottle went flying and landed in the street.

"Oh my God, I'm so sorry." Casper stooped to pick up the bottle. "Are you okay?"

"Yes." The woman looked a little ruffled, but then disarmed by the smile Casper offered her, which was apologetic and more than a little charming.

"I'm a klutz," he said, and then cast a look at the water bottle. "Shit. It's dented. I'm really sorry. I'll pay you for it."

"Oh, don't worry about it."

He handed it to her, and their fingers brushed. "Sorry, I couldn't help but overhear—are you two in the nine a.m. class?" He gestured toward Revolution. "The one that Molly Byrne took sometimes?"

"Yeah, we are," the taller woman replied.

"I heard that she . . ." Casper glanced around as if checking for eavesdroppers. Honestly, it was a hell of a performance—even I would believe he was your average celebrity gossip hound. "I heard that she relapsed. It's so sad. I can't even imagine what she was going through."

"Were you there?" I asked. "In the class she took the day she died?"

The women exchanged a look of silent consultation.

"Well, *we* weren't," the tall woman began, clearly having

reached the decision to share the juicy gossip. "But one of the other girls who was in class that day told us she overheard Molly arguing with someone in the changing room. She didn't see who it was, but it was definitely someone else from class."

"What were they arguing about?"

"She couldn't really tell. Just that it was getting kind of heated."

Casper's eyes widened. "That's wild. I wonder what they could've even had to fight about."

"Whatever it was, it can't have been good, judging by how the rest of Molly's day went," the short woman said.

"Too true," Casper replied, and a beat of silence followed. "Sorry again about the bottle."

"Don't be." The short woman raked her eyes over him for a moment, and I would've bet money that she was going to ask him for his number. But instead she said, "You look familiar. What do I know you from?"

"I'm not sure. Though I feel like I've seen you before too."

"Really? Where?"

Casper smiled. "In my dreams."

Both women groaned, but looked charmed nonetheless.

"Too much?" Casper asked.

"Points for effort," the tall woman replied. "But not even you can pull that off, hon."

The short woman turned to her friend. "No, seriously, though. Doesn't he look familiar?"

"I've heard I have one of those faces," Casper said. "Promise you won't forget it next time, okay?"

As the women retreated into Revolution and Casper and I headed in the direction of my car, I cast a sidelong glance at him. "You were a little too good at that."

"Comes with the territory," he replied.

"I didn't know being a paparazzo involved a level of improv."

"It's not just about aiming a camera. It helps a lot to have good interpersonal skills."

"Oh, is that what that was?"

He looked too innocent. "What else would it be?"

Something struck me for the first time. "Was Molly a fan of your *interpersonal skills*?"

"No."

"Did you want her to be?"

A pause. "I don't think it was possible to know Molly and not be a little bit in love with her."

"She would hate hearing that. She would gag audibly."

Casper smiled, equal parts wistful and sad. "I know."

18

So, Molly fought with someone at spin class," Fadia said. "And then she argued with her manager at lunch. Sounds like we've got a day that's pretty heavy on contention."

When I arrived back at Palm Vista, Fadia's door had swung open with a cry of "I'm making pasta salad! Come back at twelve!"

It wasn't purely because I was hungry—and in no position to turn down a free lunch—that I returned to Fadia's at the appointed time. At least, that's what I told myself as I dug into the pasta salad with farfalle and mozzarella and halved cherry tomatoes in a pesto vinaigrette. There was also crusty bread with olive oil and balsamic vinegar, and fresh lemonade in seltzer, and the promise of cantaloupe gelato for dessert. ("I know a guy who knows a guy—it's the best you'll ever have outside of Italy.") As I sat at Fadia's tiny yet chic circular dining table, I thought of Anton's question the other day—*Who* are *you?*

"I like to treat myself," Fadia had said simply as I took a large bite of mozzarella and farfalle. *Delicious.* I definitely deserved this, on account of putting on workout clothes and intending to exercise.

I hadn't consciously decided to update Fadia on the investigation—which was barely an investigation to begin with—but as we sat together and she told me stories about the other neighbors she knew at Palm Vista, her thoughts on the latest addition to a popular horror movie franchise, and her recent experimental recipes, I realized how comfortable I felt. Fadia was clearly someone with a natural gift for being warm and welcoming—my exact opposite. Maybe that was why, when the conversation eventually wound around to Molly, I ended up recounting the details of our unsuccessful trip to Revolution. Not that I was at all sure what a successful trip would have looked like—Casper and I somehow made it into the class, and then the toned receptionist stepped out and declared herself to be the killer? *She insulted my wheatgrass shakes,* she'd have said, raising her fist to the sky. *She had to die!*

"It doesn't really get us anywhere," I said. "There's no way to know who Molly was arguing with."

"The women you met outside said it was definitely someone in the class, though."

"Yeah, but it's not like the client list is posted anywhere, or like we can park ourselves out front and interview everyone who walks in there. I'm pretty sure the management would have something to say about that."

Fadia considered this for a moment. "I know someone we could ask."

Apartment 208 was on the other side of the building and up a rickety flight of metal stairs that connected to the outdoor walkway framing the Palm Vista complex. Fadia knocked on the front door three times and then waited. Nobody answered.

Fadia brought her fist down hard, pounding three more times. At my taken-aback expression, she said simply, "Headphones."

A moment later, the door swung open, revealing a girl of maybe sixteen or seventeen. She was wearing an oversized black sweatshirt and baggy camo shorts and had large headphones around her neck. Her dark, curly hair was separated into two buns, one on either side of her head, and she wore black eyeliner all the way around her deep brown eyes.

Fadia extended a bag toward her. "Chocolate biscotti!"

The girl's face split into an unexpectedly sunny smile. "Nice."

"This is my friend Rachel," Fadia said, and I blinked. Friends? "From 105. Rachel, this is Jaz. Could we come in for a minute?"

The girl—Jaz—opened the door wider, and we stepped inside. The unit, although a two-bedroom, looked a great deal more like mine than like Fadia's, at least on the surface: laminate countertops and white walls, and carpeting that probably should've been replaced long ago. But unlike mine, it was very tidy, with a better attempt at interior decoration, even if done on a budget—a neat color-block rug atop the beige floor, a modern-looking sofa, a gallery wall above the couch featuring school artwork and family photos and a framed Matisse print.

Jaz shut the front door behind us, and then turned to us expectantly.

"There's something we were hoping you could look up for us," Fadia said.

Look up, I soon learned, was a loose way of putting it. We followed Jaz into a small bedroom that was as tidy and bright as the rest of the apartment, with many of the trappings of childhood still present—stuffed animals on the bed, pop-star posters on the walls. The one dissonant feature was the desk, tucked in a corner, which housed three enormous monitors, a tricked-out keyboard, a mouse, and, underneath, a computer setup like I had never seen before, all blinking lights and faint humming.

"Jaz is a computer wizard," Fadia told me as Jaz settled into the desk chair with the look of a seasoned pilot about to take flight.

In approximately two minutes, she rolled to the side to give us a better look at the central computer monitor, which now displayed the class roster for Revolution Spin Studio.

"This is everyone who was registered for the nine a.m. class the day Molly Byrne died."

"How did you do that?" I asked.

Jaz shrugged. "Want me to print it?"

"That would be great."

She tapped a key on the keyboard and an inkjet printer on the floor beside the desk rumbled to life.

Client list obtained, the three of us headed back into the living room together.

"When's your mom off work today?" Fadia asked Jaz.

"Not until midnight. She just left a little while ago."

I took a closer look at the gallery wall above the couch. The top left photo showed a young woman with the same curly black hair, deep brown eyes, and light brown skin as Jaz. She was holding a chubby toddler who had to be a little Jaz—she had the same sunny smile, albeit with far fewer teeth.

"At least they let up on those back-to-back overnights," Fadia said.

"Yeah, it's something."

"Give me a shout if you need anything, okay?"

Jaz's eyes shone. "I wouldn't say no to more of that pasta salad you guys had at your last book club meeting."

"I might just happen to have thrown together a fresh batch. Swing by later and I'll hook you up."

"Thanks, Fadia!"

We left Jaz with her biscotti and our thanks for the list, and headed back downstairs.

"Her mom is an ER nurse. Works crazy hours," Fadia explained as we descended the rickety stairs. "Jaz is only sixteen, but she's already graduated high school. She's a total computer genius. Or, really, a total genius, full stop. She's very into app development these days."

"What kind of apps?"

"Oh, you know, stuffed mushrooms, bruschetta, anything filo based." I shot her a look, and she grinned. "Wait, no, that's my kind of app development. Jaz's apps, frankly, I'm too intimidated to ask about. But conveniently for us, she can also hack into just about anything you can think of. Except maybe the Pentagon, but honestly, it's just a matter of time."

"Have you needed her to . . . *hack* . . . for you before?"

"I mean, everyone's got parking tickets." Fadia smiled. "It pays to be neighborly, right?"

"Guess so."

"She's a really good kid. I feel for her a little."

"Why?"

"I don't know, just seems like she's been kind of lonely since graduating. Sometimes I wonder if she ever wants to get out there and . . . you know, do teen stuff."

"Teen stuff," I repeated. "Like . . . crashing the mall with three cool guy friends?"

"Oh yeah. All teen stuff these days can be traced directly back to Avril Lavigne's 'Complicated' music video."

Surprise must have been evident on my face.

"Yes," Fadia said wryly, "I might prefer horror films, but I've managed to keep up with MTV over the years. I contain multitudes." She side-eyed me. "How old were you when that video came out?"

"I was in college."

"And did you run out immediately to buy arm warmers and a skinny tie?"

"No comment." I thought of the teenager I had seen outside the building the other day. "Speaking of skater boys . . . isn't there another kid at Palm Vista?"

"Corey, in 108," Fadia said. "He and his folks moved in last year. They're really nice. He's a quiet kid—though we did go in-depth about the *Goosebumps* TV show at one of my game nights. He's got strong opinions about Stine."

"Do you know everyone in the building?"

"Not *everyone*. I didn't know you before, though obviously we've remedied that. And there's the guy in 107—we've never been particularly chummy. But he's moving out next month. I'm not saying I'm looking *forward* to it, but it'll be nice to get a fresh face in."

We reached my apartment door. I turned to look at Fadia. Today she was wearing a bright yellow knit top over a tiered peasant skirt. She had colorful bangles on each wrist.

"What did you do before"—I realized I didn't even know what her exact job was—"um, before whatever you do now?"

"I'm in customer service," Fadia said. "For an extremely boring corporation. But I used to be in consulting."

"Really?"

"Yeah. Got kind of fed up with the rat race."

"You seem to like people so much, though. Why do you work from home? It's pretty . . . solitary, isn't it?"

She paused in thought. "It can be. Sometimes I wonder if I

should get a pet, or . . . I don't know, a really high-maintenance plant, just for the day-to-day." Her eyes sparkled. "But I like to protect my peace. And part of that involves building my own community, outside of my job. Work is just one part of life. I didn't want it to be the whole shebang. There are too many things I love doing, and too many people I want to connect with, you know?"

I didn't. And I couldn't quite place what I was feeling until I was back inside my apartment; it was equal parts envy and awe.

19

Let's reconvene tonight at Richard's," Fadia had said before we parted ways. "He said he's happy to help out. He'll even host."

Discussing the investigation with Fadia was one thing, but I wasn't sure how I felt about bringing yet another person into it. But Fadia insisted that Richard could help us, and, well, she hadn't been wrong so far.

"Is this nuts?" I asked Anton in my apartment that evening. "Am I crazy for pursuing this? And getting other people involved too?"

"No," Anton said after a moment's consideration. "I don't think it's crazy. And . . ." He paused, as if uncertain of whether or not to go on.

"What?" I prompted.

He met my eyes. "It's not the worst thing in the world to accept help every now and then. You don't have to deal with everything alone."

"I know that."

Anton's gaze was a little too perceptive. "Do you, though?"

A knock sounded at the door before I could respond.

It was Casper. He had changed out of the *Sun's Out, Guns Out* tank top and back into his all-black outfit, leather jacket included. Anton clasped Casper's hand with a smile and said, "Rachel was right, you're really committed to that jacket."

"Sorry?" Casper said.

"It's probably overkill for June," Anton replied, "but I appreciate the aesthetic. Very James Dean."

"Thank you?"

"You're welcome. Shall we get this murder-mystery show on the road?"

We met Fadia outside—more introductions commenced—and then we headed up to Apartment 203.

The door swung open just as Fadia raised her fist to knock.

"I heard we've got a murder," the man at the door said. Richard.

He looked to be in his mid-forties or so, with thinning dark brown hair and a thick beard, as if the hair on his head was slowly migrating down to his face. He wore khaki cargo pants and a plaid button-down shirt open over a graphic tee, the sleeves of the button-down pushed up hastily. He ushered us into his living room, where a large whiteboard stood against one wall.

"What's that?" Anton asked.

"Murder board," Richard replied. "I know it's a cliché, but it actually helps."

Anton's lips quirked. "Love it. Where's the red yarn for connecting leads?"

Richard cast him a disparaging look. "That's really only on television."

His apartment was pretty austere, the only furniture a small square dining table, a shabby-looking couch in green plaid, and two folding chairs that appeared to have been moved from the dining area to the living area for our benefit. A small flat-screen TV sat atop a milk crate. The whole place reminded me of a girl I knew in med school, whose apartment was similarly spartan. Notably, she owned only one plate, one cup, and one set of silverware—not out of frugality but for the sake of efficiency. *Why would you need more than that? Just wash it and use it again.* I wondered how much dishware I would find if I opened one of Richard's kitchen cabinets.

After yet another round of introductions, Anton and I settled on the couch and Casper and Fadia each took one of the folding chairs, while Richard approached the whiteboard and picked up a marker. I watched as he printed *MOLLY BYRNE* in big capital letters at the top, and then added *VICTIM* underneath it, slightly smaller.

It made my stomach twist.

"Let's recount the details first." Richard wrote in a hasty scrawl as he spoke. "Fadia gave me the basic rundown, and I did a little research online to confirm: found at home, history of drug abuse, appears to be an overdose—whether accidental or intentional, unclear—but instead, we're presuming murder." He turned to us. "So obviously, she was poisoned."

Casper frowned. "Why obviously?"

Richard gave Casper a withering look. "She wasn't shot, strangled, stabbed, or drowned. No head injuries. No signs of a struggle. How do you kill someone without laying a finger on them? Poison. Whether it was arsenic or cyanide or something niche that evades tox screens, we don't know yet. Did the killer put it in her nonfat matcha latte with coconut-milk cold foam? Inject it between her toes during a pedicure? Who knows? But if she was murdered—and that's the assumption we're making here—she was almost certainly dosed with something."

"Hairline fracture of the skull?" Fadia suggested.

"The ME would catch it."

"Suffocation?"

"There'd be cyanosis."

"You people are terrifying," Anton murmured.

Fadia persisted. "There was this one episode of *CSLA* where this woman got water in her lungs but didn't die until she lay down later—essentially a delayed drowning?"

"I was there when that was pitched, and no. In real life she would've shown symptoms beforehand—coughing, trouble breathing, something of that nature. Somebody would've noticed she wasn't well." Richard spun the dry-erase marker absently in one hand and addressed the rest of us. "In case Fadia didn't tell you, I used to write for *Crime Scene LA*."

"Used to?" Anton said with interest. "What do you do now?"

"I've got a screenplay in the works. And in the meantime—"

"Rich writes for *World Adventure Club*," Fadia interjected proudly. "You know, that kids' show with the talking backpack?"

"Talking backpack," Casper repeated.

Richard looked slightly ruffled. "I got into writing for film a couple years ago, quit *Crime Scene LA*, got divorced, needed money, so I took on *WAC* just to make some steady cash. The screenplay thing is totally still underway. After seven years of plotting murders on *CSLA*, plotting the mystery of Rucksack's missing compass is not particularly mentally taxing. So I can do both."

"What's your movie about?" Anton asked.

"Mistake," Fadia muttered, barely perceptibly. "That was a mistake."

Richard's expression brightened. "It's about a television writer who receives an anonymous package on the worst day of his life. Inside the package? A cell phone. It starts ringing, and who's on the other end of the line? It's *him*, from the future. There's been a *nuclear winter*—"

"Is any of this relevant to Molly?" Casper interrupted. "The actual reason we're all here? Shouldn't we focus on her?"

Richard set his jaw. "You know, someone could really benefit from Rucksack's lessons on kindness and manners, but okay, Haircut, yes, let's get back to the murder at hand."

Out of the corner of my eye, I could see Casper's discomfited frown. One of his hands flew up and brushed through his hair as Richard turned back to the murder board.

"What we need," Richard said, "is for Rachel to walk us through what happened the night Molly died."

Everyone looked at me.

I blinked. "Why do we need to start there?"

"Because you saw Molly in the hours just before her death, making you the closest thing we've got to a witness right now. And how do all good *CSLA* investigations start?"

"With a pun," Fadia said.

"Oh yeah!" Anton's face lit up. "Like, they find a dead body in an industrial shredder, and Detective Clarkson takes off his sunglasses and is like—"

"'Just a *shred* of evidence will *tear this criminal to pieces*,'" Fadia intoned.

"Yes!" Anton clapped in delight. "Amazing!"

"I was going to say *by interviewing witnesses*," Richard said. "But thank you. The shredder plot was one of mine." He turned back to me. "So, what happened that night?"

All eyes were on me once more. Richard's expectant gaze. Anton, his expression turned serious. Fadia, her eyes bright. And Casper, his face unreadable.

"Molly texted me," I began. "She wanted me to come by when I got off work. It was . . . around seven thirty when I headed over to her house. I was only there for . . . I don't know—twenty minutes. Maybe less." Too short a time, in hindsight. Far too short.

Anton reached over and put a reassuring hand on my knee.

I swallowed. Continued: "She gave me some stuff she didn't want."

"What kind of stuff?" Richard asked.

"Just some accessories. She did that a lot."

I looked up at the murder board. Richard had printed *RACHEL* to the left of Molly's name. Underneath was written *Point of contact night of death*, and underneath that, *Got celeb castoffs.*

"It was never about that, though," I said, a shade too defensively. To say I didn't care at all would be a lie—of course I liked getting free stuff. Anyone would. But that was never why I was friends with Molly. "I usually tried to sneak things back into her place without her noticing, or leave them somewhere else in the house before I left."

You might change your mind later was something I said frequently upon receiving Molly's "celeb castoffs." And Molly's reply was always the same: *I only look forward.*

"How did she seem when you saw her that night?" Fadia asked. It was the same question Lee had asked me the morning after Molly's death.

"She was . . . in a mood."

A pile of tabloids had been spread out on the coffee table in her bedroom. The one closest to me was open to a Who Wore It Best page—Molly versus Petra Evanovich. Eighty-nine percent of respondents said that Petra wore it better. "How am I supposed to compete with her?" Molly had burst out. "She's nineteen years old and has legs up to her face!"

"But that was . . . I mean, everyone gets in moods, right?" I said now.

"Did she say what she was planning to do for the rest of the night?"

"Just that she was going to bed. I offered to stay, but . . . she told me not to."

I focused on the board, because I was certain that if I met anyone's eyes I would see reflected back at me exactly what I knew to be true: *You should've stayed.*

When I finally tore my gaze away from the board, Casper was looking at me.

"You okay?"

"It's not like I'm fragile."

"No one said you were."

"Did you see Molly eat or drink anything while you were there?" Fadia asked gently.

I shook my head. "No. But . . ." I thought of Molly's house as I walked through it on the way to her bedroom that night. "There was a fruit basket. In her kitchen. It looked new. It was . . ." I frowned. There had been a card stuck into the top of it. I didn't read the message, but I had noticed the signature. Printed in capital letters was the name Vivian. *That lifestyle woman.* "It was from Vivian Grayson."

"Who's Vivian Grayson?" Richard asked, adding her name to the board and, underneath it, *Sent fruit basket.*

"She's a lifestyle guru. Molly was one of her clients."

"What exactly do you mean by *lifestyle guru*?" Fadia asked. "Are we talking linen slip covers for summer, or crystals that will cure your drug addiction?"

"More of the latter."

Fadia reached for the laptop resting on Richard's dining table and began searching, as Richard wrote *Magic rock peddler* underneath *Sent fruit basket.* After a moment, she spun the laptop screen around to show us a photo of a slim, delicately featured woman in her late forties. She was gazing beatifically down at the camera lens, with a small *Mona Lisa* smile on her lips. "This her?"

"Yeah." I had googled Vivian myself, after my first lunch with Molly. I was curious about the person behind Molly's impulse to *manifest authentic experiences.* Apparently, Vivian Grayson had traveled the world, studying at an ashram in India and alongside monks in Nepal. Her website heavily promoted her wellness facility, known as Perihelion Ranch, along with her particular brand of lifestyle guidance, which was largely based in channeling positive energy, centering oneself, and—of course—manifesting authentic experiences.

Fadia pursed her lips as she considered the photo again. "She looks familiar."

"Have you been to one of her wellness retreats?"

"Yeah, ever screamed into a glass jar or taken a dry bath in turmeric?" Anton added.

"Can't say I have." Fadia frowned. "But I feel like I've seen her before."

"What else happened that night?" Richard tapped the board with the marker. "What else did you see?"

"Not much," I said. "I went up to Molly's room. She gave me a few things she didn't want anymore. We just talked. She said she was tired. I went home." I shook my head. "I didn't see anyone else there, I didn't . . . notice anything." *I didn't know I was* supposed *to be noticing anything.*

"She didn't complain of any symptoms? Stomachache, headache? She wasn't dizzy or slurring her words at all?"

"No."

"Hmm." Richard considered this for a moment. "There are slow-acting poisons, of course. Ones that have to build up a certain amount in your system to show an effect. But it could very well be that she wasn't poisoned until after you left. Which means that either A, the source of the poison was already in her possession but she hadn't encountered it yet, or B, someone showed up after you left."

"Someone did." I recounted my conversation with Detective Lee to the group. Amy Byrne had visited after I left that night.

Richard added *AMY* to the board. "Okay, when we're talking suspects—or creating them, for *CSLA*—we need motive, means, and opportunity. Little Sister definitely had opportunity. What's her motive?"

"Well, I know that . . ." I hesitated. Should I really reveal this? Here? In front of everyone? "Molly changed her will. Recently."

"How recently?"

"Just a few weeks ago."

Anton's eyebrows rose. "Changed it how." It wasn't a question.

"To include me," I said. "And to exclude Amy."

Shock flashed across Anton's face. "Molly put you in her will?"

Richard, if anything, looked rather impressed. "And cut Little Sis out. Brutal." He paused, examining the board for a moment. "However. If Amy was cut out of Molly's will, she wouldn't exactly benefit from Molly's death, would she?"

"Maybe she was just angry," Fadia suggested.

"*Angry* is a bludgeoning, not a poisoning," Richard replied. "Poisoning is particularly premeditated. She has to get her hands on it, she has to figure out how to administer it . . . I don't know. What else do we have?"

Casper recounted Molly's argument with Cal Price and Damon Maxwell at lunch, and I shared what I had learned from both of them.

"Cal had an angiogram after their lunch meeting, so he was out of commission for the rest of the day. Damon was with Molly at the press event that afternoon, but he was celebrating his anniversary with his wife afterward."

MANAGER & AGENT, Richard wrote on the board. "Pretty confirmable alibis, though the argument is definitely notable."

Under Molly's name, he added, *What is 'the truth'?*

"What else?"

I shared the threat against Nick at the funeral (*FUNERAL*

THREATENER went on the board), and the argument at Revolution (*Spin class breeds contention*).

"There's also the class roster," Fadia said. "Whoever Molly was arguing with should be on this list."

We passed the roster around. It featured an array of Ashleys and Stephanies and Brittanys.

"How are we supposed to narrow it down?" Casper asked.

The list reached Anton. "Well, I know who I would start with."

"Who?"

"Hailey Nichols." He turned the list around and pointed to a name near the middle. "She's an actress. Aspiring. I remember her publicist—who I strongly suspect was just Hailey doing a bad accent—hounding one of the writers at *Icon* to include her in a Seeing Double feature against Mischa Barton. But it was a no go because Hailey's not high-profile enough. Frankly, she's not even *profile* enough."

I couldn't recall hearing of her before. "What's she been in?"

"Not much," Anton said. "But it's her next project that makes me wonder. She has a bit part in *Robot Wars Three*."

I shook my head. "But Molly's not even in *Robot Wars Three*. They cast that Victoria's Secret model."

"Petra Evanovich," Casper and Richard said at the same time.

"It's part of my job to know these things," Casper said quickly.

Fadia cast a disapproving look at Richard. He held up his hands. "I'm just a fan of the *Robot Wars* franchise. From a filmmaking standpoint. You know those explosions are real, right? Mike McColm is a visionary when it comes to practical effects." He hurriedly turned back to the board. "So, we've got a healthy list of leads here. Is there anyone we're missing? Besides, you know, the major elephant in the room."

"What elephant?"

Richard fixed me with a look.

"You can't be serious." Anton frowned. "Rachel? A suspect? Why?"

"Well," Richard said matter-of-factly, "because Molly left you money." He ticked it off on his fingers. "That's motive. You were close to her. Means. And you were there that night." He ticked the third finger. "Opportunity."

"Are you kidding?" I said, even though I knew he was exactly right. Suddenly, Lee sprang into my mind. Had he had the same thoughts?

Richard shrugged. "If this were a *CSLA* plot, you'd be circled and starred. You're the most obvious suspect. But! On the bright side, purely from a storytelling standpoint, the killer's almost never the most obvious suspect. If this were one of mine, you'd get murdered in the third-act twist, thereby eliminating you from suspicion."

I stood up abruptly. Fadia glared at Richard.

"That was insensitive," he said. "I was being insensitive just then. I acknowledge that."

"Rachel is not a *murderer*," Anton said. "She loved Molly. And she didn't even know about the money until after Molly died. Right?" He looked at me. "Or you definitely would've told me about it, wouldn't you?"

I nodded. "I found out after the funeral."

And all of a sudden, it felt like the funeral again—too much. I was still standing. Everyone was still looking at me.

There was a sliding glass door to my right, leading to a small balcony. "I need a minute," I said, and slipped outside.

I slid the door shut behind me. The minuscule balcony looked out over the courtyard at the center of the Palm Vista complex. A sad pair of abandoned grills stood on a cracked concrete pad on one side of the courtyard. There was an old, splintered picnic bench. A handful of scrubby-looking live oaks added a touch of greenery.

I gripped the handrail on the balcony and took several deep breaths. It was cooler now that the sun had gone down. Music sounded from some nearby radio—someone on the courtyard must've had their window open. They were playing the Black Eyed Peas' "Don't Phunk with My Heart." Given the moment, it was too absurd to process.

The glass door slid open. "Everything good out here?"

Thankfully, it was Anton, so I didn't have to lie. I shook my head as he stepped out and closed the door.

He moved forward so we were side by side at the railing. "Everyone knows you didn't do it," he said quietly. "Of course they do. It's just . . . they're running through every possibility, right? To rule people out."

It was the same thing Lee and Ruiz were probably doing—or had already done. I thought of my conversation with Lee at Sawasdee: *Are there people of interest, then?*

Rachel, no.

"Well, can we rule me out now?" I asked.

Had Lee ruled me out? Were the police even investigating to that extent? I couldn't help but recall his words from our phone call: *Since you're a friend of hers, I'll just say . . . this appears to be a pretty cut-and-dried case.*

"I can," Anton said. "I know you. Believe me when I say the thought never crossed my mind, not even for a millisecond." A pause. "Maybe it should have. Maybe I'm a terrible sleuth. Admittedly, my powers of deduction might need work. My powers of *seduction*, on the other hand . . ."

He was trying to make me feel better. I tried to muster a smile.

When Anton spoke again, he was tentative: "You could've told me about the will, you know."

"I said it in there—I didn't find out until after the funeral."

"Yeah, but you could've told me when you found out. Or you could've said something earlier, when we were at your place. Before Mr. James Dean the Friendly Ghost showed up."

"It doesn't feel real," I said. "The inheritance. Any of it."

He nodded. "I get that. But . . . just know I'm here for you. Okay?"

It reminded me of Natalie on the phone the other day: *You're important, okay?*

"It doesn't just have to be about club openings or delicious deejays or work nonsense," Anton continued. "We can do the real stuff too. The tough stuff."

I looked over at him. I wanted to say something . . . like *Thank you for being a better friend to me than I've ever been to you.* But no words came out. I just nodded.

"Let's go back inside," he said. "I'll tell everyone you can't even kill a spider. I've seen you trap ones as big as your fist and take them outside. Whereas I'd crush them dead under the soles of my Louboutins without a second thought."

"You have Louboutins?"

"Not until you give me a pair of yours. I was speaking aspirationally. Of course, my feet would need to shrink significantly, but I think that's okay—as long as everything else on me stays the same size." He gave me an oversized wink, and I couldn't help but crack a smile.

He put an arm around me and I settled into his side. "We'll sort this out," Anton said. "Don't worry."

It was comforting, in the moment. But I knew that feeling wouldn't last.

IMDb: HAILEY NICHOLS, ACTRESS

Biography

Hailey Ashlee Nichols was born in Glendale, California, and knew from a young age that she was destined to be a star. After finishing high school, she set out to make her mark on Hollywood. When she's not sharing her talents in front of the camera, Hailey loves shopping, relaxing at the beach, and keeping in shape with spinning, yoga, and Pilates. She does her absolute best to live by her life's motto, *Live, Laugh, Love*, which happens to be one of her three hidden tattoos—try and guess the others! ;)

—IMDb Mini Biography by: anonymous

Credits—Actress (7)

Robot Wars 3: Omnitron Returns, anticipated 2009
Jossika Pierce

Bones (1 episode), 2007 Burn Victim

The O.C. (1 episode), 2006 Coat Check Girl

Impound Lot Lothario (1 episode), 2005 Drunk Barista

High School Hellraisers: Summer Vacation, 2004 Girl on Jet Ski

Fastlane (1 episode), 2003 Club Girl #2

Sleepover Mania, 2003 Bathroom Bully

Fun Facts

- Hailey is the face of MultiTime Cleaning Cloth's 2006 commercial campaign. She originated the brand's signature catchphrase, "That's icky!"
- In high school, Hailey was voted *Most Likely to Be Famous*.

20

When I got back to my apartment that night, I sank down onto the couch. I was exhausted. Molly would no doubt give me the Alyssa directive: *Take five calming breaths and drink a kombucha.* For particularly high-stress situations, she'd recommend pressing bags of green tea to your eyes for ten minutes.

There it was again—the telltale prickle of tears.

I stood up. Shook it off. Crossed over to the kitchen, got a glass of water, took a long drink.

A knock sounded at the door.

As I went to open it, I could hear the tail end of an argument.

"—would be best if you just—"

"I really don't think it's—"

It was Richard and Fadia. They both snapped to attention.

"Hi," Fadia said with forced brightness. "Sorry to just drop by."

"It's fine. What's up?"

A pause followed, in which Richard studiously examined the

doorframe, and Fadia, exasperated, stared at Richard. Finally, she nudged him with her elbow.

He tore his eyes away from the door and met mine briefly. "I'm sorry," he said. "About earlier. When I somewhat accused you of murder, and then said you would die in the third-act twist."

"No need to rehash it," Fadia said under her breath.

"Very sorry," Richard reiterated. "And for what it's worth, I actually think you're too compelling to kill off in a single episode. You would definitely get a multi-episode arc."

Fadia grimaced. "That's not—"

It was an olive branch, and I'd take it. "Thank you," I said. "I appreciate that."

"Fadia also told me that you're a copy editor. And that you quit your job."

I glanced at Fadia, whose expression turned sheepish. "It came up. You'll hear why."

Richard continued. "I actually just finished a draft of my screenplay, and I need to get it polished to send out to agents. I can't pay much, but I'm in the market for someone to give it a good proof. If you're interested in the work."

I wasn't particularly in a position to turn it down. And I had to admit, a small part of me was curious about the story of a television writer who gets a call from himself in a future where there's been a nuclear winter.

"That would be great."

Richard brightened. "Fantastic! What's your email?"

That was how a copy of a script titled *Nuclear Nucleus* found its way into my inbox the very same night.

I should've gone to bed, but I didn't feel tired enough yet. No, that wasn't quite accurate—I felt bone-tired, actually. But paradoxically, I didn't feel sleepy in the least. So I downloaded the script, curled up on the couch, and started to read.

NUCLEAR NUCLEUS—PAGE 1

SFX: A heartbeat. Slow. Consistent. Oddly sinister.

FADE IN:

INT. REX'S APARTMENT—BEDROOM—EARLY MORNING

We open on television writer REX BLAZE (36), asleep in bed. He is dangerously handsome. Rivals would describe him as coldly intimidating. Lovers would describe him as *leonine*—equally relentless in the pursuit of power and pleasure alike.

REX (V.O.)

The shifting of tectonic plates. The raw power of a typhoon, about to hit shore. How do you know when the worst day of your life is about to happen?

SFX: An explosion.

REX is startled awake. He jumps out of bed and rips back the curtains.

THROUGH THE WINDOW—THE STREET IN FRONT OF REX'S BUILDING

A driver stands in front of a beat-up Chevy truck. The sound clearly came from a car backfire—nothing more.

REX is relieved. Little does he know . . .

REX (V.O.)

How do you know when the worst day of your life is *already in progress*?

I picked up my phone. Fadia and I had exchanged numbers. I pulled up a new text window to message her.

Rex Blaze?

I had forgotten how late it was. But she answered almost immediately: Oh yeah. The character names are a real treat. Wait til you get to his love interest.

I couldn't help myself—I flipped ahead.

Tawny Livingood????

Fadia responded: Incredible, right?

Does Rex Blaze also write for a children's television show? If so, are his co-workers aware that he is equally relentless in the pursuit of power and pleasure alike??

Again, her reply came in quickly: Keep reading.

I paged through and found a scene in which Rex arrives at the writers' room to start work for the day.

```
INT. CRIME CONFIDENTIAL WRITERS' ROOM—DAY

REX enters his workplace. CRIME CONFIDENTIAL—
an undeniably average television drama about
criminal investigators, elevated into the public
consciousness only through the aid of Rex's sharp
mind and keen expertise.
```

Paid work was paid work. It was better than that listicle about celebrity dogs.

~~~

```
NUCLEAR NUCLEUS—PAGE 29

REX's grip on the cell phone tightens. THE VOICE
on the other end of the line is oddly familiar.

                    THE VOICE
      Who would know better how to fix this
      than you?

                    REX
      Why? Why me?

                    THE VOICE
      Because . . . you're me.

                    REX (with scorn)
      Be serious.
```
~~~

THE VOICE

I am. Dead serious.

REX

Okay, hotshot. Then say something only I would know.

THE VOICE

Chrysanthemums. Nineteen. Sleet. April.

CLOSE UP on REX. The combination of words has a profound effect on him. The significance of the keywords is not yet apparent to the audience—but to REX, it's the whole world condensed down to the head of a pin.

THE VOICE

I'm reaching out to you through time and space because I have information you need. You don't even know that you need it yet, but you will. Consider this a warning. From me to you. From *you* to you. I know exactly what's going to happen, and I know that you're the only one who can stop it. You're my lifeline, Rex Blaze.

REX (shakily)

This is one hell of a Phone a Friend.

I looked up from the script. Despite the absurd context, there was something weirdly resonant about that line: *I'm reaching out to you through time and space because I have information you need . . .*

If Molly could reach out to me, what would she say? Where would she point me? I let my gaze wander across the room, over piles of shoes and scattered laundry and boxes that needed to go out to the recycling bin. Something caught my eye on the floor next to my TV stand—an orange Hermès shopping bag. It held the things that Molly had given me the other night.

I crossed over and picked it up, carried it back to the couch, and emptied the contents onto the coffee table: a few boxes of Juicy Couture jewelry (*Juicy's reached the masses, which means it's basically over, but these would look cute on you*); several scarves from Louis Vuitton (*You know how I feel about jewel tones, Rachel*); and a Coach wallet, in leather, dark brown, with light brown *C*s imprinted on it. It wasn't in a box.

I opened the wallet. Unlike most of the things that Molly gave me, which were barely or never used, this wallet clearly had been used. There were several dollar bills in the money compartment. A few receipts. And in one of the credit card slots, a small folded sheet of paper.

I opened it. Written in ballpoint pen was a list of names:

PIPER
JULIA
HAILEY
AMY
WINTER

21

"Amy is obviously Molly's sister," Casper said as we sat in his car the next day. He had arrived at Palm Vista in a pristine black BMW. Upon seeing my questioning look, he had just shrugged and said, "Celebs drive luxury cars. How am I supposed to keep up in a hooptie?"

Now we sat in the plush leather seats, heads bent over the list from Molly's wallet. "And Hailey has to be Hailey Nichols, from the spin class at Revolution," he continued. "It's too much of a coincidence."

"Piper." Irina's words came back to me: *Nothing sells a magazine quite like a beautiful dead starlet.* A year ago, Piper Standish's murder was on every magazine cover and news feed. "That must be Piper Standish."

Casper nodded. "Molly knew her. They weren't friends, exactly, but they ran in some of the same circles."

"It's Molly's handwriting. I'm sure of it." I still had the note from the Chanel bag: *An authentic bag for an authentic person.* "Why would Molly make this list? And who are Julia and Winter?"

"Maybe Hailey can shed some light."

"How are we going to get her to talk to us?"

"Oh, that won't be hard."

"Why not?"

"Because she's desperate to get her face out there." Casper gestured to the back seat, where several black equipment bags sat. "This'll be our in." He grabbed one of the bags and unzipped it to show me the contents: a fancy-looking camera with a chunky lens. "Consider it an undercover mission."

"That's an upgrade from before," I said as he returned the camera bag to the back seat.

"Yeah, well, I've got resources. It's kind of my entire job."

As Casper pulled out onto the street, I glanced over at him.

"What's your plan? Like, in the long term? What kind of career progression is there for a paparazzo?"

He met my eyes as we pulled up to a stoplight. "I'm sorry, were you just possessed by my mother? Did the soul of a fifty-two-year-old woman from Garden City, Long Island, just enter your body?"

"I'm just curious what the long-term career of a pap looks like," I said.

"Maybe you can do a feature on me for *New York* magazine."

"Oh, *New York* magazine definitely won't care."

One side of his mouth ticked up.

I continued: "It's just, you told me how you got your start—getting your hand trampled and all—but what do you want to do in the future?"

"I don't know," he said. "Do I have to?"

It was a reasonable question. "No, I guess not."

"Do *you* know what you want to do in the future?"

"No idea."

"So we've got that in common." The light turned green and Casper accelerated. "I don't like to think too far ahead. What I'm

doing now is what I'm doing. What I'll do in the future is a problem for my future self."

I thought, oddly, of *Nuclear Nucleus*. "What about your past self?"

Casper gave a huff of laughter. "I try to think about him as little as possible."

Casper had a tip that Hailey Nichols was shopping at Kitson on Robertson Boulevard. There were several paps standing around in conversation when we approached the store.

One nodded in Casper's direction. He was tall and thin, with a scraggly blond ponytail. It wasn't until he spoke that I realized he was the same pap who had photographed Molly and me outside the Chanel store three months ago. The one who had called her "Dax's girl."

"Don't waste your time, mate," he told Casper now. "There's no one worth shooting in there. It's just the 'That's icky' girl."

"Got it. Thanks," Casper said as we passed by, and then he murmured to me, "Do you know what he's talking about?"

I had looked up Hailey's body of work before we set out. "Yeah, apparently Hailey did an ad campaign a couple years ago for some sponge you never have to wring out or something like that. There were a few commercials—you probably saw them at some point. She opens a door or a cabinet and sees a pixelated mess, presumably some kind of excrement or a pile of dismembered fingers or whatever—"

"I love that those are the only two kinds of messes to you."

"Not the *only* two."

"The first two to come to mind, though."

"Will you let me finish?"

Casper's eyes shone. "I'm on tenterhooks."

"So, she opens the door, sees the mess, and says her signature catchphrase—"

"'That's icky,'" Casper finished. "In a really off-putting, adult-baby kind of way. I remember now."

"How could you forget? I heard she won an Olivier Award for it."

A begrudging smile split his face. I couldn't help but smile back as we settled into a spot outside the store.

The other paps had gone their separate ways by the time Hailey Nichols, the "That's icky" forebear, emerged from the store. She was petite and tan, with a heart-shaped face and long, dark brown hair set in loose curls. She was wearing a black velour tracksuit and large white-rimmed sunglasses. She had several Kitson shopping bags hanging off one arm, a Fendi Baguette on the other. She clocked us immediately.

"Aw, I'm such a mess, though," she said with faux exasperation, one hand flying up to check her hair as Casper raised his camera in her direction. "I would've gone all out if I knew you guys would be here. I didn't even do my makeup today." To my eye, her makeup looked very much done.

"Are you kidding me, Hailey? You look fantastic," Casper said as he snapped a few pictures. "How's your day going?"

She took off her sunglasses. "Good, good. Better now that you're here. Are you with TMZ? Will this make it into Star Catcher?"

I held my camera up too. It was significantly more complicated than any camera I had ever used before, so I just pretended to be adjusting the lens.

"Tell us about your outfit," I said. It was something paps had frequently said to Molly when we were out together. "It's definitely the most interesting thing about me," I remember her remarking dryly once.

"Juicy, of course," Hailey replied, and I heard another echo of

Molly in my mind: *It's reached the masses.* "The bag is Fendi. The hair and boobs—all mine, I swear!"

"All-natural," Casper said appreciatively, in such a smarmy tone that I could barely believe he was the same person I had driven over here with. "Gotta love it." He paused to check his camera. "Just so you know, most places are looking for stuff about Molly Byrne this week. Do you have anything to comment?"

"Molly." Hailey quickly adopted a look of sorrow. "I'm totally devastated. I miss her so much."

"So you knew her?"

"Uh-huh. We were really close. We worked out together, like, all the time."

"At Revolution," I said.

Hailey perked up at the mention, as if delighted that I knew a fact about her. "Yes, the one in Brentwood, not the one in Bel Air. The Brentwood one is the original."

Honestly. LA.

"Did you have an argument with Molly there the day she died?" I asked. Might as well go *good cop, bad cop* here.

Hailey's expression turned brittle. "What?"

"That's the buzz."

"That's not— What buzz? From who? There's buzz?" She seemed troubled and pleased in equal measure.

"Is it true?"

"Of course not. Molly and I were really good friends."

I found that highly unlikely.

"You did talk with her at Revolution that day, though, didn't you? I mean, since you guys were so close. She must've talked to you about something."

She hesitated.

Casper lowered his lens and turned to me. "You know, I think we're good here. I got a tip that Lindsay is eating over at—"

"No, wait," Hailey said. "I'll tell you."

"Tell us what?"

She stepped toward us. "Honestly, this is so fucking juicy, I could sell it for major bucks, but I'm about to give it to you for free. As long as you get *these*"—she tapped on Casper's camera with one French-tipped nail—"to the right people." She gave Casper a meaningful look. "Star Catcher. Understand?"

"Sure," Casper said.

Hailey leaned in, her eyes alight with the joy of a seasoned gossip. "Okay, so Molly and I were in the changing room at Revolution that day, and I just casually mentioned the *Robot Wars Three* shoot. I'm in it, in case you hadn't heard. I'm a *named* character. We're in the middle of shooting right now, actually. Honestly, it's like my dream franchise—but anyway, I brought it up, and all of a sudden Molly totally flew off the handle. She even called me *delusional*, can you believe that? Me? Acting in a major franchise? When she probably couldn't even book an infomercial these days? *I'm* the delusional one?" She seemed to remember that she was supposed to be sad. "No, but my heart goes out to her. She'd been super sensitive ever since Dax broke up with her, and I think she just . . . reached her breaking point, you know?"

"Dax didn't break up with her," I couldn't help but say.

She gave me a disdainful look. "Right. It was totally her idea. Him cheating on her had absolutely nothing to do with it."

"Dax cheated?" Casper exclaimed. "With who?"

She shrugged. "Just the buzz. Anyway, even after all that—after she totally went off on me—she still had the nerve to ask me for, you know." Her voice dropped to a stage whisper. "The hookup."

"Sorry?"

"I used to date this guy—it's totally in the past, but he connected people here and there with, you know, whatever they might be looking for . . . *recreationally*. Molly knew that, so she asked me if I could hook her up with . . . some of her old faves. I said no, of course. I'm totally past that time in my life, FYI. And I thought Molly was too. I had no idea." Her eyes went shiny, and in stark contrast to her entire deal up until this moment, it seemed disconcertingly genuine. "I didn't know she was planning anything like that." Hailey was quiet for a moment. And then: "Get me from the left, okay?" She adjusted her hair. "Should I look sadder? Do you think this could make a memorial issue? Is it too late? What about online?"

"One more question," I asked, as Casper resumed taking photos. "Did Molly ever mention anyone named Julia or Winter? Do you know either of them?"

Hailey shot me a blank look that could give Rainbow Pup a run for his money. "No. Should I?"

I shook my head, and Casper's shutter snapped away.

"Do you think Dax cheated on Molly?" Casper asked as we sat in his parked car. Hailey had sauntered off in the direction of the Ivy, leaving us to haul our camera bags back a few blocks to where we had parked. Casper stopped on the way because he thought he saw Ashlee Simpson coming out of MAC, but he realized a few photos in that it was a false alarm.

I considered the question: Did Dax cheat? Was that why Molly broke up with him?

She would've told me. But then again—would she? She didn't tell me that she had amended her will. She didn't tell me that anything was wrong.

"I don't know," I said, leaning my head against the headrest. "She told me she got bored. That's all."

"Do you think she asked Hailey for drugs?"

Was Hailey someone you'd ask for a prescription-drug hookup in the dressing room of a Brentwood spin studio? I mean, yes—if that was your thing, Hailey definitely seemed like the type of person you'd go to. But . . . was that really on Molly's mind that morning? Was it her plan all along, even before whatever else happened later on? If that was true, then maybe it really was premeditated. Maybe it was something she was consciously planning, rather than something that happened by accident or something that was spur-of-the-moment—

"No." I looked over at Casper. "I don't think that. I think Hailey's lying."

He met my eyes and nodded. "I think so too. But why? Why would she lie?"

"Because it's a juicier story," I said. "Which could get her into a tabloid. Or . . . because she has something to hide."

Casper's phone buzzed once. He glanced at it, and then sprang into action, quickly starting the car engine.

"What is it? What happened?"

"Nick Hart is at a PT session in Beverly Hills."

"How the hell do you know that?"

"My roommate. He just texted."

"You have a roommate?" I wasn't sure why, but it surprised me. Casper seemed like the lone-wolf type. I guess I thought we were both that type.

"Two. Luke and Ryder. They're . . . an unfortunate necessity."

"What does that mean?"

"It's the only way I could afford to rent in West Hollywood. They're both in the business too. Luke just got a tip on Nick. If we hurry, we can find out who was threatening him at the funeral."

He pressed down on the accelerator, and off we went.

Excerpt from **VOGUE**, *May 2008:*

"CRAFTING A LEGACY IN REAL TIME": SITTING DOWN WITH OSCAR-WINNING DIRECTOR ADRIEN FORD

When asked about his nontraditional casting choices for the upcoming drama *Sun City,* Ford requested specificity. I explained that costars Nick Hart and Molly Byrne were not exactly conventional casting choices, given the commercial appeal of their previous films together—a blockbuster summer franchise about giant robots that even the kindest critic must admit is not exactly high art.

This was a definite misstep on my part, as it led to several minutes of backpedaling when Ford countered by asking whether I was implying that his films lacked commercial appeal (for the record, I was not). This is the reality of interviewing a two-time Best Director winner. Ford is adept at controlling a room, at guiding a conversation. I felt, at certain points throughout the time we spent together, that he was directing even me.

"I truly believe that an actor needs to feel a degree of kinship with a character to fully inhabit them," Ford said. "In Krystal [Byrne's character in *Sun City*], I see someone who has struggled, someone who is still actively struggling, but at the same time, someone who is doggedly persistent, determined in the face of challenge, scrutiny, adversity. In Tyler [Hart's character], I see someone who is more complex than what meets the eye. He's probably been underestimated in the past. He's had to prove himself, to prove people wrong. I saw similar qualities in Molly and Nick, and I knew that they were the right actors to bring these characters to life."

22

"I think it's better if I talk to Nick alone," I told Casper as we pulled up and idled near Nick's gym. "Since I've met him before. I think it'd be harder to explain why you're there. And since you're . . ."

"Short?" Casper supplied, completely deadpan. When I looked over, I caught the amused glimmer in his eyes.

"I was going to say *a pap*—"

"A short pap," he conceded.

"Yes. He might be put off by that."

"No, guys like Nick love when guys like me are around. It's perspective manipulation. We make them look even taller."

"Wait in the car," I said, and got out.

When Nick Hart emerged from the gym, he looked every bit as handsome as he had at the funeral, now in a gray tank top with low-cut armholes and black track pants with lines down the sides. Sneakers that probably cost more than three months' worth of my food budget rounded out his ensemble. He was accompanied by a burly-looking man in jeans and a black T-shirt, who stepped into my path immediately as I approached. Security.

I tried to look as friendly and non-stalkerish as possible. "I know Nick," I said. "We've met before."

"Yeah, sure," the bodyguard replied. I tried to duck around him. "Nick!"

Nick held up a hand and flashed me a smile that was polite but unrecognizing as he approached a large SUV parked at the curb.

The bodyguard was like a brick wall. He held out an arm to stop me.

"Payday bar!" I bellowed, loud and undignified.

Nick paused, one hand on the car-door handle, and looked at me fully now. Recognition dawned in his eyes.

"Oh, hey," he said. "From Molly's funeral, right?"

"Yes."

He waved to the bodyguard. "She's okay."

The guard stood down, but still eyed me suspiciously. I approached the car.

"How's it going?" Nick said. "It's . . . Rachel, right?"

I tried to ignore the odd flush of pride that he had remembered my name, and reminded myself that it was probably because I was the only crazed woman hyperventilating next to a mausoleum that he had met that day. "Got it in one. I was wondering if I could talk to you for a minute? It's about Molly."

He checked his watch. "I'm supposed to be at the studio at three . . ." He glanced around, and then nodded in the direction of a pressed-juice shop a few doors down. "How about a quick drink?"

That was how I found myself sitting across from Nick Hart at a very small café table in a violently orange and blessedly empty juice shop. The girl behind the counter had served Nick with wide, unblinking eyes, and was now standing frozen with her cell phone clutched in her hands, unable to tear her gaze away from him. She seemed to be texting, but somehow never looked down at the screen. I admired her coordination—though there was a very real possibility that her texts were just long strings of key smashes.

I glanced back at Nick. I had seen it enough times when I was out with Molly—what it was like to be recognized. To be in that halo, or adjacent to it.

Two drinks sat between us. His was bright green and mine was an unappealing mauve. Our legs were almost touching under the table. It was disconcerting—it could almost be a date, if he were anyone else on earth.

"Do you always travel with security?" I asked, pushing my paper straw around in my drink before taking an experimental sip. It wasn't terrible.

"Occasionally," Nick replied. "More so recently."

I thought of what I overheard at the funeral: *We'll be right back here with you as the guest of honor . . .*

"I, um. I don't really know a delicate way to ask this, but . . ."

"Ask away."

"I overheard something at Molly's funeral. I heard you being threatened."

He paused, his straw halfway to his mouth. "Threatened," he repeated, with a frown.

"Yeah. 'We'll be right back here with you as the guest of honor'? Something like that?"

Nick's expression cleared. "Ah. Yeah, I understand how that could sound . . . not great. But to be honest, that's just how people talk in the biz. Everything is life-or-death."

"If you don't mind my asking, what was the conversation about?"

"It was about the movie. That was my agent." He paused to

take a pull of the green juice. "Remember what I told you about *Sun City*? How Adrien Ford operates?"

I nodded. "He's . . . intense, right? As a director?"

"Yeah. So, I did an interview recently for . . . honestly, I don't remember—*Hollywood Reporter* or *Vanity*, one of those—and I said something along those same lines about Ford. My agent was pissed that I was so up-front about it. Thought it would reflect badly on the film and make me look like a d-bag or whatever for complaining about working with such a huge director. So it was basically *keep it positive or keep your mouth shut*, that kind of thing." He gave me a sheepish smile. "He doesn't really mince words."

I toyed with my cup for a moment, and then said, "Do you by any chance know an actress named Hailey Nichols?"

If Nick was surprised by the change of subject, he didn't show it. "No. Should I?"

"She's in *Robot Wars Three*. It's a small part."

"Ah. We're still shooting. I don't think we've had any scenes together. And if we did . . . I have to admit, I suck at names. Lines, I can remember. Names, I can't."

"You remembered mine."

He smiled. His eyes crinkled at the corners with it. It was powerfully effective. "Well, circumstances were a little different."

I pressed forward. "What about someone named Julia or Winter? Anyone connected to *Sun City* with those names?"

"Not ringing any bells. I'm sorry." He met my eyes. "What's all this about?"

I wasn't sure how honest I should be in the moment. I decided on a half-truth: "I guess . . . with what happened with Molly, I'm just . . . feeling kind of paranoid. And when I overheard your agent at the funeral, I thought maybe—"

"I was in some kind of danger?" He clapped a hand to his chest. "I'm touched."

"Don't be too flattered. I would've followed up with anyone I heard getting threatened."

"Okay, feeling slightly less special, but I'll still take it." He cocked his head. "What about Hailey and Winter and whoever?"

"Julia," I supplied. I decided on another half-truth. "Just checking up on some old friends of Molly. Or . . . acquaintances, maybe." I gave my juice another stir. The straw had become waterlogged and was no longer entirely solid. "Well, anyway. I know you're busy. Thanks for taking the time to—"

"Wait." Nick's brow furrowed. "Sorry, I just remembered. I think there was a Julia or a Julie at the PR firm Molly had been working with. I don't remember exactly, but I think there was some kind of issue and they had to let Julia go. Molly was upset about it. Something about . . . privacy? A security breach? It was really stressing Molly out. She spent a lot of time on the phone, talking about it with her, uh, lifestyle coach."

"Vivian Grayson?"

He snapped his fingers. "That's it. Vivian. She visited set once. Molly treated it like the Second Coming. Her vibe was a little weird, but I've never been one for that kind of thing. Energies and frequencies and whatever."

"Yeah, why buy into all that when you can just worship at the altar of the Hershey Company?"

He grinned.

"This was all really helpful," I said. "Thank you."

"Anytime." His eyes shone. "Feel free to repay me with a Payday."

WWW.CELEBRITEASE.COM

June 22, 2008
04:43 PM PST

SPOTTED:

Giant-robot slayer Nick Hart out for a PT-and-pressed-juice date with . . . *Icon* reporter and erstwhile Molly Byrne bestie Rachel West?

Ladies' man Nick has been papped with his fair share of actresses, pop stars, models, and other famous faces over the years. While West, the perfect paragon of a celebrity hanger-on, seems to be working her way up the ladder from celeb friend to . . . celeb friend with benefits?

These two look awfully cozy [SEE BELOW] . . . What do you think? Is Rach already scheming her next social level-up, or is Nick just slumming it for funsies?

(If you ask us, the answer is—both.)

23

Honestly, these fucking articles," I muttered after my phone buzzed with the tenth text from an old acquaintance asking if it was really me at the juice shop with Nick Hart. I knew via Facebook that this particular acquaintance, a girl I went to college with, was currently an aide on the Obama campaign. We hadn't spoken since graduation, and yet she still wanted to know whether or not I was "smashing the *Robot Wars* guy."

"Sorry?"

Casper and I were on our way to Vivian Grayson's ranch, Perihelion. Casper drove with authority, navigating the BMW with much more confidence than I ever had in my rust-bucket Corolla.

"It's this stupid blog. Celebritease. They're vapid and vicious and just . . . extremely annoying. They used to write about Molly all the time, and now they're posting about me, for God knows what reason." With surprising speed. The photos were up lightning fast after my chat with Nick.

I looked over at Casper.

It clicked into place. "Stop the car."

Confusion flashed across Casper's face. "What? Why?"

"Stop the car. Right now."

He pulled over to the side of the road.

My heartbeat had ratcheted up. "Is it you?"

Casper's brow wrinkled in confusion. "What?"

"Are you Celebritease?"

"No."

"Casper."

"I'm not. Honestly. I don't have a blog."

"Say it to my face."

Casper turned and looked me in the eye. "I don't have a blog," he repeated. "And if I did, it wouldn't be a vapid, vicious, extremely annoying one. It would be highbrow and deeply pretentious. A lot of long-exposure shots of the beach at dusk. Deliberately blurry close-ups of candy wrappers on the sidewalk, in Banksy-style criticism of consumerism. That kind of thing."

I couldn't smile. "You're not sending them pictures? Information?"

"Rachel, I swear."

"Swear on everything you love."

"That's not hard. I don't love much, besides this jacket. I swear."

"On your life, then."

"That's even easier. Believe me, no one's putting much value on my life, least of all me."

I grabbed his wrist. I don't know why. "Don't say that."

He looked down at my hand, and then back up at me. It was quiet for a moment, until he said, "It's not my blog. I swear to you."

I wasn't like Molly. I didn't have some innate *sense about people*. Or maybe I did—I had a sense about her. And she had a sense about him. Right now, the look in Casper's eyes, the intent there, was steady and unflinching.

I let go of his wrist. "Okay," I said. "Then maybe your industry insight can help me with this one. Whoever these bastards are, they just posted about me. *Celebrity hanger-on Rachel West spotted trying to fuck Nick Hart* or whatever."

"At the juice place?"

"Yeah, antioxidants are an aphrodisiac, didn't you know?"

Casper frowned. "I didn't clock anyone around while we were there."

"Well, they're getting pictures somehow. Unless they're getting them from you."

Casper met my eyes again. "Rachel, I mean it. I wouldn't screw you over like that."

"Not even with antioxidants involved?"

A ghost of a smile. "No."

~~~

We debated for some time about how to get into Perihelion Ranch.

"Don't we need an appointment, or some kind of . . . reference?" I asked.

"We've got one," Casper replied. "You."

"What about me?"

"Call them up. Say you want to talk to Vivian about Molly. If Molly was really as devoted to her as you say, then Vivian will talk to you. You were a known quantity around Molly. You were in her inner circle, so to speak. Plus . . ." he trailed off.

"What?"

"You're inheriting money, which puts you in exactly the right tax bracket to be one of Vivian's clients. You could use that angle."

So I called the ranch as we drove, and just as Casper had predicted, I managed to secure us a meeting with Vivian.

Perihelion was in Malibu, close to the Santa Monica Mountains. We drove up a winding drive, lined with olive trees, that led to an
~~~

impressively large Spanish-style building with a terra-cotta tile roof and a white stucco exterior, its many windows glittering in the sunlight.

When we stepped out of the car, a valet swooped in and whisked the keys away from Casper.

We were led inside, to an open foyer with an intricately tiled floor. A woman behind a reception desk informed us that Vivian would be with us shortly.

When Vivian finally appeared, she was not as tall as I expected her to be, but still willowy thin. Her hair was white-blond, but there was just the faintest hint of darkness at the roots. She was wearing white linen pants, a loose white blouse, tan leather wedge sandals, and bracelets of silver and gold stacked on each arm.

"Rachel, hello." Vivian clasped my hand in both of hers. "It's a pleasure to meet one of Molly's dearest friends."

"I think you're my best friend," Molly told me once. I tamped the memory down and forced myself to smile at Vivian.

"It's great to meet you too."

She led us into a large white-walled room with wood paneling on the ceiling. Windows lined one side of the room. Two enormous white couches sat in the middle, facing each other, and several armchairs were clustered nearby. At one end of the room was a massive wooden desk with a white upholstered chair behind it.

"I'm sure you feel an incredible loss," Vivian said when Casper and I had settled down on one of the couches. She had perched on the couch opposite us. A narrow, brushed wood coffee table ran between us, with a tasteful assortment of items arranged atop it—a tray full of sand with a miniature wooden rake, a string of large glass beads, a hand-thrown dish full of crystals. "Just as everyone here has been feeling, myself included. Molly was such a radiant presence."

"I know she really trusted in you and . . . your methods, so I wanted to meet with you. Molly left me an inheritance, and I'm just . . . trying to make sense of it all."

Vivian's face didn't change, but something in her eyes sharpened. She looked to Casper. "And if I may ask, who is your companion?"

"This is Casper," I said. "My—"

"Friend," he said, at the same time that I said "boyfriend," and for a beat we just looked at each other awkwardly.

"We haven't defined the relationship yet," I said, at the same time that he said, "We just broke up."

Vivian looked between us for a moment, her expression unreadable, and then she gave a small smile. "Well, I'd be happy to tell you a little about myself and our facilities, and about our worldview here at Perihelion."

"That would be great," I replied.

My former office mate, Tyla, would have loved everything about Vivian's operation. They certainly weren't consuming artificial dyes at Perihelion Ranch.

It was difficult to find a natural segue from how Vivian could help me *manifest natural peace and well-being* to Molly's death. But Casper found a way.

"This program—" he cut in eventually, after Vivian had extolled the virtues of the entirely gluten-free, vegan menu served at the ranch.

"Lifestyle reimagining," Vivian corrected.

"Yes. Is it similar to the one that Molly was in?"

"Every habitué is on their own path at Perihelion, and no two journeys are alike. Rachel, it sounds like you have a need for stability and direction. Whereas Molly's needs were different."

"And what were those?" I asked.

Vivian's eyes narrowed ever so slightly. "Every practitioner's journey is deeply personal—and confidential. I'm sure you understand that, and I'm sure you'd appreciate the same discretion."

"Yes. I just . . . Can I be honest with you?"

"Of course. Honesty is an imperative part of the process."

I wondered if any of Vivian's crystals were capable of transmitting the fact that I was about to be extremely dishonest with her. "I've been trying to reach out to people who were part of Molly's life, to try to . . . I don't know, share the grief? To try to find some answers or . . . some kind of closure, maybe. I've been looking for a couple people in Molly's circle in particular, but I haven't been able to get ahold of them. Since she was so close with you, I was just wondering if she ever brought them up in any of your conversations. Their names are Julia and Winter. Do you remember Molly mentioning them at all?"

Vivian shook her head. "I'm afraid not."

I glanced at Casper for just a second. Nick had told me that Molly confided in Vivian about what had happened with Julia. Was this denial part of Vivian's "discretion"? "Molly was working with Julia for PR, and I think there was some kind of an issue that really upset Molly. She didn't mention that to you?"

"Not that I recall."

"What about Piper Standish?"

Vivian's lips pursed. "I think you'd have a hard time reaching Piper now."

"Did Molly ever talk about her, though?"

Vivian paused before giving a small nod. "Molly was shaken by Piper's death. I think she related to Piper. How could she not? Being so young and finding yourself thrust into this industry. Being adored, and having that adoration transform into something so dark."

"Had Molly mentioned Piper recently?"

"No."

"Did Molly come here to see you the day she died?" Casper asked.

"Why do you ask?"

I jumped in. "Like I said, I'm just . . . looking for closure. I thought it might be helpful to sort of . . . visualize what Molly's last day was like. And maybe then I could better understand my role in it."

Vivian examined me for a beat, and then said, "She did come by. We had a brief chat. She wanted to . . . re-center herself. Then she left." For just a brief moment, I saw on Vivian's face the same regret I felt, reflected back at me.

The ringing of a phone interrupted us before I could speak. Vivian stood and retrieved a cell phone from a nearby end table. "Excuse me. I need to take this."

I nodded.

With her phone clasped in one hand, Vivian exited the room.

Casper sprang to his feet. "Let's look around."

"For what?"

"I don't know exactly, but this is Vivian's office. Maybe she has a file or notes on Molly somewhere that'll tell us what they actually talked about that day."

There wasn't much to look at, though. The room was consciously minimal. Casper flipped through a datebook lying on the desk. I examined the shelves lining one wall. They were sparsely decorated: a carved wooden bowl, several bonsai trees.

I turned to look out the bank of windows on the other side of the room. They faced a beautiful courtyard with a garden that was partially shaded by a wooden pergola, wisteria growing thickly across it.

A figure stepped out from under the pergola and into the sunlight.

It was Dax Van Sant.

And then suddenly, Vivian appeared in the courtyard. She moved toward Dax and pulled him into an embrace.

"Casper," I hissed. "Look."

Casper joined me in time to see Vivian and Dax break apart. Vivian cupped Dax's cheek. He was wearing dark mirrored shades, and his posture was slumped, his mouth downturned. Vivian patted his shoulder, and then cast a look across the courtyard.

Straight toward the windows.

I whirled around, turning my back to the glass, and pulled Casper with me.

"Did she see us?"

"I don't know. Maybe there's too much light reflecting off the windows."

"Why is she with Dax? Was she—" My eyes widened. "Hailey said that Dax was cheating on Molly. Was he cheating with *Vivian*?"

No sooner had I said her name than Vivian stepped through the door of the office.

Did she hear me? Did she know we knew?

If she did, her expression betrayed nothing—her smile was just the same as before, just as ambiguous. "I'm so sorry, I'm afraid I have to cut our visit short. Something has come up."

"Of course," I said. "No problem."

She crossed over to us and took both of my hands in hers. "But Rachel, I want you to know that I would be absolutely honored to accompany you on your spiritual journey. I sense . . ." She peered up at my face for several long seconds. I looked away, uncomfortable, and when I glanced back, she was still gazing at me. Her eyes were a pale blue, almost otherworldly. "A sadness," she said finally. "A deep sadness. Fed by isolation."

"Can you also sense that my blood sugar is low?" It popped out before I could stop myself. A noise escaped Casper, the start of a laugh, poorly transformed into a cough.

Something flickered in Vivian's eyes—it almost looked like amusement.

"We have a selection of snacks available at reception," she said. "And while you're there, Rachel, please schedule another visit. I'd love to give you a full tour of the ranch and talk with you more about your journey."

"Sure," I said, but really I would've said anything in that moment. I was eager to extract my hands from hers.

Casper's car was waiting for us in the front drive when we got outside. I watched Perihelion Ranch shrink in the passenger-side mirror as we drove away.

"What do you think?" Casper asked. "Are you going to become a client?"

"Are you kidding?"

"Mostly."

"Even if I had that kind of money, I don't think it's for me." I held up the snack I had gotten at reception on the way out. "For one thing, these soy chips suck."

Casper smiled a little. "Fair enough." It was quiet for a moment. When he spoke again, it was with an air of deliberate nonchalance. "What about the 'deep sadness,' though?"

"She doesn't know what she's talking about," I replied.

"I think we're overlooking something important here," I said. Everyone looked my way. "Why would Molly investigate Piper's murder if Piper's killer was already arrested?"

"Because he wasn't actually Piper's killer," Richard said.

I nodded. "Clearly, Molly had some reason to think that. And maybe Piper's real killer found out about her suspicions—"

"And killed her too," Casper finished.

It was silent for a moment as we all considered this.

Finally, Richard spoke. "I think we're gonna need a bigger board."

We started in on Molly's board after another round of snacks. Casper had printed the photos he took at Molly's house. He passed copies out to each of us and tacked one to our board, showing Molly's hasty scrawls on the back of the Dior box.

Entity was written in the top left corner and circled twice, with an arrow extending from it that pointed to a bubble labeled *Pictures???*

"What's Entity?" Jaz asked.

"That's the club where Piper died," Casper replied.

I frowned. "I didn't know Piper died at Entity. Is that why they rebranded?"

"Yes," Anton said. "Though the watering down of their cocktails was also criminal."

There were a few other entries on Molly's murder board: *Brady. Chrimbo. Mystery Man.* And one I hadn't noticed when we first discovered the board, probably because it had been scribbled out. The text underneath was still partially visible, though: *Dax.*

Anton's eyebrows lifted. "Molly thought Dax was involved in Piper's murder?"

"Who's Dax?" Elena asked.

"Molly's ex," Casper and I both said at the same time.

"Oof." Elena grimaced. "She suspected her own boyfriend?"

"Yeah, but she crossed him out," I murmured.

Fadia opened a Tupperware container of egg tarts and passed it to Richard. "Maybe these are people she wanted to question?"

"Because they might have information about Piper's death, or because they might be suspects?" Jaz asked.

"Why not both?" Richard countered, taking several tarts and extending the Tupperware toward Elena. When they made eye contact, he nearly dropped it.

"What about the list of names that Rachel found?" Anton asked. "How do they factor in?"

"Oh, I've got some updates there." Jaz set her plate down. "Fadia sent me the list to do some sleuthing online. I found Julia. Or, at least, the Julia that Nick Hart was probably talking about when he said she worked at Molly's PR firm."

"Did you have to hack into some HR mainframe to find her?" Anton asked with interest.

"I used Google," Jaz replied, with the kind of withering contempt that only a teenager could truly pull off. She handed a sheet of paper to Richard. "For the board."

He taped the sheet up. It was a photo of a pretty woman in her mid-twenties, with auburn hair and freckles.

"Julia Smith worked for the Beacon Group. They'd been handling Molly's PR for the past year or so. It looks like Julia parted ways with the company a few months ago."

"Why?" I asked. Maybe I was projecting, but Julia Smith's smile looked a little strained.

"Well, to find that out, I'd have to"—Jaz gave Anton a begrudging smile—"hack into the HR mainframe."

"Nobody's doing any hacking," Elena said. "Google, fine. Facebook, fine. But we're not breaking any laws."

"Of course not." Jaz's eyes were wide and guileless. "That would be wrong."

Elena looked exasperated.

"I also found some more info on Hailey," Jaz continued. "Not sure if it's relevant, but when you guys talked to her, I'm guessing she probably didn't mention that she has a criminal record."

"Did she throw a cell phone at her assistant?" Anton asked.

"Definitely not famous enough for an assistant," Casper said.

"It's actually not far off, though," Jaz said. "When she was eighteen, she was arrested for assault and destruction of property. Apparently, she had some kind of meltdown at the Bloomingdale's in Century City. She destroyed a display in the shoe department and hit a sales associate with a pair of Jimmy Choos. She ended up with community service. I found a couple of pictures, if we want to add them to the board?"

"Sure, but mainly for the schadenfreude," Richard said. He added the mug shot of a teen Hailey, and a candid of her in a neon vest, spearing a piece of garbage with a metal pole.

"I also found two potential candidates for Winter." Jaz handed two more photos to Richard. "There's a hairstylist named Winter Nie who does some work with the Disney Channel—unclear whether she was there at the same time Molly was, since that's going back kind of far." Richard taped up the second photo. "I also found a Winter Crawford, who most recently worked as a personal assistant for—"

"Alessandra Delgado," I said.

Jaz blinked at me. "How did you know?"

Alessandra's former assistant stared out at me from her spot under Richard's hastily scrawled *WINTER(?)*.

"I've seen her before. I just didn't know her name." I briefly recounted my interview with Alessandra, and how Winter was later let go.

"What do all the women on Molly's list have in common?" Fadia murmured. "Why was she looking into them?"

No one spoke.

"What about everyone else? Molly's leads?" Richard gestured to *Brady. Chrimbo. Mystery Man. Dax.*

"Well, Brady is obvious," Casper said. "Brady Pierce. That's Piper's alleged killer."

"And we know Dax is Molly's ex," Anton said. "But who or what is a *Chrimbo*?"

"That I actually know," Casper replied. "It's a nickname. He's a pap." Casper glanced at me. "We saw him outside Kitson today, when we were waiting for Hailey Nichols."

I remembered the tall, scraggly guy who told Casper there was "no one worth shooting"—the same guy who had papped Molly and me outside Chanel way back when.

"There were tons of paps outside Entity the night Piper died," Casper continued. "That's how they got photos of Brady asking Piper for a picture. Maybe Chrimbo was there too. Maybe he saw something."

"So we need to track down Chrimbo," Richard said. "We need to interrogate Mr. Ex Van Sant, and we need to find out why Molly thought Brady was innocent. It would also be mighty helpful to talk to our Julia and Winter."

"What do we do about 'Mystery Man'?" Jaz asked. "Not exactly Boolean-search compatible."

"Let's leave Mystery Man for now," I said. "We've got leads."

"I know someone else we could talk to," Anton said. I looked over at him. "But first I need to talk to Rachel."

26

"So . . ."

Anton and I stood on Richard's balcony, gazing out once again over Palm Vista's sad courtyard. I'd rarely use the word *hesitant* to describe Anton, but that was how he looked in this moment, as he blinked down at the grills below and fiddled absently with one of the silver rings on his right hand. "I have something to tell you."

I couldn't help myself: "You're joining a different murder club. This one's gotten stale. You're hoping for an investigation that involves more high-speed car chases."

He cracked a smile. "I've kind of been seeing someone."

This was not what I expected. "What? Who?"

"His name is Eliot. But you may know him by a different name." He finally looked up at me, his eyes alight. "In fact, his rhythm . . . may have already been inside you."

My jaw dropped. "You're dating BEATDRAGON? Deejay, rhythm artist, provocateur?" The very same deejay, rhythm artist, provocateur who was playing at Lithium the night I met Molly.

The one with the washboard abs and the exhibitionist Twitter profile.

That explained the glimmer in Anton's eyes—he was trying very hard not to look pleased. "Sort of. Casually. It's still pretty new."

"How? When? Not since . . ."

"No, not since that night we saw him at Lithium. I ended up going to another one of his gigs a couple weeks after that, and then, afterward, I sent him a DM saying I liked the set, and . . . you know . . . one thing led to another . . ."

"Why didn't you tell me?"

"You were pretty busy being Molly Byrne's BFF. And anyway, what was there to tell? First it was just drinks, then it was just a hookup, then a series of hookups, and now . . ." Something in his gaze softened. "I don't know. I'm honestly not sure if we're actually dating or if we're just messing around, but . . . I like him." A pause. "Don't look at me like that, all gooey eyed. I'm not under the delusion that I'm living in a Colbie Caillat song or something."

"How bubbly are your toes right now?"

"A truly deplorable sentence, Rachel West."

I smiled. "When do you think you'll meet Mr. and Mrs. BEATDRAGON?"

"I hate you."

"Can I meet him?"

"Yeah, that's why I brought it up. Eliot might be able to help us with some info about what happened to Piper. He used to gig at Entity. He was actually working there the night she died."

Mr. Eliot BEATDRAGON was actually a Mr. Eliot Schwartz. He was shorter up close than he had appeared to be in the deejay booth. He had a muscular, stocky build, dark hair that was close-cropped on the sides and curly on top, and a warm smile.

"It's great to meet you, Rachel," he said after we settled into a booth at a vegetarian place in Silver Lake the following afternoon. "Ant has told me a lot about you."

"Oh, Ant." I gave Anton a playful slap on the arm. "You shouldn't have."

"Nothing good, don't get it twisted," Anton replied, and then leaned in toward me when Eliot turned to the waiter to order. "And *Ant* is just for him. Don't think for a second that you suddenly get *Ant* privileges."

"What do I have to do to earn *Ant* privileges?"

"Nothing I'll allow, believe me."

Anton and I placed our orders too, and then, as the waiter retreated, Eliot looked across the table at me expectantly. "So I heard you guys wanted to talk to me about Entity?"

"Yes," I said. "We were wondering if you could tell us about the night that Piper Standish died."

"Ah." Eliot's expression sobered. "Is this for a story?"

"Not quite." Anton cast a sidelong glance my way. "Nothing official, anyway. We're just following a thread. And I remembered you said you were gigging there that night, so I thought you might have some inside perspective—off the record, of course."

Eliot let out a breath. "I mean, it's not really a gig I'm eager to relive. But if it would be helpful for you guys . . ."

"It would," I said. "If you're comfortable with it. Just anything you can remember from that night."

"Okay." Eliot gazed up at the ceiling for a moment. "Well, it was a really packed night, for one thing. Lots of people, lots of celebs. I was doing my show like usual, the crowd was really hyped, they were into it, it was great . . . and then someone from the club came by the booth and said they needed to clear the place out immediately. I was surprised, obviously. But I thought maybe someone had put in a call on a fire-code thing. So I cut the show and packed up while they were trying to get everyone out. People were obviously really annoyed and really rowdy. I ended up going out the back to try to avoid the crowd—there's a private entrance out there, which helps when things get nuts like that—but there were a ton of cop cars in the back alley. That's when I realized something bad had gone down." Sadness shone in his eyes. "It's so fucked-up. You see some stuff on the job, but I never thought—I mean, I'm down there spinning, everyone's drinking and dancing and living it up, meanwhile someone's upstairs getting murdered? Someone's life is *stolen* from them and we're just out there partying? It made me reconsider, like, this entire thing. Luckily, I found my way out of it, but . . ." He trailed off, fumbled with his napkin for a moment. Anton reached out and placed his hand over Eliot's. They shared a brief look that made something twinge in my chest.

I flashed suddenly, irrationally, on Lee extending a bottle of water toward me, our fingers brushing. I quickly chased the thought away.

"I actually ended up getting questioned by the police," Eliot continued after a moment.

"Really? Why?"

"They questioned everyone who was in VIP before Piper died, and I had gone up there before my set. I even saw her."

"Do you remember who she was with?"

"There were so many people around . . . It was her birthday, so they were going all out. Everyone was already pretty sloshed by the time I showed up. I didn't get to talk to Piper. She was holed up with a few friends—apparently there was some kind of drama."

"Do you know what it was about?"

"I didn't hear all the details, but it sounded like Piper was pissed because one of her exes showed up uninvited. Some sleazy older guy she'd cut it off with a while back."

"Did you see the ex?"

Eliot shook his head. "Like I said, it was really crowded." He paused. "I did run into someone you might know, though. Dax Van Sant was there."

Anton and I shared a look. *So that's why he was on Molly's murder board.* But why had she crossed him out?

Eliot continued. "I remember because it's not every day you see a pap welcomed into celeb circles. He and Molly weren't a thing yet at that point. Just goes to show you, anybody can get together."

"Yeah, look how you managed to land me," Anton said, and Eliot grinned.

Our food arrived, and we moved on to lighter topics. I got the pleasure of revealing to Eliot that in college Anton was the president of a seventies-themed all-male a cappella group called the Funktuation Marks.

"Yes, because you never did anything embarrassing in college, Rachel," Anton said. "I've seen the photos. Do I need to invoke Canadian teen pop icon Avril Lavigne?"

I ducked my head. "No. The Funktuation Marks were extremely cool. No further discussion necessary."

"We were *beloved.* Our Earth, Wind, and Fire tribute brought the house down at the spring jamboree."

"I bet," Eliot said with a smile. "Did you wear, like, the *Saturday Night Fever* suits?"

"Oh yeah. So much polyester. If someone had lit a match, we'd all have been toast."

We were finishing up our meals when Eliot suddenly snapped his fingers.

"Hey, I almost forgot—I have a gig tonight, at this party in WeHo. It's for the launch of some pointless and incredibly niche thing that absolutely no one asked for . . . tobacco-flavored vodka, or vodka-flavored tobacco—something like that. You should both come. Ashton Kutcher and a hundred more of the worst people you'll ever meet will be there."

"Ooh, babe," Anton said, "sell it harder."

Eliot's eyes shone. "Free drinks?"

"Sold!" Anton beamed at me. "Rachel, you in?"

27

I didn't know how to decline tactfully in the moment, but I told Anton on the phone later that I wasn't in the mood for a party.

However, he insisted: "The mystery can wait for one night."

"But—"

"In fact, I think it's especially important that you do something *not* related to murder."

"I don't—"

"Or thinking about murder, or questioning potential murderers about how they might have committed murder—"

He might have had a point. I wasn't sleeping well. Or eating particularly well. Besides working on *Nuclear Nucleus* for Richard, I wasn't doing anything that wasn't in some way connected to finding out what had happened to Molly. Maybe I needed to get out and turn my brain off for an evening.

"Okay, I get it," I said.

"So you'll go?"

"Against my will, yes."

"Excellent." He pitched his voice low and sleazy. "Make sure you wear that red dress I like."

"Yikes. I will be wearing jeans and sneakers."

"Rachel West, I will not allow it—unless the sneakers are high-heeled and Swarovski encrusted. Be ready at nine. In full glam."

"You better be full glam too!"

"It's cute that you think I'd allow myself to be less."

Rather than tobacco-flavored vodka or vodka-flavored tobacco, the party was in fact to celebrate the launch of an alcohol-infused energy drink called HYPER BLITZ, which was stylized in all caps like a text from Anton. HYPER BLITZ came in three flavors: Blue Vanilla Shock Wave, Cherry Peach Squall, and Raspberry Limenado Thunder.

"Which would you prefer?" Anton asked, gesturing to one of the towers of tall, aggressively neon cans stacked precariously inside the entrance to the venue. "The Squall, the Shock Wave, or the Limenado Thunder?"

"Honest to God, what's Limenado Thunder supposed to taste like?"

"Meteorologists are dying to know."

We located the deejay booth, where Eliot was setting up. There was already music playing—the relentless buildup of an EDM hook, far too loud.

Eliot closed Anton in a quick hug and pecked me on the cheek. "Have you tried the HYPER BLITZ yet?" he yelled over the pounding of the bass.

"Not yet!"

"Don't!" he replied. "It'll melt your fillings!"

Anton grinned.

Eliot gestured to the booth. "You two want to keep me company during the set?"

"Sure!" Anton yelled.

I shook my head. I didn't feel deejay-booth-hype-girl ready, even in my best attempt at "full glam," which included a halter top from Molly, and shoes from Molly, and a miniskirt . . . from Molly. I had felt strange putting them on. It was one thing when she was alive—it had felt more like borrowing. But now that she was gone . . .

"I'm going to do a quick circuit," I said.

Anton nodded. "Make good choices! But not too good! Make choices that I would make!"

Someone from the HYPER BLITZ company, who introduced himself as Jake Travis, CEO of Adrenaline, got on the mic to talk about how psyched out of his mind he was to celebrate the launch of a drink that was going to "revolutionize how we imbibe." The crowd, already plied with free drinks, acknowledged him with enthusiasm. Then Eliot—now fully switched into BEATDRAGON mode—started his set.

I went to the bar and ordered the signature cocktail, which was, unfortunately, a HYPER BLITZ martini dubbed the HYPEBLASTER. It came in brilliant neon blue, garnished with what looked like a cocktail weenie and two cubes of pepper jack. I discarded the garnish immediately, and then headed off to make a circle of the room. By the time I reached the bar again, my HYPEBLASTER was gone, and I foolishly ordered another.

I was making my way around again when a voice suddenly rang out over the pounding of the music: "Hey! Girl in green!"

I turned.

Two guys standing at a nearby cocktail table, holding cans of Cherry Peach Squall, waved me over. I looked behind me just to make sure, but the taller of them, a blond with thick eyebrows and a toothy smile, nodded.

"Yeah, you! In the green! With the legs!"

I didn't love that. But I was bored, and one and a half monstrous Blue Vanilla Shock Wave cocktails in, so I backtracked to their table.

They both seemed to be in their mid-twenties or so. The second guy was dark haired, with a five-o'clock shadow. Both wore chains, shirts that were open at the chest, expensive watches, and too much hair gel. They looked like any number of guys you'd meet at any such event.

"Settle a bet for us," the blond guy said, leaning in to talk in a way that was necessary in this type of sound environment but could also be construed as flirtatious. "Are you or are you not Rachel West?"

I blinked. "I . . ."

"I knew it!" The blond smacked the other guy on the arm. "I told you." He turned back to me. "See, anyone who isn't Rachel West would say, *Who's Rachel West?* Am I right?"

That felt like an insult, but it was also undeniably true. "Sorry, who are you?"

"I'm Luke," the blond said. "This is Ryder." The dark-haired guy flashed a peremptory smile at me. "I think we have a mutual friend. Which basically makes us friends already, doesn't it?"

I flashed on the conversation in Casper's car:

You have a roommate?

Two. Luke and Ryder. They're . . . an unfortunate necessity.

"You're Casper's roommates?"

"Ding ding ding! Give the lady a prize! Our little roomie

must've talked us up, huh? CJ's definitely mentioned you before. A lot, actually. I feel like I know you." He smacked Ryder's arm again. "Dude, don't you feel like you know her?"

Ryder gave a distracted nod. "Sure."

Luke turned back to me. He looked exactly like someone who would own a *Sun's Out, Guns Out* tank top. "How'd you end up here tonight? CJ's not here, is he?"

"Not that I know of. I came with friends."

"Nice. You should bring them over."

I glanced toward the deejay booth, where Eliot was flashing his abs and Anton was dancing, his own HYPEBLASTER martini raised in the air. "They're . . . a little occupied right now."

"This is a bust," Ryder said abruptly. "There's nobody here."

Luke shook his head. "Ashton's coming. For sure."

"And everyone else will get him too, and we'll make what? Fifty bucks? If that?"

"Sorry," Luke said to me with an apologetic smile. "It's kind of a working night for us."

I took a sip of my cocktail. "Yeah, I heard you guys are photographers too?"

"'Photographers' is such a classy way to put it," Luke said. "You're a sophisticated woman, Rachel West."

Ryder was still scanning the crowd, looking—I now understood—for celebrities who might be in attendance. "Hey, ten o' clock. Is that one of the girls from *The Hills*?"

Luke glanced in her direction. "Maybe? I can't keep up with that fucking show. All I know is that Spencer Pratt blocked me on Twitter 'cause I said he looks like a thumb. What do you think, Rachel? In your professional opinion?"

I frowned. "Does Spencer Pratt look like a thumb?"

Luke grinned. "Is that one of the girls from *The Hills*?"

It was hard to distinguish faces in the pink, green, and blue neon flashing lights. Maybe it was Lo Bosworth, or maybe it was a girl who looked like her from afar.

I thought there was at least a sixty percent chance you met some girl who looked *like Molly Byrne!*

I squeezed my eyes shut briefly. I was not supposed to be thinking about Molly tonight.

"I don't know," I said, glancing back at Luke. "Maybe?"

"Oh fuck," Ryder said suddenly.

Luke frowned. "What?"

"Fucking DVS is here."

Luke's expression soured. "That jag-off. Why should I be surprised?"

DVS. That could only mean . . .

"Dax Van Sant?" I asked.

"Shit," Luke said. "You know him, don't you? Sorry if you're cool with him or whatever. It's just, if we're being honest, that dude is the fucking worst. If he's not stealing shots from other paps or trying to photobomb, he's parking his douchebag Maserati sideways across three handicapped parking spaces."

I couldn't help but crack a smile.

"I mean, come on," Luke continued, aggrieved. "He walks around in a literal *cloud* of his own self-named fragrance that he's desperate to launch. He wears driving gloves like he's about to join the fucking Monaco Grand Prix. He wants to be famous so bad, it's pathetic. Like, you know how wanting to be cool paradoxically makes you instantly uncool? Wanting to be famous that badly makes him instantly repellent."

"I don't really know him that well" was all I could think to reply.

"Count yourself lucky."

"I really think that's Lo Bosworth over there," Ryder said, and then abruptly left the table, crossing over to the woman nearby.

"Can I get you another drink?" Luke asked.

I shook my head. "I'm good. Thank you, though."

Ryder successfully engaged Maybe Lo Bosworth in conversation. He gestured to Luke, who downed the rest of his can of HYPER BLITZ in one go and then winked at me. "Duty calls. See you around, doll."

As Eliot's set continued, I headed outside. The room felt too stuffy, which made my stomach roil. The Blue Vanilla Shock Wave was probably doing something unspeakable to my internal organs.

Several groups of smokers stood clustered outside, so I moved a little farther down the street to get some fresh air.

I pulled out my phone. One notification: a missed call from my parents. I cleared it.

And then I pulled up my contacts. I selected Lee's name before I could second-guess it.

The phone rang twice before he picked up. "Lee."

"I'm at the worst party right now," I said by way of a greeting.

"Rachel?"

"Yeah."

"Are you okay? Are you safe?"

"It's not that kind of bad," I said. Maybe Lee thought I was reaching out to him as a member of law enforcement. I wasn't sure how to dispel that notion. "It's just shitty-energy-drink bad."

"Shitty energy drink?" Lee repeated, surprise in his voice.

"Tell me, would you prefer to be leveled by Cherry Peach Squall or decimated by Raspberry Limenado Thunder?"

"Is there a third option?"

"Yes. And it tastes like carbonated Sudafed."

He let out a breath of laughter. "Make sure you save me a case."

“For your next dinner party?”

“So the ME can analyze it and add it to our tox screens.”

I smiled. But then tox screens made me think once again of Molly, which made me think of murder, and Anton said I wasn’t supposed to be thinking about murder tonight.

I wouldn’t ask Lee about Molly. He said that if there was news, he would tell me. And he hadn’t told me anything. So that meant there was no news, right?

“Sorry?” Lee asked, and I realized that I may have said some part of that out loud.

“Nothing,” I replied. “I’m a little drunk.”

“Do you need a ride?”

“No, I’m with friends. We’ll leave together. You’re awfully concerned about safety, you know.”

“It’s kind of my job.”

“Oh, so you’re not just concerned about *my* safety.” I don’t know why I said it. Except I had an inkling. I pushed past it: “It’s not a personal-interest thing. It’s because I’m a member of the general public, whom you’ve sworn to protect. Just like your idol, Detective Clarkson.”

“I didn’t actually become a detective because of television,” he said, and there was something unguarded about his tone, something suddenly . . . vulnerable. “I just wanted to . . . make things better. Help people. I thought it was a way that I could. Sometimes I wonder . . .”

“What?”

“If I’m just making things worse.” He paused, and when he spoke again, he was quieter. “The caseload is only getting bigger. There’s so much pressure to wrap things up. It’s . . . it’s not really how I imagined it would be.”

“You should’ve become a firefighter,” I said. “People actually like firefighters.”

He huffed a laugh.

“I didn’t become a copy editor because of the magazines,” I continued. As long as we were being honest. “I mean, I did, but also because of my brother. Because my brother died when I was a kid.”

There was a beat of silence. I wanted him to make a joke. Lighten the mood. But he just said, “I’m so sorry.”

“No, I’m just drunk.” This is why I tried not to drink to excess. It came out. It was always waiting to come out, and if I didn’t shut it away, clamp down tight, if I gave it the slightest bit of breathing room, it would escape.

“Are you—”

“I should go. Anton will be wondering where I went.”

“Who’s—”

“Good night, Lee.”

I hung up the phone.

It was not until later that I realized he never asked me why I called. I also realized that I couldn’t justify it myself. I just wanted to hear the sound of his voice.

28

When I headed back inside, I walked almost directly into Dax Van Sant. I narrowly missed wearing his HYPE-BLASTER home.

He blinked. "Rachel?"

"Yeah." I was sure he needed verbal confirmation, on account of his wearing sunglasses inside a dark room. *He walks around in a literal* cloud *of his own self-named fragrance that he's desperate to launch,* Luke had said. I couldn't help but notice the scent—Axe body spray meets sangria meets motor oil. If this was Eau de Van Sant, it needed work.

I knew that questioning Dax would go against the entire point of the evening. But he was here, right now, and he had also been at Perihelion Ranch, with Vivian Grayson, and at the club on the night of Piper's death. It was too good an opportunity to pass up, even if I was not exactly sober. "Hey, do you have a minute?"

He smiled, with too much teeth. "Depends on how we'll be spending it."

"In conversation," I said flatly. "Let me get you another drink."

I got another cocktail for Dax and a bottle of water for myself, and we headed back outside, where it was relatively quiet. At least we didn't have to yell to be heard. I wouldn't stray too far from the smokers this time—so there would be witnesses.

But it turned out that wasn't necessary. Just past the smokers was . . . Casper.

He was staring at his phone. When he looked up and caught sight of the two of us, his eyes widened in surprise.

"What are you doing here?" I asked.

"I . . . came to get pictures," he replied. I didn't point out that he didn't appear to have a camera. Maybe his trusty Canon PowerShot was stowed in his jacket pocket. "What are *you* doing here? With . . . Dax?"

"I see my reputation precedes me," Dax said, raising his martini to Casper and then throwing it back.

"Yeah, you're a legend," Casper replied sardonically. "So, were you having an affair with Vivian Grayson, then?"

Dax nearly choked on his drink.

Inwardly, I groaned. Even in my HYPER BLITZ–saturated state, I was planning on taking a slightly subtler approach. But clearly, Casper preferred the hatchet method.

Dax coughed, drew his arm across his face to wipe off excess HYPEBLASTER, and then set his glass down on a nearby ledge and raised his Wayfarers onto his head. "Are you fucking kidding me right now?"

"Nope. Answer the question."

Dax turned to me. "Who's this asshole?"

"A friend," I said, a bit apologetic. "We saw you with Vivian at Perihelion."

"Oh really?" Dax replied. "That's funny, because I saw Heidi Klum there getting acupuncture. Doesn't mean she's screwing Vivian, either."

"Why were you there, then?" I couldn't help myself: "Couples acupuncture with Heidi? Not sure how Seal will feel about that."

"I went to see Viv," Dax said. "To *talk*. To . . . commiserate, or whatever, about Molly. I'm the one who introduced Mol to Vivian in the first place. I would never cheat on her." He took a breath. "Molly was the one who ended things between us. You know that. If it were up to me, I would've—" When he spoke next, the words came out roughly. "I wanted to make it work. I was still . . . I was still in love with her."

Love? Molly had dated Dax, sure, but from the sound of it, he was just another one of the Mayfly Men. Were Dax's feelings that much stronger than hers?

"Did you see Molly—or talk to her—the day she died?" I asked.

Dax reached into his back pocket and pulled out a pack of cigarettes. He offered it to me, but I waved it away. He pointedly did not offer it to Casper. "I hadn't seen her since right after that bullshit article came out."

"You mean *my* bullshit article?"

"That's the one." He lit up a cigarette. "You know, a heads-up would've been cool."

"Molly didn't need your approval to talk about her own life."

"Yeah, but it would've been nice to find out we were breaking up from her, and not from some fucking tabloid."

Casper's eyebrows lifted. "She didn't end things with you before it was published?"

"No. I found out along with the rest of the nation. Lucky me, huh?"

That surprised me. It seemed unlike Molly. I had a hard time believing she wouldn't have officially ended things with Dax—in person, over the phone, or at the very least via *text*—before the article came out. But then again . . . Molly could be impulsive. And once she decided something, it was decided, no going back. *I only look forward.*

I felt a weird pang of . . . something. Not guilt exactly, but . . . something uncomfortable that I didn't want to delve too far into. Maybe it was the feeling that Dax and I were a little bit similar—both pulled into Molly's orbit.

"What do you know about Piper Standish?" I asked.

Surprise flashed across Dax's face, but then quickly dissipated. "Not much. Never really a fan of her movies. But I know she was a hot ticket before she died. Her photos sold really high."

I figured there was no point in beating around the bush. "Were you at Entity the night Piper died?"

I expected him to hedge. To deny it. But he just nodded. "Yeah, I was."

"Outside or inside?" I asked, even though I already knew the answer. I wanted to see if he would tell the truth.

"Outside to start. There were a lot of people coming through that night, but the spot got blown up quick. It's not worth trying to snap anyone if fifty other guys are out there getting nearly identical shots, so I went in and hung out with some friends. Fucking ironic."

"Why?"

"Because anyone who got photos of Piper that night ended up making a killing—pardon the expression. I know a guy who bought a Lexus off his camera roll from that night alone."

"Were you in the VIP area inside?"

"Yeah, but not with Piper's crowd. They had a private room."

"Who was in Piper's crowd?"

"I don't know. I don't really remember. I went a little too hard that night." He looked at me, his eyes narrowing. "Why does any of this matter? Piper's dead. The asshole who did it is in jail right now." Dax drew in a shaky breath. "This whole year has been so fucked-up. I need a serious energy realignment."

"So you follow Vivian Grayson's practices too?" I asked.

"Of course. I wouldn't have recommended her to Molly if I didn't."

I thought of the inconsistencies in what we knew about Vivian. Nick Hart had said that Molly confided in Vivian about Julia Smith, but Vivian had denied it. Was she being discreet, or did she have something to hide? "One more thing. Do you remember Molly mentioning anything about a Julia Smith or a Winter Crawford?"

"Yeah, Julia Smith—that's the PR girl."

Casper straightened up a little. "You know her?"

"Not personally. But Molly liked to collect strays." Dax cast a meaningful glance in my direction. "You should know that better than anyone. Julia was one of them too. Before you came on the scene."

I swallowed. "What happened to her?"

"She got fired out of nowhere. The firm said she had been leaking Molly's info. Molly was really upset about the whole thing. She put a lot of stock in being able to read people, but . . . I guess she read that girl wrong. Mol even tried to track her down later, but it was like she just . . . vanished off the face of the earth."

I shared a look with Casper.

"What about Winter?" I asked. "Winter Crawford."

Dax shook his head. "Don't know her. Molly never mentioned her." He frowned. "What's up with all the questions? Are you doing an article?"

"Nothing official. Just . . . compiling information."

"Well, consider all of this off the record."

"Sure."

Dax headed off after that, back inside for more drinks and mingling and whatever else happened further into the progression of an alcoholic-energy-drink launch party. I didn't particularly feel like sticking around to find out, and I told Casper so.

"Do you want a ride home?" Casper asked. The second offer of the evening. I flashed again on Lee—maybe he was in his living room, watching TV in sweatpants. Or writing his phone number on the backs of business cards.

Maybe he was in the shower.

It was time to go home.

"I thought you came to take pictures," I said, looking back at Casper. If my face was flushed, I could blame the drinks.

"Oh, yeah. Well. It's probably not even worth it at this point."

"So why'd you come, then?"

He looked away. "Just . . . happened to be out."

On the way to Casper's car, I called Anton and left a voicemail to tell him I was leaving. I sent a text too for good measure: Have fun! Don't make choices I would make!

"Did your roommates text you to come?" I asked Casper as we reached the car.

"They might have mentioned it," he replied, opening my door and then crossing around to the driver's side.

"You could've gotten a photo of Maybe Lo Bosworth," I said as I put on my seat belt.

He switched on the engine. "I'll find a way to survive the disappointment."

We were waiting at a stoplight a few minutes later when Casper spoke again.

"Dax was pretty forthcoming."

"Yeah."

"Like, surprisingly so."

I considered this. "You think it's suspicious?"

"I don't know. It's just, he had no reason to be that open with us."

I thought about what Molly had said at that lunch when I discovered Casper taking her picture: *Why wouldn't I want to control my own narrative?*

Was Dax being honest with us, or was he just controlling his own narrative?

FROM THE *ICON* ARCHIVE:

APRIL 14, 2008

MOLLY BYRNE TELLS ALL

On her relationship with paparazzo Dax Van Sant, Molly spoke plainly: "Sometimes you know it's over before it's even begun. It was like that with Dax. Obviously it was never going to work out. Why would a prisoner date their jailer? I mean, probably because they don't have many other options. But lucky for me—I've got plenty of options."

What drew her to a relationship with Van Sant in the first place?

"Attraction," Molly said with a wide smile. "All my relationships start with that."

29

I spent the morning after the HYPER BLITZ launch regretting my life choices (or at least severely regretting that second HYPEBLASTER) and finishing my review of Richard's screenplay. I had already pledged to send him my edits by the end of the day, and although I was a near zombie after staying up until four a.m., I never missed a deadline.

I managed to send Rex Blaze and his nuclear adventures back to Richard by early afternoon, and afterward I went out and picked up some single-serve ice creams at the gas station. Then I brought them to Jaz's door. I had gotten a text from her earlier:

got more info on julia smith

Who is this? I replied.

jaz? from 208

Ah sorry! Did Fadia give you my number?

no, she replied, and then a second later: i have your social security number too fyi

Are you going to steal my identity?

is it even worth stealing lol

I could not disagree.

Jaz and I settled down at the picnic bench in the courtyard to go over what she had learned. Winter Crawford was still a nonstarter—she didn't appear to have an online footprint, and our only connection to her was Alessandra. And since Molly had arranged my interview with her, I didn't have Alessandra's contact info. I had reached out to her agency and left a message, but I was still waiting to hear back. I wasn't sure if I ever would.

But Jaz had an update on Julia Smith: "She was definitely fired, and what Dax said was right—she was leaking information about Molly to the tabloids."

"Did you actually have to hack into an HR mainframe to find that out?"

She cast me a sidelong glance while unwrapping her Drumstick. "You really want the answer to that?"

"Probably better not to know. Plausible deniability and all that."

"Good call."

"Did you really find my Social Security number?"

Her eyes gleamed. "Did you really get a traffic ticket in 1999 for driving too slow on the highway in Missouri?"

Oh great. Apparently one of my most embarrassing moments was floating around on the internet for discovery by tech-savvy teens. "In my defense, I was just learning to drive," I said.

"My mom says that driving defensively is key," Jaz advised around bites of ice cream. "Man, they must've eaten you up on the roads when you moved here."

"I drive a lot better now." I took a lick of my own ice cream. "So, where did Julia end up after she got fired? Dax said she basically vanished."

"He's not wrong. She had been living with a roommate in Culver City, but apparently she moved out really abruptly and totally left the roommate in the lurch. Lot of angry posts on Myspace about it from the roommate. But then it seemed like the push the roommate's boyfriend needed to take their relationship to the next level? So now they're living together."

"Good for them."

"I guess. If you're into that kind of thing." She eyed me. "Are you?"

"What?"

"Into that kind of thing."

"Cohabitation?"

"Just, like. Dating and stuff."

I thought of Lee and the text he had sent me last night: *Did you get home okay?*

And how long it had taken me to craft a response: *Yes, Rachel West lives to fight another day.*

Very glad to hear that, he'd replied, and I had felt startlingly warm from it, like I was a teenager again.

I recounted absolutely none of this to the actual teenager sitting across from me. Instead I just said, "I haven't exactly had a lot of time for it lately. Why?"

Jaz shrugged. "Just wondering."

"Looking for some hot goss?"

Jaz suddenly looked way too interested in the rusted grills to our left.

"You are! You *are* looking for hot goss!"

She turned her eyes skyward. "Well, can you blame me? I'm alone all the time! Who am I supposed to talk about? Or even *think* about?"

I thought of what Fadia had said about Jaz: *Sometimes I wonder if she ever wants to get out there and . . . you know, do teen stuff.*

Jaz shook her head before I could speak. "Don't. It's not—don't feel sorry for me or whatever. I chose this. I *wanted* this. I wanted to hurry up and graduate, and I wanted to take college classes online, and I wanted to be on my computer twenty-four seven, because why wouldn't I? It's what I love most! But it's also . . . really fucking lonely sometimes." She eyed me. "Yes, I curse. Just not in front of my mom, she has a policy."

I smiled. "Gotta respect the policy."

It was quiet for a moment.

"When I graduated early, I kind of just . . . lost touch with everyone at school." Jaz picked glumly at the Drumstick wrapper for a moment. "Or maybe we weren't that close to begin with. I don't know. It's like my old friends think that I'm living it up, doing whatever I want, but it's not really like that. I'm just . . . here. And they're all there, together."

Fadia had told me that Jaz had finished high school in half the time. But I knew there was more to high school than just the coursework. I thought of Molly's fascination with "regular school," and the eager questions she'd ask me about it sometimes. *Did you have a big group of friends? Did you all eat lunch together every day? Did you walk to class together and gossip about people? Did a guy ever carry your books, or is that just made up for TV?*

I thought of the skateboarding boy I saw sometimes outside the building. "There's a kid who lives on the first floor," I told Jaz. "I've seen him skateboarding around."

"A kid?"

I waved a hand. "A youth. Like you."

"A *youth*."

I made a face. "I'm just saying, you're not the only one in the building. Maybe you could make a new friend."

Jaz rolled her eyes. "I've seen Corey from 108 around before too. Fadia keeps trying to make us be friends. Because that's totally how it works. We're both teenagers, so we'll automatically get along. Like how all old people super get along, because they've all got that one thing in common."

"Point taken." I took a bite out of my ice-cream cone. "Are you counting me among 'old people'?"

She gave me a withering look.

"Never mind. I don't want to know."

Jaz took a noisy bite of her own cone, and then, mouth full, said, "What about you and Casper?"

"What about us?"

She shrugged. "Are you an *us*?"

"We're a *we*, insomuch as *we* are looking into Molly's death together. But in that context, so are you and I."

"He's kind of cute, though. In, like, a stray-puppy kind of way."

"A stray puppy?"

"Like a cute, scruffy dog who tumbles out of a trash can in a Disney movie. The scrappy hero dog who helps foil the villain."

"I'm sure he'd love to hear himself described that way."

"It's true, though!"

She wasn't wrong, but I wasn't going to admit that. "He and I are just . . ." I was about to say *friends*, but that didn't seem quite accurate. Spending time together investigating a potential murder did not automatically a friendship make. "Coinvestigators."

"Coinvestigators," Jaz repeated. "How warm and fuzzy." She paused for a moment, considering. "I guess he does play it pretty close to the chest."

"What do you mean?"

She lifted one shoulder. "What do we know about him outside of being a pap, wanting to find Molly's killer, and committing to an all-black aesthetic?"

Before I could respond, my phone buzzed. It was Fadia.

"Can you swing by my place?" she asked when I picked up. "I just remembered something."

30

I figured out where I know her from. The guru."

When Jaz and I arrived at Fadia's apartment, she waved us in and led us over to the TV. A movie was paused on the screen. The still image showed a scantily clad young woman lying in a hospital bed, her face frozen in an oversized expression of terror.

It was, without a doubt, a young Vivian Grayson.

The styling and general aesthetic spoke of the early eighties. Vivian looked to be twenty or so.

Fadia pressed PLAY. As tense violin music spiked, a masked figure in scrubs appeared from the shadows and stabbed Vivian. She let out an ear-piercing shriek. A theatrical spurt of blood leapt from her chest, some of it spattering the camera lens.

I winced.

"Yeah, cinematically speaking, it's not great," Fadia said. "But that's her, right? Molly's guru?"

As the camera closed in on Vivian's stricken face, her pale blue eyes gone glassy, it was all too clear: "Yeah, that's her."

"It's just a small part." Fadia held up the VHS box for

Endoscope of Terror. "She's not even in the movie for more than five minutes. The credits list her as Shawna White. I'm no Jaz, but a cursory search for Shawna White turned up two more B-movie credits and a commercial for Pamprin circa 1991. Her résumé ends there. Then Vivian Grayson suddenly pops up in 2000."

"So Vivian's been lying about her identity," I said. "The ashram, the monks, that's all fake?"

"Definitely seems like it could be. My guess is, she went and presto-chango-ed her image to try to make some serious dough. B-movie extra? Not a ton of upward mobility. Lifestyle guru? Sky's the limit, given you nail the branding and hook the right clientele."

"Maybe Molly found out," I said. "She went to see Vivian the day she died. Maybe it wasn't what Vivian told us—maybe Molly went there to confront her."

"Wouldn't that give Vivian motive? If Molly was going to expose her secret?" Jaz asked.

We all considered this for a moment.

"How does Piper fit in, though?" Fadia asked.

I shook my head. "I don't know."

"Sounds like you're going to have to pay another visit to Perihelion."

"Vivian did encourage me to check out the ranch again. Tour the place and talk more about my 'journey.' That would get me in the door."

"A good old-fashioned ambush," Jaz said with a smile. "I like it."

Back at my apartment, I called Perihelion and secured an appointment with Vivian for the following day. With that sorted, I settled in to learn more about Piper Standish.

When I searched her name online, the most recent headlines were from just a couple of weeks ago. I clicked on one article titled "How Do We Ever Heal from This?: Looking Back at the Murder of Piper Standish." There was a link to a video interview with Piper's mother, Paula, who spoke with a correspondent from a major prime-time news show.

On-screen, Paula was seated in front of a tasteful background, the correspondent positioned across from her.

"She was blessed," Paula said. *"It was a God-given talent. That's what I always thought when I saw Piper act. She was truly gifted."*

Narration from the correspondent played over clips of a young Piper in various films: *"Critics and audiences agreed. From early childhood, Piper held her own on-screen opposite some of Hollywood's biggest names, receiving her first Golden Globe nomination at the age of nine, and her first Oscar nomination at twelve. But as Paula tells me, the highs were punctuated by all-consuming lows."*

"It's a difficult industry. Everyone knows that, and no one felt it more than Piper. The scrutiny, the rejection. The treatment that young women like her experience off-screen."

"In July, Piper was slated to sit down with Twenty-Twenty *for a major interview. An interview that never went forward, with the actress's death occurring just days before she was scheduled to appear on our program."*

"She wanted to speak her truth," Paula said. *"She wanted to tell people what it was really like. The cost of fame, of this kind of success. The darkness she had encountered in the industry."* Her mouth twisted. *"It's devastating. She paid the ultimate price for it."*

"Can you share Piper's truth with us now?" the correspondent asked.

"I can't speak for my daughter. I can't know exactly what she would've wanted to say, because I'll never know all that she went through." A beat. *"I'm heartbroken. I'll never get over it."*

I spent hours reading about Piper. In some ways, she shared many similarities with Molly, although their career paths were markedly different. While Molly had initially taken the family-friendly child-star route, Piper was a critic's darling as a kid, acting in major dramas from the age of five. But like Molly, Piper had her fair share of time in the media—headlines decrying nights spent partying, websites counting down to her eighteenth birthday.

I was more than a dozen search pages in when I found a website titled PiperStandishTruth.com. The link took me to a poorly formatted blog page titled WHAT REALLY HAPPENED TO PIPER STANDISH. Underneath it was the hashtag *#FreeBradyPierce.*

Where is the security camera footage? the home page read in a loud red font. *Where are the photos? The police REFUSE to see that there is NO WAY Brady could have killed Piper. The timeline DOES NOT ADD UP. If you are reading this, I AM BEGGING YOU to get the word out to #FreeBradyPierce. He is NOT GUILTY!!!!*

Molly thought Brady was innocent too. What had made her think that?

I clicked on the CONTACT form and started a message.

Excerpt from **COSMOPOLITAN**, *February 2007:*

PIPER STANDISH: HOLLYWOOD'S LITTLE IT GIRL ON GROWING UP ON SCREEN AND OFF

Cosmo: Moviegoers first saw you on the silver screen when you were just five years old. Now, at eighteen, what's your perspective on growing up in the public eye?

PS: It's definitely a unique experience. I think the general public becomes invested in you in a way. They feel like they know you, even though it's impossible to know someone just from watching them in a movie for two hours. It can be difficult too, because people have this image of you in their mind that might not match with who you are now. I'm still a little girl to a lot of people. But I'm growing every day. I'm changing. I want to be taken seriously, like anyone else my age.

Cosmo: That's so insightful. Could you share some tips with our readers about your diet and workout routine?

31

Later that evening, a call came in from a number I didn't recognize.

"Is this Rachel West? The reporter?" a reedy female voice said when I answered.

I had been a little creative in my message on the Free Brady Pierce website. But it was technically the truth. Or had been at one point. "That's me. Who am I speaking with?"

"Kimberly," the caller replied. "Kimberly Pierce. I'm Brady's sister."

I swallowed. "Do you have some time to speak with me about your brother?"

He didn't do it," Kimberly said. "But no one believes that, just because he had some pictures of Piper in his room and made some stupid comments online. They've made him out to be this crazy stalker, but I swear to God, my brother did *not* kill her. Why would he do that? He was her *fan*. If anyone actually paid attention to what he had said, or to why he was even upset that night, they'd see that."

"What happened exactly? From his perspective. If you . . . if you don't mind sharing."

"I'll tell you everything," she said. "Just like he told it to me. Are you ready?"

I had my laptop open, ready to take notes, my fingers poised over the keys and my phone cradled against my ear. "Yes."

She took a breath and let it out slowly. Then she began her story.

"He was waiting outside the club that night. That part is true, obviously. He did . . . he did know that Piper would probably show up. A friend of mine worked there—an *ex*-friend, because he turned on Brady like everyone else—and he'd tip us off sometimes when someone big was coming through. He knew Brady was a huge fan of Piper's, so he let him know her people had rented a private room that night. It was her birthday. They were celebrating her birthday."

A pause. I waited for her to continue.

"There was a big crowd out front, waiting to get in, waiting to see who would show up, all the photographers and stuff. Brady managed to get to the front of it, and when Piper showed up, he actually got her attention as she was walking by. Like, she looked *right* at him! He asked her if he could get a picture with her real quick, but then this security guy just shoved him away and rushed Piper into the club. She probably would've said yes if it weren't for that stupid guard! Brady wasn't mad at Piper that night—he was mad at *him*. That's what no one seems to understand. Anybody would be mad if they're pushed aside by some bodyguard like that—like they're worthless or something. But Brady was never mad at Piper. He would never take his anger out on her like that.

Not just her—he would never do something like that to *anyone*. Ever.

"So he waited in line to try and get into the club after that—he thought maybe he could ask for the picture again if he saw Piper inside—but the bouncers wouldn't let him in. But then, just as he was going to leave, this guy came out and called Brady over. He said he was one of Piper's people, and that she felt really bad about what happened and wanted to make it up to him with a meet and greet. They could even get that picture together. So of course Brady was thrilled! He followed this guy up to the room where she was having her thing, but it was empty. The guy told Brady to wait there and Piper would turn up, and then the guy left. Brady waited for a while, but no one showed. So he started looking around the room. There was a bathroom attached, and that's where—that's where he found her. She was in there, on the floor. He said . . . he just panicked, you know? Anyone would've. He rushed over to check on her, and of course some of her blood got on him, how could it not? She had been—" Her breath caught. "She was already dead. She'd been dead the whole time he was in there. As soon as he found her, he yelled for help. People came rushing in, and everyone thought—they just assumed he was the one who did it. Never mind that a person who just *murdered* someone wouldn't call out for help like that!"

"How long was he in there?"

"Maybe fifteen or twenty minutes before he found her."

"And the guy who invited him up there . . . ?"

"No one can identify him. I said there's gotta be footage, right? But you know what? When Brady's lawyers contacted the club, all the club manager could say was that their security cameras were 'inoperative' that night. Convenient, don't you think? Whoever it was that took Brady up there knows *exactly* what really happened.

He set Brady up to take the fall. I'd bet my life that he's the one who really killed Piper."

"What did he look like?"

"Brady couldn't remember much. White guy, brown hair. Average build."

"There was nothing at all particular about him? Tattoos, scars, hairstyle, even what he was wearing—"

"I don't know." Kimberly sounded miserable. "Brady said he wasn't paying attention. He didn't care about anything besides seeing Piper. But if Brady says this guy was there, he was there. I know my brother. I believe him." Her breath hitched. "Do you have any siblings?"

"Yes." I thought of Natalie, who had texted me the day before: *Hope you're having a good day.* I hadn't responded.

I thought of Sam, and how I used to watch over his shoulder as he played video games when we were kids. Whenever he would reach a save point, he'd let me try to play, even though I was categorically terrible at video games.

It's your reaction time, he'd say. *And picking up cues from your environment. You have to pay attention to things that don't seem important. That's how you unlock secrets in the game. Work on that stuff and you'll get better.*

"You know how it is, then," Kimberly said. "You know you can just tell when they're lying. And I know, in my absolute heart—I know Brady's telling the truth."

I didn't speak.

"Do you know what?" Kimberly continued after a beat. "If you're writing an article, there's someone else you should contact."

"Who?"

"I talked to this girl a few weeks ago—she sent me a message on the web page like you did. Said she was looking into Piper's death too, and wanted to get any info I had about that night. She said she thought she might know who actually did it."

My heartbeat quickened. "What was her name?"

"I remember it sounded kind of familiar," Kimberly replied. "She said her name was Anna Scott."

32

Anna Scott was Molly's favorite alias—she used it often for reservations and bookings. It was the name of Julia Roberts's character in *Notting Hill.*

I would cut off my pinkie toe to be as beautiful as Julia Roberts in Notting Hill.

I thought you said you'd give your pinkie toe to be as beautiful as Robin Wright in The Princess Bride.

I have two pinkie toes, Rachel.

Molly had spoken with Brady Pierce's sister too. Just a few weeks ago.

"She listened," Kimberly told me before we got off the phone. "She made me feel like . . . I don't know. Like I wasn't crazy. Like she actually believed me."

I didn't know what to do with myself after I finished the call. It was a little too late in the evening to confab with Casper or Fadia or the others, to share what I had learned, but I felt wired. And hungry. I hadn't eaten since the ice cream with Jaz in the courtyard earlier.

I peered into my fridge. Unsurprisingly, its contents had not changed since the last time I peered into it—predominantly condiments, with a couple bottles of water and a half-empty two-liter of Diet Coke for variety. So I decided to head back to the gas station down the street.

Once I was there and on my way to the snack section, a magazine on an endcap rack caught my eye. It was *Us Weekly*, the headline in big white letters superimposed over a photo of Molly: WHAT REALLY HAPPENED TO MOLLY BYRNE?

It felt surreal. It felt like nothing I could have ever imagined as a kid.

I remember going on grocery-store trips with my dad and Natalie back then, sometimes for a big shop but sometimes for just a handful of things, or even just one arbitrary yet very specific thing—*Your mom said we can't come back until we've found the ripest cantaloupe here!*

I was old enough at the time to realize that the trips functioned mainly to get us out of the house so that Sam could rest quietly. Natalie was still little, and too young to understand what was happening. So we'd tap at the bottoms of cantaloupes together and look for the greenest grapes and try to determine which was the best-smelling laundry detergent.

When we'd get to the checkout lane, Natalie would beg our dad for candy while I gazed at the racks of magazines, the impossibly glamorous celebrities shining back at me from their glossy covers. I'd slip a magazine onto the conveyer belt and hope my dad wouldn't notice, though he always did, and he always let it slide. And then we'd go home and I would escape to the backyard—I shared a room with Natalie, so it was hard to get any privacy—and pore over the pages. The outfits, the parties, the movie premieres, the relationship drama, the glamour of it all. It seemed so foreign and so shiny and so unattainable.

I never imagined a future in which I would know the person on the cover of one of those magazines. A future in which I would be staring at her and her photo would be staring back at me and she would just be . . . gone. And I would feel that loss keenly.

WHAT REALLY HAPPENED TO MOLLY BYRNE?

That's what I'm trying to figure out, I thought. *I* will *figure it out.*

I could imagine Molly's response: *That's all fine and good, but try to figure it out without frowning so much. You'll get premature eleven lines.*

I tore my eyes away from the magazine cover and headed to the snack aisle. I was loading up on chips when I caught sight of someone farther down the aisle, peering intently at a display of beef jerky.

It was Lee. In track pants, a hoodie, and a baseball hat. He was holding three energy drinks improbably in one hand and a bag of Doritos in the other.

I couldn't help but recall a conversation I had with Molly once, in which she recounted a brief fling she'd had with a Greek shipping heir. I had sheepishly asked her what it was like to hook up with guys who were that extremely good-looking.

"It's not always as great as you'd think it'd be. It doesn't matter if they're good-looking if they're missing one key thing."

"What's that?"

"They have to be *interesting*." Her eyes shone. "I genuinely think that's where attraction comes from. There has to be something interesting about them. Otherwise you might as well fuck Malibu Ken."

"You mean Nick Hart?"

"No, I mean the plastic doll. But honestly—not that far off."

Lee must've felt my gaze, because he looked up and met my eyes.

I had tried to brush it off in our previous interactions. But it was undeniable: Lee was interesting. Deeply so.

His eyes widened briefly in recognition. He gave me a half wave with the bag of Doritos.

My arms were full, but I lifted my shoulders in response.

He came over. "Need a hand?"

"I'm good. Thanks, though."

He nodded toward my heap of snacks. "You must be really into Oreos."

"They're for my fish," I replied unthinkingly.

"Really?"

"No, they're probably deadly to marine life. I don't have a fish. I don't know why I said that."

His expression was part bewilderment, part amusement. "Fair enough." A pause followed, in which we probably each wondered why the other was at the convenience store late on a Tuesday evening, seemingly purchasing the world's saddest dinner. "How are you?"

"Great. How could someone with this many Oreos *not* be great?" I gestured to his energy drinks. "Decided against the HYPER BLITZ?"

"I heard it's already been banned in ten states."

"For good reason. I barely made it out alive."

There was more genuine concern in Lee's expression than I expected.

"Kidding, obviously. You really take your role protecting the public seriously, huh?"

He didn't reply, just considered me for a moment.

"Anyway." I held up my Oreos. "I better pay for these now, or they'll be leaving in my stomach." I started toward the checkout counter. Lee followed.

"Do you tend to snack while you shop?" he asked.

I looked over my shoulder at him, my eyes wide. "Oh, never. That would be a crime."

He shook his head, and as I got in line, I could see his smile in the security-cam monitor hanging behind the register.

I paid first. And then lingered, even though I probably should've just said goodbye and headed home to eat my Oreos. But Lee's stuff rang up quickly, and then we were exiting the store together, and there was still the question that I really wanted to ask, but not in the middle of the snack aisle, with half a dozen rows of Pringles cans staring back at me: "Any updates on Molly?"

"I'm afraid not."

I couldn't help but think of Brady Pierce's sister. Her insistence that Brady was innocent. Molly had thought so too. If the cops hadn't investigated Piper's death properly—if they had missed something critical, and her true killer was still out there—what if they were doing the same thing with Molly now? Only looking at things on the surface and missing important details?

"You followed up with her manager and her agent, right?" I asked. "About the argument they had with Molly the day she died?"

Lee cast a look around, as if a crowd might materialize from thin air to listen in, before answering: "Yes. According to them both, it was just a conversation about film promo that got a little intense. It sounded like Molly's expectations didn't match theirs. That's all."

"Did Cal really have an angiogram later that day?"

"How do you know about that?"

"Did he?"

Lee nodded begrudgingly. "He did."

"And Molly's agent?"

"Damon Maxwell was at the press event with Molly that afternoon. Molly's assistant took her home afterward, and Maxwell went to dinner at Nobu. Look, Rachel—"

I couldn't help but press on. "What about the tox screen? Did you get the results back?"

Lee let out a breath. "The first screen was inconclusive, so they're doing a more extensive panel. I told you, these things take time. I know it's frustrating. And I know it's tempting to . . ." He hesitated. "To want this to be something other than what it appears to be. But—"

"Don't tell me it's cut-and-dried or whatever."

"I just know how difficult it can be to—"

"Got it. Your concern is noted." I had no reason to be short with him. But I felt suddenly exhausted. I was probably vitamin deficient. Maybe Anton was right about the scurvy.

"Did you walk here?" Lee asked.

"I did." I tried to force brightness into my voice. "I'm nothing without my fresh evening air. It's even more addictive than the thrill of live television."

There was that smile again, just a flash of it.

"I walked too," he said.

"Since we'll be heading in the same direction, why don't you take this side of the street and I'll take that side?"

"Or we could walk together."

I clutched my bag of snacks to my chest. "Without a chaperone? I don't know about that. What will the society matrons say when you take your barouche out in Regent's Park tomorrow?"

"I don't—"

I wasn't sure why he was still standing here with me. I was annoying even myself at this point. "We can walk together, sure. Good thing my place is close—you won't be stuck with me for long."

"It wouldn't be a hardship." His eyes shone in the fluorescent light spilling through the store windows. *Deeply interesting*, I remembered, and then tried to forget.

It was quiet as we passed the gas pumps and headed to the sidewalk, but then I couldn't help myself: "Did you work on the Piper Standish case?"

Lee's brow furrowed. "No. High-profile crimes like that are handled by a different division."

"Molly's death wasn't considered high-profile?"

"It was, but the situation was different. It wasn't exactly—"

"A crime," I said. "Right."

"Look . . . I want to reassure you, we're doing everything we can to get a complete understanding of what happened to Molly. And not that I'm saying I'm some genius investigator, but I do pride myself on being thorough."

"Even when the caseload is only getting bigger?" I said, thinking of our conversation on the phone last night. "Even when there's pressure to wrap things up?"

Lee's expression was serious. "Yes. Even then." A pause. "I just want you to know we're doing right by your friend."

The rest of our walk passed in silence. When we slowed to a stop in front of Palm Vista, I turned to look up at Lee.

"I'd like to believe it," I said. "That you're all doing right by Molly."

"But you don't?"

"I just . . . don't think the situation is what it seems."

His response was gentle: "You don't think it, or you don't *want* to think it?"

I could tell him everything. I could take him up to Richard's apartment and show him the murder board and everything we'd found out. But . . . I already knew that everything we had found so far was circumstantial. We needed something conclusive, something concrete.

So all I said was, "Don't patronize me, okay?"

His eyes widened. "That's not—that was not my intent."

I could tell that was the truth. Just like I could tell that Lee really did believe that the police were doing right by Molly.

I shook my head. "No, it's me. It's probably the vitamins. Or the lack thereof. Not that I have scurvy, but I also can't say I don't *not* have scurvy. Schrödinger's vitamin deficiency. I should get inside. Have a good dinner, or whatever it is you call a meal consisting of"—I waved a hand at his chips and energy drinks—"all that."

"Rachel—"

There was something about the way he said my name that made me feel like I might go crazy.

"Good night, Lee."

I headed off.

As I closed the door to my apartment, I caught sight of him still out on the street, waiting to see that I had gotten inside.

Excerpt from NUCLEAR NUCLEUS, pg. 57

TAWNY runs after REX.

TAWNY

I don't understand, Rex. I love you. And I think deep down you might love me too. Why can't we be together?

REX

You've got it all wrong, Tawny. I don't know the definition of the word love.

TAWNY

Well, Webster's dictionary says—

SFX: A distant explosion.

SFX: REX's cell phone rings.

REX

I'm a little busy right now, Tawny.

TAWNY

But Rex!

REX flips open his cell phone to answer the call as he walks away.

THE VOICE

Just keep walking.

REX

I can't help but feel a little sorry for the girl.

THE VOICE

You're making the right choice. It'll be better for her in the end.

REX

Maybe I could settle down one day. Become a family man.

THE VOICE

Maybe you should focus on saving the world first.

33

If my apartment was a reflection of my mental state, then it was pretty obvious that I wasn't at my best at the moment. After I finished my snacks from the gas station that evening and actually sat for a moment and took in my surroundings, it was all too clear: the place was a wreck.

Laundry seemed like the best place to start, because piling everything up in the hamper would effect at least some kind of visual change. But then I actually had to go do the laundry, which was how I found myself throwing open the door to Palm Vista's laundry room.

It was more of a glorified closet, just big enough to fit two washing machines and two dryers, both coin operated. I was typically a fan of late-night laundry, so the room was almost always empty when I visited.

Not tonight, though—I was greeted by the sight of Elena loading clothes into one of the washers. She looked up when I came in, lugging my overstuffed hamper behind me.

"Rachel, hi," she said brightly. "Thought I'd be the only person here this time of night."

"So did I," I replied. "Mind if I grab that one?" I pointed to the unoccupied washing machine.

"Oh, go for it. I'm not one of those monsters who claim both washers at once." She stuffed a few more clothes into her machine and then uncapped a bottle of laundry soap. "Hey, Jaz told me about the big revelation today—the guru's career swap. As a medical professional, I just have to say, I can't believe a film called *Endoscope of Terror* actually got made."

"Makes you wonder what kind of titles they pitched and discarded."

"*Comprehensive Metabolic Panel of Doom*," Elena said.

"*MRI Know What You Did Last Summer*," I replied, and she grinned.

"Nice."

As I began feeding quarters into the machine, I thought about my meeting with Vivian tomorrow. How did Vivian go from being Shawna White, B-movie extra, to Vivian Grayson, lifestyle guru? Did Molly know that Vivian wasn't who she said she was?

"Thanks for chatting with Jaz today," Elena said suddenly.

I looked over at her. She had shut the lid of her machine.

"She really seemed to enjoy talking with you," she continued.

"She's a great kid."

Elena just smiled, some unspoken amusement in her eyes.

"What?"

"Sorry," she replied. "You just said that like someone twice your age. You're pretty young yourself."

I tried to gauge Elena's age. It was hard to say—her skin was incredible. How someone could frequently work nights and stay looking so hydrated and poreless, I just couldn't comprehend. Maybe I should ask for pointers.

"I don't feel that young," I said. I didn't point out that Jaz had implied earlier that I qualified as "old people."

"I get that. I was about your age when I had Jaz, and it wasn't long after that her dad passed. Made me feel like I aged a decade or two in the blink of an eye."

"How did you—" I began, but then I changed my mind.

Elena just nodded, her gaze open and encouraging. "Go ahead, it's okay."

"How did you deal with it? With the loss?"

"Oh, not well, at first. But I was lucky. I had my family's support—my mom, my sister. And I had Jaz. She didn't know what was going on. She needed her mama to be healthy and present and to love and care for her. So I focused on that. Having that purpose helped me move forward."

"I don't know what my purpose is," I said.

It was too honest. It was more than I usually let myself say.

"Not that it's the same," I added quickly, staring into the depths of the washing machine. "I know that it's not—"

"Hey."

I looked back at Elena. She had lovely brown eyes. They were warm, like Lee's.

"You're allowed to feel your feelings," she said. "And you're allowed to not know. Having that purpose helped me. Maybe figuring yours out is what will help you."

I nodded.

"You should come by for dinner sometime," she continued. "I know Jaz would love that. I think I have a couple nights off next week."

"That would be great," I said, and I meant it.

"We could make it a movie night. Or a TV night. How do you feel about the *Housewives* franchise?"

"No significant opinions."

"Then we can help you form some," she said, lifting her empty laundry bag. "You know, I ended up watching a few episodes of that show Richard worked on, *CSLA*?" She leaned in conspiratorially. "Just between you and me, I thought it was kind of awful."

"I heard it really went downhill after Richard left."

"Is that so?" She considered that for a moment. "He's a funny guy, isn't he? Not that I think he's always intentionally *trying* to be funny, but still."

"That can be its own kind of charm," I said.

She smiled. "It definitely can."

★ MAY 2008 ★

AFTER ALESSANDRA DELGADO'S PREGNANCY ANNOUNCEMENT NETTED ME another *Icon* cover story, things at work really started to snowball. Publicists began reaching out to me, I was getting invites to events, and in our weekly pitch meetings Irina had more than once turned to me and said, "Rachel, how about you take this one?"

Molly's schedule had filled up too. We hadn't hung out in a week or so when I got a text from her: We need to catch up and celebrate.

I thought we might go to a club or a new restaurant, but to my surprise she took me back to the beachside taco truck that we had visited the first day we hung out.

"What are we celebrating?" I asked.

"Rachel West, *Icon*'s hottest new entertainment reporter," Molly replied, raising a can of Diet Coke in my direction.

I knocked my own can against hers. "Thank you. Seriously. I couldn't have done it without you."

"Maybe you could've," she said with a wink, "but not nearly as fast. You're booked and busy."

"So are you."

She nodded but didn't reply.

"What have you been up to?" I asked.

"Sort of a side project," she said. "Just . . . something I've been looking into."

"That's exciting. What is it?"

"I can't really talk about it yet." She smiled. The rote one. "I'll let you know how it goes, though."

After we ate, we went for a walk on the beach, tracing our way along the shoreline in contented silence. Every so often, Molly bent down to pick up a shell or small rock, and then slipped it into the pocket of her skirt.

"You want to know something?" she said eventually. She didn't wait for me to answer. "If I weren't me—like, if I were just a person—I would want to be you."

"Just a person," I mused. "If you're not a person now, then what are you?"

"An object." She said it matter-of-factly. "A product. Available for public consumption." She paused to pick up another shell. "I'm Sour Cream and Onion Pringles."

"Once you pop, you can't stop," I said, and Molly smiled. The real one.

"Rachel, I have some bad news."

"What?"

"I think you're my best friend."

"Why is that bad news?"

"It's not bad for me. It's bad for you."

"Why?"

"Sour Cream and Onion Pringles are horrible for your health."

"But there's a reason why they're popular. I actually read an article about how foods like that are developed. They're designed to dissolve rapidly in your mouth—something about it makes people want to eat more. So they're basically scientifically engineered to be wanted."

She smiled again, and maybe that was what encouraged me to go on: "I think you might be my best friend too."

"Good. It sucks when it's one-sided." A pause. "I always had trouble making friends growing up."

"That surprises me."

"No, it's true. Everyone wants to know the weird TV kid, but no one wants to *know* her, not for real." She let out a breath of laughter. "It's such a cliché. Growing up, I had the best of everything money could get. The newest clothes, the coolest hairstyles, the best doctors and dentists and tutors. If I chipped a nail or coughed or got a zit, ten people would come running. I know. Poor little rich girl, right?"

"It doesn't mean things can't be hard," I said, looking out at the water. "They're just hard for different reasons."

Molly moved back from the shoreline a little, out of the reach of the water, and sat down in the sand. "You said your brother was sick when you were a kid."

I took a seat next to her. "Yeah. He was diagnosed with leukemia when he was thirteen. I was ten."

I didn't continue, and she didn't prompt me to. She didn't tilt her head in consideration or pity or whatever. We just sat, watching as the waves broke gently against the shore.

"It was hard," I said finally, which, as it always did, felt like a pathetic understatement—nothing close to the excruciating reality of it. "He had to do radiation and chemo. He had a tough time with it. It put a lot of strain on my parents, and my little sister was still really young at the time." I picked up a nearby stone and tossed it in the direction of the water. It didn't quite make it. "He went into remission after a year."

Relief flashed across Molly's face. I hated to chase it away with what I was about to say, but I said it anyway.

"He was fine for a while. But when he was sixteen, he passed away."

"Is that why you wanted to be a doctor?"

"Yes."

"Like a guy who becomes a CIA hit man to catch the kingpin who killed his fiancée," Molly said, prizing a smile out of me in spite of myself. "You were going to kill cancer."

"I was going to help people. I thought. But . . ."

"But . . ."

I didn't think I could do it—lay it all bare for Molly Byrne. Describe it—what happened that night during med school—in full. Even well over a year later, I didn't think I was strong enough. "I realized that it wasn't—that I just wasn't . . . suited for it. For that type of job. I'm not the kind of person who's capable of helping other people. I can't even help myself."

"So you switched careers."

"I thought I'd be selfish. That I'd just try to be happy, maybe. Medicine always felt like . . . trying to shove a square peg into a round hole, you know? So I thought about what made me happy when I was a kid."

"The magazines."

"Yeah." It was the sound of the waves, maybe. Or the sunlight, perfectly calibrated to the golden hour. It lit Molly—her face, her hair, her eyebrows and eyelashes—in radiant gold. "You know what, though?"

"What?"

"Sometimes I wonder . . ." I shook my head. "I loved the magazines because they were what I read when Sam was sick. They were what made me happy back then, what . . . took me away from everything that was going on. But . . . what would I have liked if he had never been sick? If none of that had ever happened? I wouldn't have tried to be a doctor, and I probably wouldn't have tried to be a reporter either. So what would I have done? What would I even like? Who would I be if that hadn't happened?" I swallowed. "Do you ever think about stuff like that?"

"I think everyone on earth thinks about stuff like that." Molly's eyes turned to the water. "What if I hadn't gone to that first audition? What if I hadn't worked with Cal, or signed with Damon's agency? What if I hadn't made this choice or that choice, what if I wore the black dress instead of the white one, what if I turned left instead of right, what would my life be like? Would it be better? Worse? Would I be happy? Am I happy now?" A beat. "You're not alone in that kind of thinking. Not even a little bit."

It was quiet. And then Molly turned and looked at me with the full strength of that clear blue gaze.

"Rachel, if you had the chance to figure out who you would be without all that, would you take it?"

"I mean, it's pretty impossible without a time machine, but—"

"Just answer the question."

"I would," I said. "Definitely."

Molly considered me for a long moment. Then she got to her feet and extended a hand toward me. When I stood, she didn't drop my hand. Instead, she leaned forward and pressed a kiss to my cheek.

"Thank you," she said.

"For what?"

She just smiled. It wasn't the dazzling, genuine smile, nor was it her public smile, the one that she slipped on in social situations. It was a small, private smile.

She released my hand and moved away. "Let's keep walking."

34

I returned to Perihelion Ranch alone.

I had considered asking Casper to join me, but ultimately I held back. I felt like I might get more from Vivian if it was one-on-one.

She met me in the lobby once again, and this time she took me on a tour through the ranch's facilities—the wellness spa, the infinity pool, the yoga pavilion. It was all beautiful, expensive, consciously Zen.

We returned to Vivian's office at the end of the tour, and Vivian took a seat across from me in one of the armchairs upholstered in pristine white fabric.

"Are there any questions I can answer for you, Rachel? Anything more you'd like to know about the facilities or our philosophies here at Perihelion?"

"Actually, I was hoping I could talk to you more about . . . you." My heartbeat quickened. It was time for Jaz's "good old-fashioned ambush."

One of Vivian's impeccably shaped eyebrows arched. "What about me?"

I spoke carefully. "I have a friend who's a total movie buff. She loves horror movies in particular. She found this one from a while back, *Endoscope of Terror*. Have you heard of it?"

Vivian didn't speak for a moment. Her face didn't change, but something flashed in her eyes. Eventually she said, "I thought I had purchased and destroyed every existing copy of *Endoscope of Terror*, but clearly one got past me."

I was too surprised to remember my next question. I'd figured I'd have to do some serious maneuvering to get Vivian to admit her past. But she just met my gaze, her expression placid.

"So you were an actor?" I asked.

"A failed one, sure," she replied. "I was also a waitress, a cashier, a magazine salesgirl. I tried to model. Print at first, but that went nowhere. I tried getting gigs at car shows, but I was told my hand gestures were 'unconvincing.' I did a stint as an audience plant for infomercials. I was also an addict. At some point, that eclipsed everything else."

I thought of young Vivian—Shawna White—as she appeared in *Endoscope of Terror*, and tried to reconcile her with the woman sitting in front of me. "How did you become . . ." I waved a hand to encompass the room—the white furniture, the crystals, the bundles of sage.

"I hit rock bottom. I realized that something had to change or . . . it would all be over. It was a slow, terrible, painstaking process. But I rebuilt myself from the ground up."

"Did you really travel like you said? The ashram, the monks?"

She looked surprised. "Of course. After I got back on track and started working again—an office job, something stable—I saved every penny I could, and then I took a trip that changed my worldview completely. When I came back, I knew exactly what I wanted to do with my life."

"Did Molly know? About your past?"

Vivian inclined her head. "There are people who come to me for a quick fix. An herb they can sprinkle on their quinoa that will make them hate their job less, or a sliver of citrine that will keep them from sabotaging their relationships. They don't want introspection. They want a shortcut. So I give it to them. Why not?" She paused. "Do you know what *perihelion* means?"

"It's the point at which a planet is closest to the sun."

"Yes. Then there are people, like Molly, who come to me and that's where they are. They're as close to the sun as they can possibly get, and if they get any closer"—she snapped her fingers—"they'll burn up. I know because I've been there. The alcohol, the drugs, the stupid decisions, the even worse company . . . I lived it. And I came back from it. Those are the people I tell my real story to, because they deserve to know that you *can* come back from it. That it's just one point in your orbit." She reached down and moved one of the crystals on the dish in front of her. She seemed satisfied with its new position. "I told Molly everything. She said it—" Another pause. "She said it made her respect me more, knowing that I had been there too. Of course, every person's journey is different. I was never going to become a megastar. That was part of my issue. Molly became that star. That was part of hers."

It was quiet.

"Molly came here the day she died," I said.

"Yes."

"And then . . . you sent her a fruit basket."

She looked at me curiously for a beat before answering, "Yes."

"I saw it. At Molly's house. I was there that night. There was a card. You were apologizing for something."

Vivian dipped her head and, for the third time, said simply, "Yes."

"Was it . . ." I knew what Dax had told us, but I had to confirm it for myself. "Was it because of Dax? Were the two of you . . . together?"

Surprise was obvious in Vivian's expression. "*Dax* and I? Certainly not."

"But when we visited before . . . I saw you with him. In the courtyard."

Vivian's brows drew together. "Dax did come by that day . . . We both feel Molly's loss deeply, so I imagine you saw us in a moment of shared grief. There's of course a strict policy in place at Perihelion about romantic relationships with clients. And even if there weren't, and putting aside the obvious issues of getting involved with Molly's former paramour . . ." Her lips twitched with something like amusement. "Well, I can't say Dax Van Sant is particularly my type. I'm happy to guide him on his spiritual journey. But I don't want to be on that journey myself."

"Then why did you send Molly the basket? What were you apologizing for?"

Vivian didn't respond right away.

"Molly came to me for guidance that day," she said eventually. "I gave her my thoughts. My advice. But I think . . . no, looking back on it, I *know* . . . my advice was wrong."

"What did she want help with?"

"She had discovered something. She wouldn't tell me what it was, but she seemed to think that it could jeopardize . . . everything. Everything that she had worked toward. But she knew she had to reveal the truth. She asked me how she could be at peace with that." Vivian paused. "I told her that her journey was hers alone. Anything else was just a distraction. So if this was a distraction, she should cast it aside, continue for herself, be her most authentic self. She got upset. She said it was bigger than her, and if what she was supposed to be was authentic, then was there anything more authentic than the truth?"

It sounded just like Molly. I swallowed, my throat suddenly tight.

"She was still so upset when she left," Vivian continued. "And I thought sending over a damn fruit basket would smooth things over, when really what I should've done in the first place was support her. I should've told her that she should share the burden, whatever it was. But I didn't. And then she . . ." Vivian's eyes shone with tears. "Obviously, I failed her. I failed her completely."

I realized it all at once—Vivian still thought, like everyone else, that Molly had overdosed.

I decided in that moment not to tell her about my suspicions. I would wait until I could reveal the truth, the whole and authentic truth, just like Molly had intended to do.

Vivian looked away, blinked several times, cleared her throat. Then she said, "I'll never forget what I learned from her. I'll never make that mistake again."

35

I met Casper at a bar near Palm Vista that night to catch him up on my talk with Vivian.

Much to Casper's chagrin, the bartender carded him when he ordered a beer. Casper huffed as he quickly pulled a license out of his wallet and slid it across the counter to the bartender, face down.

"Bad picture?" I asked, one eyebrow raised.

His expression turned sheepish. "Let's just say I've gone through some hair evolutions." The bartender briefly inspected the ID and then, pacified, handed it back. Casper hurriedly returned it to his wallet. "Why didn't he card you too?" he muttered as the bartender grabbed our drinks.

"I'm not offended. It's been a very long week."

The bartender brought us each a beer. I rested my elbows against the bar top, clasped both hands around the bottle. The coldness was grounding as I told Casper about the conversation with Vivian.

"I think Molly definitely figured it out," I said when I'd

reached the end of my account. "Who killed Piper. She went to Vivian for advice that day. But Vivian didn't know what it was that Molly was really asking."

Casper took a pull from his own beer. "Where do we go from here?"

"I don't know yet." A ringtone sounded from my purse. I pulled out my phone and glanced at the screen. Then I set the ringer to vibrate, put the phone on the bar, and turned back to Casper.

"Don't you want to get that?" he asked.

I shook my head. "It's my parents. I'll call them later."

"Are you close with your family?"

"Close enough," I said, and he gave me a look. "What?"

"Honestly," he replied, "out of everyone we've talked to so far, you're the most evasive one."

"I'm not *evasive*."

He looked doubtful. "Do your folks know what's been going on here? With Molly and your job and everything?"

"They know a little bit." But even that was a stretch. They knew that I had known Molly, and they knew she had passed away, but that was pretty much the extent of it. They had no idea how much of a role she had played in my getting promoted, or how much time we'd spent together in the months I had known her. To them, she was just an extension of the "glitzy Hollywood life" I was attempting to live, the pipe dream I was trying to make a reality against everyone else's better judgment.

"They're not particularly interested in what I do, to be honest," I said. "I didn't exactly follow the path they hoped I would. They think this"—I waved a hand, encompassing the room, but really I meant all of it: *Icon*, writing, LA, the whole thing—"is just me trying to 'find myself' or whatever. And eventually I'll come to my senses and move back home and do something . . . normal."

"Don't you want to make a difference?" my mom had asked the last time we talked. It was after my promotion but before Molly's death. "Do meaningful work?"

"My work is meaningful to me, Mom."

"Really, Rachel? Writing articles about daytime TV stars and their botched liposuction—that's meaningful to you?"

"They'd be thrilled if I went back to school," I told Casper. "Finished my MD. Got a job. Settled down. They'd be over the moon."

I thought about the fantasy life I had crafted for Lee the night we had dinner at Sawasdee: the fiancée, the golden retriever, the house, the honeymoon. It was pretty much the same thing my folks would want for me, so long as the white coat came along with it.

"So they were all in on you being a doctor," Casper said.

"Yeah. And I was all in on it too, at some point. Or at least I thought I was."

"What happened?"

I shifted the bottle around in my hands. "You know, I still can't believe you're old enough to drink."

"We're practically the same age," he said, and repeated, "What happened?"

Those familiar black fingers of panic flickered at the edges of my vision. I took a sip of beer to fend them off, to anchor myself in the present. I glanced over at Casper again. He had the decency to look away.

In profile, his nose had a slight bump on the bridge. It was cute. I thought about what Jaz had said—the scrappy-Disney-dog thing. And then I thought about what he had just said to me: *Honestly, out of everyone we've talked to so far, you're the most evasive one.*

He could just as easily have been talking about himself. Jaz was definitely right on that point: *What do we know about him outside of being a pap, wanting to find Molly's killer, and committing to an all-black aesthetic?*

"What about you?" I asked.

"What about me?"

"You said you moved back to LA after you dropped out of school. What happened there?"

"Nothing particularly significant," he said with a shrug. "I was trying to study photography. I flunked out, on account of not taking it seriously. I didn't want to go crawling back to my parents after I had made a huge thing about studying photography, so I came here instead."

"And got your hand crushed trying to get a picture of Molly Byrne."

One corner of his mouth lifted. "Exactly."

I had looked up the photos after Casper told me the story of him and Molly and their trip to McDonald's. The images popped up right away, a series of snaps of Molly standing at the counter in full club wear: a black-and-white satin bomber jacket hanging off her shoulders, a mini baby blue slip dress underneath. She cast a mischievous look back at the camera as an awestruck cashier extended a McFlurry toward her. *Isn't this a trip?* Molly's eyes seemed to say. *Isn't this just the life?* She had a way of staring down a lens that made you feel as if she was looking at *you* specifically. As if, despite how magnificently glamorous she seemed, she was your friend. Someone you could know. Maybe even someone you could be like, if you tried hard enough.

I knew how the full force of Molly's gaze felt in real life. And Casper knew it too—from behind the lens of a camera.

"Why be a paparazzo, though?" I asked, and he let out a breath of laughter.

"You mean, why not go into wedding photography, or pet portraits, or get a job at a Sears Portrait Studio?"

"Well, yeah. There are advantages to those things, aren't there? Everyone who visits the Sears Portrait Studio goes there to get their photos taken willingly."

"Oh, I beg to differ. I'm positive there are some toddlers who've been brought there against their will."

"You know what I mean, though."

"It's great in theory," Casper said after a moment's thought. "Doing something for the purity of it. Making a completely honest living. But you were at *Icon*. You know how it is. Sometimes you have to do stuff you don't want to do to get to the stuff you do want to do. And I make a hell of a lot more money doing this than I would at Sears."

"But what do you actually want to do? You said you didn't know. That it was Future Casper's problem."

He smiled. "I guess what I want right now is to have enough money to keep not knowing."

Suddenly, my phone buzzed again.

"One second."

I picked it up, ready to silence another call from home. But the buzzing persisted as I stared at the name emblazoned across the screen, completely and entirely unable to make sense of it:

MOLLY BYRNE

Excerpt from NUCLEAR NUCLEUS, pg. 89

REX

You're telling me I'm going to die?

THE VOICE

Everyone dies, Rex. Everyone who has ever taken a breath in this life takes a last one.

REX

But in the future—

THE VOICE

I'm telling you to live now. Live as hard as you can, as much as you can, because you never know when it will all come to an end.

REX

But you know how. And when. You know everything—

THE VOICE

Goodbye, Rex.

REX

Wait! Hello? Hello!

REX stares down at the phone as alarms sound and Air Force One enters a nosedive. The call has ended.

36

"Hello?"

I stood on the sidewalk outside the bar. I had beelined out there and accepted the call with shaky hands.

There was loud, pulsing music on the other end of the line.

"Hello?" I repeated urgently.

"You," a female voice replied.

For one blistering moment, my heart leapt to my throat. It was Molly's voice. It was her. And in that moment, stupid, blind relief coursed through me. *This whole thing was just a mix-up. She didn't really die. She's not really gone. I don't know how, but it's all just been a huge, colossal mistake—*

But then she continued. "First on the fucking speed dial. Of course you are."

Her words were slightly slurred. And there was a rasp to her voice, a burr to it that had never been there before.

All at once, I realized: it wasn't Molly. Of course it wasn't.

"Amy," I said.

"Try not to sound so disappointed."

The pulsing beats in the background faded slightly, as if Amy had moved from indoors to outdoors too. She was definitely drunk. Her voice was far looser than it had been in our previous encounters.

"What's going on? Why are you calling me from Molly's phone?"

"'If Molly Byrne was lightning in a bottle, then Amy Byrne . . .'" Her voice hitched. "'Amy Byrne is static electricity in a Capri-Sun pouch.' That's what people think. That's what they think I am. Molly is Oreo. I'm Hydrox. Molly's Gucci. I'm . . . fucking . . . Kmart. Can you even imagine what that's like? To be the shitty off-brand version of something people actually want?"

"Where are you?"

"Why does it matter?"

"Why did you call me?"

"I wanted to see—just wanted to know—who she was talking to . . . that day." Her words were becoming more slurred. "I just . . . wondered . . ."

"Amy, are you okay?"

"Just . . . had to see . . ." Her voice grew weak.

"Amy?"

The line went dead.

WWW.CELEBRITEASE.COM

June 26, 2008
03:32 AM PST

Another day, another twist in the Molly Byrne saga:

We here at the Tease take no joy in reporting that MB's lil sis Amy Byrne was rushed to Cedars-Sinai late last night. According to our sources, Amy collapsed while out on the town in Hollywood. It's uncertain at this time whether the Budget Byrne suffered from overindulgence at the club or whether something more sinister is at play (Drugs? Health issues? A chronic case of need-for-attention-itis?).

At the time of this posting, Amy is said to be in stable condition, but no other details regarding her collapse have been released.

What's next for the besieged Byrnes? If you ask us, they should hire a priest for an exorcism, kill a chicken in the backyard, or maybe leave town for good. This is just too much bad juju for one family tree.

37

I tried calling Amy back multiple times, but she didn't answer. Eventually the calls went straight to voicemail.

"I'll reach out to some contacts," Casper said before we parted ways at the bar. "See if anyone's spotted Amy out tonight. If I hear anything, I'll definitely let you know."

I slept fitfully that night. I felt suspended in that moment of hearing Molly's voice and then realizing it was actually Amy's voice. The momentary relief followed by crushing disappointment, followed by some kind of . . . embarrassment, because of course Molly was gone. Of course she was. And then the grief of knowing I would never talk to her on the phone again. I would never hear her voice on the other end of the line.

I didn't cry, not even in my dreams. But I wanted to, profoundly.

When I woke up the next morning, I had several missed calls and a text from Casper:

Amy at hospital, check online

A brief internet search brought up headlines that ran the gamut from the calm and clinical (ACTRESS AMY BYRNE ADMITTED TO HOSPITAL FOLLOWING HEALTH ISSUE AT NIGHTCLUB) to the sensational and downright fictional (MOLLY BYRNE'S GRIEF-STRICKEN SISTER RUSHED TO ER AFTER HARROWING NIGHTCLUB COLLAPSE—DRUGS AND ALCOHOL TO BLAME?).

I picked up my phone to call Casper just as it buzzed with an incoming call.

It was Lee.

"Hello?"

"I'm sorry, I know it's early, but—"

The chances that he was calling just to hear the sound of my voice seemed extremely minimal. "What is it? What's going on?"

"Amy Byrne called me," Lee said. "She's asking to see you."

It took me a moment to process this, and then I was standing and launching into a frenzied search for my wallet and keys. "Is she okay?"

"Yes."

"Why did she call you?" I located my keys under a stack of unopened mail. "Did you give her a business card with your personal phone number handwritten on the back of it?"

"I—yes."

"You *do* do that for everyone! Remind me to ask you later if you dedicate time to doing them all at once or if you write them out on an as-needed basis."

"That's not—"

"What's her room number? Are you there now?" I grabbed my wallet and slipped on a ragged pair of flats. "You know, it would be more expedient just to get it printed on the backs of the cards when you order them, but then you'd lose that personal touch, wouldn't you?"

"Slow down. Yes, I'm here now, with Ruiz." Lee gave me Amy's room info. "Drive safely."

"I was planning to drive extremely recklessly, but you know what? I'll reconsider."

"Rachel."

"I'll be there soon. No traffic stunts, I promise. Though it would be great if you could arrange a motorcade."

Lee let out something that I could describe only as a combined laugh and long-suffering sigh.

"Is that a no on the motorcade, then?"

"Just drive safely," he said.

"Got it. See you soon."

I called Casper after hanging up with Lee, and we met up in the parking lot at the hospital. Lee and Ruiz were waiting outside Amy's room when Casper and I arrived. Ruiz was leaning against the wall, her arms folded. She looked every bit as put together as she had the first time I met her. Lee straightened up as we approached. He eyed Casper for just a moment before looking at me.

"Thanks for coming," he said. "Amy insisted. She said she wants to talk to someone she trusts."

"And you're sure she meant me?"

"It's not Ruiz and me, that's for sure. According to Amy, we're 'fucking this whole thing up royally.'"

"That's not all she said," Ruiz muttered, examining her nails.

"Right. She thinks her collapse was due to—"

"I don't mean that part, I mean the funny part."

Lee colored slightly. "I don't see how that's relevant."

One of Ruiz's perfect eyebrows lifted. "She said you're as stupid as you are hot. Should that not go into the write-up?"

"There's not going to be a write-up," Lee replied. "And she also said your eyebrows are uneven."

Ruiz pushed off of the wall. "Yes, obviously the girl's judgment is clouded."

"What exactly happened last night?" Casper asked, in that somewhat annoyed tone he tended to get when people were straying from the Matter at Hand. "Why is Amy here?"

"I'm sorry, have we met?" Lee asked.

"This is Casper," I explained, and then quickly added, "my colleague," before Casper could jump in with some other unlikely identity. He might declare himself to be my husband or my stepbrother or my chauffeur—who knew at this point? "He knows Amy too. Is she okay?"

Lee nodded. "She's stable. Blood work is fine. She said she hadn't eaten at all yesterday, so there's a strong likelihood she passed out because of that. But . . ."

"But what?"

"She doesn't think that's the case," Lee said. "She thinks she was poisoned."

Casper and I shared a look.

"So, what are you going to do about it?" Casper asked Lee.

Lee looked between us and then met my eyes, an unspoken question all too plain on his face: *Sorry, but who is this guy again?*

I didn't always agree with Casper's hatchet approach, but being direct seemed like the best move at this moment. "Yeah, what do you guys do next here?"

Lee shook his head. "There's not a lot we can do, I'm afraid. The docs could order a more extensive tox screen, but they don't really feel there's cause for that. Passing out at a nightclub is more often than not for exactly the reasons you'd think."

I thought of the inane Celebritease post about Amy that I read this morning: *overindulgence at the club.*

And then I thought about my conversation with Lee the other night: *I just don't think the situation is what it seems.*

"Yeah, but if she thinks she's been poisoned—" Casper began.

"With all due respect," Ruiz said, "people also think that their next-door neighbor is a serial killer, or that aliens are communicating with them through their microwave. We hear a lot of stuff that doesn't exactly warrant a full-blown investigation when a little common sense is applied."

"This isn't about *common sense*," Casper said fiercely. "You're not even—"

I cut in before he could continue. "Could I talk to you for a minute?" I asked Lee. "Alone?"

I ignored the frown Casper gave me as we headed away. Lee followed me a little ways down the hall, past the nurses' station, where several nurses were gathered around a computer monitor. One of them let out a sudden peal of laughter, and I had the distracted realization that they were watching an *SNL* Digital Short.

"You really aren't going to do anything?" I asked, looking up at Lee.

"Like I said, there's not a lot we can do. The hospital didn't call us in. Amy called me herself, and I came because Molly's case is still technically open. But frankly, it sounds like she hasn't been taking care of herself—understandable, considering what she's been going through—and that, combined with the clubbing—"

"I just don't understand how you're so quick to write it off."

"And you're so quick to assume that it's something catastrophic," he replied. "What's that saying? When you hear hoofbeats—"

"Yeah, no, I've heard that one before."

"Another quote you hate?"

"Why does it always have to be a horse? Statistically, there's got to be *some* instance when it's a zebra."

"Rachel—"

"It's fine," I said. "I'll talk to Amy. You guys can go." I wasn't in any position to dismiss them, but saying it felt good nonetheless. And it felt even better to push past Lee and start back down the hallway.

"Hey." Lee caught up with me and put a hand on my arm to stop me. I turned back, and for a moment we just looked at each other.

Then I dropped my eyes to where his hand was still loosely circling my wrist.

He withdrew it. "Sorry. I just—I know this is complicated."

"It seems pretty straightforward to me."

It was quiet. Except for the audio of another Digital Short playing softly from the computer speakers. We were right near the nurses' station now, and when I glanced over, all four nurses were staring at us, rapt, instead of at the screen. I tried to ignore them.

"You don't believe her," I said.

"I believe that she thinks something happened to her last night. I also believe that she's been through a terrible loss, and is under an incredible amount of stress, and, self-reportedly, is not eating or drinking as she should be."

When I looked back at Lee, his gaze was gentle but firm. Unyielding.

"I don't know what else you want me to say here," he said.

I couldn't define exactly what it was that I was feeling—whether I was upset or disappointed, or upset at being disappointed. "Say you'll take Amy seriously. That's what I want you to say. Say that you'll look beyond the surface and do your fucking due diligence."

Lee took a step closer to me. His voice softened. "I am truly sorry for what Amy's going through. And for what you're going through. But we've done due diligence. I know it's hard to—"

Anger flared in my chest. "You said you wondered if you were making things worse. Well, what if you are?"

"Rachel . . ."

"It's fine. I'm sure you're really busy, so let's just call it here."

"Call what?"

"This," I said, and then amended it: "This conversation." And then back again: "This."

What was *this*? There was no *this*. But Lee was looking at me as if there might be.

I felt like I might crumble under that gaze. So I turned and walked away.

38

When Casper and I entered Amy's room, she was in bed, looking pale against the sheets and startlingly young without makeup on. She looked up from her jewel-encrusted phone and glowered at me. "Took you long enough."

"What happened? Are you okay?"

The glower shifted seamlessly into a sneer. "As if you actually care."

Casper snorted. "Did you want us here just so you could be rude to us?"

"I wanted *her* here," Amy replied. "You showed up uninvited. As usual."

"Are you all right?" I tried again.

"No, I'm not fucking all right!" Amy snapped. "I got poisoned!"

"Tell us what happened," Casper said, more gently than I expected.

Amy glared at him for a moment, but then it was as if all the fight went out of her. She sank back against her pillows. "I don't even know. I just know that *those two* are useless." She waved a hand to indicate the door, and presumably Lee and Ruiz beyond it, though they were probably now on their way out of the hospital. "Not to mention condescending as fuck." I guess she managed to get a little bit of the fight back, because she continued: "They don't believe me! The doctors didn't believe me either—they weren't even going to call the police at all! I had to call them myself, and a whole hell of a lot of good that did me!"

Casper opened his mouth to speak, but I put a hand up to stop him.

"Walk us through last night," I said. "Please. We'll listen."

Amy took a breath. "I was at the club and everything was fine," she began slowly. "But then, all of a sudden, I started feeling sick. I called you and went outside, and then . . . I guess I just collapsed."

"Sick how?" I asked.

"Headache. A bad one, like a migraine. And just kind of . . . dizzy and gross."

"Do you think someone slipped you something?"

"I didn't drink anything." I must've looked skeptical—she hadn't exactly sounded sober on the phone last night—so she continued. "Don't look at me like those cops did. I didn't 'accidentally' take something. I didn't drink something and forget that I drank it. I'm dieting for a shoot. I was fasting the entire day. Literally."

"Where were you before you went to the club?" I asked.

She looked away. "Molly's house."

"What were you doing there?"

"Just looking after the place. Someone has to." *This is her* home, *and this is her stuff.*

I thought of the phone call last night, of the absolutely jarring experience of seeing Molly's name on the caller ID. "And you found Molly's phone?"

Amy nodded. "I knew it would still be there. She used to . . ." Her expression suddenly crumpled, as if she were going to burst into tears, but she quickly got control of it. "She used to keep it in the bathroom at night, in a box of tampons. Fucking absurd, right? That Vivian Grayson woman told her the phone's *energy* or whatever would disrupt her sleep." Her eyes glistened. "I just wanted to see who she talked to that day. I just wanted to understand . . . what I *can't* understand . . ."

It was quiet for a moment. When I glanced over at Casper, his gaze was downturned.

"Anyway." Amy wiped at her face roughly. "I passed out at the club. They brought me here. And it wasn't what those fucking cops think it was. I wasn't just *tired*. It wasn't just *low blood sugar*. Something was wrong. It was *not normal*. Which means . . ." She swallowed. "Maybe your bullshit murder theory isn't as bullshit as I originally thought. If someone dosed me . . . then maybe they did the same thing to Molly. And if you're investigating, then . . . then I might as well just tell you what I know."

"What do you know?" Casper asked, but Amy didn't answer right away.

"You saw Molly the night she died," I said gently.

Amy hesitated, and then nodded.

"What happened?"

"We fought. But we fought all the time, so it's not like that was anything new."

"What did you fight about?"

Amy rolled her eyes. It reminded me, with a pang, of my little sister, Natalie. Amy was only a year or two older than her. "Whatever, it's not like I'm embarrassed about it. That's the whole point. We fought about my sex tape."

"Your—"

"Sex tape," Casper repeated, a little too loudly.

I glared at him, and then turned back to Amy. "Okay. What about it?"

"I want to release one and Molly was trying to stop me."

"You want to release one . . . on purpose?"

"Yeah. It's basically a launching pad these days—it can jump-start your entire career. And if they're getting leaked all the time anyway, why shouldn't I just leak one myself? Pretend it was an accident and reap the benefits."

"So you already have one," I said.

"What are you going to call it?" Casper asked. "*Byrne Notice*?"

"I've been brainstorming titles," Amy replied. "But that's not half bad."

"What did Molly say that night?" I prompted. Someone had to get us back on track.

Amy ran one hand through her hair, and then said, somewhat begrudgingly, "She knew what I was planning, and she was trying to stop me. She even . . ."

"What?"

"It's so fucked-up. She even cut me out of her will."

"Because of the sex tape?"

"Because of her whole *thing*. That Vivian Grayson bullshit about *manifesting authenticity*. That's what set off the fight that night. She told me she cut me out because she wanted me to figure out who I was without her, without any of it. She was all, 'If you were born somewhere else, to other people, who would you be? What would you even want?'"

I blinked.

"I told her it was idiotic. Like, what's the actual point of thinking like that? I was born to who I was born to, and I am who I am, and I want what I want. And what I want is to be way more famous, and have more money, and more recognition, and more *everything*. What's so bad about that? Why can't I just be who I am? And why was she so fucking . . . unsatisfied with who she was? When she was the one who grew up getting everything? All the attention, all the jobs, all the fans. What *didn't* she have served up to her on a silver fucking platter? If she even knew what it was like to be me, if she knew what it was like to be *her* sister—" She cut herself off. I wondered if she remembered what she had said to me on the phone last night: *Molly is Oreo. I'm Hydrox.*

"Then she started going on about Piper, and I just had to—"

"Hold on—what about Piper?" Casper asked.

Amy shot him a disdainful look, but responded, "Well, that's where I got the idea for the tape. I mean, lots of people have them, but talking to Piper about hers gave me the idea—not that her situation was the same at all—"

"Wait." I couldn't believe what I was hearing. "*Piper* had a sex tape?"

"Yeah, but not on purpose. One of her exes recorded it without telling her. It was this whole thing. He never released it, but she told me that after they broke up, he was a real dick about deleting it. So, like I said—not the same situation, but still. It got me thinking."

"Who was the ex?" Casper asked.

"I don't know. She never said. She was seventeen when they started dating, and they had to keep it kind of low-key—maybe he was married or something. She just said he was a major mistake."

The wheels in my head were turning. "Were you there that night at Entity, for Piper's birthday?"

"Yeah, but I left early. Some asshole spilled a drink on me and it ruined my dress. God, you sound just like Molly. Why did she even care so much about Piper? It was classic Molly. Hung up on someone who's basically a stranger—and not to mention *dead*—rather than her own fucking sister." Amy's eyes suddenly shone again with tears. "And that's why my last ever conversation with her had to be another fucking fight. I mean, I guess it makes sense. Maintain the status quo or whatever." She drew a hand quickly across her eyes. "Yes, I know what *status quo* means," she added, in a way that reminded me of Molly so keenly that my chest ached.

I swallowed. "How did you leave it that night at Molly's?"

She shook her head. "I was so pissed off, I just left. That's it. I swear. But . . ."

"But what?"

"Someone was heading down her street when I left that night. I passed a car heading toward her house."

I frowned. Lee told me that no one else was at Molly's that night. That the security guard had confirmed it. "Did you notice anything about the car?"

"It was a Maserati. A red Maserati."

If he's not stealing shots from other paps or trying to photobomb, he's parking his douchebag Maserati sideways across three handicapped parking spaces.

"I know someone with that car," Amy continued. "I'm not saying it was him for sure, but, like, what are the odds? Who else would it be, in that car, that night, on Molly's street?"

"Who?" Casper asked, but I already knew.

"Dax," Amy said. "And that's not all. When I went through Molly's phone, he was the last person she called."

39

I wanted to make it work. I was still in love with her.

That's what Dax told us. Did he go to Molly's that night to try to reconcile with her? Did she reject him? Did she accuse him of killing Piper? Had he?

He was at Entity the night of Piper's death—he told us that himself. And if he was also at Molly's the night she died, then he stood at the intersection of a particularly incriminating Venn diagram.

"Seriously, though," I said as Casper and I made our way down the stairs to the first floor of the hospital. "Did the police even *bother* checking Molly's phone records?"

"Just because she called Dax doesn't necessarily mean he was there that night."

I couldn't help but flash on Lee. He clearly didn't believe Amy, but I did. "But Dax *was* there. Amy saw him heading toward Molly's house. What are the chances that another red Maserati just happened to be heading down Molly's street?"

"But Amy was at both places too," Casper pointed out, pausing in front of the stairwell exit. "She was at Piper's birthday party, and at Molly's that night."

"Why would Amy kill both of them, though? Maybe there's motive if she was fighting with Molly, but remember what Richard said—anger is a bludgeoning, not a poisoning. And what motive would she have for killing Piper?"

"What would Dax's motive be?" Casper countered.

I paused, thinking back through what Amy had told us. "Maybe he's Piper's sleazy ex. The one who recorded her."

"Now, that I could believe."

A cluster of photographers was waiting outside the hospital when Casper and I exited. A few of them turned their cameras in our direction.

"How's Amy?" the nearest, a woman with a short shock of red hair, called. "Rachel, are you two feuding?"

"No comment," Casper replied, and we made our way past the crowd—until Casper stopped abruptly and turned back. "You."

His eyes were fixed on a rangy man with a long ponytail.

It was Chrimbo. The very same Chrimbo who appeared on Molly's murder board.

"I've been trying to get ahold of you," Casper said.

Chrimbo shrugged. "Well, you've got me."

Chrimbo agreed to speak with us on condition of one venti iced mocha Frap with ten shots, extra whip, extra syrup, and chocolate shavings. Once that was procured, he was happy enough to sit across from us in one of Starbucks's well-worn leather chairs and tell us what he knew.

"Molly contacted me, sure," he said after taking a long pull from his straw. "Before she died, obviously. Didn't need a Ouija board to communicate with her." He let out a bark of laughter at his own joke.

"What did she want?" I asked.

"Pictures from the night Piper Standish died," Chrimbo replied matter-of-factly.

I met Casper's eyes briefly, and then looked back to Chrimbo, who was now licking a dollop of whipped cream off of one finger. I almost asked him if he wanted to be alone, but instead I said, "How did she know you had them?"

Chrimbo shrugged. "Probably checked a photo credit somewhere. Bunch of mine from that night made the tabloids, and you know how big a story it was. I had a brilliant angle of Piper going into the club, got her walking right by the guy who did it. Molly wanted to see the pictures. I said the ones worth seeing have already been published. She said she wanted to see all of 'em, even the rubbish ones. I said certainly, for the right price. She sent me the cash, I sent her the photos. There we have it."

"She didn't say why she wanted them?" Casper asked.

"No, sir, and I didn't much care. Made nearly as much from her as I did from the original run."

If Molly wanted those pictures, then we needed to see them too. "Can you send us what you sent Molly?" I asked.

"If you're willing to make it worth my while too."

"As a *favor*," Casper specified.

Chrimbo sneered. "As if I owe you one."

Casper's eyes narrowed. "Last year. Super Bowl Sunday. Who tipped you off at LAX?"

The sneer disappeared. "Well, that was—"

"Halloween at Hyde. Who said to go around back?"

"Fair enough, but I didn't—"

Casper fixed him with a stare. "Ben Affleck. Long John Silver's."

Chrimbo's jaw tensed. "Fine," he said. "I'll send them over."

WWW.CELEBRITEASE.COM

June 26, 2008
12:22 PM PST

Look, we don't often dip into anonymous submissions here at the Tease, but we just have to follow up on a totally unbiased, definitely legit, and completely anonymous submission we received this week. Here it is verbatim:

SPOTTED: Actress and A-lister on the rise HAILEY NICHOLS seen partying the night away with VS angel and *Robot Wars 3* costar PETRA EVANOVICH. See pictures [BELOW] of the besties leaving 1OAK.

Dear readers, let's break this thing down point by point.

"Actress"? Maybe . . . if one can claim an acting career out of a paltry list of unnamed characters that reads like a computer-generated response to the question "Whatever happened to that girl at my high school who went to LA to 'make it big' and failed miserably?"

"A-lister on the rise"? No comment. Fish in a barrel. Next, please.

"Partying the night away"? Oh yes. Hailey and Petra seem to

be living it up as they exit the club separately, walk ten feet apart, and get into different cars . . . Petra's blank stare really says "I'm having the time of my life!"

Finally, we have to round out this whole thing with a truly delicious quote from Petra's camp:

"Ms. Evanovich would like to make it clear that she does not know that girl."

Brutal. Exactly how we like it.

40

Our next order of business was to track down Dax.

"I'll call Ryder," Casper said as we headed to the parking lot. Chrimbo had gone off on his own, now turbocharged with a worrying amount of espresso.

"I thought your roommates hated Dax," I replied. "They didn't have particularly kind things to say about him at the HYPER BLITZ party."

"Oh, they definitely hate him. That's why they keep tabs on him. Dax is a notorious poacher—he'll swoop in and steal shots from paps who have been waiting for hours. Outlets don't care who was there first, or how long you waited—they just care who got the best photo. And Dax is good at getting it."

Ryder didn't pick up the phone, so Casper tried Luke, who didn't answer either. We were sitting in Casper's car, trying to figure out what to do next, when one of them finally called back.

"Did you see my text?" Casper said in lieu of *Hello*. "Uh-huh . . . yeah. Okay. Great." Then he hung up. "Dax is at the opening of some new rooftop bar. If we hurry, we can catch him."

The bar was called Wanderlust, and it was on the roof of an aggressively trendy hotel on the Sunset Strip. A pool sat in the center, surrounded by brightly colored chaise lounges and umbrellas. A bank of private cabanas stood along one side, and the bar extended along the opposite side.

The place was packed, and loud music pulsed in very BEATDRAGON-esque fashion. I wondered briefly if Eliot was actually here—and with him, Anton—but a quick look at the deejay booth dispelled that thought. The deejay was a beautiful woman wearing a bikini and a fedora, holding one side of a pair of massive headphones up to one ear and expertly navigating the turntables.

Casper and I circled the pool three times, scanning the crowd for Dax, but he was nowhere to be seen.

"What now?" Casper asked as we passed the bar again.

I caught sight of a waiter entering one of the private cabanas. He pushed aside the curtain, momentarily revealing—"Dax! Over there!"

I started toward the cabana.

"Wait, wait, wait." Casper grabbed my arm.

"What?"

Chagrin flashed across his face. "I don't know, what if he's . . . dangerous?"

"We're in the middle of a crowded bar, in the middle of the day. And there's two of us. Worse comes to worst, we can take him."

Casper exhaled a short breath. "I like your confidence."

I smiled. "Well, we're kind of a good team, right?"

He smiled back.

We reached the cabana just as the waiter was exiting. I caught the curtain before he shut it ("Thank you, we'll be joining") and slipped inside, Casper right behind me.

There was just enough room in the cabana for a cushioned sofa and a low rattan table. The table was covered in empty glasses. Dax was sprawled out on the sofa, holding a fresh glass—containing a pale green cocktail with a sprig of rosemary in it—against his chest. He blinked up at us blearily.

"What is this?" he slurred.

I thought of Jaz: *A good old-fashioned ambush.*

"Ready to tell us the truth about Molly?" I said brightly.

"What are you talking about?" He squinted up at me. "Rachel West, are you following me?"

"Turnabout is fair play, right?"

"I don't know what that means, but fuck off. Actually—" He struggled to sit up. "Actually, don't. Don't fuck off. Did you see her? Did you see Amy? Is she okay?"

He seemed genuinely concerned. Extremely drunk, but also concerned.

"She's fine," I said.

He squeezed his eyes shut and sank back against the cushions of the couch.

"Why do you even care?" Casper asked, disdain evident in his voice.

"Why do I—" Dax shook his head. "She's Molly's little sister. I told you that I—I told you I was still in love with Molly. I care because Molly would fucking care."

I wanted to be righteous about it, but it came out softer than I intended: "If you really loved Molly, then why didn't you tell us the truth?"

"What truth?"

"That you were there the night she died."

Dax blinked up at me, dazed. "How the hell do you know that?"

I shrugged. "It's true, isn't it?"

He held my gaze for a long moment, and then looked away, his face crumpling. "We were still hooking up," he said finally. "After we broke up. Just . . . whenever she'd call. I'd drop everything and go over there. I had an agreement with the security guy. Molly didn't want it getting out that we were still fooling around—after the breakup articles and everything, she just didn't want to deal with it. So Paulie would let me in and look the other way."

"What happened that night?"

Dax's eyes grew shiny. "She was already dead by the time I got there, I swear to God." He swallowed. "She had texted me, asking me to come over. I was out with some friends, but I told her I'd ditch them as soon as I could. She said it was important, so I should hurry. She even called me, but it was loud at the restaurant and I missed it. I tried calling her back, but she didn't answer, so I just headed over there. Paulie was off duty by that point, but Molly had sent me the code to get in." He took a gulp of his cocktail and then ran a hand over his face. "I went up to her room. I thought maybe she had fallen asleep. But when I went over to her bed . . . when I saw her, she was . . . well, obviously she was dead."

My voice came out tight. "Why didn't you do something? Call nine-one-one?"

"I panicked," he said roughly. "I mean, for fuck's sake, I knew how bad it looked. The ex shows up in the middle of the night, he's the only person there, and she just so happens to be dead? There was nothing anyone could've done for her at that point, so I just . . . I just left." He looked up at me, his expression full of drunk earnestness. "I feel like a total piece of shit for it—of course I do. But life is for the living, you know? If the roles were reversed, I'd want Molly to do the same thing."

"You didn't do anything else?" Casper said. "You didn't take anything, or touch anything?"

Dax looked conflicted for a moment. "I did. I knew she had pills in her bathroom, so . . . I moved a few of the bottles to her bedside table."

Casper looked aghast. "Why?"

"I told you, I panicked. I didn't want to be accused of anything."

"So you decided it would be better to leave your fingerprints everywhere?"

"I . . . had gloves," Dax admitted, shamefaced.

I flashed on something Luke said at the HYPER BLITZ party: *He wears driving gloves like he's about to join the fucking Monaco Grand Prix.*

Scorn was all too clear on Casper's face. "Yeah, because that's not suspicious at all."

"I just made the rational conclusion, and added a little support for it," Dax replied defensively. "That's all."

"You think she overdosed?" I asked.

"What else could have happened?"

"We don't know. That's the whole fucking point," Casper said, anger in his voice. "You tampered with a *crime scene* to cover your own ass. So no one would look further into her death."

"A crime scene?" Dax repeated. "You think—I told you, I didn't do anything to her—"

"Yeah, even if that's true, someone else might have. Did you ever think of that? No, obviously not."

None of us spoke.

Dax shook his head. "But there wasn't anything like—you know, there wasn't anything you'd expect to see, no signs of a struggle or any of that *CSI:LA* bullshit. She was just lying there. I thought—" His voice hitched. "If it wasn't drugs, I thought maybe she just—I don't know. There was this girl in my high school who got so thin, her heart just stopped one day. I thought maybe . . . Why would someone want to *kill* Molly?"

"That's what we've been trying to figure out," Casper said bitterly. "And it would've been a hell of a lot more helpful if you had just told the truth before. Assuming you're telling the truth now."

"I am," Dax said. "I swear." He threw back the rest of the cocktail, and then, rather than setting the empty glass down on the table with the others, he clutched it once again to his chest. "I should've answered the phone sooner. If I had seen her call sooner . . . if I had gone over there earlier . . . do you think it could've made a difference?"

Dax was too late that night. I was too early. It hurt far too much to think about.

I shook my head. "I don't know."

WWW.CELEBRITEASE.COM

June 26, 2008
04:05 PM PST

This just in:

Not twenty-four hours after the collapse of C-list sibling Amy Byrne, Molly Byrne's former flame Dax Van Sant was spotted out on the town with former *Icon* magazine reporter Rachel West, also known as Molly's very last BFF of the week.

This comes hot on the heels of Rach's pressed juice tryst with *Robot Wars* leading man Nick Hart, just last week. Has the giant-robot slayer been jilted for a mere pap? Rags-to-Hollywood-riches former *Icon* reporter West gained more than a few cast-off pairs of Louboutins during her time as MB's bestie—maybe she was eyeing Molly's man at the same time?

Judging by the pictures [BELOW], the tone between these two does seem a little more pleasure than business.

And the plot. Gets. Thicker. Who else is loving this?

41

"A prime suspect emerges," Richard said that night, circling Dax's name on the murder board with gusto. "Now we're really getting somewhere."

We had all gathered in his apartment for an emergency meeting. Fadia barely had time to throw together a Niçoise salad.

"I don't know, though," I murmured. Something had been bothering me since our conversation with Dax earlier. "Assuming Dax was lying to us today—which I'm not sure of—then we'd go with the theory that Dax was Piper's ex. And in that case, he most likely killed Molly because she discovered that he killed Piper."

"Sounds plausible," Fadia said.

It wasn't an outlandish theory. But the pieces didn't quite fit. "Why would he poison Amy, though? After everything? What would he gain from that?"

"Maybe he wanted to prevent her from telling people she saw his car heading to Molly's the night she died," Elena guessed.

"But that assumes Dax knew he had driven past Amy that night," I replied. "There's also the question of how Amy got poisoned in the first place. She said she didn't eat or drink anything before she collapsed. She was doing a fast for a photo shoot."

"How else could poison get into her system?" Anton asked.

"Injection," Elena suggested. "Though it'd be challenging to disguise."

"Hmm." Richard spun his dry-erase marker around in one hand a few times as he contemplated. "What if the poison was something like Midas Touch?"

"What's that?" Jaz asked.

"It's from an episode of *CSLA*," he said, a note of pride in his voice. "A transdermal poison. It was my idea. I named it too. The symptoms were yellowing of the nails and the sclera—the 'everything you touch turns to gold' part? It's not an actual poison, obviously—Midas Touch is fictional—but transdermal poisons are very much real. They're transmitted through touch. Absorbed through the skin, faster if the victim touches their eyes, nose, or mouth. The killer could have used a transdermal poison to coat some object that Molly came into contact with."

"And if Amy happened to come upon the same object . . ." Fadia began.

I blinked. "The phone."

"What?"

"Amy called me on Molly's phone last night. What if it was the phone?"

Suddenly, a text alert chimed. Casper pulled out his phone.

"It's Chrimbo," he said. "He sent the files."

He logged into his email on Richard's laptop and brought up the photos from Entity the night Piper died. We all crowded around to peer at the screen.

Several of the shots were familiar. I recognized the one we had used for the cover of Piper's memorial issue of *Icon*. It was a shot of Piper in profile, smiling over her shoulder, lit up in the haze of dozens of flashbulbs. Many of Chrimbo's other photos were clearly unusable—partially obscured by other cameras or photographers. But they told a story as we clicked through them: Piper getting out of an SUV, a security guard nearby holding an arm out toward the crowd, several other people trailing behind her—

"Wait," I said suddenly. "Go back."

Casper clicked back to the previous picture.

Piper was in one corner of the photo, almost out of frame. Another woman was behind her, a few feet away. She had on standard club wear and was carrying two purses. I knew from Molly that it wasn't unusual for a celeb to carry an empty bag that went with their outfit, while keeping their necessities in a separate purse guarded by an assistant.

It wasn't the two purses that caught my eye, though. It was the woman holding them. A quick glance up at the murder board confirmed—

"That's Winter Crawford," I said. "Right?"

I looked to Jaz, who nodded. "Yeah, that looks like her."

I thought of something Alessandra said during our interview: *I was willing to take her on because I felt for her circumstances.* "Was she Piper's assistant?" Were those "circumstances" Piper's death?

"Look who's behind her," Casper said, advancing through a few more photos. Another woman entered the frame, wearing a cream-colored bandage dress. Her face was turned away in one shot, but in the next—

"Julia Smith!" Jaz exclaimed.

The frames advanced. A third woman appeared, wearing a sparkly blue minidress. The photos showed this woman catching up to Winter and Julia, linking arms with them, and entering the club just behind Piper.

It was Hailey Nichols.

I frowned. "Hailey told us she didn't know Julia or Winter."

"She also said her hair and breasts were real," Casper replied.

"Touché." I stared at the picture of the three women at the door to the club. "So Hailey was part of Piper's entourage the night Piper died. And so were Julia and Winter."

"Piper, Hailey, Winter, Julia," Fadia said. "That's four out of five from Molly's list. We're just missing—"

"Amy," I supplied. "She was there that night too."

"So that's what they all have in common," Anton said. "They were all at Entity the night Piper died."

"They have something else in common," Fadia murmured. We all looked over at her. She pointed to the center of the murder board, where the picture of Molly stared out at us. "Molly."

Fadia ticked off points on her fingers as she spoke. "Amy's connection is obvious. And Casper, you said that Molly knew Piper." Casper nodded. "Julia Smith did Molly's PR until she got fired. Winter Crawford was Alessandra Delgado's assistant—"

"Until she also got fired," I interjected.

"Right, and Rachel, you said Molly talked to Winter while you were interviewing Alessandra."

I nodded.

"And Hailey Nichols was in Molly's spin class," Fadia finished.

Elena's brow furrowed. "If Hailey lied about knowing Winter and Julia, maybe she also lied about what she and Molly fought about the day Molly died."

"Sounds like we really need to track Julia and Winter down," Anton said. "Get a second and third opinion."

Jaz perked up. "I actually have an update on that! It's been a no go on Winter—she's totally offline—and you haven't heard back from Alessandra's agency yet, have you, Rachel?" I shook my head. "So no progress there. But remember Julia Smith's roommate? The one who was super annoyed because Julia skipped out on their lease? She just got engaged. There were a bunch of people congratulating her on the Facebook announcement. Including someone named J. Lowell. Her profile picture caught my eye." She took over Richard's laptop and, after a few rapid-fire keystrokes, showed us the screen. On it was a private Facebook profile; only the profile picture was visible.

"That's Julia," I said.

Jaz nodded. "Looks like she made a new account under a different name. So I did a little digging."

"You're pretty good at that," Anton commented.

"I know, right?" Jaz's eyes gleamed. "She's a student at Glendale Community College now. I got a copy of her schedule."

"And how exactly did you do that?" Elena asked with a frown.

"It's open access," Jaz replied innocently.

Elena's answering expression was heavy on skepticism. "Really?"

"For . . . employees of the registrar's office."

"Oh, and you're definitely one of those."

"I could be! Anyway, the point is, we know where Julia's going to be and when. In class, on campus! We can find out what she knows!"

42

Finding out what Julia knew was easier said than done. The first order of business was to intercept her. The second was to convince her to talk, and I had a feeling that wouldn't exactly be easy. A person doesn't typically move out, change their name, and start a new career because they're super eager to dwell on the past.

Before we left Richard's apartment that night, Casper said he wanted to come along with me to meet Julia. But in the morning, he texted saying that something had come up and we'd link up later. So I waited alone in the second-floor corridor of the Health Sciences building on the Glendale campus. If Jaz's info was correct, Julia was set to get out of class any minute.

I watched intently as people began to emerge from the classroom—groups of two and three chatting, solo students checking their phones. I waited as more and more people streamed out, and waited still as the flow eventually dwindled. But there was no Julia in sight.

I was starting to think this was a pointless endeavor when

suddenly the door swung open one more time and there she was, dressed casually in leggings and a sweatshirt, her auburn hair tied up in a messy bun, a messenger bag slung over one shoulder.

I moved toward her. "Julia?"

"Yeah?"

"Do you have a minute to talk?"

"About what?"

"Piper Standish."

Her expression, open and curious just a second before, quickly hardened. "Sorry, no." She moved swiftly past me.

"I'm Rachel," I said, hurrying to fall into step with her. "I'm a friend of Molly Byrne's. She helped me out when I was having a tough time—just like she did for you, right?"

"I told you, I don't want to talk." She quickened her pace.

"You never leaked Molly's info, did you?" I said, and Julia slowed to a stop just ahead of me. Her shoulders were tense. "You were set up. Because you knew something. Something someone didn't want getting out. So they got you fired." I paused. "Threatened you, maybe? And Winter . . . did the same thing happen to her?"

Julia took a breath, and then turned back to face me. "Look . . . I don't know who you are, but I'm trying to start over. That's . . . literally all I want, and that's what Winter's doing too. Neither of us wants anything to do with any of that. So just leave me alone, okay?"

"Molly was looking into Piper's death. I think she figured out what really happened."

Julia's grip on the strap of her bag tightened, her knuckles going white. She looked down at the floor for a moment, and then back up at me, her expression mournful. "That's what I was afraid of."

"Please, if you could just—if you could tell me what you know—"

She took a step toward me, her voice low and shaky: "I don't know who killed Piper. Honestly. I don't. But if that person got to Molly too, then that's even more reason to leave it alone, isn't it? Anyone who goes digging is in danger."

"You must know something, though. You must've seen or heard *something*."

She shook her head. "All I know is who was there that night. And who tried to make it look like they weren't."

"Who—"

"That's it. That's all I can say. I'm sorry. Please don't contact me again."

She hurried away.

43

All I know is who was there that night. And who tried to make it look like they weren't.

Julia's words echoed through my mind on the drive back to Palm Vista. Who was there that night? Everyone on Molly's list: Julia, Winter, Hailey, Amy. Dax Van Sant. Who tried to make it look like they weren't? What did that mean?

When I arrived back at Palm Vista, deep in thought, I found Jaz sitting outside my apartment, her back pressed up against the door. She quickly climbed to her feet as I approached.

"Hey," I said. "Everything okay?"

She looked uneasy, and not in that uniquely teenaged way—in a startlingly grown-up way that immediately put me on alert. "I, um. I wanted to talk to you. Alone. I . . . sort of found something."

"What is it?"

"Can we go inside?"

I opened the door and let Jaz pass by before I shut it behind us and turned to her. "Whatever it is, you can tell me. It's okay. I'm kind of hard to shock these days."

She took a tentative seat on the couch. "Well . . . I was doing some looking around online . . ."

"Did you see something confusing that you need me to explain?" I couldn't help but try to lighten the mood. "So, when two people are in love . . ."

Jaz actually cracked a smile. "Shut up." But it just as quickly faded. "It's just . . . I was sort of curious, because of what we had talked about before. About Casper."

I thought of the Disney dog tumbling out of a garbage can. But I knew what she really meant: *What do we know about him outside of being a pap, wanting to find Molly's killer, and committing to an all-black aesthetic?*

"I was just looking," she continued. "I figured he might have his own website, like, as a photographer. And I found a few domains registered in his name. They were pretty random URLs, but when I visited them, they redirected to . . . and I mean, they *all* redirected to . . ."

"Disney garbage pail dog dot com?" I said. "Leather jacket for the aesthetic dot com?"

She didn't smile this time. "You know that blog Celebritease?"

Stop the car.

Casper had looked me right in the eyes.

Jaz continued hesitantly. "So I searched the domain registration for Celebritease, and it was under a company called CJ Inc. I checked the IP for CJ Inc, and the location is an apartment building in West Hollywood. I think . . . I mean, it's got to be him, right? CJ Inc? Casper Jones? He's the one who runs that site."

I don't have a blog. And if I did, it wouldn't be a vapid, vicious, extremely annoying one.

I had taken Casper at his word. I had believed him, for absolutely no reason except that Molly had been okay with him selling pictures of her. What kind of a foundation of trust was that? Honestly, how stupid could I be?

"I'm sorry," Jaz said when I didn't speak. "That blog has been saying really awful stuff. And he's been—"

"Lying to us." From the beginning. Boldly and straight to our faces. "Clearly."

"I thought you'd want to know."

I swallowed, and forced the words to come out in an even tone: "Yeah, of course. Thanks, Jaz."

She nodded unhappily. I gave her an awkward pat on the shoulder. Amusement flickered briefly across her face. "What was that?"

"I don't know. Just . . . trying to be comforting."

"You're kind of terrible at it."

"I know," I said. "Sorry."

In a move that completely surprised me, Jaz suddenly surged forward and caught me in a tight hug. I barely had time to hug back before she pulled away.

"I should get back home. My mom's off work, so she'll be wondering where I am." She paused at the door. "Do you think . . . should I tell everyone else?"

I shook my head. "Don't. I'll tell them."

With a solemn nod, she left the apartment.

44

I had already arranged to meet Casper at a coffee shop near Palm Vista to go over what I had learned from Julia. But now I had a completely different agenda.

I got there early—too early, but I couldn't bear sitting around my apartment any longer. I didn't even go inside the coffee shop. I just waited out front, trying to school myself, trying to plan for the interaction. I would be angry, of course, but in a completely controlled way. I would maintain the upper hand. I wouldn't lose my cool or let him know how much this was affecting me. I wouldn't give him the satisfaction.

I couldn't stand still, though. I paced back and forth. I took a seat on the window ledge outside the café, then, a moment later, stood up, walked partway down the block, changed direction, walked back.

When I spotted Casper approaching in the distance, I headed to intercept him.

"How'd it go with Julia?" he asked as we neared each other. "What'd she say?"

"I asked you point-blank," I replied, and it came out so much more hurt than I had intended. Clearly, my attempts at schooling myself had failed miserably. "I asked you, and you lied to my face."

He frowned. "What are you talking about?"

"Jaz looked you up. Guess what she found."

He just blinked, guileless. "What?"

Fresh anger bloomed in my chest. "Seriously? You're going to pretend?"

"Tell me what you're talking about."

"Celebritease," I said. "Guess who owns the domain. CJ Inc. Okay. Coincidence? Maybe. Sure. But then guess what just so happens to redirect to Celebritease. Every domain owned by Casper Jones. Hmm. I wonder who the owner of CJ Inc could possibly be. I wonder why it's registered to an apartment building in WeHo that just so happens to be your apartment building. What kind of a massive fucking coincidence is that?"

Casper didn't speak for a long moment. When he finally met my gaze, there was something complicated in his expression, some emotion I couldn't place. "I . . . I can explain. At least, I know there's part of it I can explain. Okay?"

"You really don't need to. Honestly, it's on me. I'm the idiot. I believed you when I had literally no good reason to." I passed a hand over my eyes. I wanted to blame the situation, the grief, anything—but it was on me. There was no denying that. "All those terrible things they said about her—that was you. How could you do that to Molly? How could you stand there and pretend to care about what happened to her and then turn around and shit on her for clicks?"

"That's not—"

"You lied to me. And you said—you *swore*—"

"Rachel, listen to me." He took a step toward me.

I backed away. "Don't."

He and I are just . . . coinvestigators, I had told Jaz. But I knew in this moment that that wasn't the truth. Maybe I hadn't come to think of Casper as a friend exactly, but maybe it's because it was more than that. I had come to think of him as an ally. A partner in all of this. Someone in my corner. More importantly, someone in Molly's corner.

For a moment, Casper and I looked at each other. There was a part of me that just wanted him to say *I'm sorry, I'm sorry, I'm so sorry.* But he didn't.

"I can explain," he repeated.

I wanted to get even angrier. But instead, hurt thrummed through me, potent and profound.

"You can go to hell, okay?" I replied. Then I turned and started off in the opposite direction. *Classic Rachel West avoidance tactic.*

Casper wouldn't allow himself to be avoided, though. He was hot on my heels as I headed swiftly down the street.

"Rachel—"

I pulled out my phone. I needed Anton, or Fadia, or—

The screen was black. Of course my battery chose this moment to fail me. Or, more aptly, it was another moment of me failing myself. I could've plugged my phone in. I could've looked into Casper's background at the fucking start of all this.

I rounded a corner and ran smack into someone.

It was Lee.

"Hey, I just—" He looked at me, and then at Casper, who had stopped a few feet short of us. "What's going on?"

Casper ignored him. "Rachel, please let me explain."

"I don't want to hear it." My voice was close to breaking. It made the situation, the need to get away from him, seem even more desperate. I wasn't going to cry, not here, not like this, certainly not in front of him.

"But—"

Lee's gaze darted from me to Casper again, and then he moved to stand between us. "She said she doesn't want to talk to you."

"Hey, this is between Rachel and me, okay? I'd appreciate it if you'd stay the fuck out of it." Casper glowered up at Lee.

"She doesn't want to talk to you," Lee repeated, calm and collected.

Casper glared at Lee for a second more, and then tried to sidestep him, just like I had tried to get around Nick Hart's mountain of a security guard by the juice shop only a few days earlier. It felt like a lifetime ago. "Rachel, I'm sorry. I know I should've told you from the start, but I—"

"Walk away," Lee said evenly.

"Please, just—" Now Casper's voice sounded close to breaking.

"Fuck off," I said. "I mean it."

Casper's posture deflated.

He didn't walk away, like Lee had suggested. He didn't have to, because I walked away instead.

Lee caught up with me, and it was only when we had neared Palm Vista and Casper had disappeared in the distance that Lee spoke.

"What was that about?"

I ignored the question. "What are you doing here?"

"You texted me. You said you had important info about Molly?"

I had. And I had completely forgotten about it. After meeting Julia Smith, I had sent Lee a message. As much as Julia wanted to leave the past behind, she was a lead into both Piper's and Molly's deaths. Even if Lee was unreceptive, I had to share what she told me.

"Your phone went straight to voicemail, so I was going to swing by," he continued. "What was that?" He gestured back in the direction of the café, uncertainty in his expression. "Bad breakup?"

We could be cousins, I'd said when Casper and I had met with Alyssa, right at the start of the investigation.

We could be dating.

"No." If only it were that simple. It was all playing back in my mind, rapid-fire. Casper wasn't after justice for Molly. That was now painfully clear. Had it all been fodder for Celebritease? Had he ever actually been invested in any of this? Or was he just another media vampire, looking to suck Molly's death dry for as much attention as possible? And here I was, his unwitting accomplice. Leading him from person to person, from source to source, just so he could get pictures and info and tear me down too. It was nauseating. It was devastating. What would Molly say if she knew? Would she ever forgive me?

I thought, suddenly, of that night. The last night I saw her. The last night she was alive.

★ JUNE 2008 ★

MOLLY HAD TEXTED ME: CAN YOU COME OVER? IT'S IMPORTANT.

I was still at the office, but I told her I'd head over when I finished up work. I arrived at Molly's house just as the sun was dipping below the horizon. Paulie let me in through the side door. "She's up in her room."

I cut through the kitchen and headed down the hall and up the stairs to Molly's bedroom. That grand suite with the enormous four-poster bed and the giant windows looking out onto the valley. Molly sat on the floor in the center of the sitting area, surrounded by random piles of jewelry, scarves, bags, hair accessories, shoes . . .

"I'm going through some stuff," she said when I walked in. "I thought you might want some of it."

I set my purse down on one of the chairs.

"That's why you wanted me to come by?" I was expecting something a little more pressing than a decluttering.

"I'm so happy we're the same shoe size," she said, ignoring the question as she strung half a dozen silver bangles on one arm. "I have these Valentino heels you'll love. I'm never going to wear them again."

Something was wrong, and I could tell. She was cheerful, but it wasn't the airy cheer she evinced in happy moments. It was forced. It was misdirection.

"Is everything okay?"

Molly didn't reply. At least not to the question. "Take these bracelets." She stood up and grabbed a few small pink and brown boxes, then came over and handed them to me. "My stylist sent them, but you know how I feel about Juicy."

"Molly—"

She turned back to the piles of accessories. I put the boxes down on the wide Lucite coffee table. Strewn among the items were a handful of celebrity magazines, haphazardly leafed through. I noticed a page that had been ripped from an issue of *Star* and partially crumpled—it showed Nick Hart and Petra Evanovich posing side by side at a press conference. His smile was broad and confident, his eyes bright blue in the light of the flashbulbs. Petra's smile was slight, her expression coy.

"I was in Who Wore It Best this week, did you see?" Molly said, her voice brittle.

So many outlets had one of those sections, including *Icon*. I assumed she meant *Us Weekly*, which was the original pioneer of comparing celebrities who had the misfortune of wearing the same outfit. My eyes caught on the Who Wore It Best page among the open magazines. Molly in a green Grecian-style dress, tucking a strand of hair behind one ear. In another shot, Petra posing in the same green dress, her lips pursed, her gaze piercing.

"What do you think of those scarves?" Molly pointed to a pile of colorful fabric on the chair where I had rested my purse.

"They're pretty."

She walked over to one of the windows and looked out for just a moment, then moved to the large silver-framed mirror hanging on the wall nearby and contemplated her reflection. She turned away, seemingly unsatisfied with what she saw.

"Seriously, how the fuck could my stylist put me in the same dress as Petra? How am I supposed to compete with her? She's nineteen years old and has legs up to her face!"

"You're twenty-four."

"Yeah, and thirty is basically forty in Hollywood, which means I'm practically over the goddamn hill."

"Molly—"

"I know," she said. "I know. It's not even about that. I wish it were. I wish all of this was just some petty thing that the old me would care about. The inauthentic me. I wish it were that simple. I wish—" She cut herself off abruptly, turned away, and then just as quickly turned back. "You do anything you can to keep them watching, Rachel. Anything. You play the sweet, innocent schoolgirl, and then you get implants so you can play the sexy girl. You get fucked on a waterbed and launched through a window. You shoot a scene eighteen times so a director can capture one singular tear tracking perfectly down your cheek, because God forbid you look the slightest bit ugly when you cry. And then they end up adding the fucking tear in post!" Her eyes blazed. "You do anything that anyone asks you to do, whether you want to or not. And it's not enough. Nothing's ever enough. If you complain, you're 'difficult.' If you try to blow off steam, you're 'spiraling.' They love you until they don't, and then it's all over. First you're a pity, and then you're a punch line, and then you're forgotten, and somehow they've convinced you that, out of every shitty thing that could possibly happen, that's the very worst. That's the very worst thing you could ever be. Forgotten. But there are worse things. There's shit that's *so* much worse." She met my eyes, and her voice broke. "I'm just so tired."

My voice stuck in my throat. "Why don't you lie down?"

"That's not what I mean."

Silence.

"They're already saying there's Oscar buzz for *Sun City*," she said. "My agent says it could be the most meaningful film of my career. The start of a whole new era. I could get better roles, more authentic roles, I could become . . . the actor I've always dreamed of being." She blinked rapidly. "What happens if I burn it all down?"

I shook my head. "That won't happen."

"I can't stop thinking about that thing you said, you know, that thing of like, who would I be? If it weren't for any of this. Who would I be and what would I want and what kinds of choices would I make? What would my choices even *be*? What the fuck are they now?"

"Molly, did something happen?"

A complicated series of emotions crossed her face. But all she said was, "Yeah, Hollywood continues to Hollywood. Men continue to be the fucking worst. And we're just, what? Collateral damage? Sour Cream and Onion Pringles?" Her eyes shone with unshed tears. "Ray, I'm so fucking tired. Of all of it."

This was my opportunity. In the numerous times I've played that evening back in my mind, this was my biggest missed chance, my biggest failure. I should have said something. Anything. I should have pressed her further. I should've said, *Tell me what happened. We can figure it out. Let's just talk about it.*

But I didn't speak. I didn't know what to say. I'll always regret it.

In the moment of silence that followed, Molly's expression shuttered. It turned into the look that she gave the sales associates at the Chanel store. The polite smile that had followed the real one in the bathroom at Lithium the night we first met. It was Molly retreating.

She crossed over and picked up the scarves, then pressed them into my hands. "You keep these. They'll look so pretty on you."

I shook my head. "You might want them later."

"I have so many already. I want you to have them."

"Why?"

The smile didn't waver. "Because you appreciate beautiful things."

I didn't want the scarves, but I knew she would be sad if she found them later, so I accepted them. I would sneak them back into her house another time.

"Take this stuff too." She picked up a thick-papered shopping bag, orange, with the Hermès logo on the front. She scooped up the Juicy jewelry boxes and tossed them in before handing the bag to me. "I'm going to lie down. I need some sleep."

I nodded.

She crossed the room and climbed into that big bed. "Thanks for coming over."

"Anytime." I hesitated. "I could stay if you want?"

"It's okay. I'm okay."

"Call me if you need me," I said. It felt insufficient.

But she just smiled at me again. A glimmer of the real one. "I already did. And you came. Thank you." She laid her head down. "Good night, Ray."

"Good night."

That was the last time I ever saw Molly Byrne. Sinking under the covers. Disappearing.

I left the room and softly shut the door behind me.

45

I let Lee into my apartment. I closed the door behind us and rested my forehead against it.

Call me if you need me.

I already did.

I took a breath. And then another. It did nothing to steady me, nothing to shake loose the image of Molly in her bedroom that night, righteous and devastated and exhausted—*Ray, I'm so fucking tired. Of all of it.*

I was tired too. It ran bone deep, right down to the marrow.

"Are you okay?" Lee asked.

Not remotely, I wanted to reply, but I didn't. Instead, I turned and faced him and said, "I don't know what to do." Embarrassingly, my voice broke on it. "I don't know what the fuck I'm doing besides making things worse."

Lee stepped toward me. I looked up at him for a moment, surprised to see the concern in his eyes. Before I could react, he closed the gap between us and pulled me into a hug.

I didn't pull away. But I didn't hug back either. "What are you doing?"

I could feel his voice resonate in his chest. "You looked like you were about to cry."

I swallowed hard, resting my head on his shoulder. "No. I don't do that."

"Why not?"

Because I couldn't let myself. It was like sending a bucket down into a well. I knew that no matter how many times I brought it back filled, over and over again, I would never reach the bottom.

I could see the Hermès shopping bag from Molly next to my couch. Nearby were the scarves she had given me that night. I would never be able to return them to her now.

I thought of my brother, Sam, and the strangeness of turning seventeen and realizing that I was now older than my older brother would ever be. I thought of my mom pressing a figurine into my hands shortly after Sam died. It was one I had given him, a character from some anime he liked—I had saved up my allowance for months to get it for him for his birthday. I remembered so clearly his smile, brief but potent, when he opened the box. *He would want you to have this,* my mom said, but it made no sense. It was Sam's figurine. I had gotten it for *him.* But it came back to me in the end—something I didn't want but couldn't bear to part with. Something that represented both the person I had lost and the person I had been, who was gone now too. I was a sister who could never buy her brother a present again.

It wasn't fair. None of this was fair.

Fair *is a place with cotton candy and carousels.*

I pulled away slightly and looked up at Lee. He and I had never stood this close before. From this vantage point, his eyes were particularly brown and particularly open.

He held my gaze, and then shook his head minutely. "I'm sorry about last time," he said quietly. "I thought a lot about what you said—"

I didn't want to talk. I didn't want to think. I didn't want to be inside my own head.

"It's okay," I said thickly. "It doesn't matter."

A crease appeared between his eyebrows. "But—"

"It's okay," I repeated, resting my hands on his chest. For a moment, I stared at them resting there. He was so warm. Everything about him was just—warm—

I turned my face back up toward his.

I leaned in . . .

And he stepped back, putting space between us.

"Rachel—"

Fuck. "No, never mind," I said.

He cleared his throat. "I don't know exactly what's going on right now, but I know this isn't the best idea."

The air felt cold suddenly. I felt cold, even though blood was rushing through me. All of a sudden, I was perilously close to tears again. "If you don't want me, you can just say so."

"Believe me, Rachel, that's not the problem." He shook his head. "You have no idea."

"Then why not?"

He reached out and took both my hands, squeezed them gently. His expression was annoyingly earnest. "Because you are not okay right now."

I broke away. "Just say it's a conflict of interest or something. It's way less condescending."

"Rachel—"

I didn't care if he was right. I just wanted to feel something that wasn't grief or anger or despair. But if he wouldn't let me have that, I'd double down on anger.

"No, I get it, you're good, you're noble, you're heartbroken. And I was sad and lonely and I latched onto you because you showed up at my door one day and were nice to me, and how fucking pathetic is that? You were doing your job and I just—"

His jaw set. "I think you know it wasn't just that."

I couldn't stop the words from firing out, clear and targeted. "And I need you to know that I don't actually want you. I'm just upset, and you just happen to be here."

Lee's usually readable face shuttered. He looked at me for a long moment.

"What?" I said. "Do you need me to be more direct? You should go. Please go."

"I don't—"

I felt like Amy Byrne, tossing Casper and me out of Molly's house. "Just fucking leave me alone, okay?"

Lee looked as if he was going to speak, but after a moment's silence, he just nodded.

Then he left.

Excerpt from NUCLEAR NUCLEUS, pg. 103

REX faces down his ARCHENEMY. The mastermind behind this whole disaster. A shadowy figure cloaked in a black shroud.

REX

Show yourself.

ARCHENEMY

Not yet.

REX

Coward! *Show yourself!* You've taken everything from me!

ARCHENEMY

Oh, Rex. Don't you know what they say?

REX draws his gun and fires. The gun clicks uselessly—out of bullets. A FLASH OF LIGHTNING illuminates ARCHENEMY's ghastly face and his eerily wide, sinister smile.

ARCHENEMY

Things can *always* get worse.

46

Lee's business card was still sitting on my kitchen counter, now off to the side with some junk mail and a take-out menu from a nearby Chinese place. I picked up the whole pile, card included, and threw it in the trash.

The rejection stung. The acknowledgment that Lee was right stung even more. I was not okay right now. Kissing him wouldn't have made anything better.

But it would've gotten me out of my brain, I thought traitorously. *At least for a moment.* I just wanted to be anywhere else. A thousand miles away. Another planet.

I needed to push through. I had to share the truth about Casper with the group. I texted everyone—except Casper—to meet at Richard's apartment that night.

I'LL STOP BY YOUR PLACE BEFORE MURDER KLATCH, Anton texted back.

Don't, I replied. I'll see you at Richard's.

YOU GOOD?

I didn't respond.

Natalie called me. I ignored that too. She called again.

"What happened with your job?" she said when I finally answered.

I was momentarily thrown. "What? Nothing."

Her tone hardened. "You want to think about that for a minute and then try again?"

I rubbed a hand over my eyes. "Natalie, I don't really have time for this right now—"

"'Molly Byrne's former flame Dax Van Sant was spotted out on the town with former *Icon* magazine reporter Rachel West'? Ring any bells? Seriously, you act like I don't have access to the fucking internet."

I blinked. I hadn't even realized, but it was there in the latest Celebritease post: *former Icon* magazine reporter Rachel West. *How did Celebritease know I quit my job?* was a question I probably would've pondered for far too long. Like a colossal idiot. Of course Celebritease knew. Casper knew everything. What would be next? *THIS JUST IN: Molly Byrne left massive inheritance to moronic failure Rachel West.*

I took a breath. There was a second when I wanted the dam to burst. A second when I could feel the cracks beginning to expand, the truth just waiting to spill forth: *I have been having the shittiest time here. My friend is gone. I don't know what to do. I don't know how to fix anything.*

But all that came out was: "So you're keeping tabs on me now? Did you set a Google alert?"

"Yeah. How else am I supposed to know how you're doing when you never share anything with anyone?"

"I don't—"

"Did you quit or were you fired?"

"It doesn't matter."

"Of course it does! It's your life, Rachel! Don't be like Sam."

My heart squeezed painfully. "That's not— Don't do that. Don't bring him into this."

"He was our brother," she said softly. "We're allowed to talk about him. We're allowed to . . . to remember him. The good parts and the bad." She let out a breath. "I just wish you would open up."

"And I wish I were on a tropical island with a margarita." I couldn't help myself. It was who I was, I guess. It was imprinted in my DNA.

"Rachel—"

"I can't talk right now. I have to go."

Exasperation was heavy in her voice. "Of course you do."

I hung up the phone.

LIAR, Richard wrote under Casper's new entry on the murder board that evening. The other Casper-specific bullet points read *PAPARAZZO*, *FOLLOWED MOLLY*, and *CELEBRITEASE*.

Richard frowned at it. "Disappointing."

It was a remarkable understatement.

"So, what now?" Fadia asked. "Where do we go from here?"

I stared at the board. At the various names and photos and Richard's notes. And Molly at the center of it all: *VICTIM*.

There was only one conclusion in my mind: "We don't."

Fadia's brow furrowed. "What do you mean?"

What was there to be drawn from any of it? What had we proven besides the fact that Molly had an extremely shitty final day on earth? And that people, given the chance, lied. And lied again.

"This whole thing was a bad idea from the start," I said. "It was Casper's bad idea, and I went along with it."

"But we're onto something," Richard said. "We really are."

"It's not our job, and we should've just stayed out of it from the beginning."

"What about justice for Molly?" Elena asked.

I thought of Lee, and then quickly pushed that thought aside. "The police will handle it."

"Like they did for Piper?" Anton said. "Seriously, Rachel. After everything we've found out so far, you just want to give up and leave it to someone else?"

"It's not *giving up*. It's being realistic. What have we actually proven?" I looked from face to face, from Anton to Fadia to Elena to Jaz to Richard. "Tell me. What proof do we have of anything?"

"We have tons of testimony," Elena replied. "Dax Van Sant moved the pill bottles at the crime scene. Molly's sister really was cut out of the will—"

I shook my head. "How do we even know anyone was telling the truth?"

Jaz blinked up at me, earnestness in her gaze. "Just because Casper lied doesn't mean everyone else did."

It wasn't enough. "I'm done. With all of this." When I met Anton's eyes again, his expression was annoyingly soft. "What?" I couldn't keep the bitter edge out of my voice.

His tone, in return, was frustratingly gentle. "Come on," he said. "What do I always say? *Classic Rachel West avoidance tactic.* Aren't we seeing it in action right now? Isn't this the same thing that happened with med school? And with *Icon*? Something gets hard, and you run away from it."

He wasn't wrong, but that didn't stop anger from flaring in my chest. "Yeah, okay, so what? Maybe that's my whole MO. What do you want me to say? Sure, I'll keep playing detective because it's a fun distraction for all of us. I'll keep digging into Molly's past and tarnishing"—my voice caught, embarrassingly, but I pushed through—"her memory. Sure, I'll keep at it just so no one can accuse me of being a quitter." I stood. "I can't. I can't do that. I can't do any of this anymore." I felt, suddenly, entirely depleted. I met Richard's eyes. I figured he, of everyone there, would be the last one to meet me with softness. I was right. He just looked at me steadily.

"Thank you for—" I started to say, but I couldn't quite finish the sentence. "Thanks anyway, for trying."

47

As soon as I got back to my apartment, I decided that getting drunk would be an excellent idea.

I went to the Pink Palmetto, the bar near Palm Vista that Casper and I had gone to the other night. The first time I ever came here was with Anton, after my dad had encouraged me to get to know my "local watering hole."

Watering hole, Anton had remarked as we took in the Pink Palmetto's interior. *Sounds about right. They've definitely got the* hole *part down.*

I took a seat at the bar and ordered a rum and Coke, and then another. I'd brought my romance novel along, and by the third rum and Coke, I'd stopped trying to read and was instead describing the issues with the small-town-secret-millionaire trope to the bartender, a twentysomething guy with ear gauges and gelled-up hair. He seemed amused enough through my drunken haze, but in reality he was probably just as annoyed with me as I was with the small-town-secret-millionaire trope.

"The thing is," I said, "he thinks that nobody knows. But

everybody knows. I mean, he drives a fucking Bugatti. How can she *not know*? Is she inept? Maybe." I sloshed a bit of my fourth rum and Coke. "Maybe she's like me."

"Are you inept?" the bartender asked with a raised eyebrow. There was a glimmer of something in his eyes—maybe he really was more amused than annoyed.

"Oh yeah. Absolutely. Ask anyone who knows me." I waved a hand, and then had to pause to catch my balance on the bar. "They'll tell you that Rachel West is fucking *inept*. Actually, they won't. They won't say anything, because I've run away from all of them. That's what I do." I took a long pull of the drink. "That's my whole—whole *mopus oderandi*."

"*Mopus . . .*"

"That's not right, is it?" I set my glass back down. "Modus. Modus *oderpandi*. Operandi. Fuck Latin. Honestly."

"What's your modus operandi?"

"Running away."

"And what are you running from?"

"I don't even know." I shook my head. Disconcertingly, my vision suddenly swam with tears. "Or . . . maybe I do."

Before I moved to LA, I rarely drank. I thought of that night at Lithium, and then of the HYPER BLITZ party, and my conversation on the phone with Lee outside. Drinking brought everything to the surface.

The evening grew hazy. I tried to read more—I think. I tried to talk to other people at the bar—maybe. My phone rang at some point—it was Casper.

It suddenly seemed, at that moment, like the perfect time to have things out with him. To tell him exactly what I thought of him.

"Ghost," I said, instead of *Hello*, when I had finally figured out which button to press to accept the call.

"Rachel?" There was a note of surprise in his voice. Maybe he'd just wanted to leave a voicemail. Like a coward.

"Ghost," I repeated. "A friendly little ghost."

"What are you—"

"That's what she said you were, remember? Molly. She trusted you, so I trusted you, and how fucking stupid was that?" The bartender was looking my way, so I nodded in his direction. "*Inept*, right?"

"Where are you? Are you somewhere safe?"

"Why does it matter?"

"Because you sound very drunk."

"And you sound like a liar. Because you are one. You're a lying ghost."

"Where are you right now?"

"I am at my *local watering hole*," I said. "But not for long." I stood, too fast, and almost lost my footing. "I'm leaving." The fighting spirit had left me already. My righteous indignation. I forgot that I was going to have it out with Casper. Instead, that energy had been redirected toward trying to stay upright. "Goodbye."

I hung up.

I paid my bill, somehow, and then left. As I headed down the street, I kept one hand out to catch myself in case I fell. My apartment felt much farther away than it had coming here. In fact, it felt like it just kept getting farther and farther away, no matter how much I walked.

Was Lee's house closer? If I went there, would he give me another bottle of water? Would he let me sit on the porch? Or would he turn the lights off and pretend he wasn't home? I couldn't blame him. It was me. It was all me. I had made a mess of everything.

At some point I decided that I needed to rest, so I sat down on a random stoop and closed my eyes, just for a moment.

And after how long, I have no idea, I felt a hand press gently against the side of my face.

"Rachel?"

I jerked back. I had the distinct feeling that I had been having a dream, but then again, maybe this was the dream? Where was I? What was I doing? I was outside, in the warm night air, and Casper was kneeling in front of me.

"Are you all right?"

I looked around. I was slumped over in a doorway.

"What are you doing here?" I asked blearily.

"Looking for you. Let's get you home."

I shook my head, and even though it felt like just the slightest movement, the earth spun. "I'm not going anywhere with you. I'm going to live here." The concrete step underneath me was cool and grounding. I placed my hands against it, and suddenly, sense memory overwhelmed me. I had felt the same coolness against my palms as I crouched outside a bank of elevators in the parking garage at Memorial Hospital. "Maybe I'll just die here."

"Rachel."

"Maybe I could've actually become a doctor," I said. "Maybe I could've done it if it hadn't happened. Maybe if I had finished school, then I would've been . . . ready for it." My voice hitched. "Or maybe it would be the same thing, no matter when it happened, maybe I'd just fucking—"

"What are you talking about?"

"I didn't think it'd happen so soon." Tears were streaming down my face now. The doorway, the sidewalk, the streetlights, Casper—they were all far away. "I didn't think I'd have to see it so soon."

"See what?"

Blood. Stillness. The loss of someone far too soon, for such an unspeakably devastating reason. "Sam," I said, his name choking in my throat. "It just made me think of Sam." And all of a sudden I was thirteen again, pushing open his bedroom door. Alyssa's words came back to me: *It sounds crazy, but there was just this* emptiness *in the room.*

I knew it. I knew that emptiness. My knees giving way. A sound ripping from my throat—just wordless, guttural sound. I knew it. And it came back to me with startling, earth-shattering clarity that night in med school, when I was shadowing in the ER. The boy rushed in on a stretcher—a boy who had felt just the same pain that Sam had. The frenzy of the people around me as they worked on him. All the while I stood frozen, unable to do anything—unable to move, unable to tear myself from the past.

"The patient—he died. They tried, but they couldn't—there wasn't anything anyone could do. And I just—I just—" I shook my head. *I just lost it.* "That's what he looked like when I found him. My brother. That's what he— How could we let that happen? After everything. How could he survive everything he'd been through and then . . . It's so unfair. He deserved so much more. He was hurting so much, and we didn't—I didn't—" My vision blurred with tears again. "I thought I could handle it, but I can't. I thought I was stronger than that, but I'm just—I'm the weakest fucking person, Casper."

For a moment, I met Casper's eyes. They were kind and open and sad—sadder than I had ever seen them. "I don't think that's true at all."

"You don't know me. And I don't know you."

"Please," he said gently. "Let me help you home."

"Was Molly right?" I swallowed. "Are you a friendly ghost?"

"Yes." He nodded. "Yeah. I am."

48

I woke in my bedroom, fully dressed, to morning sun pouring through the blinds. Only my shoes were missing. I think a blanket had been thrown over me, but I must've cast it off sometime in the night—it lay in a heap on the floor.

I sat up. And then promptly threw up in the waste basket that had been placed next to the bed.

I lay back down. After several steadying breaths, I tried to sit up again, more slowly this time. The inside of my mouth felt fuzzy and horrible.

Eventually I got myself out of bed and went into the bathroom. Threw water on my face. Brushed my teeth. Then I stepped into the living room and let out a shriek.

It took me a moment—the moment in which I was shrieking—to realize that the figure on the couch was Casper. He had clearly been sleeping, but he sprang to his feet immediately.

"What? What happened? What is it?"

I braced myself against the doorframe of the bathroom, my

heart pounding. There was a good chance I might throw up again. "What the hell are you doing here?" I choked out.

Casper raised both of his hands, as if he were trying to calm a spooked animal. "I brought you back last night. I didn't want to leave you alone. You were pretty wasted." He pointed to my small, sad, lumpy couch. "I slept here the whole time, I swear to God."

"Okay," I said. "Get out."

"Rachel—"

"No, I have no interest in anything you have to say. I don't—"

"I also stayed because I realized something about the case."

"There *is* no case. We're not—"

"Chrimbo only had pictures of Piper *entering* the club."

It was reflexive: "Yeah, because she left in a fucking body bag."

Casper was undeterred. "No, I mean, with how busy the place was that night, he would've stayed to get exit photos. Those are just as good, if not better. You wait to see who leaves with who, who's drunk out of their minds, the whole nine yards. Any pap worth their salt would've camped out."

Even though there was a part of me that didn't want to believe anything Casper said, there was a greater part of me that just couldn't help myself: "But Chrimbo didn't stay that night?"

Something like relief flashed in Casper's eyes. "No. He didn't stick around. So I tracked him down yesterday and asked him why. He told me that partway through the night, some guy came out and paid him to go a few blocks over to this other club, Aurora, and take pictures there. The guy said that there were big names over there and it would be worth just as much as he had paid him, if not more."

I blinked. "So?"

"So, Chrimbo went and took the pictures. He told me he'd send them over to me. Whoever the guy was, he has to be the mystery man on Molly's murder board. And there's got to be some reason why Mystery Man sent Chrimbo to that other club."

There was the same earnestness in Casper's expression as there had been the day we first met, in the alleyway near the *Icon* building. When he had handed me a page from my own article and tried to convince me that Molly hadn't overdosed. That it really was zebras, not horses. I hadn't believed him in that moment, but eventually I came to realize that he was right. And everything we had learned since—everything he and I had learned together, regardless of who he was or why he was doing it—had supported that truth.

I didn't trust him. But I couldn't shake Molly—*I have this sense about people.* And *better the devil you know.*

Casper was the devil I knew, I guess. He still wanted to find the truth. And I knew in my heart that I did too. I couldn't forsake Molly after everything. I couldn't give up now. And I couldn't exactly do it without Casper—I needed to see those pictures.

So I pointed to my laptop, sitting on the coffee table between us. "Pull up the photos."

He hesitated.

"What is it?"

"I can explain," he said. "About Celebritease."

"Is there a version of it where you weren't lying to me this whole time?"

His jaw tensed, a mournful look in his eyes. "No."

"Then I don't want to hear it." I gestured again to the computer. "Now. The photos."

Chrimbo's late-night exit photos from Aurora showed a number of celebrities leaving the club, in various states of dishevelment. Casper and I clicked through them until—

"Wait."

Nick Hart was exiting Aurora in jeans and a partially buttoned dress shirt, his hair artfully pushed back with a pair of sunglasses, an easy smile on his face. And there, in the corner of the photo, was . . .

Hailey Nichols.

The same Hailey Nichols who fought with Molly at spin class the morning of her death. The same Hailey Nichols who was desperate to dish out gossip about Molly when she thought we could get her into the tabloids. The same Hailey Nichols who was at Piper's birthday party.

The photos showed her hurrying after Nick, grabbing his arm, and looping hers through it. He gave her a smile that looked slightly aggrieved.

"But Hailey Nichols was at Entity," Casper said. "With Piper's entourage. Why would she be papped coming out of Aurora with Nick Hart?"

I thought of what Julia had said—*All I know is who was there that night. And who tried to make it look like they weren't.*

"Because she killed Piper," I said. "And she needed to establish an alibi. Getting papped leaving a club with a huge star like Nick would do just that." I couldn't tear my eyes away from the photograph—Hailey, the sequins on her dress winking in the light of the flashbulbs, a smug smile on her face.

Casper frowned. "But why would Hailey kill Piper?"

My mind raced. I thought of Jaz's report of Hailey's past: *She destroyed a display in the shoe department and hit a sales associate with a pair of Jimmy Choos . . .*

And Richard's thoughts on motive: *Angry is a bludgeoning, not a poisoning.*

Piper's death was a bludgeoning. *Acute head injury.* Piper's killer was definitely angry.

"Piper had everything Hailey wanted," I said slowly. "The fame, the recognition, all of it. What if she was jealous? What if they fought and Hailey just . . . lost control?" Like what had happened with the sales clerk. Only this time, the consequences were deadly. "Molly must've figured it out and confronted Hailey at Revolution that day. So she killed Molly too." I shook my head. "Hailey told us that Dax was cheating on Molly, and that Molly asked her for drugs. She was lying to make Molly seem unstable. To make it seem like she really did overdose."

Hailey's eyes had glistened with tears when Casper and I talked to her outside Kitson: *I didn't know Molly was planning anything like that.* It had seemed genuine in the moment. Was she a much better actor than her résumé would indicate?

"But Hailey must've had an accomplice," Casper said. "Someone covering for her after she killed Piper. Mystery Man was the one who told Chrimbo to get the pictures at Aurora, and the one who set Brady Pierce up to take the fall by getting him to wait in Piper's VIP suite. Who's Mystery Man?"

I continued to click through the photos. I frowned. There was Piper again, entering the club.

"The rest of these are from Entity, not Aurora," I said.

"Yeah, Chrimbo said he found a set of photos that he hadn't sent to Molly. These are the ones he rejected right off the bat. He thought he'd wiped them, but he found them on a backup drive."

We continued through the photos—shots that were completely out of focus or almost fully blocked by other cameras or people. There, in one corner, was a blurry Piper, waving at the crowd. There was the back of Hailey's head as she caught up with Julia and Winter.

And there, just behind them, at the edge of the frame, was a glimpse of a man in a suit, with slicked-back hair. He was holding a cell phone up to one ear, his face partially obscured. I recognized his watch first.

This was a gift from Molly when we got the Sun City *contract.*

It was Molly's agent. It was Damon Maxwell.

49

I called Maxwell Artistic Management, and the usual nasal-voiced receptionist answered.

"Veronica, it's Rachel West," I said without preamble. "Molly's friend. I'm wondering if Damon is in the office today?"

"He's not."

"Do you know where I could find him? It's pretty urgent."

"I'm sorry, he's on set with a client."

"With . . ."

"Nick," she said, as if it were obvious. "Nick Hart."

"Nick is *Damon's* client?" I said, and Casper's eyes widened.

We'll be right back here with you as the guest of honor.

"Yeah, Nick used to be with William Morris, but Damon worked his magic and signed him last summer. He's a huge get." Veronica lowered her voice. "To tell you the truth, after losing Molly and all, I'd be worried about the agency's position if Damon hadn't landed Nick."

My next question was already bubbling over: "Hey, can I ask—did Damon also represent Piper Standish?"

"No," Veronica replied. "Not for lack of trying, though."

"What do you mean?"

"Well, Damon's always looking to expand his client base, and Piper was a real star. He definitely courted her, but she was happy where she was. That's why he was so thrilled to lock Nick down. They finally put that superhero-movie deal through—you might've seen the announcement in *EW.* A five-film contract, can you believe it?"

"That's great," I said woodenly. "Good for them."

We said our goodbyes and hung up.

"So Damon is Nick's agent," Casper said. "Which means—"

"He was the one threatening Nick at the funeral," I replied. "And if Damon was involved with Piper's death—and Molly's—then he might be willing to do the same thing to Nick."

One of Casper's contacts reported that *Robot Wars 3* was shooting on location at an industrial park in South LA. I called Molly's assistant, Alyssa, as Casper and I drove there, and after a hurried greeting I got straight to it: "That day—the day Molly died—you said you misplaced her purse at the press junket."

"Yeah . . ."

"How did you get it back? Where did you find it?"

"I didn't," she said. "Damon did. He brought it to me."

What Alyssa told us when we spoke to her at the coffee shop flooded back to me all at once: *I took her home afterward. I wasn't feeling well, so I didn't stay long.*

"Did you use Molly's phone after that?" I asked.

A series of short, high-pitched barks suddenly came through from the other end of the line.

"Sorry," Alyssa said hurriedly. "It's Rainbow Pup. I think he's hungry. Or angry. It's hard to tell. What did you say?"

"Did you use Molly's phone that day?" I repeated, unable to keep the urgency from my voice. "After you got the purse back?"

"Yeah, just for a minute. She asked me to send a text."

"To who?"

"To you. Asking you to come by her place."

I squeezed my eyes shut briefly. "Okay. Thank you. That's really helpful."

The shooting location was a flurry of activity when we arrived—grips loading in equipment, background actors milling around, PAs running here and there. Casper and I managed to join the fray unnoticed. We were passing by craft services when I heard a jovial voice ring out above the crowd.

"No, get that stuff away from me, I'm serious," Nick was saying. "My trainer said he'll flay me alive if I stray from the nutrition plan. These muscles don't just happen on their own, you know."

We headed into the craft services tent. Nick was standing in there, in conversation with several other people—Damon was nowhere in sight—and he glanced in my direction, turned back to the group, and then did a double take.

"Rachel?"

A woman at Nick's elbow frowned over her plate of salad. "Isn't that the juice-shop girl? The one you said you *weren't* dating?"

Nick cut through the group and closed me in a one-armed hug. He was costumed just as you'd expect a giant-robot-slaying vigilante to be—a slick leather jacket and pants, combat boots, a variety of holsters filled with a variety of weapons, and an artful scrape above one eyebrow.

"Sorry, ignore Jess," he said to me, throwing a cheeky grin at the woman with the salad. She rolled her eyes but smiled back.

"She's on my PR team, so she's contractually obligated to track and squash all internet rumors."

"You should be paying me triple for as much squashing as I have to do for you."

"What can I say? I love a pressed juice." Nick turned his smile on me. "What are you doing here?"

"Do you have a second to talk?" I glanced around. "Um, privately?"

Jess rolled her eyes again, playing it up for the group. "Oh, but of course. Nick, you'll be the death of me. Just remember you're the one apologizing to hair and makeup if you mess up"—Jess waved a hand at his general figure—"any of that."

"Indecent acts on set? I would *never*." Nick shot an oversized wink at the group, and then turned back to me. "You want the grand tour?" He glanced over my shoulder, registering Casper's presence. "Who's your friend?"

Nick wound us through the shooting area, pointing out various tents and trailers and luxury portable bathrooms. I was eager to get the tour over with, though, to get somewhere where we could talk privately, so that we could warn Nick—before Damon made an appearance.

"When Damon threatened you at the funeral," I said, interrupting Nick as he guided us past the armory, "it wasn't about some interview, was it? It was about Piper Standish."

It made sense. If Nick had realized that something was off about that night with Hailey Nichols at Aurora, or if Molly went to him about it and he raised any sort of suspicion to Damon, Damon would've wanted to keep him quiet.

Nick frowned. "Sorry?"

"Look, can we just—" I took his arm and pulled him through

a nearby door, into a smaller offshoot of one of the larger warehouses. It was empty, and not lit for shooting.

"What's this all about?" Nick said, looking between Casper and me, confusion on his face.

I cut to the chase. "Damon covered up Piper Standish's murder. We think he was involved in Molly's death too. And if that's true, then—"

"Wait, wait, wait." Nick held up his hands. "Hold on. You think Damon's a *murderer*?"

"An accessory to murder, at the very least," Casper said. "Definitely an accomplice."

Nick shook his head. "No, they already got the guy who killed Piper. And everyone knows that Molly OD'd—"

There wasn't enough time to explain. "Look—"

"Why would Damon be involved in any of that?" Nick continued.

He had pinpointed the exact question that was still nagging at me. What did Damon Maxwell stand to gain by helping Hailey Nichols? She wasn't some huge star Damon was eager to sign—*She's not even* profile *enough.* So why would Damon help her?

My mind raced. Piper's birthday party at Entity. *Piper was pissed because one of her exes showed up uninvited. Some sleazy older guy she'd cut it off with a while back . . .*

It slotted together in my mind. "Piper's ex," I said. "The asshole who taped her without her permission. The one she was going to confront on her birthday. Was it Damon?"

Had Nick found out? I thought of what I overheard Damon say to Nick at the funeral: *Stop trying to be clever, and keep your fucking mouth shut.*

And then Veronica on the phone today: *They finally put that superhero-movie deal through . . . a five-film contract, can you believe it?*

Damon needed Nick as a client. Why would he jeopardize Nick's career by using him as an alibi for Hailey Nichols at Aurora?

I met Nick's clear blue, Malibu Ken gaze. "Or . . . was it you?"

"What are you talking about?"

My heart rate quickened. I could feel panic flickering at the edges of my vision, but I couldn't let it overtake me, not now. "The night Piper was murdered, you showed up at Entity. Not through the front—through the private entrance in the back." The same one Eliot left through when his set was cut short that night. "You didn't want her to know you'd be there."

Nick shook his head. "I wasn't at Entity that night."

All I know is who was there that night. And who tried to make it look like they weren't.

"No, you were three blocks over at Aurora, conveniently getting papped with Hailey Nichols. Is that why she's in this movie? You threw her a bone because she threw you an alibi?"

Confusion was still writ large on Nick's face. Too large. "Rachel, I have no idea what you're talking about. Is this some kind of bit? Am I being punk'd?" He glanced at Casper. "Is that guy in on it?"

I glanced at Casper too. Could he run for help while I distracted Nick? There was only one door into the room, and Nick was standing directly in front of it.

I tried to keep my voice even. "Seriously, you're gonna let a nonactor steal the big monologue where you explain exactly why you did it?"

"Did *what*?"

"You killed Piper. Because of . . . what?" I thought of the TV clip of Piper's mother's interview: *In July, Piper was slated to sit down with* Twenty-Twenty *for a major interview. An interview that never went forward, with the actress's death occurring just days before she was scheduled to appear on our program . . .*

"The bombshell interview she was going to give?" I continued. "Where she was going to reveal that you recorded her—when she was underage—without her consent? You had a five-picture deal in the works, and you couldn't let anything—like, oh, a sex scandal with a teenager—jeopardize that. So you thought maybe you'd scare her into silence. And when she wouldn't back down, you got angry and killed her."

Did Damon also represent Piper Standish?

No. Not for lack of trying, though.

"Damon happened to be there that night, trying to schmooze Piper into signing with him," I said, another piece rapidly falling into place in my mind. "When he discovered what you'd done, he said he'd help you cover it up if you signed with him instead. So he framed Brady and fixed your alibi at Aurora, with Hailey Nichols to vouch for you." Anger coursed through me. "Molly fought with Hailey the morning she died because . . ." My voice caught, but I pushed through. "Because Molly figured it out. She was trying to get Hailey to come forward about you. But Hailey refused because she didn't want to risk her role in the movie. Instead she called you and warned you that Molly knew what you had done. When Molly showed up at the press event—what? You stole her purse? Coated her phone in poison, handed it off to your agent, and considered it a job well done? How did you even get a transdermal poison?"

Nick just stared at me for a long moment. Then he said, "I'm a celebrity, babe. I can get anything I want."

I flashed on Molly and her Pinkberry, how it seemed like she could get whatever she wanted, whenever she wanted it. All she had to do was say the word. Did that really have no bounds?

Nick gave a short exhale. "Just have to say, you were right—a nonactor really shouldn't do the monologue." His expression turned rueful as he pulled a gun from one of his many holsters.

"Genuinely, this whole thing has just gotten completely out of control. And for such stupid reasons."

I swallowed. "So, what now? You're going to kill us too?"

Casper spoke, his voice tight. "That's a prop."

Nick looked at the gun for a moment, and then slipped it back into the holster with a sigh. "You're right." Then he pulled another, smaller handgun from inside his jacket. "But this one isn't."

"Yeah, sure." Casper sounded about as confident as I felt. "Why would you bring a gun on set?"

Nick gave a sheepish shrug. "What can I say? I'm a suspenders-and-a-belt kind of guy. I'm a top star, and there are some real nutcases out there. I carry it everywhere." He smiled, and it chilled me. "Right next to the Payday bar."

"We're on a busy set," I said.

"That's true. But this part isn't exactly jumping, is it? You know why? Because they're planning to blow up this building in about"—he consulted the large, industrial-looking watch on his wrist—"ten minutes. The explosions in Mike McColm movies are real, after all. It's pretty convenient." He gestured to Casper with the gun. "You. Go stand up against the wall."

Casper hesitated, looking at me.

Nick flipped the gun's safety off. "I'll give you three seconds."

Do it, I mouthed, and Casper backed slowly toward the wall opposite the door.

"It was an accident, for the record," Nick said. "Piper. Maybe I pushed her too hard. But she came at me first." He shook his head. "I just wanted to talk to her. If she hadn't come in with that energy, wanting to fight, wanting to accuse me of doing fucked-up shit—"

"She was a teenager."

"Don't kid yourself, she knew exactly what she was doing. And then she wanted airtime, and what a great way to get it—some sob story about how a big star took advantage of her, the poor little defenseless kid—when the truth is that she was fucking *bitter* and wanted to ruin shit for me because she didn't like how things ended between us. She wanted to screw up my career, my *life*, everything that I've built, just because I didn't turn out to be the boyfriend of her dreams. What happened to her was her own fault. Don't dish it out if you can't fucking take it."

"And Molly?"

"She figured it out. It was the damn PR girl's fault. She knew I was there that night, and then she gets all buddy-buddy with Molly, and the next thing you know, Molly starts asking questions. So I get the PR girl fired—problem solved. But then there was the other one. The assistant! She gets to talking to Molly too somehow. I get her fired too, but it doesn't matter, because now Molly's full-bore *investigating* like she's fucking *Dateline*. She was going to go to the press. She was going to make me out to be some kind of murderer." He considered me for a moment. "Just like you're planning to do, huh? I should've known when you brought it up at the juice shop that you were going to end up being a real pain in my ass."

"Too bad you couldn't get me fired—I'm already unemployed."

He smiled. "I'm not a total idiot, though. I know how this scene goes. You try to keep me talking while one of you dials nine-one-one behind your back."

He wasn't wrong. He advanced on me and grabbed my arm, wrenching my phone out of my grasp and throwing it against the floor. It smashed apart. At the same time, Casper surged toward Nick.

Nick shot him without hesitation.

I let out a strangled cry. Casper looked at me for a split second, a devastating mix of shock and surprise on his face, before crumpling to the floor.

"I said to stand against the wall. I said that. He could've just listened to me." Nick took a deep breath, exhaled. Shook his head as if to clear it. "Okay. It's okay. This is fine. We can work with this." He trained the gun on me. "Okay. Here's what I got. You're the fangirl I threw a bone to, who gets obsessed and comes after me. We've already been seen together, so that's not a big stretch. It worked great with the Piper fanboy we pinned that whole thing on. So you come in, you try to shoot me."

He swung the gun toward Casper's motionless form. "That guy—he's the hero. He selflessly jumps in front of top action star Nick Hart and saves my life. He'll probably get mentioned in the In Memoriam section of the Golden Globes, maybe the Oscars if it's a slow year." He gestured to himself. "I run out of here, bar the door, and then go grab the first stupid PA I see, *oh shit, she has a gun, she shot someone, please, you have to help, please*—but before anyone can do anything, *bam!* This place goes up in flames. They find your bodies afterward. It makes for some great headlines. Ticket sales for the movie increase tenfold, because everyone wants to see Nick Hart's stalker get blown up. I go on *Twenty-Twenty* and cry my eyes out. It's a win-win-win. Not for you guys, obviously, but, you know, that's kind of just the nature of the situation. You have to break a few eggs, right?"

"Nobody's going to—" I started. I was going to refute his plan, keep him talking to buy us more time, just like he said, just like they did in the movies.

"I won't shoot you, if that makes you feel better," Nick said. "We did have some good banter."

Before I could react, he swung the gun up and brought it swiftly down on the top of my head.

50

I wasn't knocked out cold. The world didn't immediately cut to black. It wasn't nearly that pat.

It did hurt immensely, though, and while my first instinct was to let out an extremely loud stream of expletives, instead I fell to the floor and just lay there, eyes closed.

True to his word, Nick ran from the room and slammed the door shut behind him. I heard the metallic click of a lock.

I sprang up and flew to where Casper lay, motionless.

I peeled his jacket back. Blood was blooming steadily across his T-shirt underneath. My heart seized in my chest.

"Casper." I grabbed hold of his face. He blinked, his eyes unfocused. "Casper, look at me. Please."

He grasped my sleeve weakly. "Get out," he rasped. "Go."

There wasn't a chance in hell that was going to happen. I looked around the room wildly. If this place was really going to blow up, was it wired with explosives? Could I, a person with absolutely zero knowledge of explosives, disarm a literal bomb? What would Rex Blaze do? Which wire had he cut to disarm the bomb attached to the rudder of Air Force One? Why was I thinking of *Nuclear Nucleus* in this moment? *Focus, Rachel, focus, holy shit—*

There was a window set high in the wall opposite the door—if I located one of the explosives, could I throw it through the window like some kind of bootleg flare? Could I get up there somehow, break the glass, climb out? What about Casper? Casper . . .

His breathing was shallow. None of it mattered if I couldn't save Casper.

I thought desperately back to med school. That night at the hospital spliced in, unbidden. The blood—there was so much blood—

School. The lecture on traumatic bleeds. *Identify the source of the bleeding. Apply firm and constant pressure. The skin should bow beneath your hands.*

I could do this. I could. Get the bleeding under control. Get Casper up—get us both up—get to the door, and . . . break it down, I don't know, I'd figure it out as I went—

One thing at a time.

Identify the source.

I placed my hands on the wound and pressed down hard. Casper's breath hitched.

"Don't worry," I said. "You'll be fine. Just look at me."

Apply firm and constant pressure.

"I bet right now you're wishing I had finished school," I said, a hysterical breath of laughter bubbling up. "Or you're wishing we'd never come here. Or that you'd never met me. You're wishing I never got the stupid idea to leave my life behind and come to LA. You're thinking, why didn't Rachel just tough it out? Why did she think any of this was a good idea?" I thought of Molly: *What if I hadn't made this choice or that choice? What would my life be like? Would it be better? Worse? Would I be happy?*

My voice caught in my throat. "If neither of us had ever met Molly, what would we be doing right now?"

Casper shook his head. "Worth it," he choked out. "It was worth it."

I nodded. My eyes filled with tears. "It was, right?"

He grabbed my wrist. "Ray . . ."

No one called me that but Molly. "Casper."

"I'm not— Fuck." His chest heaved. Tears were pooling at the corners of his eyes. "I'm not—"

Suddenly, miraculously, the door swung open.

Constant pressure. I couldn't let up.

Footsteps pounded. Someone yelled, "In here!"

Casper's grip on my wrist loosened. His hand fell away as a stream of people burst into the room.

WWW.CELEBRITEASE.COM

June 28, 2008
2:17 PM PST

Look. We here at the Tease are going to be real with you:

There was no way in a hundred thousand years of frozen-over hell that we could have ever predicted this. But apparently Nick Hart is a fucking murderer.

(Allegedly.)

51

Fortunately, my text to Lee had gone through before Nick smashed my phone against the floor, and Lee sent officers to the film site. Nick was apprehended easily—by the time he reached the "first stupid PA" he saw, the production team had already clocked that something was wrong. In large part because the section of warehouse that we were in was not in fact the section of warehouse that was slated to blow up that day. It was actually intended for a short scene that was meant to shoot later that afternoon—and plant mics had already been placed throughout the room. When the sound engineer overheard our conversation and realized that it might be real—not part of some rehearsal, or Nick just fooling around—she reported it immediately.

Everything after the warehouse door opened was a blur to me. I couldn't have told you how many people came onto the scene or who pulled me away from Casper or how I got into an ambulance, I couldn't have placed the faces of the paramedics or the nurse who did my intake at the ER. Someone asked me for an emergency contact and I gave them Anton's number. Someone asked me if I knew Casper's emergency contact.

"No," I said. "I don't know."

Casper was taken into surgery, and I was taken to get an X-ray. Police officers—not Lee—came to take a statement. The doctor ordered a CT scan. Anton had arrived by the time I got back from it.

"Holy shit, Rachel," he said when I was settled in my hospital room. He moved toward me, but then hesitated, as if unsure whether I was in the right state for a hug. I reached out and pulled him into one.

"Is Casper okay?" I mumbled into his shoulder. "Have you heard anything?"

"Yeah, I overheard the nurses talking. It sounded like his surgery went well. He's in recovery right now."

"What did they say exactly?"

"I'm the wrong person to be asking about complex medical stuff, but I know someone definitely said 'everything's looking good.'"

I let out a breath. "Thank God."

He pulled back and looked at me. "How are you?"

I shook my head. I couldn't even begin to articulate it.

"You did it," he said. "You found Molly's killer."

That part felt entirely surreal. Grief and anger still coursed through me, mingled with relief and, at the back of it all, something I couldn't quite define. A weird sense of . . . pride? Anton was right—we had done it. We had found Molly's killer. We had uncovered the truth behind her death.

"And you effectively destroyed the *Robot Wars* franchise," Anton added.

"No, Nick did that all by himself."

"True. Obviously on account of being a murderous sociopath.

But in a just world, his wooden acting would've done the trick on its own."

I cracked a smile. But it quickly retreated.

"I'm sorry," I said. "About yesterday." Had it really been only a day ago? It felt like a lifetime.

"Don't even think about that right now. You're literally hooked up to . . . *devices* . . ."

"This is just a heart rate monitor."

"Yeah, and I can see your heart rate spiking."

"Because I suck at apologizing. But I mean it. I'm sorry. You were right. I was trying to run away. You've done nothing but be here for me, even though I've been a shitty friend—"

"Rachel. You're allowed to mess up."

I shook my head. "But—"

"You are." He took my hand. "And I am too. Keep that in mind when Eliot eventually decides to leave me for one of Rihanna's unreasonably hot backup dancers and I'm drunk and crying at the club and need someone to come pour me into a cab."

"I will be that person," I said. "But it's not going to happen. You're hotter than Rihanna's hottest backup dancer."

"You're right," he said sagely. "I am." He squeezed my hand. "Everyone's here to see you, you know."

"Everyone?"

"The whole crew. Fadia, Richard, Jaz, Elena."

"They came?"

"Of course they did. We're still a murder klatch, aren't we?"

I gave a small smile. "Right. I mean, I guess we're whatever the murder klatch becomes after the murder is solved."

"We might have to become a book club."

"That's doable. I just read one about a secret millionaire . . ."

Anton smiled. Then his eyes widened. "Oh, that reminds me!

How could I forget? An extremely handsome detective came to see you too."

There was a light rap on the door, and then, as if summoned, Lee stuck his head in.

Anton looked back at me, his eyes now comically wide. "I did that," he whispered. "I just made that happen. Is this *The Secret* in action? Am I a psychic witch like Fadia?"

I couldn't gauge by Lee's expression whether he had heard the phrase *extremely handsome detective*, but I really hoped he hadn't.

"Maybe you could grab the others," I told Anton. "I'd really like to see everyone."

"Sure." Anton stood. "I'll go do that. And we'll be back in . . . a reasonable amount of time." He headed to the door. "Maybe a little longer than you'd expect. For totally legitimate reasons."

Anton left, and then it was just the two of us. Lee met my eyes, and his face was readable once more: concern, relief, exasperation, and something else that was harder to parse—worry? Guilt? Regret? Or were those just my own feelings, reflected back at me?

"It was a zebra," I said.

He looked for a second like he might either laugh or cry. "Fucking hell, Rachel."

"You got my text."

"Yeah, thank God I did. What were you thinking?"

"You're here to lecture me? Shouldn't there be at least a twenty-four-hour grace period when you've been a victim of blunt force trauma?"

He squeezed his eyes shut briefly. "I'm sorry. How are you? How do you feel?"

"I've been better. But . . . at least I'm here. And not shot or blown up or otherwise wiped off the face of the earth by the most repulsive of *People*'s sexiest men alive."

"You were right. About everything."

"I wasn't right about who did it, though," I said. "I thought it was Hailey Nichols, heavily assisted by Damon Maxwell—who, by the way, is extremely involved in all of this—"

"I know. Nick gave him up immediately. Maxwell fled the set, but we picked him up at his office."

"Good." I swallowed. "Molly figured it out first. That it was Nick. That's why he killed her." My voice stuck in my throat. Maybe it was the adrenaline wearing off, or the pain medication or the combined psychic weight of the last forty-eight hours. But I let the tears gather without attempting to push them back. "It's so fucking unfair."

"It is. I'm sorry."

It was quiet.

When Lee spoke again, his voice was soft. "I should have listened to you. It never should've gotten to this point. I'm so sorry."

I shook my head. I was sorry too, but it had nothing to do with the case, and everything to do with what had happened between us at my apartment. *I need you to know that I don't actually want you.* I didn't know how to bring it up. How to take it back.

So I just cleared my throat, trying to get the roughness out of my voice. "I talked to some officers earlier. I don't know if I'll have to do a more detailed testimony . . ."

Lee nodded. "You might have to give an additional statement. But so you know, the case is being transferred to another unit—the one for high-profile crimes." The one we had talked about in the gas station parking lot, what felt like ages ago. "It's probably for the best. I'm not exactly impartial anymore. I don't know if I ever was." He shifted his gaze across the room, and then back to me, discomfort obvious on his face. "Look, about what happened between us—"

"I was kind of out of my mind," I said. "You did the right thing, and I was really vicious about it, and I . . . I'm sorry."

I didn't mean what I said that day. The only honest part was me wanting to kiss you.

I continued: "If we could just . . . forget that it happened . . ."

He considered me for a moment, and then nodded. Neither of us spoke.

"So . . . I guess this is it then," I said finally, ignoring the fierce pang of regret in my chest.

"Maybe I'll see you at Sawasdee," Lee replied, a hopeful note in his voice. "Or . . . at the Circle K."

The pang of regret transformed into something small and warm that I didn't want to examine too closely. "Maybe I'll buy you a beer. Or . . . some Oreos."

One corner of Lee's mouth lifted. "I'd like that."

~~~

"I just grabbed whatever I had on hand" was the first thing Fadia said when the Palm Vista crew poured through the door of my hospital room a few moments after Lee had departed. She pulled an enormous Tupperware from her even larger purse and opened it. "Mini profiteroles and chocolate-dipped madeleines. You should get your blood sugar up." She turned to Elena. "Shouldn't she get her blood sugar up? For the shock?" Before Elena could respond, Fadia continued. "I'm pretty sure you should, for the shock. Take four or five, or six or seven, take as many as you want."

Baffled, I took a mini profiterole and a madeleine. And then I burst into tears.

"What? What is it?" Richard said, looking panicked. He turned to Elena too. "Is it the shock?"

"Do you not like dark chocolate?" Fadia asked, looking equally panicked.

"Maybe we should give you some space," Elena said, glancing at Anton, who looked poleaxed.
~~~

"I'm not in shock," I sobbed, even though I might have been. "I'm just . . ." Relieved? Devastated? Touched? "I'm sorry," I said. Was apologizing like a muscle? Was I getting stronger the more I exercised it? "For . . . trying to shut this whole thing down, when all you guys ever did was try to help me."

"Oh," Fadia said. "Don't worry about that."

"But—"

"Here." Jaz grabbed the Tupperware from Fadia and thrust it at me. "Take four or five more, and tell us everything that happened."

So I pulled myself together and filled them in on all the details of what had happened with Nick. We talked and talked, the six of us crammed into my little hospital room, and I couldn't even say how much time passed. It was only after a nurse stopped by to check in on me for the third time that Elena let out a sigh.

"We should probably let you get some rest, Rachel."

"I'm staying," Anton said, in a tone that brooked no argument. "Little Miss Concussion here needs a chaperone. But I'll walk you guys out."

Jaz hung back. "Um . . . could I talk to Rachel alone for a minute?"

"Of course," Elena said. "We'll be in the hall."

"Thank you for coming," I called as the group headed out. At the door, Elena caught my eye and gave me a warm smile.

"Of course."

When we were alone, Jaz turned back to me. "So . . . I did some more looking."

That hadn't boded well the first time she said it to me. It was with some apprehension that I asked, "What did you find?"

Her expression was enigmatic. "It's . . . kind of more of a *who* than a what."

She reached into the front pocket of her massive hoodie and pulled out several sheets of printer paper folded into quarters. She handed them to me, and I unfolded them. The top page was a photo of a man, in his late twenties or so, with a shaved head and a thick beard.

"Who's this?"

"Casper Jones."

I looked at the photo again, then up at Jaz. "But—"

"At least, he went by the name Casper. As a paparazzo. His real name is Julian Jones. He's the one who registered CJ Inc and Celebritease. He used to live in West Hollywood. Guess who he lived with."

I blinked.

Jaz handed me another printout. It was a security camera photo of two familiar faces.

"This is from a street cam across from the juice shop where you met Nick," she said.

"Those are Casper's roommates." The very same roommates I met at the HYPER BLITZ launch. *Settle a bet for us. Are you or are you not Rachel West?* "That's Luke and Ryder."

Jaz nodded. "I really only scratched the surface, but if I pulled enough footage I think we'd find one or the other of them at just about every spot where Celebritease papped you in the past couple of weeks."

"So . . . *they* run Celebritease?"

"Sure looks like it."

"And Casper . . . our Casper . . . was in on it?"

Jaz shook her head. "I don't know. But this guy"—she tapped the picture of Julian—"definitely started the whole thing." Julian stared back at us from the page, a defiant gleam in his eyes.

"But if this is the real Casper Jones, then . . . who's our Casper?"

A smile lit up Jaz's face suddenly. "Once I knew what to look for," she said, "that was surprisingly easy to find out."

52

Eliot came by the hospital in the early evening with some food for Anton and me, plus a large bouquet of flowers and something in a brown paper bag that he tried to hide until Anton explicitly pointed it out.

"I didn't know what to get for someone after something so bonkers traumatic," Eliot said, his expression turning sheepish. "So I brought a six-pack of HYPER BLITZ because I thought it would be funny. I should've gone with the teddy bear, I'm very sorry."

I grinned. "No, this is right up my alley."

"Don't drink it, though. Combined with the meds, it might actually kill you."

"Noted."

After we ate, I cajoled Anton into going out to get some air with Eliot.

"You don't have to sit vigil at my bedside. I'm fine."

"What if you have some kind of delayed post-concussion collapse? What if you lose your mind and drink the HYPER BLITZ?"

"In either scenario, trained medical professionals are just the press of a button away."

"But what if—" He hesitated. I could see it on his face: he was worried about my emotional state more than anything else.

I shook my head. "I'm okay. For real. Go take a walk with your boyfriend."

Anton's eyes widened. "That's not—we're not—"

"We haven't exactly defined the relationship yet," Eliot said. He slipped his hand into Anton's. "I don't know about you, Ant, but I kind of like the sound of it."

Anton nodded, trying very hard to suppress a smile. "I'm willing to discuss."

After they left, I waited a few minutes before I slipped out of my room and went to track Casper down. Jaz had given me his room number before she left, along with another fierce hug.

When I reached Casper's room, the door was ajar. I saw Casper before he saw me. He was wearing a hospital gown, lying in bed with a huge bandage on one shoulder, his arm in a sling. His eyes were closed.

For a moment, I just looked at him.

His eyes opened. He blinked once, twice. Looked in my direction.

"Rachel?"

"Mm."

I had absolutely no idea what to say. He stared back at me, and I could tell he felt the same way. Nothing was entirely sufficient to capture . . . all of it. Everything we had just been through.

I stepped into the room. "You okay?"

He nodded. "You?"

I nodded.

"I heard they got him," he said.

"They did."

Casper shut his eyes briefly. "Thank fuck."

"How are you feeling?" I asked after a silence.

"I've definitely been better." He swallowed. "But I'm alive. Thanks to you."

"You wouldn't have been shot if it weren't for me. I should've . . . It should've been me."

"But it wasn't. Which is great, because I couldn't have kept you from bleeding out. I was a photography major."

I let out a weak breath of laughter. Then it was quiet again.

"I'm glad you're okay," I said finally. "Cameron."

He met my gaze.

"Cameron James Finch," I continued. "Formerly of *The California Kids Crew*. The ill-advised *Mickey Mouse Club* rip-off of the mid-nineties."

He squeezed his eyes shut again, and this time he looked relieved and chagrined and embarrassed all at once, all in one quick moment. And when he opened his eyes, he just looked like Casper. Unruffled. Or, rather, like Cameron, I suppose. I was still wrapping my head around all this.

The other photo Jaz had given me was a headshot of a short, round-faced kid with large front teeth and a mop of curly hair. He was wearing a collared shirt that was way too big for him. His arms were folded across his chest, and he was shooting a big, toothy grin at the camera. He looked like the mischievous kid next door who comes over unannounced and raids the fridge. He looked like a character who definitely had a catchphrase.

"Tell me," I said. "Tell me what you were going to say when you said that you could explain."

"I'm not Celebritease," he replied. "Because I'm not Casper Jones."

"You're Cameron Finch. You were a child star."

"I was a child *actor*. There's a big difference. Child stars are successful."

"You were on a TV show, though."

"Yeah, at a doomed cable network that canceled us after two seasons. And then I failed about a thousand auditions, hit puberty, got even less castable, and never landed another part again."

"You knew Molly," I said. "When you were kids. You worked together."

He nodded. "Molly was on *The California Kids Crew* too. Before she got cast as Betsey Blue." A ghost of a smile passed over his face. "She was . . . you know, exactly what you'd think. The coolest and prettiest and most interesting girl in the world. She did me a favor by acknowledging my existence."

I could imagine it clearly: the round-faced kid from the headshot trailing after a young Molly on a TV set.

"How did it happen?" I asked. "How did you . . . become Casper Jones? And why?"

For a moment, Casper just fiddled with the cord attached to his heart rate monitor.

"I . . . had left the industry," he began. "And LA. But then I fucked up in college, and my family situation was . . . not the best . . . and anyway, I just wanted to come back. So I moved back out here, just crashing on couches, looking for a place to live. Eventually I saw a roommate-wanted ad, and it was for Luke and Ryder's place. They were both already working as paps. They told me this Casper guy had been living with them for a few months but then suddenly up and left town for good. He was a pap too, and had sold pictures to a few places. Luke and Ryder convinced me that it would be so much easier if I just . . . stepped in for him. I could take over his room, his contacts, they'd lend me the cameras, share tips, anything I needed. I was pretty broke at the time, and it all just . . . seemed like this amazing shortcut."

I shook my head. "How did it even work? You don't look anything like that guy."

"It's not like I ever tried to get a bank loan in his name."

I thought of Casper at the bar, sliding his ID face down to the bartender. He didn't want me to see the name on his license.

I thought too of the photo Jaz gave me of the real Casper Jones. Their coloring *was* similar, but the real Casper had that beard, and the buzzed head, and thick eyebrows . . .

"What about the paps who knew him, though? The original Casper?" I asked.

"There's a fair amount of turnover."

I couldn't help myself: "Really? I thought it was an incredibly stable career path."

He smiled a little. "If anyone questioned it, I just told them I'd gotten into cryotherapy and this crazy fad diet from the Balkans, where you only eat beetroot and paprika. People told me I looked ten years younger. And that I'm way better looking without the beard."

"Seriously? That worked?"

"It's not like we're in the business of taking pictures of each other. I'm not sparing a second glance at whoever's standing next to me at a club entrance when some huge name walks out. I probably wouldn't notice if Chrimbo got swapped out." He paused, his expression turning serious. "But, Rachel, I had no idea that the real Casper Jones started Celebritease. Or that Luke and Ryder took over running it after he left town. Honestly. I was telling the truth in the car that day when you asked me. I would never do that to you. Or to Molly. Ever."

I didn't speak.

"Luke and Ryder were tracking me," he continued. "I think they thought that, because I had been in the industry before, I'd have more connections. After you confronted me yesterday . . . I had an inkling of what might've happened. I found a bug in my car, and I knew it had to be them who put it there. That's how they were getting info. And when I confronted them, they confessed right away. They—" He cut himself off abruptly, jaw tensing.

"What?"

"They laughed it off. Said it was crazy that it took this long for me to figure it out." He shook his head. "Needless to say, I'm moving out of their place." A pause. "But everything else was just like I told you, I swear. That night at the club with Molly, getting my hand broken—all that stuff happened. I just left out the part where Molly recognized me. She knew right away who I was. That's why she helped me, and that's why she let me trail her. She always said she never minded helping out a fellow California Kid."

"Didn't she wonder why you were calling yourself Casper now?"

"She liked it," he replied. "She said I couldn't pull off being a pap named Cam anyway. I think her exact words were, 'It would be insipid. And yes, I know what *insipid* means.'"

I could imagine, with perfect clarity, Molly saying it. I swallowed against the lump in my throat.

"Why didn't you tell me in the first place?"

"*Oh, by the way, I was on TV as a kid, and also, I'm working under a fake name*? When do you reveal something like that?"

"When you're sitting on a sidewalk, drunk out of your mind. I've found that's a pretty good moment for a big reveal."

One corner of his mouth lifted briefly, but then his expression turned sad.

"You're right," he said. "I should've told you the truth from the start. I'm sorry."

I didn't know what to say. Maybe I was bad at accepting apologies too. There was a part of me that wanted to reach out, grab Casper's hand, give it a squeeze. But I didn't. I just cleared my throat and said, "So, what am I supposed to call you now?"

He let out a short exhale. "Is it weird that I don't even know? I've been Casper for a few years now. I've actually gotten really used to it. I think part of the reason it was so easy to take on was because . . ." He paused. "I don't know. I guess I didn't want to go back to being the kid who was in the business before, and who failed so terribly at it. I wanted to start fresh. Be someone new. Someone better."

"Maybe you can split the difference," I said with a half smile. "Be a little bit of both. Maybe you're Casper Finch now."

He gave a small smile back. "Maybe I am."

ICON ONLINE

JUNE 29, 2008

Details continue to unfold regarding the alleged murder of actress Molly Byrne.

Actor Nick Hart and the actor's agent, Damon Maxwell, were taken into custody after an on-set confrontation in which a shooting allegedly occurred. According to sources, Hart became erratic following accusations of his alleged involvement in the grisly nightclub murder of actress Piper Standish.

Robot Wars 3 costar Hailey Nichols has come forward with the shocking claim that she was blackmailed by Hart and Maxwell to provide an alibi for the star on the night of Standish's death.

Byrne's former flame, paparazzo Dax Van Sant, was on the scene and captured the photos below as Hart was escorted into the courthouse.

"Justice will be served for Molly," Van Sant told reporters. "That's the most important part of all of this."

Byrne's former manager, Calvin Price, also spoke to *Icon*: "It's unspeakable. Molly was a true gem; she had the biggest heart. Those two [Hart and Maxwell] deserve the worst of what's coming to them."

Representatives for the Byrne and Standish families have released a joint statement requesting privacy during this difficult time. Representatives for Hart and Maxwell could not be reached as of the time of reporting. Sources have confirmed that filming for *Robot Wars 3: Omnitron Returns* has been halted indefinitely.

53

I was back in my apartment the following day—trying to rest like Fadia and Anton had made me promise I would—when a knock sounded at my front door.

It was a delivery man, bearing a large fruit basket.

I unpacked the contents on my kitchen island: dragon fruit, star fruit, yuzu, grapefruit, and maybe a pomelo (again, I wasn't entirely certain). I knew it could have come from only one person, and the card confirmed it:

Thank you. Here for you anytime. xVIVIAN

I picked up a star fruit, contemplated it for a moment, and then gave it a rinse before beginning to slice it. Maybe I would embrace fresh fruit in this weird new phase of my life. Here in the aftermath of everything.

I was just polishing off the last piece of star fruit when a text message came in from an unlisted number.

Anton had swung by earlier and dropped off a new cell phone

("You can pay me back with your riches when they're out of probate"), and I had been getting messages and calls on it nonstop since the news about Nick Hart had broken. From family members, old school friends and acquaintances, former coworkers at *Icon*, even Irina—*especially* Irina, in fact, along with dozens of other outlets looking for quotes and interviews.

I had stopped answering. I was even considering burying my brand-new phone next to the abandoned grills in the courtyard, but then I happened to glance at it when this latest text came in.

come to mollys, the message said.

Another text quickly followed.

its amy

Prove it, I replied. Say something only Amy Byrne would say.

hydrox, she replied.

That was hard to ignore. So I went to Molly's.

The gate swung open as I pulled up, and when I reached the house Amy was already standing at the open front door in a purple velour tracksuit and Uggs, her arms folded, one hip cocked.

"I heard you almost died too," she said when I got out of my car.

"Something like that. You think we should start a club?"

She didn't smile, but she didn't glare either. She just examined me for a moment, and then she turned and headed into the house. When I didn't follow, she paused in the foyer.

"Well? Aren't you coming?"

So I headed inside too.

The formal living room featured a massive white sectional with a liberal assortment of fuzzy throw pillows. Amy sat down on one section and I sat down on another. She picked up a fuzzy pink pillow and held it against herself.

"What did you want to talk about?" I said when it seemed like she wasn't going to start the conversation.

"Our horoscopes," she replied, and then rolled her eyes. "What do you think I want to talk about?"

"I'm a Virgo."

"You're annoying is what you are."

Avoiding the topic wouldn't change what had happened. It was best to rip the Band-Aid off. "You want to know what happened with Nick."

Anger, pure and unadulterated, flashed across Amy's face. "I'm not wasting my breath on that worthless piece of shit. He can rot in prison, and he fucking will."

"Then what do you want to talk about?"

Amy waved a hand, encompassing the living room. The house at large.

"I don't want it," I said when I realized what she meant. "The house. The money. Whatever I need to do, or sign, or whatever, just . . . tell me. I'll do it."

Amy let out a short breath of laughter.

"What?"

"No, it's just . . . I thought about it a lot after I was in the hospital. And here I was about to tell you that I won't fight you for it. My parents won't either. They'll do whatever I want. And if Molly wanted you to have it, then . . . you should have it." A pause. "But thank God you said what you said first."

"I mean it." It was the truth.

"It's not about . . ." She swallowed. "It's not about the money. It's that this was her home. This is the place she chose, the things she liked, everything she thought was important, or beautiful, or . . . meaningful . . ."

I thought of Sam's figurine, the one I had gifted him for his birthday. I still had it, wrapped in paper in a box under my bed.

"I know you weren't just a stranger to her," Amy continued. "I know that. I just . . . I can't bring her back. But I still want to hold on to her . . . in any way that I can."

I nodded. "I understand."

Amy looked off across the room for a moment, blinked rapidly. When she looked back at me, her gaze was clear. "I guess Molly was right about you," she said finally.

"What do you mean?"

"That you're genuine. That you have no ulterior motive." Something like amusement flashed in her eyes. "Don't get me wrong, I'm not going to adopt you like she did. I'm not like that. We're not going to be friends. Or hold hands and skip off into the sunshine."

"That's fine."

"But . . . thank you."

"For what?"

Amy toyed with the edge of the throw pillow. "For being her friend. For being there for her."

I shook my head. "I wish I'd done more."

"Me too," Amy said. "I wish you'd done more too."

When I looked over at her, one corner of her mouth lifted in a small smile. She had a dimple in her left cheek, just like Molly.

"Kidding," she said, and her eyes shone as she added, "mostly."

I was still parked outside Molly's house when I called Natalie.

I had talked to my family while I was in the hospital. My mom wanted to fly out. I told her it wasn't necessary. My dad was worried about the medical bills. I told him I'd figure it out. Natalie just told me to get some rest.

I wasn't sure if she'd pick up the phone. But she did, on the second ring.

"What's going on?" she said instead of *Hello.* "Are you okay? Did something else happen?"

"Yeah," I replied. "I just foiled a kidnapping at In-N-Out. I'll be on the news at ten."

Relief was evident in her voice, with a dash of exasperation. "Sounds like you're feeling better."

"I am," I said. "And . . . I'm sorry." My breath hitched. "I'm really sorry, Natalie. I know I should have—"

"It's okay."

"It's not. I'll be better," I said. "I want to do better." I thought about what Amy said at Molly's funeral: *That's all that I wanted from her, to have her as my sister. To have her here. I wish she had known that.* "As your sister."

She exhaled. "Don't get carried away. Just come home at Christmas. Answer the phone when I call you. Tell me how you're actually doing."

"I will," I said. "You have to do the same, okay?"

"Deal." A pause. "So, how are you actually doing?"

"I'm . . ." I couldn't quite find a word to sum it up. Exhausted? But better than before. Definitely better. "I'm just happy to be here."

From: alyssas8023@yahoo.com
To: rwest901@yahoo.com
Subject: Thank you and Question

Rachel,

I heard you're back home recovering from the whole Nick Hart ordeal. I wanted to reach out to say I hope you're doing well, and to thank you for what you've done for Molly by uncovering the truth. I'm not sure how many calming breaths she would recommend given what you've been through, but I hope the kombucha I sent over to your place is a help.

In case you're at all curious, I've just landed a job as Alessandra Delgado's executive assistant. Apparently, the assistant she hired at Nick's recommendation was "a total disaster—is there any surprise?" Alessandra sends her warm wishes to you as well, and an invitation for a trip on her fiancé's yacht anytime you would like (but speaking as her new assistant: please check with me prior to any bookings to make sure the offer still stands and that the yacht is available).

My schedule is about to become particularly hectic, as Alessandra is currently splitting her time between LA, NYC, and Monaco. Plus, with the baby on the way . . . it's going to be a bit of a circus!

Which leads me to my question: how do you feel about pets?

Best,
Alyssa

54

I can't keep him." Molly's toy poodle, Rainbow Pup, sat perfectly still on my couch, unblinking. Anton and I stared at him. After a moment, Rainbow Pup let out a small huff, spun in a circle, and curled up into a tight ball.

"Wait, that thing's alive?" Anton burst out.

"What's alive?" someone called as my front door swung open.

I looked up as Fadia entered. "I guess we're all just traipsing in whenever we want now, huh?"

"You wouldn't leave your door unlocked if you didn't want me to come on in," she replied with a wink. She crossed over to the kitchen and set a casserole dish on the counter. "What are you guys—" She caught sight of Rainbow Pup, and her face split into the brightest smile. "Oh, what a precious little guy! Are you pet sitting? Adopting? Can I hold him? What's his name? I love him already."

Anton and I looked at each other.

With my enthusiastic blessing, Fadia adopted Rainbow Pup and granted me unlimited visitation rights. I was thrilled to see him settled into a new home, no longer forced to live out of Alyssa's Louis Vuitton Neverfull. I had no doubt that Fadia would put as much care into being a pet owner as she did into being a hostess, and a home chef, and a friend—which is to say, Rainbow Pup would receive top-tier care. It was hard to tell if he really appreciated it. It was hard to tell what he felt about anything, but Fadia insisted there was an "old soul" contained within that fuzzy five-pound body.

Several days after Casper was discharged from the hospital, we all met at Richard's apartment.

An apartment that now suddenly featured . . . about twice as much furniture as it had before. The television was sitting atop a real TV stand rather than a milk crate. There were four actual chairs around the dining table, and an upholstered armchair near the couch, and a low wooden coffee table, and even an area rug.

"I went to IKEA," Richard said, coloring slightly, when Anton had pointed out the change. "There was . . . a sale. So I thought I'd just . . ."

"Buy out the showroom?" Anton said brightly.

"Fadia mentioned that it would be nice to have more places for people to sit," Richard said in a rush. "If people . . . happened to keep coming by. Anyway, make yourself at home." He hurried off to the kitchen. Anton and I shared an amused look.

The murder board still stood in its place of prominence in the living room. Someone—presumably Richard—had circled the photo of Nick Hart in red marker and written *CULPRIT* across it.

The entries for Casper and me had been updated too. In addition to *PAPARAZZO* and *FOLLOWED MOLLY*, Casper now had *IDENTITY TWIST* and *ALMOST A CASUALTY* written underneath his name. My entry now said *ALMOST A CASUALTY* too, and beneath that, with two stars preceding them, the words *ULTIMATE SLEUTH* were written.

Richard returned with a plate of snacks as I looked at the board. "It's helpful to do a postmortem—pardon the term," he said. "Purely from a storytelling standpoint. Get a sense of the whole arc."

"Ultimate sleuth?"

"Well, yeah. You solved it in the end. That's what the sleuth does. I was wondering which one of us would turn out to be the main sleuth. I had my money on Fadia, to be honest. Or—" His eyes caught on Elena and Jaz, standing by the spread of food that Fadia had laid out on the kitchen peninsula. Elena let out a peal of laughter at whatever Jaz had just said. Jaz rolled her eyes but tried not to look pleased.

Elena glanced our way, the laughter still alight on her face. Richard quickly looked away.

"Anyway." He cleared his throat. "It was you. Well done."

"Thanks."

"No." He stood awkwardly for a moment. "Thank you. For your help with *Nuclear Nucleus*. Your edits were really helpful. I've sent it out to a few agents, and I actually have a meeting about it next week."

"Seriously? That's fantastic."

"Yes, well." I could tell he was trying not to look pleased. "I'll keep you posted."

Casper joined us then, his arm still bandaged and in the sling. "'Almost a casualty,'" he read from the murder board. "My parents will be so proud."

"The *almost* makes a world of difference," Richard said, clapping a hand on Casper's good shoulder. "Good to see you up and around." Then he moved to join the group in the kitchen.

"Don't worry," I told Casper. "I'm 'almost a casualty' too."

"Don't remind me."

It was quiet for a moment as we both contemplated the board. Then Casper picked up one of Richard's dry-erase markers, uncapped it one-handed, and drew a line through *PAPARAZZO* under his name.

"Just updating it," he said when I gave him an inquisitive look. "I'm not just moving out of Luke and Ryder's place. I'm done. With all of it."

"So, what are you going to do now?" I asked, as Fadia approached us.

Casper shrugged. "Maybe the Sears Portrait Studio is hiring," he said with a half smile. "I'll just have to find a new place to live."

Fadia's eyes lit up. "I know somewhere you could rent! That standoffish guy in 107 is moving out next week. Which means we'll have an empty unit right here at Palm Vista."

"The rent *is* pretty decent," I said when Casper glanced my way.

"Plus, the tenants are top-notch," Fadia added.

"No, you can't all live here," Anton chimed in from the kitchen. "I'll feel left out."

"You can move in with me," I replied, and Anton made a face. "Maybe I'll drop by more often instead."

"I would be a great roommate!"

"Office mate? Yes. Friend? Absolutely. Roommate? No. Who wants bubbly?"

I contemplated the murder board one more time as Anton poured drinks and Fadia distributed them. At the center of the board, the photo of Molly smiled out at the room. It wasn't her real smile—the full-out, thousand-watt one. But maybe that one was better preserved by memory. It was how I wanted to remember her.

"What about you, Rachel?" Casper asked, accepting a glass from Fadia and handing it to me before taking another. "What are you going to do next?"

"I don't know."

And I didn't. Not exactly. I thought of Molly's question: *If you had the chance to figure out who you would be without all that, would you take it?* Maybe that was why she wanted me to have the money—or at least the possibility of having it. And even without it, that's what I wanted to do moving forward. That's what I wanted to figure out.

I had no idea that some weeks later, after I would sign the documents relinquishing my claim to Molly's inheritance, a check from Amy Byrne would arrive in my mailbox in the amount of five million dollars. With an accompanying note: *If we ever meet again, drinks are on you. But let's never meet again.*

All I knew in this moment was that I had the opportunity to figure out who I wanted to be. And that I wasn't alone.

"To Molly," I said, raising a glass.

"To Molly," everyone echoed, and we all drank.

acknowledgments

This book was not originally intended to be a throwback. When I first started *Rachel West*, the year was 2009, meaning that 2008 was the extremely not-distant past. Over the course of the intervening seventeen years, I've worked on many other projects, but this one was always somewhere in the back of my mind. I knew the time would come eventually when I would sit down and finish Rachel's story.

You are reading these words now (if you've made it this far!) because I did indeed manage to sit down and finish Rachel's story. It took on new meaning to me as I approached it in the 2020s with the ability to look back at the 2000s as a whole—at how far we've come, how far we haven't come, and the many ways in which the media and the internet and pop culture have evolved, for better and for worse.

I'm not sure if this is the same book it would have been if I had finished it in 2009. For one thing, the incredibly talented Mary Baker at Berkley probably would not have been my editor, because I'm pretty sure (correct me if I'm wrong, Mary) that she was a freshman in high school at the time. A present-day Mary took a chance on this book and helped shape it into the story it is today, and I am so grateful for her keen insights, generosity, and enthusiasm. I'm thankful as well to the stellar team at Berkley for lending their prodigious talents to help bring this book to life.

This would also not have been possible without my intrepid agent, Bridget Smith, who has found homes for eleven of my books in our twelve years together. Thank you for everything you've done to help *Rachel West*—and, you know, my dream of being an author—become a reality!

Many thanks to the amazing community of authors in St. Louis. Particular thanks go to Samantha Markum, whose immensely helpful advice and expert brainstorming skills guided me through a number of tricky spots in this book. I also consider myself extremely lucky to benefit, as both a writer and a reader, from the incredible indie bookstore scene in St. Louis. Thank you in particular to the Novel Neighbor and Left Bank Books for spreading the love of books to the city at large. Special thanks to Stephanie Skees and Kassie King of the Novel Neighbor for their fierce championing of authors and for many excellent brunches.

Last but certainly not least, this book would not exist without the love and support of my amazing parents, sister, brother-in-law, nieces, family, and friends. I am unendingly grateful to you for brightening my days, for keeping me fed, and for continuing to ask, "How's the book going?" even when it might result in a significantly longer answer than you were expecting or hoping for. Thank you for putting up with me.

Photo by Jing Nie

Emma Mills is thrilled to make her mystery debut with *Rachel West and the Fallen Starlet*. She is the author of six young adult novels, including *First & Then*, *Foolish Hearts*, and *Something Close to Magic*, and the middle grade graphic novel series *The Greenies*. When she is not writing, Emma can be found reviewing scientific documents, tending to her large collection of succulents, and deep-diving into various fandoms. Emma lives in St. Louis with her dog, Teddy, who is best described as a big personality in a tiny package.

VISIT EMMA MILLS ONLINE

EmmaMillsBooks.com
elmify